Praise for
WHEN HARRY MET MOLLY

"A delectable debut...I simply adored it!"   —Julia Quinn,
New York Times bestselling author of *What Happens in London*

"At once frothy and heartfelt, *When Harry Met Molly*
satisfies! This book is better than dessert!"
—Celeste Bradley,
New York Times bestselling author of *Rogue in My Arms*

"Kieran Kramer pens a delightful regency confection...a
wonderfully bright debut."   —Julia London,
New York Times bestselling author of *A Courtesan's Scandal*

"A delicious romp that will keep you laughing. A fun
heroine and a sexy hero make this a delightful read."
—Sabrina Jeffries,
New York Times bestselling author of
The Truth About Lord Stoneville

"I couldn't put it down...a charming delight!"
—Lynsay Sands,
New York Times bestselling author of
The Hellion and the Highlander

"A wickedly witty treat...an exquisite debut!"
—Kathryn Caskie,
USA Today bestselling author of *The Most Wicked of Sins*

"*When Harry Met Molly* is a delightful, page-turning
read! New author Kieran Kramer will capture both your
imagination and your heart."   —Cathy Maxwell,
New York Times bestselling author of
The Marriage Ring

WHEN HARRY MET MOLLY

Kieran Kramer

St. Martin's Paperbacks

This is a work of fiction. All of the characters, organizations, and events portrayed in this novel are either products of the author's imagination or are used fictitiously.

WHEN HARRY MET MOLLY

Copyright © 2010 by Kieran Kramer.
Excerpt from *Dukes to the Left of Me, Princes to the Right* copyright © 2010 by Kieran Kramer.

Cover photograph © Shirley Green
Photo illustration © Jim Griffin

For information address St. Martin's Press, 175 Fifth Avenue, New York, NY 10010.

ISBN: 978-0-312-61164-4

Printed in the United States of America

St. Martin's Paperbacks edition / November 2010

St. Martin's Paperbacks are published by St. Martin's Press, 175 Fifth Avenue, New York, NY 10010.

10 9 8 7 6 5 4 3 2 1

To my wonderful husband Chuck

ACKNOWLEDGMENTS

I'm so excited to be able to thank the many kind people who've helped me become a published writer:

My fun and fiesty agent, Jenny Bent: I can't adequately express how grateful I am to her for launching me on this journey.

My brilliant editor, Jennifer Enderlin: a bedrock of support and inspiration always. Her mentorship has meant the world to me.

The team at St. Martin's Press: they're simply fabulous, and it's a honor to work with such caring, talented people.

My fellow writers, especially my friends at Lowcountry Romance Writers of America—every member has great stories to tell—and the Beau Monde chapter of RWA, in particular, Nancy Mayer and Sue Pace.

A special thank you to Cherry Adair for first picking my contest entry out of a pile and sending me to the national RWA conference. She has one of the biggest hearts of anyone I know.

I'd also like to thank other writers who have inspired me with their awesome talent, wisdom, fortitude, and grace: Debbie Macomber, Jennifer Crusie, Nora Roberts, Jane Porter, Christina Dodd, J.R. Ward, Jayne Ann Krentz,

viii ACKNOWLEDGMENTS

Susan Elizabeth Phillips, JoAnn Grote, Sharon Brennan Wray, Susan Wiggs, and Virginia Kantra. There are more, so many that I can't name them all here. Every writer I've met has gifted me with something of herself, even if it's simply the acknowledgment that we share the joys and angsts only writers can know.

Of course, without my family none of this would have happened at all. A special shout-out to my sister Kristin, who organized a sibling gift to me, my first laptop, so I could take my stories anywhere. My husband Chuck and my children, Steven, Margaret, and Jack, have provided me with endless hugs, encouraging words, and cups of tea. The rest of my family, on both sides, have also been un-flagging in their support. I love you all!

PROLOGUE

1808

Thirteen-year-old Lady Mary "Molly" Fairbanks, daughter of the widowed Earl of Sutton, seethed with emotion on a daily basis, whether she was cleaning her teeth, breaking the shell on her morning egg, or riding her favorite mare. She was sure no one else felt quite as deeply as she did—about anything. Which was why she must vent her passions to all the company at the Duke of Mallan's annual Christmas ball.

If she didn't, she would *die.*

At the very least, her *soul* would.

The tradition went back well over a hundred years. She wouldn't be the first child to present a riddle, joke, or poem to the adults before they withdrew to the ballroom. But she would be the first to recite an original verse signifying her deep, fervent love for Roderick, the duke's eldest son.

She'd called him Robert in the poem. A little subtlety was required; otherwise, she feared he'd have to break off his engagement with her sister Penelope right then and there at the ball, and that wouldn't be proper.

He should wait until after the ball was *over.* Molly

hoped she could stay awake that late, in case he felt the need to ride over to her father's neighboring mansion and propose after midnight, which would be Christmas Day.

Penelope wouldn't care anyway. She'd been kissing Roderick's younger brother Harry in the arbor. All that would go into the poem as well. Because a woman in love *must* speak the truth, mustn't she?

Although, of course, in Molly's poem Penelope had become Persephone and Harry, Barry. No one would ever know of their perfidy.

Except Molly. And through gorgeous verse, Roderick would guess that she and he were meant to be together—that is, after she grew a little taller and started and finished her four years at Miss Monroe's Academy for Young Ladies in London, where, according to Penelope, the girls had chocolate and brioche every morning and were encouraged to buy fine lace and new bonnets whenever the mood struck them.

Molly couldn't *wait* to go to London!

It was time. The company was clapping for a little boy who'd just told a silly riddle. Molly wiped her hands on her new white muslin gown with the bottle-green sash and scalloped hem and stared at the company gathered before her, imagining them in their underthings so she wouldn't be nervous.

Then she drew a deep breath and began to recite the poem she was sure would change her life forever, and for the better:

A LOVE RECTANGLE OF TRAGIC PROPORTIONS

Robert, Robert, wherefore are thou, Robert?
While Persephone's in the arbor,
Bestowing kisses on young Barry,

You clutch the golden ring
She's to wear when you marry.

Persephone, Persephone, why does thou wound
Robert so?
Barry is but the moon
While Robert is the sun.
Can't you see Robert is all
And Barry is, um, none?

Barry, oh, Barry, why not find your own true love?
My sister isn't yours
She belongs to another,
But if you steal her away,
Perhaps I'll marry your brother!

There.

Molly folded her paper up and noticed that silence reigned in the ballroom. She knew she was a good poet, but really, was she *that* good?

She looked up at Roderick and saw that his was mouth hanging open. As was Penelope's. And Harry's.

Indeed, everyone's mouths were hanging open.

She swallowed a happy lump in her throat.

Love had lent her verse . . . wings.

She blinked several times. Still, no one spoke. Yet no one clapped, either.

Roderick looked at Harry. His lips became a thin line. "You slimy bastard," he said quietly.

Harry backed up a step. "Roderick—"

Penelope stared at Molly. "How could you?" she choked out. And then her face turned beet red and she began to cry—loud, gusty sobs.

Roderick jumped over the tabletop. "I'll kill you!" he

roared at Harry, his fists clenched, eyes wild. And then he leaped on Harry and began pounding him.

Harry socked him in the jaw.

There were cries from all the women. The duchess fainted in a heap on the floor. Immediately, a footman picked her up and began to carry her from the ballroom.

The duchess lifted her head. "Boys," she said weakly. "No incidents, please. Especially not at Christmas."

Molly clutched her throat. What was happening? Why—why—?

"Roderick! Harry!" shouted the duke. "Stop this instant!"

But they didn't stop. They careened around the head table, wrestling, punching, kicking.

"Roderick!" Molly yelled, her heart racing. "My love!"

But she couldn't get to him. The room filled with noise: talking, shouting, crying, screaming, the sounds of breaking glass. Crowds of adults and children alike surged toward the fight.

Molly squeezed through and saw Harry lying on his back on the floor, surrounded by smashed china and broken goblets. Roderick swayed unsteadily on his feet. Both of them breathed hard and loud, their chests heaving.

Lord Sutton stood from the head table. "Lady Mary!"

Oh, no. *Mary*. When Papa used her formal name, Molly knew she was in trouble. He pointed to the door leading to the ducal grand hallway. "Go—to—your—room!"

"But I don't live here, Papa!" Molly cried.

Lord Sutton's face was white. "I don't care. Go to any room. Any room but this one!"

Molly's eyes flooded with tears. She blinked them away and began to walk slowly backward.

But then Harry stood up and grabbed Roderick's shoulders. He pushed him back, parting the crowd with the force of his shoves, until Roderick's body slammed against a wall.

Molly didn't even feel her feet hit the floor as she rushed across the room. She jumped on Harry's back, locked her legs around his waist, and pulled on his hair until his eyes were looking straight into hers, albeit upside down.

"You beast!" Molly screamed, and tugged harder on his hair. "Leave him alone!"

Harry staggered to the left, gave one mighty heave of his torso, and Molly fell to the ground.

Ouch. That hurt. That *really* hurt. But Molly had no time to nurse her wounds. Roderick came out from behind Harry, pulled back his fist, and delivered a blow to Harry's nose.

Molly heard the crunch. Blood spurted everywhere.

Harry leaned forward, grasping his nose. "I never—" he gasped, then looked slowly up at Roderick. "I never meant to hurt you," he said.

There was silence all around.

"Nooooo," Penelope was moaning, cowering in a corner with several of her good friends. "Roderick, please. Stop." She wrung her hands, tears trickling down each cheek. "I love you."

"Do you?" Roderick barked at her. "Do you *really*?"

Penelope nodded. "Yes," she said, her voice trembling. "Ever so much."

Roderick's fists unclenched. He gazed with disgust— and something close to pity—at his younger brother.

And he spared no glance for Molly as he stalked to Penelope's side. Penelope threw her arms around him and hugged him hard. His embrace was more restrained, but Molly could see by the look of pure joy in Penelope's eyes that he'd forgiven her.

Molly's heart sank. Everyone forgave Penelope. She was perfect, after all.

"You shall join the army, Harry," the duke said, his

voice tired and . . . and sad. "And while you're in it, you shall think on the meaning of loyalty. Of duty to one's family."

Harry's eyes narrowed. "I know all about duty, Father. You won't let me forget it."

Molly cringed at his bitter tone.

"You have *more* to learn," his father reprimanded him. "It will take you several years. And when you do learn what you must, you may rejoin the family with my blessing. Until then, you are *not* welcome here."

"Not even on Christmas?" Harry's face blanched beneath the blood smeared across his cheeks. He looked first at his father, then his brother.

"I'm afraid so, my son." His father sighed. "Your presence here tomorrow would simply extend everyone's misery, would it not?"

Harry picked up a goblet of wine, drained it, and set it down on the head table. "To your happiness," he said to Roderick and Penelope, neither of whom said a word.

Harry then looked at Molly. "And *you,* you little nosybody, may our paths never cross again."

"They shan't any time soon," Lord Sutton said. "The events of today have convinced me that my daughter requires a firmer hand than I can provide her here at home or at Miss Monroe's Academy in London. She shall be sent away. The day after tomorrow. To Yorkshire."

Away? Not to London but to . . . to Yorkshire?

And the day after Christmas?

"No!" Molly cried. "How could you send me to Yorkshire? It's cold and windy and—"

"It's for the best." Lord Sutton's tone was steely. Several people beside him nodded.

Molly's eyes spouted tears. "But—but why so soon after Christmas?"

Lord Sutton said nothing, merely drew his brows together.

And then the worst of it dawned on her. "Oh, no," she said, trembling. "I can't miss the wedding, Papa. It's a mere two weeks away, and I'm to stand next to Penelope and hold her flowers."

She loved Penelope. Yes, Molly did, even though she wanted to marry Roderick, too!

It was all so confusing. At that moment, she loved and hated her family all at once, and she needed someone to hug her and tell her everything would be all right.

Mama, her heart cried. *Help me!*

But Mama had long since gone to heaven.

Nevertheless, Molly waited. She waited for Mama or the angels or *somebody* to make things seem less horrible. But Penelope didn't step in and tell Papa to let her stay. No one did. Not even Roderick—and she'd written the poem for him.

The wretch.

The crowd was silent again. Harry turned to leave, his hand gripping his nose.

"Go," Lord Sutton told Molly. Then he looked toward Cousin Augusta. "See that she's taken home immediately and put to bed."

"Of course," Cousin Augusta said, and pushed her glasses up her nose. "No presents for you tomorrow, missy. This Christmas incident shall never be forgotten, not as long as I draw breath."

Cousin Augusta was a mean old bat. And just yesterday, she'd wandered about the house looking for her glasses when they'd been right on her nose!

Molly fell in line with Harry.

"I hate you," she whispered to him.

"The feeling is mutual," he said quite cheerily.

And with those parting words, the two young trouble-makers walked away from the people they loved best, both of their futures gravely altered by a single act of passion, both of them believing they were alone and destined to be alone—

Forever.

CHAPTER 1

June 1816

Lord Harry Traemore knew the man next to him in the private room at his club in London—Lord Wray, who'd slithered to the floor and begun snoring—might appear to most passersby to be passive, even sleeping. But Harry and his old schoolmates from Eton, their reasoning skills gently manipulated by rather copious amounts of brandy, realized this prone position of Wray's was actually his attempt to bravely endure his fate.

After all, Wray was to be married in the morning. And everyone knew his future wife was . . .

Exactly like his mother.

"I'm sad," Harry's friend Charles Thorpe, Viscount Lumley, said, an empty snifter dangling from his hand. "A good friend's freedom is being taken away."

Lumley was rich as Croesus, with the most twinkling blue eyes Harry had ever seen and a grin that could light up Vauxhall Gardens at midnight better than any fireworks.

"It's not right," said Captain Stephen Arrow. His naval uniform, crisp and distinguished with its gold braid and buttons, offset the casual manner in which he sprawled in his chair. "He put up a good fight, didn't he?"

Harry sloshed some brandy into his mouth. He couldn't even taste its flavor anymore. His tongue . . . it felt numb. And his lips, for that matter. It wasn't often he drank this much—contrary to the stories told about him, which he did nothing to deny.

But tonight was different. Tonight he felt the brush of the nuptial guillotine close to his own neck. He didn't want to marry. Not for a long, long time, not until he was truly cornered by familial obligation. And as far as he knew, that would likely never happen.

Harry was simply a spare. Only if his robust older brother Roderick somehow stuck his spoon in the wall before his wife Penelope produced a son—the next heir to the House of Mallan—would Harry's potential as a bridegroom begin to matter. Penelope had already produced four daughters—his splendid little nieces Helen, Cassandra, Juliet, and Imogen—so it couldn't be long now before she gifted Roderick with the son the whole family craved, even prayed for.

Because it wouldn't do, Harry knew from whispers in the servants' hall and the perpetually disappointed expressions on his parents' faces, for disgraced Harry—the returning war hero who was *not* a hero but should have been—to be merely one person away from inheriting the ducal title.

No, that wouldn't do at all.

Which was why Harry was so averse to marriage in the first place. Why take on yet another person in his life who would only disdain him?

Wray smacked his lips and shifted on the floor.

"At least he's out of his pain," said Nicholas Staunton, Lord Maxwell, in that unruffled tone of his. Cool, mysterious, and rather unconventional despite his strong aristocratic lineage, Maxwell, Harry was well aware, was unlikely to voice an observation unless he were truly moved to do so. He raised a quizzing glass and observed Wray further. "I understand he's had a hell of a year. Dozens of debutantes and their mothers chasing him without cease."

"Poor sod," said Harry, looking down at Wray. "He was even thrown into a carriage by two masked thugs and almost forced to elope with the Barnwell girl, but he leaped out on the London Bridge and nearly got run over by a coach-and-four instead."

A loud popping noise—followed by another pop and a creak—sounded from the logs burning in the fireplace.

The sound even woke Wray. He opened his eyes, gazed at nothing, and said, "No. I won't eat my porridge. Please don't make me," before he went back to his snoring.

"God save his tormented soul," Arrow entreated with great solemnity.

And then the bookcase opened. The one near the fire.

Yes, *opened.*

Harry rubbed his eyes.

"What the hell?" said Arrow.

Harry knew, of course, that every great house had a secret door to somewhere, but he'd no idea his own club did.

A buxom female—rather matronly in dress and age, actually—stumbled out from a dark passageway, a spitting candle in her hand. The curls at her temples had gone to gray beneath the half-handkerchief pinned to her hair, and her gown, while a pleasing midnight blue, couldn't disguise her spreading hips. She placed the candle on the mantel, turned to the men, and curtsied.

"You're a woman," Lumley said slowly.

Considering the fact that women weren't allowed on the club premises, Harry could forgive Lumley's stating the obvious.

But before she or anyone else could respond, a man emerged from the opening behind the bookcase, as well—a portly man with a merry grin and a bottle of cheap gin in his hand.

"I'm dreaming," said Lumley, shaking his head.

"Au contraire," the man said, and proceeded to belch. "You most certainly are not dreaming, Viscount." He patted his stomach, lifted the bottle to his mouth, drank, and wiped his mouth with his sleeve.

Then he swayed.

"Oho!" he said, and chuckled when the woman grabbed his elbow.

"No dancing, Your Highness." She giggled and took the bottle from him. "We need music for that."

Long before she'd even set the bottle on a side table, every man in the room had stood—except for Wray, who was still fighting his battle against cruel Fate on the floor.

"Your Royal Highness!" Captain Arrow said, and saluted the swaying man. "Captain Stephen Arrow, at your service."

By God, it *was* him. The Prince Regent himself. Harry almost saluted, too, but then he remembered he wasn't a sailor, so he bowed deeply, right near Wray's snuffling mouth.

Prinny rubbed his chin. "Yes, it is I," he said. "My delectable companion and I were on our way to the secret bedchamber—"

There was a secret bedchamber at the club?

Harry and Lumley exchanged looks of shock. Maxwell ran his narrowed gaze over the bookshelf. Arrow remained standing at attention.

"Captain Arrow," Prinny said with a huff of laughter. "At ease. Please. I can't think when you look as though you're about to call out orders to fire a hundred cannon at the Spanish fleet."

Arrow's shoulders relaxed.

And there followed a general lessening of tension in every man, Harry noted. Maxwell took a puff from his cheroot. Lumley grinned, and Harry uncurled his fingers, which he'd balled into fists at his sides.

Yes, Prinny was in his cups, but he was also in a good mood.

"As I was *saying,*" His Royal Highness went on, "Liza and I were passing through, and we couldn't help overhearing your conversation, gentlemen." He opened his snuffbox with a grand flourish, pretended to inhale some—everyone knew he really despised the stuff—and returned it to his pocket. "And I'm shocked—nay, dismayed," he went on, "at the state of affairs in this room. Can't be good for the Empire when its best and brightest are gloomy."

He leveled an eye at Harry. "Yes, I include even you in that description, young man. Despite everything I've heard about your bedding the captain's wife while your unit suffered an *ambush,* of all things"—Liza gasped—"you can't be a complete disgrace if the Duke of Mallan is your father."

Harry's chest knotted. "Thank you, Your Highness," he gritted out.

But inside, his heart grew harder. And smaller.

Prinny looked around assessingly. "We must correct this situation. What you need is hope—hope that you may avoid legshackles. And not just a vague hope." His expression brightened and he raised his right index finger. "You'll need a surety!"

"Yes!" Liza clapped her hands.

"We need to make it *impossible,*" Prinny said, "for any matchmaking mamas, silly debutantes, and conniving bettors to rob your bachelor days of their necessary frivolity. Who's got a quill and paper?"

No one did. Harry wondered what the Prince was about.

A coach-and-four rattled by the window, and through the door, there were the regular sounds of club life: voices rising and falling, the scrape of forks and knives against plates, the clink of bottle against glass.

Life was going on as usual, Harry thought, except for here in this room. He wished he could talk to the other bachelors, but no one dared look at anyone but Prinny.

Prinny nodded his head at Arrow. "Captain, please see to it that paper and quill and writing desk are brought immediately. I have a decree to prepare and sign. Here. And now."

Captain Arrow saluted. "Of course, Your Highness."

Not thirty seconds later, he was back with Prinny's requested materials, which he handed off to Liza with a swooping bow.

Liza blushed, Harry wasn't surprised to see. Women always fell apart around Arrow.

"Take this down," Prinny said to Liza, who settled into a chair, the quill poised above the blank paper, prepared to write.

"Please begin, Your Highness," she said.

Prinny adjusted his cravat. "By order of the Prince Regent," he said, "let it be known that the annual Impossible Bachelors wager shall commence the first week of August in the year 1816 and every August thereafter. The participants shall be conscripted by the Prince Regent and his advisors, who shall have sole control over the circumstances of the bet."

Harry's neck muscles tensed, and the sound of Liza's quill scratching across the paper only made it worse. He craved nothing more than to get up and *leave*.

But, of course, he couldn't.

After a bit more scribbling, Liza looked up, her quill at the ready.

"The winner of the wager," Prinny continued, "shall

be granted an entire *year* of freedom from the trials, tribulations, and, ahem, joys of marriage. As well as from the dreary events leading up to the eventual acquisition of a wife."

His grin was decidedly saucy. "He shall not be chased after by matchmaking mamas at social events." A twinkle gleamed in his eyes. "He shall not be forced to attend tedious balls at Almack's"—he paused and grinned—"although if he cares to attend to observe and flirt with the newest crop of debutantes, he shall not be denied entrance by the patronesses."

Liza's mouth curved up in a smile, and she continued to write furiously.

"And he most certainly shall *not*," Prinny said, his eyes stormy, "be trapped into marriage by a young lady's relatives—or by bettors seeking to make their fortunes."

Almost as one, the gentlemen in the room looked down at Wray, snoring on the rug.

"Pity this comes too late for him," Prinny murmured.

Liza made a small tsking noise and inclined her head in sympathy.

But then Prinny gripped his lapels, threw back his shoulders, and resumed his speech. "Those who cross the Prince Regent in his wish to see at least one of his bachelor subjects free from shameless pursuit for the period of one year"—he paused and narrowed his eyes—"shall forever be given the cut direct by His Royal Highness and his loyal subjects."

Harry met Maxwell's eyes, which reflected back his own gut feeling. Prinny meant business, obviously. And since *he* meant business, they must follow suit.

The Prince Regent released a long-suffering sigh. "The price of pursuing seemingly impossible freedom and privilege is always high, is it not?" He arched a brow. "Therefore, the losing bachelors shall be required to draw straws."

He looked first at Lumley, then Arrow, then Maxwell, then at Harry. "The recipient of the shortest straw," he said grimly, "shall propose marriage within two months to a woman of his club board's choosing."

He leaned back on his heels and crossed his arms over his expansive belly. "That is all."

Liza laid her quill down and blew on the paper holding Prinny's latest decree.

A cold stone boulder rested in the pit of Harry's stomach. He most certainly didn't want to marry. But he'd prefer to avoid the altar *his* way—as Prinny's way involved a hefty measure of diabolical risk.

Prinny sauntered to the desk and signed the decree, hiccupping as he handed the quill to Liza. "I'm amazed at my own genius," he said with a chuckle.

"*I'm* not, Your Highness." Liza cast him an adoring glance.

Prinny curled his chubby hand around hers. "The first year's wager shall be in your honor, my dear. I shall call it the Most Delectable Companion contest. The ladies shall be rigorously tested according to my exacting if unscrupulous standards—and the lucky bachelor who brings the finest mistress shall win a cherished year of freedom." He looked up. "Are you ready, gentlemen?"

Harry swallowed hard. Follow Prinny's orders, and any one of them might very well be legshackled by Christmas if they lost the wager!

"Your Highness," Arrow said in his authoritative naval captain's voice. "According to my ship's sailing schedule, I shall be rounding Cape Horn at that time."

"No, you shall *not*," Prinny insisted. "I shall see to it that you're reassigned, Captain Arrow."

Harry caught the slightest hesitation before Arrow spoke. "Very good, sir," he said.

But Harry could see the red creeping up his friend's

well-tanned neck. He wasn't happy about this wager, either.

Dear God was written all over Maxwell's usually implacable face.

Lumley exclaimed something like "Wha'?" before remembering to shut his mouth.

"I shall send each of you details of the circumstances of the bet imminently," Prinny said sternly. "You'll follow it to the letter." He snorted. "I'm quite sure I'll be entertained."

Harry's spirits sank even lower. Prinny and his compulsive need to be entertained! Couldn't he simply reinstitute the tradition of the court jester?

Prinny's gaze narrowed. "Harry, you're to host. Maxwell, record. Arrow and Lumley, you shall form the arbitration committee. Keep me informed as the wager progresses, gentlemen. And that's an order."

"As you wish, Your Highness." Harry forced himself to sound amenable, although he'd no desire to be under the strict watch of His Royal Highness in a caper over which he had no control. He'd already undergone five years of imposed military service, courtesy of his father, and then he'd stayed in long enough to do his damnedest to help Wellington win at Waterloo.

He'd been home only a year, hardly long enough to enjoy his freedom.

Liza stood and handed the decree to Prinny, who immediately passed it off to Harry. "See that it's hung to the right of the fireplace in the front room of the club." He chuckled and took the candle from the mantel. "Congratulations. You're all the Prince Regent's Impossible Bachelors now. Except Wray, of course."

He nudged Wray with his foot. Wray flung out an arm and snorted.

"I believe I shall name one more Impossible Bachelor,"

Prinny said. "To fill the vacant spot Wray would have occupied had he not been vanquished by feminine forces
already." His brow creased in thought. "Possibly that rat
Sir Richard Bell. He's seduced so many virgins that it's
time he sweated a bit, eh?"

And before anyone could respond, he swooped into the
hidden passageway, pulling Liza by the hand.

The bookcase shut upon them both.

There was total silence in the room until the creeping
footsteps of Prinny and his lady were no longer audible.

"Dammit all to hell," Lord Maxwell said, his voice
dangerously low.

Arrow ran a hand through his hair. "I don't *want* to be
reassigned! And I most certainly don't want to be called
an Impossible Bachelor. It doesn't have nearly the ring to
it *admiral* has."

Lumley threw himself into a chair. "I've nothing to do
except oversee my estates. And perhaps acquire a few
more. So I think I shall quite enjoy this wager. Especially
if Sir Richard shows up. I'd like to pound his face for ruining the Glasbury girl last year. She's a nun now, did you
know that?"

"Yes, I knew that," Harry spluttered, "and I agree with
you about Bell. But really, Lumley. *Enjoy* the wager? What
are you thinking? One of us will wind up *married* at the
end of it!"

"I forgot about that part." Lumley sighed. "I don't even
have a mistress at the moment, much less a delectable
one. Which means, right now, I'm favored to get legshackled!"

"You and I both," said Arrow. "We must get cracking.
Maxwell's Athena is sublime, and Harry's girl is—who is
she now, Harry? The blonde, or have you moved on to
that redhead you met at the Cyprian Ball?"

"That's beside the point at the moment." Harry had difficulty keeping up with all the women in his life. He'd rather not think of them unless he had to, which was usually right before he saw them—when he'd open a drawer near his bed table and pull out a little bauble from a collection of baubles his jeweler had put together for him to save him the tedium of selecting little gifts himself. "We're Prinny's puppets. He's shrewd when he wants to be, but the only thing that interests his addled brain these days is mindless entertainment."

"There's nothing more annoying than an intelligent person who's gone to seed," Maxwell said with a hint of contempt. He raised his brandy glass and drained it— then filled it again.

Wray sat up with a groan. "I'm awake."

"Obviously," said Maxwell. "And no doubt with the devil of a headache already."

"Gawd, yes." Wray's hair was sticking up all over his head.

Maxwell poured another brandy and handed it to his soon-to-be-married friend.

Wray took a large gulp. "I daren't let Prinny know," he rasped, "but I came to when he opened that demmed bookcase. No telling what shenanigans he would have had me participate in before the wedding tomorrow had I been any more lucid."

He raised himself to sit on a leather chair, wincing as he did. "Don't be so down, gentlemen. Imagine . . . one of you at Almack's, looking over the girls, and no one—not even Lady Jersey—being permitted to say a word to you about their gowns, their pedigree, or their worthiness as potential wives."

"There *is* that," Arrow said hopefully.

"So before you go feeling sorry for yourselves," Wray said with a grimace, "remember, I'd give anything to be in your position."

He was right, of course. And if Harry were truthful with himself, he must admit that beneath the resentment he felt about being pulled into Prinny's scheme, there was a spark of hope . . .

That *he* would win the wager. And be able to walk into any ballroom in London and not have to worry about someone trying to marry him off.

He patted Wray's shoulder. "You're a good man."

It was his way of saying farewell to a noble bachelor, and everyone there knew it.

Wray tried to buck up and grin, but it turned into another wince. He got up and stumbled toward the door. "I've got to go, gentlemen. I—I'll see you"—he hesitated—"*after* I'm married. At church. Or a musicale. Or something equally boring."

And he shut the door behind him.

There was a grave silence, but Harry turned to the others. "I'd like to raise a toast," he said.

Arrow, Lumley, and Maxwell each wore almost identical somber looks, but they lifted their glasses anyway.

"To the Impossible Bachelors," Harry said with spirit. "And this impossible wager. May we survive it handily, with our freedom intact."

"Here, here," the others said in chorus.

Everyone drained their glasses.

"One more thing," Harry said with a grin. "I propose the damned bookcase is nailed shut before we leave tonight. All in?"

"All in!" they cried.

Just as he knew they would.

CHAPTER 2

August 1816

Thanks to the Providence School for Wayward Girls, which took her in hand at age thirteen, twenty-one-year-old Molly Fairbanks was no longer a silly romantic—she was a silly romantic with superb posture. She sat perfectly straight in her chair at the rather seedy inn where she and Cedric Alliston were taking a bit of nuncheon before eloping to Gretna Green.

Not that she could actually eat. She was much too excited. And confused. The way she suspected a bird let out of a cage is confused moments before it flies away to freedom.

To honor her emancipation, she'd forgone her usual dreary traveling dress. She'd worn instead her favorite white muslin gown paired with her late mother's gloves and a navy blue and white striped silk parasol Penelope had just sent her from Italy, where she and her family were on a six-month painting holiday.

"Cedric—" Molly toyed with her glass of ratafia. "If Papa weren't so damnably rich—and far away at the moment—would you still be running off with me?"

"What a sh-illy question," Cedric said, working his jaw in a grand manner as he cut his sausage. He often spoke as if he were clenching a knife between his back teeth, which should have seemed terribly Londonish to a girl who'd been rusticating in Kent an age with an addled crone of a cousin, and before that, a cold, stone school high atop the wind-scoured Yorkshire dales.

But as Molly had never *been* to London, she couldn't be impressed.

"The elopement izzh what it izzh," Cedric said, glancing at the gold watch he wore on his emerald green waistcoat. "And we are what we are."

Molly blinked. "I don't understand you."

Which was nothing new. Cedric was like a puzzle. And she was like a person who, um, didn't *like* puzzles. Particularly the kinds with one piece missing. Cedric seemed one of those.

He sighed, his perfectly chiseled jaw framed by the exceedingly high points of his shirt collar. "Our nature is sh-tamped upon us, Mary. Every piece of broken pottery your father and I pull from the earth reveals the human condition. And we can't esh-cape it."

"Oh," she said politely. How did every conversation they had come round to broken pottery?

Cedric pointed his fork at her. "Unlike your perfectly proper sister Penelope, you are nothing more, or lesh, than a well-bred young lady—of too high spirits, I might add—who requires constant direction from a better mind. And I . . . I am the brilliant treasure hunter—of noble visage," he added with a loft to his brow, "who shall provide that tutelage. It's our lot in life."

He shrugged and popped a piece of sausage in his mouth.

Oh, pish posh. Molly pursed her lips. Cedric was no treasure hunter. He was an impoverished social climber—

Cousin Augusta's husband's nephew—who served as an assistant to her father. And Penelope wasn't perfectly proper, either. Any girl who kissed her fiancé's brother couldn't qualify as perfectly proper, could she? And Molly loved her long-married sister all the more for it.

Molly knew ladies weren't supposed to seethe, but really, why was it that only gentlemen were allowed to speak boldly? And why were they permitted to boast about themselves—even contradict themselves!—while ladies must remain meek and . . . and boring?

"Someday," she said, leaning toward Cedric, "someday you shall call me Molly. And you'll never go back to calling me . . . Mary."

"I beg to differ." He slurped at his wine.

"*I* beg to differ."

"You can't. I already did." He set his goblet down with a *thunk*.

"We both can. You don't have a license to differ *alone*."

Cedric scoffed. "You make no sen-sh."

"I beg to differ," she said.

Although secretly, in her deepest heart, she realized Cedric had a point. She *must* have lost her mind to have agreed to stay at home, pour out Cousin Augusta's tea, and listen to her complain of a brass band playing in her ears—while Papa traipsed about Europe hunting treasure with Cedric for the past three years.

And when Papa *did* return to visit Marble Hill, Molly spent each night at the dining room table (sitting quite straight) while Cedric and her father prosed on about chunks of broken, thousand-year-old vases for *hours*.

Molly didn't like dirt. Or dark, broken things pulled out of the ground.

She liked flowers. Romantic novels. Fresh air. And dancing.

And although Cedric did look rather like Apollo, with

his shining halo of golden curls, patrician nose, and long, golden lashes framing cerulean blue eyes, she didn't love him. He was too much of a boor *and* a bore—and sometimes even a *boar,* the way he snuffled and snorted when he ate—to love.

Of course, part of her—the silly romantic part which had read *Pride and Prejudice* thirteen times—thought it would be awfully nice if he loved her. Because maybe then she'd come to love him back. Someday. After her senses had been dulled by age or . . . or perhaps after he'd done something heroic.

She watched him shake out his lacy cuffs and lean back in his chair, chewing with his nose in the air.

Very well. He'd never do something heroic. But she had no other options. Clearly. Other than spinsterhood. Or being driven mad by Cousin Augusta's imaginary brass band.

At least, being married to Cedric, Molly could finally see London and Paris and kick up her heels while Cedric and Papa were away.

But her daydream of a future as a social butterfly was interrupted when a man and a woman swept into the taproom, drawing not just her attention but everyone's. The woman was extremely beautiful, if a trifle overdone, in a tulip pink gown with a neckline that showed her décolletage to great advantage.

"She's lovely in a tartish way, is she not?" whispered Molly to Cedric.

The vision in pink lowered her brows, flicked her curls back, and stuck her hand on her hip. But her male companion at the bar either didn't notice her or was ignoring her. He wore a simple lawn riding shirt and buff breeches tucked in tall black boots, one of which rested jauntily on a brass rail near the floor. Molly couldn't help but observe the impressive breadth of his shoulders and the glossy blackness of the hair spilling over his collar.

Cedric placed his fork and knife on his plate and gazed at the woman in pink. "She is Aphrodite," he said simply. "Come to life."

Molly watched as Aphrodite compressed her lips, wended her way through the tables without her consort, and approached a table adjacent to theirs. Looking over her shoulder, the beauty saw Cedric and smiled slowly, like a dewy rose blooming at the kiss of the sun.

Cedric drew in a breath.

Molly wondered if Cedric ever thought *she* was fine-looking. She doubted it. No matter how often she pulled on her nose in front of her looking glass at home, it stayed short and snub, not aristocratic and elegant. Her mouth, she knew, was wider than the river Thames. Her eyes were a Wedgwood blue, but Miss Dunlap, the headmistress at Providence School, said they were too impertinent to be ladylike, and Molly's hair . . . well, it was her greatest annoyance. It was the color of molasses and as thick as it, too, always slipping out of its pins.

"Hello," said Molly, and gave the woman a little wave.

Aphrodite inclined her head in cool acknowledgment of Molly's greeting, but her expression grew much . . . warmer when she looked at Cedric. There was silence between them, but Molly sensed an invisible golden thread extending from Cedric to the woman. And that thread thrummed with tension. It was the call of one beauty to another, the recognition that one perfect specimen of physical form had found its ideal mate.

But that was a silly thought, Molly said to herself. She was here with Cedric and they were going to Gretna together.

He pushed his chair back, stood up, and strode to the woman's table. "Please allow me to assist you," he said to her, and pulled out a chair.

Molly felt her face flush. Cedric never pulled out *her*

chair. Somehow there was always a servant around to pull out her chair, so until this very moment, she'd never noticed Cedric's lack of attention that way. Though, come to think of it, he hadn't pulled out her chair for her in this very taproom thirty minutes ago.

Her heart clenched. So what if Cedric and Aphrodite looked perfect together? Looks weren't everything. Attraction between like minds was much stronger than any physical attraction, wasn't it?

Of course, Molly and Cedric didn't *have* like minds. But perhaps someday they would.

If Cedric completely changed.

It *could* happen, Molly thought quickly. She'd once heard about a woman who fell off a horse and woke up believing she was the Pope!

But what did it matter now, anyway? Cedric was now firmly ensconced back in his own chair. Crisis over.

"Shall we have some fruit and cheese?" he asked her.

Cedric *never* asked for fruit and cheese.

"Good idea," she said, but her heart sank.

She knew. She knew he simply wanted to stay longer at the taproom so he could gaze at the Aphrodite look-alike.

He gave a self-satisfied smile and waved over the barmaid. Molly's stomach felt raw and anxious. Everything around her was crystal clear in the most uncomfortable way. She could see the pores on Cedric's nose, the crack in their tabletop, which was filled with an unknown gooey substance. The smell of sour beer and sweat filled the air. Even the aroma of sizzling sausages passing by on a tray above the barmaid's head overwhelmed her with its . . . greasiness.

She felt a dull, heavy ache near her heart, an ache that throbbed. And throbbed harder. And wouldn't go away. She must admit it. Cedric was a conceited prig. And she'd be wasting her life if she ran away with him. Just as she'd wasted the past three years pouring tea for Cousin Augusta and trying to be the scholarly, obedient girl her father wanted her to be—on top of the five before that she'd spent with the teachers at Providence School, who'd done their best to wring every last bit of fun from her soul.

When was the last time she'd been . . .

Herself?

Free?

And truly happy?

"I need some air," she said, and stood.

Cedric nodded.

When she walked by the table with Aphrodite sitting there, alone, Molly tried to forget about her own snub nose and untidy hair and drew her shoulders back because she was a fighter, even though most of the time she forgot that fact about herself. But at this moment of truth, when she sensed that she was second-best, she strove to appear strong and goddesslike herself. She would be above the fray.

So she focused instead on the line of dusty deer antlers above the bar and didn't particularly fathom that she and the man who'd accompanied Aphrodite—and was approaching his table with two tankards—were on a crash course.

Someone soft and sweet-smelling smacked right into Lord Harry Traemore, second son of the sixth Duke of Mallan. And a split second later, something warm and foamy splashed across his chest.

His beer, of course. A sad waste. Being the spare to the heir of a dukedom, Harry was used to squandering time and energy thinking and talking about beer. And loose women. And outrageous curricle races to Brighton at midnight.

It was the duty of the spare to be a sad waste himself,

wasn't it? To give one's servants something to talk about and one's unerringly perfect family a mission in life. Of course, it wouldn't serve for his family to know that since he was a little boy, he'd wished *he* could be perfect, too, like them.

But it was too late for that. Harry had made his mark on the world, and it was a most imperfect mark—quite damning and irrevocable, impossible to refute. He'd waste no more time grieving over what he couldn't *be*. What he couldn't *have*. The only alternative was to be as imperfect as imperfect comes.

At least he'd be the best at *something*.

"Oh, my goodness!" the petite woman in front of him said, the thick brown knot at the top of her head unraveling. "I do apologize."

"No, no," he said. "Quite all right. I was trying to get around those two"—he nodded at a couple of old men nearby—"and didn't see you, either."

Which wasn't exactly true. He'd been staring at the sulking Fiona in her revealing pink gown and gloating over the fact that her mere presence at the competition would ensure him a solid win at Prinny's game—and another year's freedom from the parson's noose. He'd soon kiss that ridiculous pout off her mouth. It was only there because he hadn't allowed her to bring her yapping lapdog on the trip.

Harry didn't *believe* in lapdogs. He was all for large, rangy dogs that drooled over sofas, but—

Good God. The brunette woman was looking up at him with impish brown eyes. It couldn't be. But it was—

Molly Fairbanks. *Lady* Molly Fairbanks. What was she doing at a seedy inn in the middle of nowhere?

"You," she breathed.

"You," he said back.

"It can't be." She took a step backward.

"It is," he said, and backed away, as well.

"Why here?" she asked.

"Why not?" he said.

He noticed neither of them could go far in the maze of chairs and tables. They were trapped, forced into a position of proximity.

"I still hate you," she said. "Just so you know."

"The feeling is mutual," he said curtly. His insides roiled, but he held the tankards in his hand steady.

"Please get out of my way," she insisted, her round little chin pointing high in the air.

"With pleasure," he returned.

But neither of them moved. Granted, he was rather more trapped than she was, being larger and surrounded by more jutting angles of tables and chairs.

But then a mass of people surged from behind Molly, spilled around them on both sides, and filed past to join their brethren at the large table. Molly joined the swell, bumping against a large lout who leered at her, his teeth stained yellow and broken, and narrowly evading jostling a rosy-cheeked matron with a grinning babe on her hip.

And then she broke free.

Harry watched her head toward the door to the stable-yard. She was escaping him, no doubt, he thought grimly.

As well she should.

CHAPTER 3

Molly had to get out of the taproom so she could breathe and decide what to do. But she already knew what to do. Her wicked self was speaking to her, and she refused to let herself stop it. Her wicked self always came out around Harry.

It was telling her that she must go inside and dump a tankard of beer over his head.

She bunched her skirt in her fists and stared fixedly at John Coachman, who sat patiently atop Cedric's coach, snoring into his chest. From the corner of her eye, she saw a brood of hens pecking at the dirt beneath an oak tree.

Pouring beer over Harry would, indeed, bring her some sort of solace. But she'd matured, hadn't she? She didn't have to be quite so obvious in her disdain for him. Even more deliciously satisfying would be for her to hie herself back to her table—back to Cedric—and make it look as though they were an extremely happy couple in love.

She'd pretend that Cedric was a huge catch. She'd make some remark about an amazing naked statue he'd uncovered and say that Prinny himself was anxious to see it.

Harry would be suitably impressed, and he would rue the day he ever did her wrong.

Which wasn't necessarily one specific *day,* now that Molly thought about it. He'd done her wrong on many days—just by being *Harry.*

Any doubts she had about going to Gretna with Cedric were now completely quashed.

"I'll marry Cedric, and we'll be ridiculously happy," she said out loud to no one and turned back to the inn door.

She resolutely pushed herself through the throng inside to her table, where Cedric sat, moodily plucking at grapes and chewing on something, as slow as a cow at cud.

He hated fruit. She knew it was costing him dearly, this ruse by which he could stay and gaze at his Aphrodite.

"Cedric!" Molly called to him, her hands clasped to her bosom. "My love!"

He looked up at her and said nothing.

She smiled brightly and, seating herself, sensed the overwhelming presence of Harry at the table beside her.

"I have no desire to try your meal," she heard Harry say.

She stole a glance. Aphrodite was holding out her fork, not speaking, but obviously insisting that he taste something on the tines.

"No, *thank* you," Harry said with more force. A lone black curl fell across his brow, and he was in desperate need of a shave.

Molly suppressed a scoff. Of course, even when Harry *did* shave, he appeared in desperate need of a shave. That blue-black shadow on his jawline never went away. He looked like a lascivious pirate disguised as a gentleman, whether he was dressed as he was now or in evening clothes.

If he were any other man, she would dream about being ravished by him (whatever that entailed; Penelope wouldn't tell *all*). But as it was, Molly slowed the pounding of her heart by recalling the time he'd brought her a second small Queen cake at his parents' last anniversary celebration, when he knew very well a lady stopped at one—and then had the effrontery to say, "I know you want it. You have the appetite of a man."

Oh, he was wicked!

Now she watched as the pink-gowned beauty waved the fork in front of Harry's face. Finally, he took his large hand and pushed the fork back in her direction. "Please," was all he said.

But Molly knew that voice. It was forceful, annoyed. She'd heard it several times the past year, at the baptism of her niece, at Christmas, and at a family funeral.

Aphrodite burst into soft, beautiful tears, dropped her fork to her plate, and stood up from the table. Her bosom heaved in a most . . . visible fashion.

"My God," Cedric said, mouth agape, staring at that bosom. A pulpy grape sat in the middle of his tongue.

"Do swallow that," Molly said, feeling sour and mean and ready to spar with someone. "You've been chewing on it this age."

But Cedric ignored her. His mouth stayed open as he watched Aphrodite walk away. Her rich brown hair spilled in glorious curls down the center of her back, exposing her creamy shoulders. Her lovely pink dress was adorned with a matching cream sash that fluttered silkily behind her.

And then Cedric turned back to Molly, livid, judging from the slant of his magnificent brows, and spat the grape out on the plate. "How can you think of grapes at a time like thish?" he sputtered.

Molly felt like slapping his face. But she widened her eyes instead. And prayed to think of something compelling—and romantic—to say back to him.

* * *

Harry eyed Molly's companion. What a milksop. Of course, he knew who Cedric Alliston was, the smarmy bounder. His affectations at Eton were legion, the most prominent being a tendency to speak as if his jaw were glued shut.

Harry suppressed a smirk and watched as Molly tried to forget the chewed-up grape in full view on Alliston's plate.

"Exactly," she was saying. "How can I think of anything but our Gretna wedding, my love?"

Oh, dear God.

Alliston got up. "I shall check on the horsh-es," he said.

Right. Harry had no doubt he'd be checking on the whereabouts of the lovely Fiona. Harry had seen the lust in his eyes, which the fool hadn't even bothered to disguise in front of Molly.

Molly smiled and waved. "I'll be waiting!"

When Alliston left, she turned to Harry. "I'm sorry you obviously haven't found true love yourself," she said lightly, striving her damnedest to sound like a woman adored.

"If what you and Alliston have is true love, then I don't want it," Harry threw back. "Besides, it's awfully hard to find true love when you're trudging all over Europe with the King's army *for five years.*"

She stiffened. That hadn't been her fault. He'd been the one to kiss Penelope, after all!

She lifted her chin. "I hear you were a perfect disgrace in the army. You should try peeling potatoes every morning, noon, and night at a miserable school *for five years.*"

Neither one said another word. Several minutes passed. Harry finished his meal. Molly scraped at her plate, squinting in annoyance because the sun was winking off his boots, which she suspected he buffed with champagne. His chest hairs were curling rudely from the gaping vee at his neck, and when he yawned quite loud enough to wake the dead, his overly tanned neck corded from the effort.

"Goodness," she admonished him from under her breath.

Harry grinned at her, exposing brilliant white teeth, but his eyes were rather slitted, as if he were cursing her at the same time. "I had rather too much fun last night," he said in an offhand manner and stretched out his legs.

Too much *fun*?

Molly glared at him, not one bit surprised at his audacity.

The crowd at the large table exited the taproom. The only people left were Molly, Harry, and two old men at the bar. And of course, the innkeeper and the flirtatious barmaid. They'd done a booming business today.

Molly sighed. "Well, I shall go meet my intended outside."

"And I shall meet my beautiful companion." Harry pushed back from the table, threw some coins down, and stood, looming above Molly.

"You mean your lightskirt," she said.

"Yes," Harry replied. "And thank God I don't have to take her to Gretna. I can simply take my pleasure with her and be on my way."

"You—" Molly breathed.

"No, *you*," Harry said back.

She stood, skewered him with a look, and stepped smartly around him, quite as if he were nothing more than a chair, or a bucket, or a broom. She strode toward the inn door. Harry moved in that direction, as well. Each went by different paths, through different tables. Molly started to walk faster, but to her dismay, Harry did, too.

And then it was a race—who would get to the door

first? Of course Harry won, with his longer legs, a fact which annoyed Molly no end. When he stopped at the threshold, she pushed under his arm and emerged first in the stableyard.

But Harry didn't seem to notice. He was staring at a carriage moving at a smart pace out of the yard onto the road. A flash of pink could be seen inside its window.

Harry's lightskirt had been wearing pink!

"Oh, my," Molly said, and couldn't help the note of triumph in her voice. Wouldn't it be splendid if the beautiful Aphrodite had left Harry for another man?

"What the hell?" Harry snarled. He obviously didn't care that Molly saw his rage. She was as nothing to him, as he was to *her*.

He took off at a run.

Molly gazed down the road, too, at the carriage, at Harry running toward it. The coachman whipped the horses into a frenzy of speed, and Molly couldn't help but enjoy seeing Harry fall well behind its wheels.

And then she recognized something. The back of Cedric's carriage. It had gotten a mighty scratch on it from the time he'd chained a naked statue to the roof and wrapped the chain around the carriage body.

Harry's lightskirt was inside Cedric's carriage.

"Cedric," she whispered, and she began to run, too. She lifted her skirts with her left hand and followed Harry onto the road, her boots flying.

"Cedric!" she cried, and waved her shuttered parasol above her head. "Please don't leave me!"

But the coachman flashed his whip again. The horses strained at their bits and galloped even faster, seemingly anxious to leave the inn and its stableyard far behind them.

CHAPTER 4

Molly stood on the road beside Harry and watched the vehicle carrying Cedric and his Aphrodite disappear around a bend in the road. Her ears began to buzz. In the distance, the chickens, the oak tree, the woman and child climbing into a wagon in the stableyard—all became wavy, like ribbons of taffy.

God, no. This couldn't be happening to her. Everything, *everything* . . . was wrong, upside down.

She blinked slowly, several times, to make the waves go away. When they did, she found her feet again, one of which she promptly stomped at Harry.

"Now see what you've done," she said. "I'm stranded here because *your* fit of temper caused *your* lightskirt to throw herself into the arms of *my* intended!"

Harry brought his face a mere few inches from her own. "And *your* intended obviously had had enough of *your* bossiness. So much so that he took off with *my* lightskirt!"

"You shouldn't have a lightskirt," said Molly. "What would your mother say?"

"And you shouldn't be running off to Gretna Green with a spineless fop."

Molly refused to blink. "He wasn't spineless. Simply . . . sensitive."

Although she had no idea why she was defending Cedric. It was Harry's fault, of course. He always brought out the irrational in her.

Harry scoffed. "Alliston sensitive? He is about as sensitive as a tree stump."

She crossed her arms. "And your lightskirt is about as intelligent as . . . as an insect."

Harry's smile was wicked. "She doesn't require intelligence for what I need her for."

If he intended to make her blush, Molly wouldn't give him the satisfaction. She turned her back and put up her parasol.

Never in a million years would she ask Harry's help.

But help was what she needed. She was stranded at a remote hostelry in the middle of England, unchaperoned and without even the excuse of going to Gretna Green with her intended to protect her reputation.

If anyone back home found out what was happening to her, she was a fallen woman.

Harry watched Molly march onto the dusty road, the silliest of striped parasols open above her head. She stared down both ways with a wrinkle on her brow. He recalled that there were no farmhouses or places to stop for at least ten miles southward, but the north road led her even farther from home.

"Here now!" he called to her.

She turned around. "I've nothing to say to you." She put her chin in the air and headed south.

Harry trotted after her, grabbed her elbow, and swung her around. "You're not going to disappear and leave me in an awkward situation."

Her cheeks were spotted pink. "Oh, and I'm not in one

myself? Any gentleman would have noticed I am! But no, you're no gentleman. The whole world knows *that*."

She hit him on the chest with her reticule. It felt empty, except for maybe a coin.

He sighed. "That doesn't help anything."

She inhaled through her nose and let her breath out in a gusty sigh. "I'm sorry. A lady doesn't hit people. Even though you deserve it, cavorting with a woman who's no lady at all, running off with any man she sees!"

He scoffed. "Are you telling me *you're* a lady? You put a thistle in my seat and a rock in my wine goblet last time I dined at Marble Hill."

"That was a long time ago."

"It was at Penelope and Roderick's bon voyage celebration before they took the girls to Italy. Barely four months ago."

"Yes, but how is that worse than pulling someone's chair out a little too far? You did it the very evening after your dear aunt Cora expired! I almost fell on my bottom at supper, in front of all your grieving family, thanks to *you*."

"I did it for Aunt Cora," he said. "She liked practical jokes."

"A poor excuse," Molly replied.

They glared at each other. Neither one spoke for a minute, and then she said, rather thickly, "We're both in trouble."

He hoped she wouldn't become a watering pot. It was the last thing he needed, to be in the presence of a stubborn shrew who was also *crying*.

"Perhaps we should help each other out of it," he said very reluctantly.

Oh, how it cost him!

"That's what I was thinking," she said, brightening a bit.

Thank God. Although seeing her brighten was something he usually wouldn't encourage.

"Exactly what *is* your situation?" she asked him.

"I'm traveling to a house party, a rather lively one. I can take you with me."

"Lively?"

"Let's just say it's not the sort of house party *you*'d typically attend. Or most members of the *ton,* for that matter. It's . . . unique. This year I've been designated the host."

She waved him off and kept walking.

"And I need a mistress to take with me!" he called after her, refusing to look or sound ashamed.

She wheeled around. "I should have known you'd propose something scandalous." And then marched off again in an even greater huff.

"You'd be my *false* mistress, not a real one, you foolish chit!" As usual, she had his blood boiling.

She turned again, stopped, stuck an index finger on her chest. "Me? Foolish?"

"Yes, *you.* Walking into certain danger on that road." He felt his nostrils flare like a bull's. There was not a person in the world who could rile him the way Molly Fairbanks did.

"Dangerous?" She put a fist on her hip. "How is walking on a road more dangerous than attending a gathering with you, where there'll be sure to be drunken louts falling everywhere and lightskirts gadding about half clothed? And why would anyone need a false mistress anyway? It's a ludicrous concept."

Harry crossed his arms and prayed for patience. "First of all, we shan't be drunk *all* the time."

Molly rolled her eyes.

"There *is* some strategy involved."

"Such as?"

"If I show up with no mistress at all," he explained,

"I'll lose the wager immediately. So I must bring *some-one*. Your presence will at least keep me in the game."

She opened her mouth to rip into him—he saw the flare of battle in her eyes—but he put his index finger in the air. "I'm willing to make you a mistress *in name only* to protect your virtue." She should be pleased. "Although no one else shall know of our arrangement, of course."

He'd be the only man at the house party with a false mistress. Did she not appreciate his sacrifice?

She lowered her brows. "I knew it was something like that. What exactly do you mean by 'game'?"

"We compete. Whoever brings the finest mistress wins."

"Ugh." She rolled her eyes. "Do go on."

"Each woman shall be judged on her beauty—extra points for beauty, actually, especially if we can *see* much of it."

Molly's brow wrinkled. " 'See much of it'?"

"Yes." He bit his lip, not caring to explain. "And then, of course, she shall be judged on her conversation. And her wit." He snapped his fingers. "If she's skilled at gambling with ha'pennies, laughs frequently at men's jokes, and notices when their brandy snifters need replenishing, so much the better."

"You're joking."

Harry shrugged. "Not at all. To sum up, she'll be judged on almost all the things that make a female, shall we say, mesmerizing to a man."

Molly sighed and tapped her foot. "What do you win if you bring the, um, finest of the mistresses?"

"*She* gets the glory of winning the title—'the Most Delectable Companion,' " he said as if he were announcing the tightrope walker at the traveling circus. "And a crown of paste," he remembered to add.

She twisted her face up. "That's all? She receives no tangible reward beyond a worthless title and tiara?"

He shifted, suddenly feeling doubtful. Molly had a way of making him feel like a . . . a dunderhead. He hadn't felt that way since—

Since he'd *last* seen her!

"You should at least give the Most Delectable Companion loads of money," she said, her chin back in the air. "God knows she'll deserve it. Any lightskirt of yours would require the patience of a saint!" She paused only long enough to get her breath. "What does her consort win?"

"Another year of freedom from the parson's noose," he said with relish, because he knew she would hate to hear him say it. "And every matchmaking mama, all the dragon ladies who rule Almack's, and every bettor at every club in London will know he's off the market. Thanks to a royal decree put forth by Prinny himself."

"Prinny?" Her lip curled. "You mean the Prince Regent will give you permission to enjoy shirking your duty by your family."

"What duty?" Harry said coolly. "Roderick shall be the next Duke of Mallan, and Penelope will be sure to produce a son soon. He'll already have four big sisters to boss him about. The line is thriving, I assure you."

"But *you* must marry, as well." She sounded exactly like his mother. *And* his sister-in-law. *And* his father and brother.

"I am the spare," he ground out. "I can stay a bachelor as long as I'd like. They merely need me if Roderick sticks his spoon in the wall before his son is born, and my brother is a hale, hearty fellow who shall be around for another seventy years at least."

"But your mama will want more grandchildren," Molly persisted, twirling her parasol as if they were conversing about the weather.

She must quite enjoy bickering, Harry thought. Perhaps it was her favorite pastime.

He felt his mouth become a grim line. "I'd rather not discuss it. It is, quite frankly, none of your business, Molly Fairbanks."

"Ohhhh," she growled, and lowered her parasol to glare at him. As if he couldn't see the intensity of that fierce look unless the sun were full upon her face.

They were getting nowhere. Fast. And she was working herself up to hitting him again with that blasted reticule.

"Let's get back to business, shall we?" he said. "The men whose mistresses *don't* win the contest must pull straws to see who must get legshackled to the woman handpicked for each of them by the board of their club. So we have an obvious winner *and* an obvious loser."

Molly brightened. "If you lose this year, you'll have to marry Anne Riordan."

"How do *you* know?"

"Easy. Your papa's on the board, and he tells everyone he believes she'll have a calming influence on you." She inclined her head and smiled. "I will quite enjoy that, seeing you and Anne married."

He narrowed his eyes at her. "You always were cruel."

She laughed. "Tell me, Harry, what would I get out of being your—ahem—false mistress?"

He crossed his arms. "Safe, anonymous travel back to Marble Hill. I assume your father is traipsing about Europe somewhere and that you somehow pulled the wool over his cousin Augusta's eyes?"

"How did *you* know?"

"Easy. You're extremely predictable."

She narrowed her eyes. "I don't like how you said that."

He shrugged. "Take it as you wish."

She bit her thumbnail. "But the gentlemen at the house party. What if they recognize me in town? Now that I'm not marrying Cedric, I shall have to have a Season."

"You'll wear loads of face powder and rouge."

"They'll itch." She knew from experimenting with Cousin Augusta's.

"And you must use a false name."

"I'll forget it. I know it."

He sighed. "You can't afford to forget it."

"Then it must be Delilah," she said. "It's the only name I'll be able to remember."

"Why Delilah?"

"I don't know. But I already know I won't forget it."

Harry shook his head. He would never quite understand women and the way their minds worked, especially Molly's—thank God.

"You needn't be overly worried about being found out," he said. "The gentlemen will be mildly pickled half the time—when we're out shooting—and severely so the other half. Plus, they'll be looking *down* almost always." He cocked one brow.

Her face grew red. "Do you mean—" She glanced down at her own bodice.

"Yes."

She shuddered. "This house party sounds awful."

"It will be." He grinned. "Positively dreadful."

She narrowed her eyes, kicked a stone in the road, and then whirled back to face him. "Why me?" she demanded. "Why not ask that buxom barmaid back at the inn to be your *real* mistress? She's a willing handful, isn't she?"

He resented having to venture into truth territory, where vague notions about saving damsels in distress claimed priority over his own more immediate needs and wants.

"Believe me," he said. "I thought about asking her, even if she is a bit rustic. But I can't allow a gently bred lady to be thrust out into the world unprotected. Even if that so-called *lady*"—he put as much sarcasm in the word as possible—"is *you*."

"Oh." She drew back.

"Oh," she said again, softer this time, and bit her lip.

He'd gone too far. And yes, he felt guilty. Roderick would have his hide if he'd heard Harry address his sister-in-law so.

But Molly was so . . . provoking. Always had been. From the time she'd discovered, at age four, a sack of acorns he'd spent two weeks gathering for a game of war with Roderick and redistributed them to the squirrels at Marble Hill.

She shook her head. "I won't go with you. But thank you for asking." Her voice was small. She lowered her parasol and took off down the road again, this time looking not so much like Napoleon. Her arms were wrapped around her middle, not swinging boldly. Her stride had shortened, as well.

She stumbled over a rock.

"Wait!" he called to her.

She recovered and kept walking.

He strode after her. "Will you *stop*?"

She quickened her pace.

He caught up to her, and she began to run.

Dash it all, he would have to run, too!

In one fell swoop, he lifted her over his shoulder and turned back to the inn. She screamed and kicked and beat him with her parasol, but he paid no heed to her pathetic attempts to make him submit to her shrill threats and simply kept walking.

"Thrash and scream to your heart's content," he said, ignoring the ringing in his ears. "Perhaps it will tire you out."

A remark which his captive took to heart.

Seemingly by the grace of God alone, Harry made it to the stableyard without too much bodily damage.

"Ready?" he called to his coachman, who'd been ready

this age, and was agog at the sight of his master toting a screaming virago who was, at the same time, obviously a well-bred young lady, over his shoulder. Harry opened the door to the carriage, stuffed Molly in, and jumped in himself, pulling the door quickly behind him and holding it shut. He put his hand on the other door as well to keep it sealed.

The carriage rocked forward and began a brisk roll out of the stableyard. They were on the road north again.

Molly clenched the seat cushion and drew in huge lungfuls of air. "I told you I hated you, Harry," she said between breaths. "But the truth is I hate you with a capital *H*. That's even more than I hated you before."

He would allow her that diatribe. As penance for his "you're no lady" dig.

"Nevertheless," he replied coolly. "We're stuck together. For one week."

Inwardly, he sighed. Then reassured himself—if he could handle Waterloo, he could most certainly deal with Molly Fairbanks.

CHAPTER 5

Molly glared at Harry through slitted eyes, leaned back, and looked out her window. "Don't expect me to say a word," she muttered. "The entire trip."

"I was counting on it," he replied, cheerily enough.

Damn him.

She was still reeling from having been carried upside down by him and flailing madly at his back. But what was a girl to do but rebel when insulted by one's own worst enemy?

The carriage rolled on. They passed several farms—farms where she could have taken refuge, perhaps, if Harry hadn't acted like a pirate and made off with her as if she were some sort of booty.

She was to be his mistress. His *false* mistress.

She tried not to think too hard about what being a contender for the title of Most Delectable Companion would entail. Would he have to . . . kiss her? In front of everyone else, to act as if she were his actual mistress?

Her heart raced at the thought, so she glowered at him. Because it really was vile, the idea of her own innocent lips touching his double-speaking ones—even though his lips were quite tempting to the average girl. They were strong yet pliant-looking, and they were usually quirked in a pleasingly masculine expression.

But she wasn't your average girl.

"I know what you're thinking," he said. "You wish you could speak. But you already said you wouldn't, and I'm holding you to it."

She slitted her eyes again.

"We shall be stopping in the next hour. There is another inn, a more respectable one. I shall escort you to a private room and guard your door while you change into one of Fiona's gowns and apply her cosmetics."

Her eyes widened.

"What?" Harry drew his brows together. "Are you wondering if Fiona has many gowns?"

Molly nodded. Violently.

"Indeed she does," Harry replied. "And bonnets. The latest creations from Paris, I believe."

Molly grinned, but then immediately stopped, attempted to look sick and depressed, and stared out the window.

"Too late," he said. "I saw it."

"Oh, you—" She clamped her mouth shut.

"Hah! You said something!" He chuckled.

Indeed, he looked entirely too pleased with himself.

"I think I *shall* talk," she said, in a wicked voice. "I think my silence pleases you. So I *shan't*"—she paused for emphasis—"be silent any longer."

Sure enough, he got a wrinkle on his brow and his mouth moved down into a frown.

Splendid!

"As a matter of fact," she added breezily, "I should like to discuss this house party. Who will be there?"

Harry shifted in his seat. "You already know of most of them if you read the London papers."

"I'm not supposed to," said Molly. "Papa says they give me *ideas*."

"Which means you read them anyway, don't you?"

She refused to dignify that remark.

Harry gave an easy laugh. "We'll be in the company of the other men conscripted by Prinny to be his Impossible Bachelors," he said. "Nicholas Staunton, Lord Maxwell. Viscount Charles Lumley. Captain Stephen Arrow. And the baronet, Sir Richard Bell."

"Lord Maxwell." Molly started with her left index finger. "I've never heard of him."

"He's a very good friend, a trifle mysterious and rather a recluse."

"Who's his mistress?"

"That would be Athena Markham—"

"She who treads the boards?"

"Right. It could be he's thrown her over for someone else. I've no idea."

Molly gave a huff. "Lord Maxwell would be a fool to throw over Athena Markham."

"Why is that?"

"She's divine. Penelope told me so. She saw her in *King Lear.*"

"She certainly tends to attract an audience, on or off the stage. And she's quite beautiful." Harry sighed and looked quite as if he were already sporting a ball and chain, with Anne Riordan holding the lock and key.

"What?" Molly sat up higher in her seat. "You think I have no chance against Miss Markham?"

Harry merely gave her a very droll look.

"You've no idea of my acting abilities," Molly said. It was bragging, she knew, but she was *good*. At least she knew she would be if only someone would give her a chance to be in a play!

"You're right," he said, his chin in his hand. "I've no idea."

She knew he hadn't meant that as a compliment.

"Let's move on," she said, grasping her middle left finger. "That viscount. Lumley. I've heard that everything he touches turns to gold."

Harry frowned. "Yes. He's the best of fellows. But he's easily taken advantage of—not in business, but in matters of the heart. I've no idea how he's made it this far without being legshackled. His better friends, and I count myself one of them, have come to conclude that it's luck. Not skill."

"Yes, particularly as he's worth twenty thousand a year," Molly replied.

For once, they were in agreement. But then she realized Harry was boasting. "Do you really think it takes skill to remain a bachelor as long as you have?"

"Certainly." His tone was a trifle too smug. "It's like feinting to the left or right, or ducking, when you're fencing. Some of us have the natural ability to dodge and survive—others do not."

"So you've evaded parson's mousetrap how many times?"

"Countless," he murmured, and then smiled, but it was to himself, she saw, a small smile of recollection.

She didn't like that smile. It meant that he was thinking of all the girls (besides Penelope) whom he'd kissed—and perhaps done more with—and escaped without any consequences.

The roué!

"Someday you'll be caught," she reminded him.

His face took on a foreboding expression. "Yes, as I was once before, thanks to *you*." He was referring to the Christmas incident, of course. "But I've a few years left," he added.

"Do you think Anne will wait that long for a proposal?"

"No," he said. "Which is another reason for me to delay."

"But someone else will crop up," Molly said darkly. "Perhaps she'll be worse than Anne."

Harry sighed. "I know."

He looked so sad and desperate that she almost felt sorry for him.

Almost.

Back to business. "Tell me about the third person, that captain." She wriggled her ring finger to show him she was still counting.

"Oh, yes," Harry said. "Captain Stephen Arrow, another old friend. He's a dashing fellow who takes to the high seas whenever a young miss gets too adoring. Of course, he's fought in many battles, so we mustn't begrudge him his excuse."

"An easy out, being a ship's captain," said Molly. "If every man had a ship, we'd have no males left on land at all."

"Yes, I'd take facing cannonballs over a woman's expectations any day," said Harry.

"*Ha.*" Molly glared at him. "Who's the fourth again?"

"A baronet, Sir Richard Bell." Harry sighed. "I despise the man. But he's certainly a tried-and-true bachelor."

"How so?"

"He's been seducing young debutantes without getting caught for close to twenty years."

"Surely not."

"Oh, yes. I don't know what he tells them, but they never tattle to their parents, who would, of course, demand he be brought up to scratch."

Molly wrinkled her brow. "I don't like the sound of him."

"Stay away from him. The past several years, he's had a particular aversion to me."

"Why?"

"I don't know. I've always wondered. He's older than

Roderick, and we run in different circles. So I don't see why he'd even notice me. But he does. He goes out of his way to be unpleasant." Harry shrugged. "I simply ignore him."

"Hmmm. Probably your best bet."

"And he always keeps the same mistress," Harry went on. "It's a mystery why she stays with him. Of course, his wealth probably lured her in, but she could do much better. Her name, I believe, is Bunny."

"Is she a strong contender for the title of Most Delectable Companion?"

"Yes." Harry grinned. "She is what most men would describe as the perfect mistress."

"Why?" Molly nudged at his crossed knee. "What is it about her that makes her perfect?"

She knew she shouldn't enjoy talking about mistresses, but it was so much more interesting than hearing Cedric prose on about naked statues or Miss Dunlap lecture on the virtues of self-discipline.

"Bunny has the face and figure of a goddess," Harry said. "And the disposition of your most favored servant, the one who answers your every beck and call and asks nothing in return."

Molly made a face. "Ugh. Is that what men really want? She sounds like a pet. A favorite dog."

Harry chuckled. "Oh, no." His tone was silky. "She is nothing like a favorite dog, I assure you."

Molly felt her chest tighten. "I don't like men who want women who are constantly currying their favor."

"Of course you wouldn't like those men! Because you don't curry anyone's favor—except maybe Cedric's. Weren't you as affable as a lapdog with him?"

She refused to answer because, by God, she had been!

"I knew it," Harry said. "You were his slave."

"Never," Molly lied.

She despised Harry for bringing up Cedric and her fawning behavior with him, which she'd instituted as soon as she'd realized she wanted him to run off with her. Hopefully, Harry hadn't also deduced that she'd coerced Cedric into kissing her that very morning. Because every woman should be kissed at the start of her elopement, shouldn't she?

Cedric hadn't deserved a kiss from her, she realized now. And judging from his bland response, he obviously hadn't *wanted* it, either, which was an even more lowering thought.

"You're best rid of him," Harry said easily. "It's not in your nature to be obedient."

"Stop talking about my nature," she said. That was personal, and what did he know about *hers*?

And then he seemed to read her mind.

"Believe it or not, Molly Fairbanks." His voice was low, intimate. "I know you."

She felt gooseflesh on her arms and a strange thrumming in her middle. "Don't talk to me in that . . . that way! It's indecent. I shall tell the duke."

He laughed. "I wouldn't, if I were you. It's only how a man addresses his mistress." He sat up and his expression grew serious. "Get used to it," he said in a neutral manner. "I shall have to address you that way at the house party."

"No." Molly crossed her arms. "It's quite inappropriate."

"The whole week will be inappropriate," he reminded her.

"Hmmmph."

"While we are on the subject"—he had a way of ignoring her *hmmmphs* that quite riled her—"let's go over some expected behavior."

"Oh?" She prayed he wouldn't mention kissing him.

She would have to close her eyes and pretend he was Cedric, although, blast it, she didn't love Cedric!

All right, then. She would pretend Harry was a hero in a gothic novel, that's what she would do. She'd even give him an imaginary name. She was Delilah. So he'd be . . .

Samson.

She closed her eyes a moment, envisioning a noble Samson cradling her in his strong, golden arms. *Oh, Samson!* she would sigh. And then he'd kiss her. Just like that.

She opened her eyes again.

"Are you all right?" Harry had a squiggle on his brow. "Your mouth was hanging open. I was sure you were about to faint."

"I'm fine, thank you very much." She laced her fingers together. "Do go on."

"About *kissing,*" Harry said, his eyes locking onto hers.

She'd never noticed them before. They were a warm, rich brown with little golden glints in them. Her stomach tightened, and for some reason, the air seemed to grow hot in the carriage. Perhaps someone should open a window, she thought—

And then her world went black.

CHAPTER 6

Seeing Molly slack—without a fight in her—nearly undid Harry. He had the instant thought that he would be sent to hell for teasing her if she died.

So he must see to it that she recovered. Immediately.

He slapped her gently on the cheek. "Molly! Wake up!"

Nothing happened. He glanced down and saw the regular rise and fall of the rounds of her breasts, peeping from the top of her modest neckline.

She was obviously in no danger of dying. He ignored the vague sensation of relief that swelled his chest and shook her gently by the shoulders. "Wake *up,* Molly!"

Her skin was alabaster white, her eyelids almost translucent. She was like Briar Rose in that Brothers Grimm tale, but—

You'd have to pay him a million pounds to kiss her to wake her up, and even then he wouldn't do it.

"Women and their megrims," he muttered, and grabbed a flask out of his pocket. Carefully, he dribbled a bit of brandy into her half-parted mouth.

She made a spitting noise and then her eyes began blinking madly.

He leaned over her. "Feeling better?"

She sat bolt upright. "What in heaven's name—" Her puckish brown eyes registered confusion first, then annoyance.

Which meant she was back to her old self.

"You fainted, I believe." Harry grinned. "I had no idea you were that sort of female."

"I am certainly not *that* sort of female, if you mean weak and insipid. I simply didn't get enough to eat today."

"That and perhaps you're worried about your duties as a mistress."

"*False* mistress," she corrected him. Her cheeks grew a tiny bit pink. "And I am *not* worried. I'm quite capable of performing my duties. Even though I have no idea what they are, beyond the card playing and the laughing and the appearing beautiful all the time." Looking out the window, she scooted deeper into her seat and crossed her arms over her breasts.

Harry leaned back, amused, because she was obviously worried about her duties, and nothing gave him more satisfaction than seeing Molly Fairbanks ill at ease.

Even so, he decided to grace her with a small, reassuring smile—*not* to be kind, he reminded himself, but to calm her so she'd perform her forthcoming role exceptionally well. Otherwise, he'd likely be sitting across the breakfast table from Anne Riordan sooner than later.

"Speaking of your responsibilities as my false mistress—"

"Yes?" she said rather fast.

"To make it appear as if we have a genuine relationship," he said, "we will have to . . . *kiss* every once in a while. If we don't, someone may catch on that you aren't a real lightskirt, and then I am doomed."

She made a face that proved pretty girls can turn into the veriest hags at a moment's notice if they so choose. "I don't *want* to kiss you, Harry."

He rolled his eyes. "It doesn't have to *mean* anything."

"Are you sure?"

"Quite." Harry strove to sound like an old, trusted friend. "A kiss is simply a kiss. Two mouths meeting. Nothing to fear."

She appeared to be thinking. "I *do* kiss my horse sometimes," she said. "Usually on the nose, but"—she put her hand to her mouth—"once I kissed him on the lips."

She laughed outright. Some would say in a charming manner.

Not Harry, of course. But he could give her, at the very least, a modicum of a smile. "Kissing a man might be slightly different from kissing a horse," he said, attempting to match her lighthearted tone.

But her eyes suddenly lost their impish quality. They became stormy. Defiant. Hurt.

Ah, thought Harry. Cedric had either kissed her. Or *not* kissed her.

He dared not ask which.

"Do it," Molly said, closing her eyes. "Right now."

Harry hesitated. He should have known she would try to take him off guard. She always wanted the upper hand.

Very well, then. He would show her who had the upper hand!

And if she had any memories of Cedric's kisses, he would erase them. Because Harry prided himself on his kissing abilities. Not that he'd ever told anyone that. But still. He'd never left a woman disappointed.

"Ready?" he said.

She nodded, very fast, and squeezed her eyes even tighter shut. Her fists were clenched in her lap so hard her knuckles were white.

He took her by the shoulders and bent forward, wary. But her lips immediately conformed to his. They were soft and cushiony, and despite the fact she'd had brandy mere seconds ago, she tasted sweet, like strawberries. How had a sharp-tongued wench like her managed that?

He gained courage at her passive acceptance of the kiss, although he sensed, and was mildly entertained by, the stiffness of her posture. Praying that she'd not balk—because the chaste kiss they were now sharing wasn't nearly the kiss a man and his mistress would share at a ribald gathering—he teased her mouth open further.

Harry heard her small intake of breath at the invasion, but he trusted in his kissing skills, pushing farther and farther into the sweet boundaries of her mouth until he sensed himself reacting, really reacting.

And it was because she was responding. She sort of melted into him across the space separating them in the carriage, and he pulled her onto his lap, and he pressed her lower back just so, to settle her.

She was molded perfectly to his body now. She lifted her hand and placed it tentatively around his neck, gripped him, and drew him even closer. One part of his mind was appalled at himself, kissing a girl whom he wouldn't mind seeing fall off a cliff, and the other demanded that the pleasurable sensations continue.

Of course, the side demanding pleasure won.

And then she said something like, "Mmmmm," deep in her throat, a wholly unexpected response which took him to the next level of . . . of need, he supposed. Not that he needed to kiss Molly.

He needed Fiona, the lightskirt to end all lightskirts, whose company he'd been deprived of—thanks to the woman sitting on his lap right now.

Abruptly, he pulled back and took a measured breath.

"Samson," she murmured, like a baby whose toy has been taken away, and opened her eyes. But they were heavy-lidded, her gaze dreamy.

"What did you say?" His own voice was rough—with

irritation, he was sure, brought about by unsated desire for Fiona.

Molly's eyes widened. "Nothing." And with a polite, nervous smile, she stumbled backward into the opposing seat.

He didn't know how to respond. He could have sworn she'd said *Samson*. Who the bloody hell was *he*? Then light dawned. He was playing the Samson to her Delilah. Molly was pretending he was someone else while he kissed her. No woman, as far as he knew, had ever had to pretend he was someone else to enjoy his kisses! While he'd been very aware throughout the whole, insanely delicious kiss that she was Molly.

Yes, Molly the termagant. And Molly the shrew. But Molly, nonetheless.

"I suppose that was adequate practice," she said, and looked out the window at the passing countryside. She appeared bright as a daisy now, her lips cherry red.

"Yes, I suppose so," Harry answered, his mood completely soured.

"That fainting spell was a fluke," she insisted. "I'll be the best false mistress *ever*."

"Um," was all he responded. He wasn't interested in talking to a female who'd used his body to enjoy a fantasy kiss with a biblical figure.

"But Harry." She nudged his knee again. "I'm getting safe passage back home simply for being with you, correct? For giving you that fighting chance. Because if you show up without a mistress, you forfeit the contest and head to the altar with a squint-faced bore."

"Right. Thanks for reminding me."

"Good." She smiled. "Because if I *win*, I want something *more*."

He felt his palms dampen. He hadn't even contemplated the prospect that Molly could win. He should have been better prepared. He should have thought of all the angles this scenario could take. There was a very remote chance she *could* win.

She was pretty, in the way an apple sitting on a blue plate is pretty. Most definitely *not* the way a velvety rose in a crystal vase is pretty (her sister Penelope was that). But pretty nonetheless. He should encourage Molly to win. In fact, he was embarrassed that she'd thought of the possibility first.

"That's right," he said. "If you win, I shall be prepared to reward you a little something extra. Perhaps a bonnet, or a new gown."

"No," Molly retorted. "If I win, I want something much more substantial than a new bonnet or gown."

Every woman of his acquaintance *loved* new bonnets and gowns! He felt his brows come together. "What, exactly, would you want?"

Knowing Molly, she would hit upon something that would hurt him to have to pay. He would do the same thing if he were in her position. It was the nature of their . . . *relationship*. If you could call it that.

The carriage was well sprung, but Harry felt tension gather in the muscles of his back. "Do go on with your pronouncement."

"My *demand*," she corrected him.

"Your demand, then," he said, feigning nonchalance.

But when she opened her mouth to speak, he braced himself for the worst.

CHAPTER 7

"If I win, I want you to find me a husband," Molly said to Harry, her heart pounding with excitement at the thought of taking London by storm in the coming Season. "A *good* one."

A strange look of relief appeared on Harry's face, as if he'd been expecting her to exact from him a ship full of silver and gold if she were to win the Most Delectable Companion title. She had gone rather easy on him, she realized now, but she couldn't regret her choice of prize.

He bit his lip, hard, as if he were trying not to laugh.

Which made no sense, as her plan was brilliant.

"Don't you see?" she said. "In town I must steer clear of men like you and Cedric if I'm to make a good match. I'll rely on your expertise as an Impossible Bachelor to detect that tendency in my suitors. It should make the going much easier."

She was very pleased with her plan, so pleased she'd regained her appetite. She took a lovely green apple from a basket on the seat next to Harry and bit into it.

Harry still didn't say a word. "A good match," he finally croaked, his eyes appearing rather glazed. "For *you*."

She swallowed a chunk of apple. "Have you the head-ache?"

He shook his head.

She needs must explain further, obviously. "I daren't make a mistake, Harry. If I don't marry this Season, I'll be firmly on the shelf. And I don't want to be Cousin Augusta's companion forever."

While she waited for him to say something, *anything,* she surreptitiously adjusted her bodice with one hand (it was still somewhat askew from their kissing practice), nibbled on the apple, and tried not to blush at the remembrance of Harry's kiss.

That morning Cedric's lips had been cold as ice and he'd never opened his mouth, *or* hers.

The sensations she'd felt with Harry's kissing were entirely different and . . . completely unsettling. In fact, she looked forward to more kissing practice. Even if it *was* with Harry. She would continue pretending he was Samson, of course.

Finally, Harry cleared his throat.

"Yes?" She lowered her apple, now more a core than anything else.

She knew him. He'd do something, *anything,* to deny her her wish. But she so wanted to go to London. She *so* wanted to dance! And find a husband, too, she supposed—someone who would understand her.

Harry had a solemn expression on his face, even though his lips kept twitching. "If you win the Most Delectable Companion title," he said, "I will do my very best to locate a gentleman with serious intentions toward you. In fact, I would like nothing more than to see you settled."

"Thank you." She opened the door to the carriage and tossed the apple core out, then returned to a demure position and clasped her hands in her lap.

"Preferably on the Continent," he added. "Or the far north of Scotland."

"Very funny."

"With someone who can . . . *contain* you."

"Enough." She slapped his leg, but she was too excited to give real credence to his insults. He *had* agreed to her terms, after all.

She grabbed a roll from the basket, and leaning back on the squabs, said, "Do your best to see that he's handsome, Harry. And he should not be either too old or too serious—I've had enough of serious with Cedric."

"But Molly—"

"Yes?"

"You do know you must be like honey to attract a bee." He was talking nonsense.

"I want no bee," she said. "I want the best bachelor on the market. And *you* shall find him! Have you any cheese in that basket?" She rummaged through.

"In the bottom," Harry said, then added, "I can't do it alone. You must entice this bachelor. That's where the honey plays a part."

"Oh, bother with honey," she said, topping her roll with cheese and taking a bite. "Although I am perfectly good at enticing if I have to. Look at Cedric."

"There is Cedric," Harry granted rather dubiously. "Tell me, how many gentlemen, all told, have brought you flowers?"

She was reluctant to answer. She was also loath to tell him that the only reason Cedric had eloped with her was because he wanted her father's wealth to back his own digging expeditions.

So instead she ate her bread and cheese and watched a field of cows pass by her window. They swung their tails, and one cow nudged another. When Molly's neck grew pained from twisting, she finally returned her gaze to Harry.

"No man has brought me flowers, actually," she confessed.

Even though Cedric had had no idea he was to elope with her until *she* told him to, he should have brought her flowers. She hoped Harry's lightskirt was taking her former fiancé for all he was worth.

"All the more reason for me to tutor you in the ways of men, then," Harry said. "Because aside from a decent fortune and good name, the skills you must have to win a proper husband are actually very similar to the skills you'll need to be an excellent mistress at the house party. Which I was about to detail for you anyway, before we started practicing our—"

"Kissing," she interjected quickly, wishing they could do it once or twice more. But she didn't want him to know that he was any good at it, so she supposed she would have to wait until the house party to try it again.

"Yes, well"—Harry gave a short laugh—"in either case, whether you are mistress or wife, you will have to be . . . beguiling."

"I can do that," she said, starting on her second roll and slice of cheese.

His lips twitched again. Really, he must have a tic of some sort.

"Watch the other mistresses at the house party," he advised her. "Notice how they act around the men. Every night we'll cast a vote for our favorite mistress of the day—we can't select our own, so this is an opportunity for you to work your charms on the other men."

She sat quietly for a moment. "What will the other men find, as you say, beguiling?"

"What most men do. A beautiful woman, of course, is always a pleasure. And if she doesn't speak too much, if she is mysterious at times, dangling only occasional tidbits of warmth in her speech and manner, then men will find her most intriguing. They will want to see what fire lurks beneath the surface."

Molly scoffed. "That sounds very complicated. And silly."

Harry sighed. "You *asked*."

"What else is there?" Molly wiped her mouth with her handkerchief. "I'll try to be so good at it, they won't mind that I natter on now and again."

Harry sighed. "Men like biddable women, Molly. Someone they don't have to take too seriously, someone who entertains them but knows when to leave them to their other duties and interests."

"Then I'm disgusted with *all* men."

Harry jetted a breath. "Do you want me to help you find a husband or not this Season?"

She felt like sulking but couldn't afford to. "Yes."

"If you have any hope of that happening, then you'd best listen to what I have to say. Because if you don't win the Most Delectable Companion title, I most certainly will not be looking out for your interests in London."

"And if I don't win the Most Delectable Companion title, *you* might have to marry this year."

They glared at each other.

The carriage pulled up to the inn. Thank God. She needed to get away from Harry. Their *relationship*—if you could call it that—was entirely too provoking.

In a private room at the inn, Molly opened Fiona's trunk and gasped.

Goodness. She was looking at a veritable treasure chest filled with shimmering, rich fabrics! In hues that a respectable young lady was never permitted to wear.

She bit her lip to restrain her excitement. Fiona was so very lucky, wasn't she?

Had been lucky, Molly corrected herself, her chest expanding with a glorious, warm feeling. *She* was the fortunate owner of the trunk now!

Pressing a dainty undergarment to her breast, she felt extremely possessive already, although she had no idea what the dainty undergarment *was*. She peered through its diaphanous panels and wondered, but only for a moment.

Because there were elaborate slippers. Fringed and beaded shawls. Two bonnets wrapped in paper, both of them stunning. (The others must be in those hat boxes strapped to Harry's carriage). And nightclothes so sheer, Molly could see right through them.

But the gowns . . . oh, the gowns! In the next few minutes, Molly tossed dress after dress aside, oohing and aahing at the varied fabrics, the elaborate detailing of each one, until she found a dress that was—

Breathtaking.

The most beautiful shade.

And entirely unsuitable for a proper young lady.

It was a bishop's blue muslin sheath spangled with matching bugle beads at the waistline and elaborate flounces at the hem. The bodice plunged to nothing, rather like a sharp cliff.

She sighed, trying not to think of Miss Dunlap and her lectures on modesty.

All Fiona's bodices plunged to nothing. Molly had dutifully looked but found no tuckers to put into those bodices.

"Oh, dear," she said aloud to no one (Harry was having a tankard of beer downstairs). "These gowns are a disgrace!"

She laid her favorite gown on the bed and glared at it.

For another five minutes, she tried to be upset and disappointed at the disgracefulness of that gown. She would ignore it. So she searched through the trunk once more and found a bottle of perfumed oil, quite exotic smelling. She also discovered, of all things, several dyed feathers.

She'd no idea why Fiona would carry such feathers.

But her gaze kept returning to the gown on the bed. Her heart raced. Somehow, she knew wearing that daring dress would feel like a great adventure.

The truth was, she'd be delighted to don it.

She held it up. She should wear a shawl to cover her exposed flesh. And . . . and if Harry required her to re-move the shawl, then—then she would simply have to do so, against her will.

It would be all *his* fault.

Besides, she shouldn't worry overly much even if she *were* half naked. The men would be drunk. And they wouldn't recognize her because she would be disguised.

Yes, that was it! Miss Dunlap couldn't fault her for wear-ing scandalous gowns if she were disguised.

Feeling rather righteous—she was a good girl, after all—Molly sat at a dressing table and applied Aphrodite's— rather, Fiona's—face powder and then rouge to her cheek-bones. She did the same for her lips. She also located a stub of kohl, with which she rimmed her eyes and black-ened her eyebrows.

And then she remembered that Fiona had had a beauty mark.

After another moment's work, Molly was done. She couldn't help but gasp at the image in the mirror. Gone was the Grecian look she so favored—and there was absolutely no trace of the milkmaid look she preferred on Sundays.

Now she resembled a . . . a real tart.

Wrapping a shawl around her shoulders, she skirted around the trunk and opened a door to the hallway. Harry was already there, looking impatient, but also rather serious. As serious as a man about to buy a horse, which was serious, indeed.

He circled her. "Remove the shawl, please."

Biting her lip, she looked down at the floor and did as she was told. And felt an instant draft. She would die of a horrible illness now and be sent to hell.

"Well," said Harry, in a soft, surprised voice.

She looked up and met his eyes. There was something new in his expression. Something that made her heart beat faster. His pupils were large and black, and his mouth curled up in the slightest smile.

"You look . . . perfect," he said, his gaze heating something in her.

"Really?" She gave him a rather wobbly smile back.

He nodded. "The dress fits you better than it did, um, Fiona." He cast a quick glance at the bodice. "Especially there."

"Oh, right." Molly nodded, looking down at the tops of her breasts straining against the fabric. "Thank you."

He walked around her. "Now don't forget. It looks more pleasing without the shawl."

Suddenly, Molly felt better. She had a job to do. And that job was to look more pleasing. She had no time to waste on frivolous thoughts of hell.

"Then I shall *not* wear the shawl." She dropped it on top of the open trunk.

Harry's gaze lingered once more on her bosom. "Um, perhaps in the carriage you *should* wear the shawl."

"Of course." She looked down at the scandalously deep neckline. "I wouldn't want to spill crumbs or anything."

"Right," he said briskly.

She retrieved the shawl. "Are you sure I'll pass the test?"

Harry's eyes gleamed like—

Like she wasn't sure.

But it scared her. And excited her. And sent tingles down her spine. He looked at her as if he would slay a dragon for her and demand she pay him afterward with something akin to what they'd done in the carriage.

Which was perfectly all right with her. She'd gladly pay him that way!

Any nice person would repay someone that way for slaying a dragon!

He took her by the shoulders and pulled her close. "I think you look as if you belong at this house party." His voice was a bit rough around the edges. "No one would possibly guess you don't belong, unless, of course—"

"I open my mouth." She grinned.

He gave a little laugh. "Exactly."

The strange tension between them was gone, thank goodness. Now she could breathe again.

He chucked her under the chin. "Just remember what I said in the coach. Be beguiling. Mysterious."

"Biddable," she repeated, and watched him shut the trunk.

"Yes," he said, as he heaved the trunk over his shoulder.

God, she hated biddable. But even as he carried a large trunk which hit the side of the door on the way out of the room and caused him to swear, Harry looked tremendously pleased with her, which, she supposed, was a good thing. She needed him on her side. They must appear compatible. Otherwise, someone might catch on to their ruse, and she would never win the contest.

Because now returning home scandal-free was not enough. She wanted that husband. He was her ticket out of what would surely be an even more ho-hum existence at Marble Hill, now that Cedric was out of the picture. And as soon as she got this husband, she could cease with the silly nonsense involved in entrapping a man, except for the dancing part and the beautiful-gowns-and-bonnets part.

She would be mistress of her own household in London, and she would tell her doting spouse that she had no intention of shutting up or wearing pale muslin every day, and he wouldn't object because Harry would have found the right man for her, one who enjoyed her conversation and wanted her to dance all the time and ride her horse and attend humorous plays.

She would read scandal sheets and pore over dress patterns and read exciting novels, just like all the other women she knew, and she would most definitely stay away from conversations about ancient relics. She'd still pour tea for Cousin Augusta when she went home to visit Papa, but she'd have friends with her who would divert Cousin Augusta from the brass band in her ears.

Yes, being biddable *now* was a means to an end—Molly's freedom. And there was nothing she desired more than that.

CHAPTER 8

Despite the comfort of Harry's carriage, which sported tasseled curtains and seats of the softest leather, Molly was relieved to arrive at their final destination in the late afternoon. As soon as she'd reentered the carriage that afternoon, all resplendent in her newfound finery, she recalled the kiss she and Harry had shared in the vehicle's cozy interior. She remembered sitting on Harry's lap, smelling his deliciously woodsy man smell, running her fingers through his silken curls, and being crushed to his chest while he kissed her senseless.

It was torture, as if the carriage itself kept whispering, *"That kiss,"* in her ear, especially when she caught Harry staring at her shawl, around the area of her bosom, and once or twice licking his lips. And then something compelled her to accidentally on purpose drop an apple *and* her shawl. She and Harry had both searched for the apple on the floor for ages—it rolled around quite a bit—and their hands kept touching.

And her shawl had conveniently fallen off, which meant even *longer* searching for the apple because Harry kept forgetting to search and stared again at her bosom.

Yes, Molly thought, the afternoon's journey had been

torture. A delicious kind of torture—but torture, nonetheless.

She must get out of the carriage before she burst with wanting to be kissed again, and by Harry, of all people.

Not a moment too soon, John Coachman brought them round to the front door of the house.

"Welcome to my favorite hunting box," Harry said, and held out his hand.

Molly took it and imagined yanking him close for a practice kiss that would harm no one. Instead, she jumped down to the gravel. "Oh, is it yours, then?" she said mildly. "A gift from your father?"

Harry hesitated. "The duke knows how much I love it here," he said, sounding a bit gruff. "So yes, he gave it to me."

"How generous of him." Molly gazed at the neat façade of a three-story gray stone manor. A gravel walkway lined with bright red geraniums led to a front door painted blue. It was tucked neatly into the side of a small, forested hill. "It's lovely," she added.

And it was. She'd quite like to churn butter here. Or knit. Not that she knew how to do either. But she *could* borrow a good book from the library. And she could eat biscuits and drink milk while reading it.

She found herself smiling.

Harry offered her his arm, and she took it gingerly.

"We keep a very limited retinue of servants," he said. "All men, except for Cook. The house isn't particularly grand, but considering what will go on here, it needn't be."

Molly paused, her cozy daydream dissolving like mist. What would actually go on here? She was supposed to be Harry's mistress. And all the other women here would be mistresses, as well, which meant there would be lots of dalliances, and she knew what *that* involved—bare skin being exposed in private nooks or even bedchambers, secret kisses in the garden, and . . . and worse than kisses, according to all the little tidbits of information she'd picked up from Penelope.

"There's a stream that meanders through the forest, and ends up in the lake on the other side of the hill," Harry added, and strode to the front door.

Molly hesitated there. "Really? I adore lakes."

Harry threw her a sly glance. "I always swim in it naked. And I never come here without swimming in it at least once. I've told my guests they have that option, too. It's quite private."

"Harry." She scolded him with a glance, but she felt a bit breathless. "Aren't you the least bit concerned that a lady such as myself might be exposed to unseemly sights?"

"You're the one who took off to Gretna, did you not?" he said with a grin that made him look like a devilish boy in need of a comeuppance. "Should I sacrifice a chance to remain free for another year because of your harebrained idea?"

"I'm not the first person to attempt an elopement to Gretna," she said, her chin rising a fraction, "nor the last."

"It wasn't the elopement that was harebrained—it was whom you decided to elope *with* that makes me doubt your judgment."

"As your choice of lightskirt makes me doubt *yours.* Fiona never said a word, that whole time in the inn. What kind of woman doesn't speak? *Ever?* It's unnatural. Perhaps all her teeth were missing. Was that it?"

He gave her an impenetrable look. "Truce, Molly. We can't *afford* to argue. There is much at stake here."

She sighed. "Oh, very well." Arguing with Harry took her mind off more pressing concerns, such as how she was going to be a false mistress. And how she was going to stop thinking about him swimming naked in that lake.

He opened the door. "Anybody home? We're rather informal here," he told her over his shoulder.

Molly walked in behind him and saw a butler walking at a snail's pace up the hallway toward them.

Before he arrived, Molly glanced around and saw a man's evening shirt flung on top of an ornate blue Chinese vase on the hall table, red patches of paint shaped like a pair of lips on the sleeve.

"Harry," she whispered, pointing at the shirt.

"Up to no good already, I suppose." He chuckled and stuffed the shirt deeper into the vase.

Typical man.

Molly forbore to huff, as the butler reached them and bowed. "Good day, Lord Harry. It's good to have you back. It might interest you to know that just this morning, we received a cask of exceptional brandy delivered by a messenger from His Royal Highness with his best wishes for a successful week."

Molly drew in an appalled breath. *A whole cask of brandy?* The men would be constantly drunk, constantly drunk and pawing at the women. She knew this for a fact because Penelope had warned her that husbands, when they drink, sometimes do naughty things to you with their hands under the supper table when you have company, especially if the company are old schoolmates who are equally drunk.

Molly yawned into her fan and then began to wave it languidly in front of her face to disguise her rising panic. *And* her interest. Harry had nice hands. How would they feel running over her thigh while they sat together at the table eating their turtle soup?

Would she flinch? Would the soup go everywhere?

Or would she do nothing?

She suddenly felt very hot.

"According to the messenger," Finkle went on, "Prinny

shall be awaiting the results of the wager with great interest."

"Is that so?" said Harry mildly. "I was hoping he'd rather forgotten about us. Left us to our own devices."

Finkle's face remained somber. "No, indeed, he has *not* forgotten, Lord Harry. To quote the messenger, the drunken old fart is bored and is seeking—ahem—a bit of fun."

Harry sighed. "With copious amounts of exceptional brandy on the premises, no doubt we'll have some amusing stories to tell His Royal Highness by week's end."

Molly hoped none involving *her,* of course.

A footman appeared at her right and took her wrap. "I shall see to it that this is placed in your room, madam," he said, looking vaguely over her head.

"Thank you," she said, and wondered if he thought her rouge and gown were scandalous. Then she wondered if he was thinking of her *naked,* because she was, after all, supposed to be a mistress.

Oh, God. Was *everyone* thinking about her naked?

She whirled around to see the butler's face, but thankfully he appeared more interested in Harry than in her at the moment.

"Are we the last to arrive, Finkle?" Harry asked, putting his arm around the servant's decrepit old shoulders.

"Indeed you are, sir," said Finkle. "The others were beginning to wonder if you didn't have a . . . a young lady to bring to the house party."

Molly blushed.

Harry threw back his head and laughed. "They would doubt *me*? You wouldn't, would you, Finkle?"

"Never, sir."

"Good man." Harry gave the appearance of slapping him on the back, but Molly could tell it was more of a gentle pat.

Finkle almost smiled, and then, just as suddenly, he appeared to be falling into a deep sleep, his head lolling on his shoulders.

Harry gestured to Molly to say something.

"Wh-where is everyone?" Molly piped up.

Finkle blinked, opened his eyes. "Why, they are at the lake, dear lady. Taking a dip."

She caught Harry's gaze. He smiled, and she froze. That little smile couldn't mean that his guests were all taking a dip together . . . *naked,* could it?

Molly felt herself blush. "Will—will they also be swimming later in the week?"

"They might be so inclined," said Finkle.

"I hope not," she said, and restrained a shudder.

"Why is that, my lady?" Finkle responded politely.

"I—I would rather not catch cold."

"Ah, but it is the height of summer," Finkle said. "The lake will never be warmer than it is right now. You might change your mind when you see it. Especially in the moonlight."

Did—did Finkle assume that everyone went in the lake . . . *naked*? Was he envisioning *her* going in the lake naked, in the moonlight?

And for that matter, was the footman? She swung around to look at him, but he was already gone.

She attempted to smile at Finkle, but she sensed it appeared more as if she had an upset stomach. "I suppose I shall have to see the lake. Eventually. Although we might be so busy, I might never get around to it."

"Oh, we'll make time." She was sure Harry said that with a wicked glint in his eye, and she swore Finkle responded with an old man's leer.

Were they thinking of her naked again? She would never know, really. But if they were, how could she make them stop?

She was terrified and embarrassed to be a mistress, even a fake one, if it meant everyone was thinking of her naked all the time! Especially Harry! Because she was already thinking of *him* naked, and that wouldn't do.

That wouldn't do at all. Cousin Augusta and Papa would disapprove, and so would Miss Dunlap.

People shouldn't see each other naked. Molly already felt naked when Harry kissed her, and that was bad enough. Maybe if she acted sickly, everyone would leave her alone all week. No one wanted to imagine a sick person naked.

"I—I have the headache," she said. "And, I think, a crumbling spine." She'd once heard an old woman at church complain of that. She put her hand on her lower back for emphasis.

But no one seemed to care. Finkle's chin rested on his chest and he began a light snore. All Harry said was, "Why don't you rest in your room until we gather in the drawing room tonight before supper?"

She was feeling rather exhausted, to tell the truth. "What time will that be?"

"I'll send a footman up to let you know."

"Fine." She could hide from the fact that, even though she'd yet to set eyes on a lake, she was already in well over her head.

Harry watched Molly ascend the stairs, daintily lifting her hem as she did so. He hardly recognized her in that revealing gown and the paint, especially the kohl around her eyes, which made her look a bit like Cleopatra. Which was a good thing. It wouldn't serve to have any other bachelor at the party be able to identify her here *or* in town.

She was climbing the last few steps now, her back ramrod straight, her hips stationary. *The way a lady would walk,* Harry thought with concern. He knew the other mistresses would move with a sinuous languor born of long experience with the lustful imaginings of men.

Perhaps Molly would learn through observation. Or a little brandy might loosen her up.

But even if she never lost that ramrod-straight back, Harry couldn't help feeling heat in his belly at the sight of her climbing the stairs. She was round in all the right places. And her back was so delicate and fine! When he'd run his hand up and down it in the carriage, he'd felt a crazy impulse to lower her onto the carriage seat and make mad, passionate love to her—to show her all the things he sensed her untouched body longed for that she was missing and could be doing.

With him.

And he with her.

He suddenly realized it was going to be a difficult week, in more ways than one.

At the top of the stairs, she turned and saw him watching her. "You're still here, Harry?"

He gave her a small bow. "Indeed, I am. I just thought of something. There's a certain walk I'd like to teach you. May I?"

Her cheeks flushed. "Of course."

He ascended the stairs three at a time and stopped right behind her. "It's the mistress walk," he said, placing a light hand on both her hips. His face was in her hair, which smelled sweet, and his mouth nearly touched the delicate rim of her ear. "Imagine yourself having to use your hips—and nothing else—to touch something out of reach," he said quietly. "Every step you take, you're reaching out to touch that thing with your hip. Don't move. Let's try it in place." He gently pushed her left hip to move her to the right, which she did.

"Like this?" she asked him, sounding a little nervous.

She was so anxious to please. And her hips . . . so pliable.

"Yes," he said in professorial tones. "Exactly. Now do that with the other hip."

He kept his hands on her as she moved her other hip.

"Now back and forth," he said. "Slowly."

She did as he asked, and he pressed his eyes closed, letting his hands ride her undulating hips. She was tantalizing him without realizing it, of course, and he was no gentleman to enjoy this practice so, but—

He forced himself to step back. "All right, that's enough."

She turned to look up at him, her brown eyes huge. "Are you sure I did it correctly?"

"Yes." He smiled at her. "Now try to make that same side-to-side hip motion as you go forward. Slowly. As if you're walking through a large vat of honey."

She nodded back, biting her lip, and did as she was asked.

"A little less side to side," he said, hiding a grin.

She instantly complied.

His breath caught in his throat. "That's perfect," he managed to say.

And it was. He rather felt like picking her up and taking her to bed.

She turned to him with a grin. "Are there any other things you can teach me?"

He was tempted to kiss her on the tip of her nose. "Er, yes, of course. But for now, rest. Would you like me to send the footman up with a book?"

She smiled. "Yes, thank you."

He could tell that she needed a distraction from her impending role as false mistress. Maybe an hour with a book would settle her nerves.

"Would a volume of William Wordsworth's poetry do?" he asked.

Her eyes lit up. "That would be just the thing."

He hid a smile. Molly Fairbanks was quite the easiest person in the world to understand.

In the small but well-stocked library, Harry easily located the volume he sought. He'd read it many times himself and kept it on a shelf close to the desk.

He rang for the footman, who appeared immediately, and handed him the book. "Please take this to the young lady upstairs."

The footman hesitated a fraction of a second.

Perhaps, Harry thought, most mistresses didn't read poetry. None of his ever had. They'd been more preoccupied with sleeping until noon, practicing their smoldering glances in any looking glass they could find after they woke up, and shopping.

However, one could never make assumptions. No doubt Lord Maxwell's mistress, Athena Markham, was very familiar with poetry.

Harry gave the lad a stern look. "Deliver it with the utmost respect. Every visitor to this house is my guest."

"Yes, sir." The chastened footman turned on his heel and left the library.

God forbid anyone else this week question Molly's tastes. Or Harry's, for that matter.

He needed a drink. A large drink. So he poured himself a double brandy from his father's supply in a decanter on the desk.

Soon his other guests would return from the lake. And when they did, he'd have to put his seriously limited acting skills to the test. He must pretend Molly was the most alluring woman in the world. Even though she obviously wasn't. She could certainly pass muster, but win the contest? With her testy temper and outspoken ways?

Harry strode to the library window and looked out upon the house grounds. His father had no idea Prinny's wager was being conducted on the most beloved of the family's minor properties. Which satisfied a small, angry part of Harry's soul.

He didn't need his father's approval. Nor his love.

But why had he told Molly the hunting box had been a gift from the duke? How stupid . . . how childish of him, to invent such a story! And he didn't even know why he'd said it.

There was a rumble of noise from outside—deep men's voices, laughing, and the higher-pitched giggles of women. The houseguests had come back from the lake. And Harry was their host.

"I won't think about you all week, Father," he murmured aloud. "Nor my duties to you. Prinny's orders."

And he left the library to go greet his guests.

CHAPTER 9

Several hours later, after a thorough reading of several of Wordsworth's poems *and* after Molly had recovered from the shock of finding out that her bedchamber was connected to Harry's by a dressing room, she placed her hand on the knob of her door and took a deep breath. She'd changed gowns (the one she wore now was even more scandalous than this afternoon's) and fixed her hair.

It was time, time to be a mistress.

A false mistress.

She walked out into a quiet hall. Candles burned in the simple sconces standing sentry outside every door. Turning right, she made her way back to the oak staircase.

As she did, she nearly bumped into a an elaborately dressed gentleman, a good ten years older than Harry. The candle flame highlighted his carefully arranged chestnut locks. His waistcoat was beaded and embroidered, and his coat fit like a glove.

He would have been terribly handsome if it weren't for his unfortunate nose. Not that Molly didn't appreciate a fine, Roman nose, or a distinguished craggy one such as her father's—but this man's was almost, um, long enough to hang a hat on, if she were to be truthful.

"And who might *you* be?" he asked her. From the sensual tone of his voice and the curve of his lip, she could tell he believed he was every woman's dream.

Molly remembered Harry's advice: Be biddable.

"I'm Delilah." She curtsied.

"Sir Richard Bell." He paused, lifted her hand, and kissed her knuckles. Then he smiled. It was a well-practiced smile, one designed to weaken knees.

But Molly's were comfortably locked. "I shall see you in the drawing room, shall I?" she returned brightly, and before he could answer, slipped around him.

"Not so fast," he growled, and caught her elbow. Then he leaned toward her to . . . to *kiss* her!

Molly slapped his face.

"You bitch," he said low. "What kind of lightskirt are you?"

"I'm not *yours,* that's for certain." She threw up her chin and continued down the hallway, ignoring her stinging hand.

"You aren't very obedient, are you?" he called after her.

For a fleeting second, she felt almost guilty. But then she came to her senses. Surely Harry wouldn't expect her to endure pawings from other men, especially a scoundrel like Sir Richard.

So she pretended not to hear him and made a beeline for the stairs, slipping down them in Fiona's slippers, which thankfully were only a tiny bit tight. She approached the well-lit room where she knew everyone, save Sir Richard, had gathered.

Before she entered, she took a breath and steadied herself. Her stint as a false mistress had begun on a rather frightening note. But she must do her best despite it.

She must believe she could actually win the contest.

She strode in, smiled at everyone around her—at the

ladies lounging in their finery on the sofas, and at the men, who were playing cards in the corner—and sank onto an Egyptian-style chair in the midst of the women. There. No one said a word to her. She appeared to fit in. Which was a good thing.

But her relief was short-lived. Three of the women were now staring at her in a most unfriendly fashion, including Athena Markham, the actress.

Oh, dear, was all Molly could think. She so admired Miss Markham's acting talent. It was a pity she didn't seem approachable.

Molly supposed all the other women in the room wanted to win the Most Delectable Companion title, too. And she was obviously part of the competition, which must explain why they appeared so cold, except for the fourth mistress. She didn't look at Molly at all. She was focused on the door, which she watched with anxious, almond-shaped green eyes, in between sipping furtively at a drink. Perhaps she was waiting for Sir Richard, which would make her the unfortunate Bunny.

"Lovely day, isn't it?" Molly said.

"I hadn't noticed," one woman replied, her shiny brown hair drawn back in a tight chignon.

She had a stark beauty, Molly thought, like a painting she'd seen once of a saint on her way to being martyred. Perhaps it was her golden eyes. They seemed to see right through Molly, deep into her very soul.

"I've been too busy beneath the sheets," the woman said, and knocked back a small glass of an amber liquid in one gulp.

"Um, all right then." Molly folded her hands in her lap. They were shaking just a tad. "I'm Moll—I mean, Delilah. What's your name?"

"Joan." The beauty narrowed her golden eyes, but even half-lidded, they were intense. Hypnotic. Molly could see how a man might think her gaze captivating. It was hard to look away.

Joan smiled, a small, mean smile. "Feeling guilty about something, Delilah?"

Molly put her hand to her throat. Yes! Yes, she did feel guilty about something! She was lying right now, pretending to be a mistress. But she shook her head. "Of course I don't feel guilty about something. Why—why do you ask?"

Joan shrugged. "I know a lot about guilt. It eats away at your soul. Until you're nothing more than a shell."

"Oh," said Molly.

That's what Miss Dunlap always told her, too!

How odd to hear words like that from a mistress at a social gathering. Joan and Miss Dunlap didn't look at all alike. And they certainly had opposing occupations. But somehow, they reminded Molly of each other.

Dear God, the last thing she needed was another Miss Dunlap to remind her that she was doing something very bad!

"Why do you wear a preponderance of rouge?" Athena tossed her dazzling mane of auburn hair, which complemented her gorgeous ivory skin and emerald gown. She gazed at Molly's cheekbones with an amused expression. "Subtlety is more sophisticated, don't you think? And so much more unexpected in a mistress." Her arm was draped clear across the small sofa, quite as if she owned it. "We must keep our men guessing, mustn't we?"

"Of course. They love mystery, don't they?" Molly swallowed. "But I—I . . . I have a sickly constitution."

She couldn't very well admit to them that she was trying to disguise her appearance!

A third mistress, a very tall one who hadn't spoken yet, fluttered her hands like a bird in flight and pointed to Molly's hair. Then she giggled. "Seagulls," she said. "In crow's nest."

Hmmm. A foreigner making fun of her attempts to beautify her hair with Fiona's feathers.

Molly was tempted to tell the girl that her strawberry blonde hair, worn in a braided crown at the top of her head, could serve as the nest of a large *goose*. But one should always be particularly friendly to guests in one's country, even if they insult one.

"I quite enjoy my feathers," Molly said.

"I use my feathers for a different purpose altogether," Joan said, rather slyly.

Athena laughed. "Me, too. I employed the feather treatment just last night!"

"Was it a success?" Joan winked.

"Oh, *yes*." Athena winked back.

Molly's eyes flew wide. The . . . the feather treatment? Perhaps Fiona employed the feather treatment, too.

What *was* the feather treatment, exactly?

Of course, she couldn't *ask*. She must change the subject. "What's your name?" she inquired of the tall woman with the foreign accent.

"Hildur," she responded, expanding her already voluminous chest. "I come from Iceland."

Heavens. Molly noticed that every word Hildur spoke sounded as if she were inviting someone to ravish her. Perhaps it was her large mouth and the languorous way she spoke. Or perhaps it was the way her finger played with the ribbons at her very low neckline.

Athena flipped her hair again. "Hildur sneaked aboard Captain Arrow's ship. She claims to be of the nobility. She had the notion Lord Byron would fall in love with her if he were ever to meet her, so she's come to England. I told her he's moved to the Continent, but she doesn't believe me."

"I don't think she understands much English beyond what Captain Arrow taught her on the ship," said Joan with a snide laugh.

"Either that or she's stupid," said Athena.

Joan laughed again.

"Fall overboard, please," Hildur said, in her slow, lush voice, looking at Athena and Joan. "*You* and *you*."

A directive which shut everyone up for a moment.

Molly hoped to defray the tension by leaning toward Athena and smiling. "Are you Miss Markham, the actress?"

Athena's mouth bowed slightly. "Why, yes. Have you seen me perform?"

"No, but my sister has. And she says you're very gifted."

But Athena didn't thank Molly. Instead, she yawned.

How rude. Molly pulled back and sat stiffly in her chair. She might make a bad mistress, but she certainly had wonderful posture and better manners.

It was going to be a long week.

"Whatever they say about your rouge and hairstyle, I think your gown is quite appropriate," blurted out the fourth girl, the one Molly was sure must be Bunny.

"Do you?" Molly swung to see her better. "I wasn't sure if it was a trifle overdone."

Molly's gown was a dull gold satin sheath with Grecian trim composed of silhouettes of small people frolicking among letters of the Greek alphabet. The trim marched boldly across the appallingly low scooped bodice and around the hem.

"Yes," said the girl. "It's *very* overdone. And those silhouettes are quite entertaining."

Molly looked closer at the silhouettes and gasped. She wasn't sure what the tiny people were doing, but there were several male and female figures whose limbs were entangled in a shocking manner.

"I'd say your gown is perfect for this gathering," the girl finished with a smile.

"Thank you," said Molly, blushing. She paused. "Are you Bunny?"

The girl nodded, but she couldn't say more because at that moment, Sir Richard walked in. It was as if an atmosphere of poison immediately enveloped the room. Or perhaps it was Sir Richard's cloying cologne.

Molly had to restrain herself from visibly showing her revulsion at his presence.

Bunny, dressed in a carmine gown with a scalloped hem, swallowed, and stood up stiffly. She began to walk to Sir Richard, her hips swaying slowly.

It was the mistress walk! The one Harry had taught her! Molly felt a little less nervous. She was catching on to this mistress business—*she* knew the proper walk. *She* knew about feathers and how one uses them to—to—

She had no idea. But next time someone mentioned them, she would wink the way Athena and Joan had.

By the time Bunny arrived at Sir Richard's side, she'd opened up like a flower. Her eyes began to glow and her lips parted, quite as if she had an amazing secret to share.

She'd become a vibrant, gorgeous mistress.

Molly bit her lip, amazed at Bunny's transformation.

The men at the card table stood as well and dropped their cards. They were laughing and talking, clearly finished with their game.

Molly sat up even straighter. The other bachelors were approaching! She tucked a curl behind her ear and tried to look tremendously beguiling, which she wasn't sure how to do, so she stole a glance at Hildur.

Hmmm.

Molly mimicked Hildur by pursing her lips, lowering her chin, and watching the men cross the room, all the while batting her lashes. But her neck began to hurt and her eyes to water. Her lips felt funny, too, all scrunched up like a pillow.

So she stopped trying to look beguiling.

Good thing, too. She could concentrate on Harry. His jet-black hair reflected the light from numerous candles, and he was freshly shaven. He looked splendid, even intimidatingly handsome, in his dove gray evening coat, black breeches, and immaculately starched cravat stuck with a discreet diamond pin.

He caught her staring, and his mouth curved in a slow, devastating grin that made her want to hop up from her chair and pace about the room and . . . and kiss him until that odd, frenetic, molten energy he caused in her was released somehow. But instead she bowed her head and pretended that her slipper had come loose.

When she glanced up again, she could also observe the other bachelors, who now stood before the women in a row. And an impressive group they were in their elegant waistcoats.

Molly instantly recognized Captain Arrow. He wore a uniform with braided epaulets at the shoulders. Tanned and virile, he was obviously born to command.

Viscount Lumley was easy to spot, as well. He had beautiful eyes and a grin that probably got him whatever he wanted.

She'd already met the odious Sir Richard, who lounged at the edge of the group, so the fifth gentleman—the one who'd maintained a cool albeit pleasant demeanor at the card table—must be Lord Maxwell. Ridiculously handsome, he exuded complete confidence and an intensity of purpose that could easily intimidate lesser mortals.

"Now that we're all gathered . . ." Harry looked pointedly at Molly and held out his arm. "Shall we?"

Shall they what? Oh, of course! She must join him. She and Harry must seem like two peas in a pod.

She stood and took his arm, her heart racing. He smelled

wonderful, like clean linen and soap, and his arm was firm and muscular beneath his coat. She would like to cling to that arm all night long, rather the way she used to cling to a favorite fuzzy blanket she'd had as a little girl.

Everyone else joined up two by two, as well. But Molly noticed that every single woman was now laughing and vivacious and somehow glowing with . . . promises unspoken.

That was it—the secret to being a good mistress must be unspoken promises!

But what *were* those promises?

Molly swallowed hard, found it difficult to breathe, and clutched her shawl around her neck.

Athena laughed and whispered in Lord Maxwell's ear. Captain Arrow pinched Hildur's bottom and she slapped his arm, giggling all the while. Joan rubbed against Viscount Lumley as if he were a lamppost and she were a cat. Sir Richard bent Bunny backward and kissed her neck, quite as if he were nibbling on an ear of corn, the disgusting man.

Poor Bunny. Although the almond-eyed beauty gave every impression of enjoying Sir Richard's attention.

Molly looked at Harry, who stood stoically waiting for the romping to cease. Either that, or he was attempting to figure out what to do with *her.* "Where are we going?" she asked him, their noses mere inches apart.

"To break the ice," he said.

"The ice hardly needs breaking here."

"The night has just begun," Harry murmured, his words tickling her ear.

What a shame. Molly was already exhausted from being a mistress. She did feel a delicious sensation thrumming in her middle caused by the mere sight of Harry. But she would prefer to go to her room this very minute, slide under the sheets, read more of Wordsworth's poems, and fall asleep. Alas, no. She must act as if being a mistress were the most exciting thing in the world!

"Off to the kissing closet," Harry said to the party gathered around him. "Prinny believes there's no better way for the contestants to begin to know each other. The ladies shall enter one at a time, and the man who draws the short straw shall follow. The two must remain in the closet for three minutes."

Molly could hardly believe her ears. *A kissing closet?*

There was a chorus of enthusiastic responses, especially from the men. And Sir Richard, she noticed, was looking at her with peculiar intensity.

Now Molly was no longer tired—she was simply terrified.

CHAPTER 10

When Athena entered the closet, a sensual smile on her lips, Molly stood mute. Her heart beat so hard when the men chose their first straws, she was afraid she might die. Except for enjoying Harry's kisses in the carriage and the few moments they'd shared as he taught her to walk the way a proper mistress should, she was having a horrible time at the house party.

How would she make it through a whole week of being a false mistress?

Harry smiled. He had drawn the shortest straw! The Romeo. Molly was tempted to be upset with him, but why? There were other ladies' men in the world—why should she be aggravated with him? He wasn't pretending to be decent, after all. At least he was honest about his lack of scruples.

Lord Maxwell raised a brow. "See that she's entertained."

Harry didn't look at Molly even once. He merely opened the door to the closet and disappeared inside with Athena for three agonizing minutes.

No one else seemed to find those three minutes excruciating besides Molly. Indeed, there was more laughter and drinking and silly, flirtatious antics than ever, almost as if the knowledge that the two people in the closet were kissing was a potent energizer of the crowd, an aphrodisiac of sorts.

Finally, the two came out, to much hooting and laughter. Athena looked much satisfied, and her lips were redder than ever. Harry looked exactly the same, which for Molly proved all the rumors that he was a jaded bachelor.

"You don't kiss and tell, do you?" Lord Maxwell asked Harry.

"Never," Harry said, playing the gallant. He leaned over Athena's hand and pressed it to his lips.

The good-natured bantering continued through Hildur's turn. Lord Maxwell drew the short straw for her. Everyone laughed when Hildur came out and said, "Do not throw *him* to the sharks."

Bunny was next. Captain Arrow was her partner. When she came out, she looked as beautiful as ever, but she said nothing. She simply smiled prettily. Sir Richard gave Captain Arrow the cold shoulder and pulled Bunny to him with a proprietary air.

Which left but Sir Richard and Viscount Lumley to draw straws. Molly and Joan still had to take their turns.

"Into the closet, Delilah," said Harry.

No one moved.

Harry nudged Molly in the back.

Oh, yes! *She* was Delilah!

She entered the closet, which to her dismay she found completely empty. She was hoping to hide behind a pelisse or a man's overcoat.

Dear God, don't let Sir Richard be the one, she prayed.

Harry shut the door in her face, but before he did, she gave him a mute look of appeal. He, in turn, signaled to her with his gaze that she must endure.

Now she was alone. In the dark. Her knees began to

tremble. She heard the wild laughter outside the closet, and then the "Oho!" which meant that some man had drawn a straw for her.

A moment later, the door opened and shut quickly. All she could see was the outline of a man's head. She couldn't tell if it was Viscount Lumley or the despicable Sir Richard.

She gulped, put her hands out in the dark, palms up, instinctively wanting to protect herself, especially if it were Sir Richard.

But her hands pressed against a very trim waist. It was Viscount Lumley. Thank God! Although she did *not* want to kiss him. At *all*.

"Wait!" she whispered.

"Why?" He grabbed her hands and squeezed them in a friendly way.

"I—I—" Her mind scrambled. What could she say that would make him delay the inevitable? "I wanted to ask after . . . your mother first."

"My *mother*?" he whispered, sounding flabbergasted.

"Yes, how is she?" Molly hoped his mother was still alive. No man could turn down answering a question about his own mother's health!

"Actually, she's quite well, thank you. Except for her gout. She and Father both get that on occasion."

"Really?"

"Yes, they do. It's a shame what old people go through, isn't it?"

"Indeed."

Their hands were still clasped.

"Do you have any brothers and sisters?" she asked him.

He had five, he said, and at her insistence, he told her the names and ages of each one, and whether or not they were married.

"Lovely," she replied.

There was another pause.

"Are you ready?" he asked at the same time that she said, "Do you like a good cherry tart?"

"Hmmm, I suppose I do," he said slowly. "Although I think I prefer apple. Why?"

She squeezed his hands back. "If Cook will let me in the kitchen, I'll make you one."

"I'll look forward to that," he said, utterly polite.

There was another pause. She felt sweat trickle down her back. The closet was quite stuffy. "It's rather hot in here," she said.

"Indeed," he answered.

"They're awfully loud out there, aren't they?" A rhetorical question, really, but perhaps he would respond.

"They are," he said.

And then someone opened the door. Their three minutes were up. Viscount Lumley dropped Molly's hands, and they walked single file out of the closet, he first.

"Well?" asked Sir Richard.

The nosy-body.

Molly's chest tightened. She didn't like that Sir Richard seemed particularly interested in her, although perhaps she was imagining that.

"We talked," Lumley said in a disbelieving voice.

"You talked?" Joan asked Molly.

Molly smiled. "Yes. He has a wonderful family." She turned to the viscount. "Thank you, Viscount Lumley, for the scintillating conversation."

There was a chorus of boos.

Viscount Lumley looked only a bit dejected.

Molly whispered in his ear, "Remember, the *tart*."

"Oh, yes!" he said, and grinned.

Harry looked at Molly with a bemused expression.

And then it was Joan and Sir Richard's turn. Of course, Molly doubted Joan would ever be afraid of anyone, but couldn't she sense the malevolence rolling off Sir Richard in waves? No one else seemed to, either, except Harry, who spoke to him as little as possible.

Their kissing episode went off without a hitch, and it was thankfully time for supper. Molly knew she must make a good impression in the dining room if she were to win any votes for the day's best mistress.

But she didn't know how.

The other women were sparkling, almost giddy—except for Joan, who maintained her intense, subtle allure—and Molly could hardly put two words together. Neither could Hildur, of course, but she said many incongruous things that made people laugh, like, "Aye, aye, Captain," to the footman who served her. She also oozed exotic, sensual charm with that jesting pout of hers.

Supper was plentiful and delicious, but by its end, Molly was weary from watching the others enjoy themselves. Her brain hurt from all the thinking she'd done, as she tried to figure out ways to enter the conversation and sound witty and charming all at the same time.

"Pass the salt, please," she said at one tiny lull. Everyone turned to look at her, which she supposed was good. She stared back, searched for something else to say, and finally came out with, "I read a very good book the other day."

It had actually been quite dull. Her father didn't approve of her reading novels, so she'd read a tome on Egyptian embalming methods. Which she knew backward and forward, thanks to her father and Cedric, so it was nothing new.

"What was the title?" Harry asked politely.

She couldn't very well *tell* them. "I forget," she said. "But—"

She took a moment to think of a proper way to describe the way the Egyptians pulled people's brains out of their noses.

But it was too late. Hildur made a funny remark, and the conversation turned to other directions. Molly was never able to interject again.

Finally, after another hour of sheer torture for her, Harry rose from the table. "It's time for the men to adjourn to the library," he said, standing tall and straight.

All the men had been drinking profusely, as well as the women, except for Molly. But no man appeared to be showing any ill effects, except for Sir Richard, who had the effrontery to belch at the table and then immediately demand a kiss from Bunny.

Molly sensed every woman at that table shuddering beneath their festive exteriors!

"Each day we'll cast a vote for the one lady who stands out above the rest," Harry said. "We'll sign our voucher to ensure that we can't choose our own companion, of course."

"What if there's a tie?" Joan asked.

"Prinny's advisors have ruled that we shan't name a daily winner," Harry explained. "We'll leave the votes to accrue in a jar until the end of the week. The daily vote counts three points. You'll also be able to win points for the occasional game you shall compete in during the week, as well as at the finale. When all the points are totaled, we shall have our winner. If there is a tie at the conclusion, we'll cast another vote until someone wins the Most Delectable Companion title. Fair enough?"

Everyone nodded, although Molly felt that somehow things were still not very fair. She wasn't sure *how,* though.

"Right, then," said Harry. "Men, follow me for our first vote."

All the men stood.

"When will you come back to us?" Athena asked in a dramatic stage voice, her arm raised and extended toward

Lord Maxwell. She looked and sounded exactly like Rapunzel in her castle, crying out to be saved.

Molly couldn't help but draw her eyebrows together. Athena's remark probably clinched the actress the day's votes, save Lord Maxwell's, of course. He wasn't allowed to vote for his own mistress.

"We'll return when our business is done," he reminded Athena.

"Very well." Athena sighed prettily, a small curve of a smile on her parted lips.

Molly almost choked with disgust at Athena's biddableness!

But then she remembered Lord Maxwell *might* vote for her. So she smiled at him in what she hoped was a winning fashion. She wasn't sure if she had remnants of the turtle soup in her teeth, so her smile was rather weak.

Lord Maxwell gazed at her with an expression bordering on aloof.

Then Joan, her eyes half lidded again, said, "I believe I've dropped my fan." Slowly, she stood up and bent down to the Aubusson rug. She patted it as if she were searching for her fan, a move which exposed her perfect cleavage to all the men.

"Why, here it is!" said the amiable Viscount Lumley, pointing to a fan lying on the table.

"Indeed!" said Joan. "I'd forgotten, Viscount." She gave him a slow, sizzling smile.

Molly almost huffed. Joan hadn't even attempted to be a good liar! She'd known her fan was there all along! Molly was sure everyone else knew it, too, but no one appeared annoyed.

In the next instant Hildur unraveled her braids, shook out her hair until it swirled in tousled glory around her face, and said, "Hildur is a mermaid. Choose Hildur."

Whereupon all the men laughed uproariously, save

Maxwell, who merely lifted his mouth upward in a show of appreciation.

Molly was shocked at the other women's brazen attempts to sway the men's votes. But then again, she supposed mistresses were supposed to be brazen.

So far, she was a terrible mistress.

She looked at Bunny to see what *she* would do to win the men's votes.

"I'm a country girl," Bunny said in that light, frothy voice of hers. "Give me a field of flowers or a stack of hay to frolic in, and I'm happy."

Then she tucked a tiny flower from a vase on the table deep into her bodice.

The small act of putting the flower between Bunny's ample breasts was so sensual the men were speechless. Which meant that Bunny had won the day. Molly was sure by the evil way Athena looked at her. But now everyone was looking at Molly.

"She has nothing to say," said Joan. "She is more like a governess than a mistress. Ask Lumley."

Everyone laughed but Molly and Harry. He gave her a look as if to urge her to say something clever.

Molly felt her face heat up, but try as she might, nothing would come out of her mouth.

"After we vote, I shall take this so-called governess upstairs," said Harry in a suggestive manner. "We'll see if she has anything to teach me."

What a vulgar thing to say!

But then Molly remembered. Lewd remarks would be flying this week. She was dying to tell everyone the truth, that Harry was lying through his teeth, that she would *never* be caught in a compromising position with him, even if he did happen to be, in her completely unbiased opinion, the most kissable man in the room.

But she couldn't do that, of course. Lumley and Arrow

hooted their approval of Harry's salacious remark and, along with Sir Richard and Maxwell, followed him out of the dining room to vote for their favorite mistress of the evening.

The other women stopped laughing and sat quietly, small smiles of amusement still lingering on their faces. None of them seemed too worried about the night's voting.

Except for Molly. Her face beneath its layer of powder and rouge felt hard as stone, and just as unmoving. She knew *no* one would vote for her.

CHAPTER 11

Harry led the men out of the dining room with a heavy heart and a sense of foreboding, but he wasn't going to let them guess he was feeling pessimistic about Molly's chances to win the contest. It was obvious she'd been a tremendous failure on her first night at the house party. At this rate, she would never win the title of Most Delectable Companion, which meant that the most he could hope for at the end of the week would be to avoid pulling the shortest straw and thus avert the disaster of having to propose to Anne Riordan.

He supposed he should be grateful to Molly for not making him the instant loser of the entire week. At least her presence assured him of having a small chance to survive the Season as a bachelor for another year. But he felt as if his luck were running out.

His first inkling of doom had come when Fiona ran away from him at the inn. No woman had ever chosen another man over him! Granted, he'd never been besotted with her beyond the bedroom, so what did it matter?

But then Molly had appeared, heaping scorn upon him for having a mistress at all. Up until now, even his mother hadn't dared to comment on his wastrel ways in so forth-right a manner.

Harry's sense of control, which he'd always prided himself on, was slipping. In fact, he felt almost desperate as he watched the other men put their votes on small slips of paper and then drop them into the large, blue vase. He knew not one of them contained the name Delilah.

By the end of the week, the vase would be full of paper, and they would remove the names to see who had won the most votes. Even if Molly won all the games during the week, if she got no nightly votes from the men, she would most likely be unable to win.

Lord Maxwell poured two brandies. "Interesting choice of mistress," he said, dropping his quill on the table and handing a glass to Harry.

"I should say so," echoed Captain Arrow, holding his own empty snifter out to Maxwell for another splash.

"Very interesting indeed," said Viscount Lumley, still looking stunned from his encounter with Molly in the kiss-ing closet.

Sir Richard lowered his cheroot. "I don't think you could have brought anyone less likely to win, Traemore," he said, smoke curling around his face.

There were mumbles of protest around the table, but they were not very loud or strong, Harry noted. Obvi-ously, everyone agreed with Sir Richard.

As he did himself.

Nevertheless, he would put on his best game face. "The competition for the title of Most Delectable Companion will continue," he said calmly to them all, and then he turned to look pointedly at Sir Richard. "And I promise you," he said evenly, "that you'll soon see that Delilah is a contender."

His promise sounded hollow even to his own ears.

Sir Richard smiled, but it was bitter and mean, not at all kind or amused. The other men said nothing.

"I shall see you in the morning, gentlemen." Harry moved toward the door, keeping his shoulders back, but inside, he felt the veriest loser.

"Off to see what your 'governess' can teach you?" asked Sir Richard.

Harry paused and turned around. "You're awfully interested in my mistress, Bell. Will that translate into a vote for her tomorrow night?"

Sir Richard was cool. "I'm not interested in your mistress, Traemore. I'm interested in seeing you lose."

"You would be, wouldn't you?" said Lumley. "Seeing as how Harry is well liked by all, and you're an aging rake with nary a friend but your valet, and even him you must pay."

Sir Richard half rose from his chair.

Lumley matched the movement. "Just try it, Bell." His tone was menacing.

"Gentlemen." Harry raised his hand. "If we're forced to be together, as this bet has ensured we shall be for at least a week, let's stay civil."

Sir Richard sat back down, his eyes still narrowed at Lumley.

Harry saw that Sir Richard was most definitely going to be a problem during the competition. But he refused to show his worry in his expression. Without another word, he bowed and left the room.

His more immediate concern was to find Molly. The girl needed propping up, or their whole house of cards would fall by the morrow.

"I'm appalled." Molly dragged her feet as Harry pulled her along the corridor upstairs toward their bedchambers. "A kissing closet? Why, I never imagined such a thing could exist!"

Harry chuckled. "I didn't, either. Prinny has a wicked sense of humor."

"It's not funny," Molly said. "If the whole week is like tonight, I'm going to hell, for certain. And it will be *all* your fault."

Harry stopped her. "My dear, console yourself with the fact that if you go to hell, you began the journey long before this week."

She gasped.

He chuckled. "Seriously, Molly, you're not going to hell. What else were you to do? I certainly couldn't take you home the moment Cedric abandoned you. I'd have forfeited the wager, and my future depends on it. You *had* to come here."

She sighed. "I really don't think my staying any longer is a good idea."

"Of course you'll stay." Harry strove to sound firm and calm. "Tonight was only our first night."

They stopped outside her room.

"But I've never felt so stupid in my life as I did tonight," she whispered, looking up at him with those brown eyes, which were bleak now, not at all impish.

Harry fought against feeling sorry for her. By failing to portray herself as a desirable mistress, she was possibly ruining his chance at freedom, just as she had done that long-ago night at the Christmas ball, when her silly poem had forced him into military service.

"I know you can do better," he said. "I've seen the fire in you. You need to show it to everyone else."

Molly sighed. "I'm supposed to be biddable *and* have fire?"

Harry thought for a moment. "Yes. I know that sounds

contradictory, but a woman's fire is banked. It's not evident *all* the time. It smolders. I should have explained better in the carriage."

"I don't have *any* fire." Molly's shoulders sagged. "Not like those other women."

Harry knew it was the brandy, but suddenly, his nemesis looked very appealing. He remembered holding her on his lap, the way she'd fiercely grabbed his neck, as if she couldn't get enough of his kisses.

And he remembered the way she'd looked in that blue gown at the inn. Voluptuous, tempting—

Of course she had fire! And she'd damned well better remember it, or he might very likely be legshackled by Christmas.

He grabbed her wrist. "Let me remind you that you are no iceberg, shall I?"

"Harry." She looked up at him, and he could tell she was afraid.

But also open to the idea.

"I won't hurt you," he whispered, encouraged.

Her brow furrowed. "But you've been drinking. When men drink too much, they do things. Inappropriate things."

"I am certainly not drunk," he said evenly. "And this is merely kissing practice. Remember? Designed to give you some confidence."

She said nothing.

"Molly?"

She still said nothing, merely looked at her slipper moving in a figure-eight pattern on the floor.

"I'm going to kiss you," he murmured, and cupped her jaw with his hand. "You'd best run now if you want to escape."

She looked up at him then, and something turned over inside his chest.

She didn't want to escape.

How unusual in Molly.

And how inexplicably enchanting.

Molly could hardly breathe when Harry put his lips on hers. He pressed her back against the door to her bedchamber, sliding his hands up the door to pin her between his arms.

It was a delicious trap she had no desire to escape. Harry first kissed her mouth, and then when she could hardly bear the pleasure of it anymore, he moved to her neck. There he dropped soft, sweet kisses on her pulse and collarbone, made even sweeter by the moan of pleasure she let escape when she lifted her chin to give him better access.

How could a rake like Harry understand her so well? Know her every need and desire? Even know what she didn't know she wanted until after he'd done it?

Such as the caressing he was now doing with his hand on her waist. The caressing that was moving upward, closer to her breasts but not quite there.

He pulled back, his gaze hot, his face fierce and handsome and compelling. "I'm going to open your door, Molly." His voice was rough, the same way it had been in the carriage after he'd kissed her.

She liked that voice. Very much.

He kissed her again, and she felt his hand move behind her, encircling her waist, and then felt the door give beneath their weight.

They walked backward into her room, and Harry kicked the door to the hallway shut behind him. Their lips were still locked, and he slid his hands up and down her back. Then he went lower, cupping her rear end in his hands and pulling her even closer against the hard length of him.

Which felt . . . perfect somehow.

So perfect she forgot it was Harry as she ran her hands up and down his back, too. And she forgot about him again when he locked one of her legs between his own, bending her back just enough to place a kiss on the top of her breast, exposed above Fiona's impossibly low neckline.

She couldn't help but moan at the pleasurable sensation. He murmured something deep in his throat, and then he yanked at her neckline with his teeth—his teeth!—and nudged it farther down.

And then his tongue began the most delicious exploration of her—

Molly's eyes flew open.

She couldn't forget. This was Harry. The bachelor to end all bachelors! One of Prinny's own Impossible Bachelors.

"That's enough," she gasped, and pushed him away. "You've had plenty of kissing tonight. You kissed Athena, too, don't forget."

He laughed softly and grabbed her waist. "That meant nothing," he murmured against her neck.

His mouth tickled in the most pleasurable way. But with everything she had in her, Molly pushed him away again. "This means nothing, as well," she said in her best Miss Dunlap voice. "The fact is, Harry, I would simply rather not participate in nothing unless I have to. After all, I'm not your real mistress."

"Yes, but—"

"Thank you for instilling confidence in me again," Molly interrupted him. "But I think it best that you save your displays of so-called affection for when others are present to see them."

Oh, she hated to say that! Because he was quite adorable just now, with that jet-black curl falling over his eye and the obvious disappointment in his gaze.

He sighed. "Have it your way. But remember, *Delilah,* if you fail at this mistress game, you are on your own this coming Season."

She felt all mixed up inside when he left through the dressing room to go to his bedchamber—angry at him for being so shortsighted yet craving him, too, somehow.

He was her only friend at the house party. It was going to be a long, lonely week if even Harry were to give her the brush-off.

She listened as he opened a drawer. And then she heard his boots come off and imagined him cursing her under his breath. And then she imagined him taking off his breeches, and—

No. She must not imagine him taking off his breeches.

Slowly, she undressed, and then she put on a stunning embroidered shift which clung to her curves and was completely see-through. If she wore it—which she would because it was quite the most beautiful thing she'd ever seen—she was sure she'd go to hell if she were to die the next day in a freak accident.

Although she was probably already going to hell for letting Harry kiss her so.

She'd best pray.

After she'd finished a rushed plea to God to send her an extra angel to help her resist Harry and prevent her having an untimely death in the meanwhile, Molly decided to give herself some extra protection against both Harry and her own decadent impulses by dragging a chest over to their connecting door.

Not that she *really* believed he'd take advantage of her without her permission.

Or that she'd wake up pretending to have had a nightmare so she could have the excuse of running into his room, where she'd cuddle next to him under the bedclothes and they'd resume kissing so her pretend night-

mare—about a ghost? or a monster? she couldn't decide
which—would be irrevocably banished.

Although the nightmare idea was tempting. *Very*
tempting.

She blew out her candle, crawled under the covers, and
tried to sleep.

But she couldn't. She had the noble thought that she
must do better in the morning—first, by trying to win over
the other mistresses, and then by somehow charming the
men, even the vile Sir Richard, if she could do so without
getting too close to him.

But she also couldn't sleep because the bureau in front
of the dressing room door reminded her that Harry was
just on the other side. And thinking of Harry reminded
her of how much she enjoyed his mouth, his hair, his
whole body, pressed against hers.

It made no sense. This was *Harry* she was feeling all
these feelings about!

She was desperate, she decided, blinking into the darkness. That was all. She was almost a spinster, and no man
had ever brought her flowers. She was to be excused for
feeling all mushy inside when she thought of Harry kissing her.

But she couldn't let those mushy feelings continue. She
must cease them immediately. So she thought about the
time a much younger Harry had planted all her dolls head-
first in a little vegetable garden she'd cultivated long ago.

That got her blood up.

She heard a noise and sat up, her heart pounding.
"Harry?"

Someone was scratching at her door, from the hallway.
But Harry was in bed. And he would have knocked on the
door connecting their rooms, if he'd needed to knock at all.

Molly crept to the door and made sure the key was in
the lock. "Who's there?" she whispered.

"Sir Richard," the voice whispered back. "I just wanted to say good night. Will you open the door?"

"No!" she hissed. "Go away!"

He laughed. "Something's different about you. And I intend to find out what it is."

She heard his footsteps move down the corridor.

Thank God.

Returning to her bed, she drew the sheets up to her chin and stared at a beam of moonlight illuminating a corner of her room. If Sir Richard found out she was no mistress, he might find out her real name, and he'd tell everyone, and then she'd be properly ruined. Not even a bounder like Cedric would want to marry her. She'd be stuck with Cousin Augusta forever, and everyone would whisper about her behind her back.

Except for Harry's family, of course. They were perfectly proper, but they were also fun, sometimes entertaining on a lavish scale and, other times, inviting just a few neighbors over for an afternoon picnic or an evening of music. It wouldn't do for the duke and duchess to think badly of her. They were Penelope's family now.

A tiny tear escaped Molly's eye.

Penelope!

It was at times like this that Molly missed her sister. *And* her mother. Because there was no one she could turn to in this house for comfort. No one at all.

Especially not Harry.

CHAPTER 12

Despite a restless night's sleep, the next morning Molly was ready to face another day as a contestant in the Most Delectable Companion contest. This time, she told herself, she would do well. She dressed in her least revealing gown, which was still outside the boundaries of good taste as it was a shocking shade of spring green. And she read the note Harry had slipped under her door: *Have a good morning. Yours, Harry.*

Yours? She blushed, remembering their kissing session last night. She supposed he *was* hers. At least for this week.

You should let him be yours even more, a tiny voice in her head urged her.

Molly cleared her throat and tried to ignore that wicked voice as she walked downstairs to the breakfast room. Once there she saw only one footman, the same one who'd helped her the day before when she'd first come to the house. Again, he looked right through her, as was appropriate, but she wondered if he were having any illicit thoughts about her or perhaps the other mistresses.

Because they *were* mistresses. Even if *she* was simply pretending.

She filled her plate and sat at the table, all alone.

Thankfully, Joan came in a few minutes later.

"Good morning." Molly smiled and took a sip from her tea.

"I abhor country hours," Joan muttered, and brushed by Molly rudely on her way to the sideboard.

"The men are already out and about, exploring the countryside on horseback," Molly said when Joan returned to the table.

But Joan merely gave her a flat stare and stirred sugar into her tea.

The other mistresses trailed in one by one over the next half hour, and none of them ate terribly much. Molly, meanwhile, enjoyed eggs and a rasher of bacon, toast and marmalade.

Athena eyed her plate. "You do eat like a horse, don't you?"

"Yes," she said with a smile. "I have a good appetite."

Joan snickered and stretched her arms above her head. "I have a good appetite, too." She winked at Athena again. "But not for breakfast. At least that's what Lumley tells me."

Everyone else laughed, especially Hildur, who laughed heartily at everything, probably because she didn't understand much of what was being said and wanted to fit in.

Molly herself wasn't quite sure what was funny, so she kept quiet. She remembered her kiss with Harry in the carriage, and that gave her an idea. She had developed an appetite for kissing after that episode and so had given in easily to Harry last night.

Perhaps Joan had meant the same kind of appetite as that!

So she eventually did laugh, but she was a trifle late.

Everyone stared at her.

"For someone vying for the title of Most Delectable

Companion, you're a featherbrain," said Joan to her. "At least Hildur has an excuse. She can't understand the language."

Molly couldn't think of anything clever to say back. So she said what she was thinking. "You remind me of some teachers I used to know. I never once saw them laugh. Some students said it was because they were naturally hateful. But I think it was because our headmistress was difficult and wouldn't let them write their families, as penance for their supposed failings. Miss Dunlap thought we were all wicked."

Joan simply blinked.

There was an awkward silence, which Bunny was good enough to break. "What an interesting story, Delilah," she murmured, and patted Molly's hand.

No one else said another word, until Athena suggested they adjourn to the drawing room.

All the women, except Molly, carried bags of some sort. Hildur sat on a sofa and pulled out some knitting. Athena opened a sketchpad and looked out the window. Joan sat at the pianoforte and began a charming prelude.

Molly sat next to Bunny on another sofa and opened a book on ancient Rome which she found on the tabletop. Bunny nudged her. "Don't you have anything to work on?" She pulled out a lovely piece of needlepoint.

"No," said Molly. "For five years I went to a very strict school where my chore every day was to peel potatoes for each meal. I never developed any feminine skills. But my father loves a good tart, and Cook never made one to his satisfaction. So I stepped in and learned three years ago."

"You live at home?" Bunny looked vaguely shocked. "And make tarts for your father?"

Molly felt her heart quicken. "Oh, no," she said breezily. "I meant in the old days. Before I—before I—" She didn't know quite how to say it.

"Before you became Lord Harry's mistress?" Bunny whispered.

"Yes," she said.

"Do you make *him* tarts?" Bunny asked her, all the while pushing her needle through her canvas.

"Yes, every Tuesday and Friday." She hoped she wouldn't go to hell for all the lies she was telling this week.

"That's wonderful," said Bunny, sounding wistful.

"Do you do anything . . . special for Sir Richard?" Molly set aside her book.

Bunny's eyes darkened. "What he thinks of as special and what I think of as special are two very different things." She shuddered and closed her eyes.

Molly couldn't even imagine to what Bunny was referring. "What do you mean?"

Bunny opened her eyes. "You don't want to know."

Molly felt her skin prickle. "I hope he doesn't do anything to make you feel uncomfortable. Or sad. Or frightened."

The way he does me, she wanted to say.

Bunny half smiled. "Nothing you should worry about," she murmured. "It's all right."

But Molly could tell it wasn't all right. It wasn't all right at all.

Bunny cleared her throat. "Let's talk again about cozy things, shall we? Things that a loving wife would do for her husband, like that baking of yours. Do you also mend Lord Harry's stockings?"

"No. I'm no good at mending. Just potato peeling. And tart baking."

Bunny giggled. "I design my own gowns. "

"Really? How fascinating."

Bunny giggled. "You're the first person to find me at all fascinating, Delilah." She paused, took out some thread and a needle from her basket. "Here, I'll teach you to sew."

And Bunny proceeded to do just that. She found an old piece of cloth, which she folded in two, and made tiny stitches in it. "See?"

Molly peered at it.

"You can do that, too," said Bunny. "Give it a try."

Molly painstakingly sewed the seam. She pricked her finger only twice.

Bunny took it from her and examined it. "Very good!"

Molly smiled. "Thank you for being kind," she whispered. "No one else is friendly at *all*."

"That's because everyone wants to win the title."

Molly frowned. "But what good is a crown of paste?"

There was a shocked silence in the room. Apparently, she'd voiced her question a little too loudly.

Bunny gave a nervous laugh. "But Delilah—it's the very idea that one might be named the Most Delectable Companion. Being an excellent one takes a great deal of skill. Don't you agree?"

Molly had once again forgotten that she was supposed to be a mistress.

"Oh, yes," she lied. Because she really wasn't sure of the skills involved. Although last night was giving her an idea. And of course the idea had to do with her being naked, and Harry being naked. Perhaps on the floor. Or the bed. Or against the door. Any of those places would do.

She felt herself blush. "That's why if I win, I'd prefer to receive money. A hundred pounds should do it."

Joan huffed. "That's more than most people earn in several years!"

Molly shrugged. "A tiara of paste won't sustain me if"—she hesitated, but then decided to be brave—"if, um, Lord Harry throws me over someday."

Again, there was an awkward silence.

"You've put me in a very bad mood, Delilah," Athena said, her winged eyebrows lowered dangerously.

"Me, too," said Hildur, crossing her arms and glaring at Molly.

"I'm sorry," she said. "I—I just meant that we *all* deserve something better than a tiara if we win."

"Would you be quiet with your outrageous speech?" Joan said. "You're boring me to tears." She struck a jarring chord on the pianoforte, her chest heaving with . . . something like discontent.

But Athena diffused the tension when she stood and flung back her hair, quite as if she were onstage. "We've no time to indulge this sort of prattle. The men approach!" Quickly, she put her sketchbook in a drawer and fussed with the ringlets around her face.

Indeed, Molly could hear the horses' hooves galloping across the yard. Her heart started beating at a fast pace. She didn't know why she was excited to see Harry again. But perhaps it was because being alone with the other mistresses had its own stresses.

Hildur hid her knitting behind a curtain. Then she lifted her bosom higher in her dress and threw her shoulders back.

"You're blocking my profile," Athena warned her.

Hildur didn't appear to understand.

"Move." Athena waved her hand. "I must be seen to advantage."

Hildur glowered at her, then threw herself onto a chair and sulked prettily.

Joan put the music away on the pianoforte, and Bunny stuffed her needlework under a table. They both took up strategic positions lounging on sofas near the drawing room entrance.

All of them appeared completely indolent, Molly thought, as if they'd merely been waiting for their men to return and accomplished nothing else in the meantime.

Predictably, the men came in with much noise and

dropping of equipment near the front door. Molly had no time to think of how she should appear when Harry saw her. She merely stood there, like a stump, and watched the drawing room entrance.

All the men poured through together, like puppies.

Which amused Molly no end. Their faces were red and their hair was tousled. Harry looked extremely handsome, and for a fleeting second, she felt a surge of heat and possession grip her.

She was proud he was "hers." And oh, how she wanted to mark him with her kisses! She wanted to fling her arms about his neck and look into his eyes and know that he would do things to her that would turn her knees to blancmange any time she wanted him to.

Because her wish was his command.

And in her daydream, he would desire nothing more than to pleasure her senseless and hold her when she was afraid—and laugh with her when she needed a friend. And then go back to kissing her, of course.

But then she remembered. Harry was most definitely not hers. Nor did he want her. And why should he? The other women, except for Bunny, had made clear yet again this morning that she made a terrible mistress.

"Delilah," Harry said with much energy and enthusiasm. Yes, he was merely putting on a show for the room, but a small part of him was actually happy to see her. And another part was worried about her.

She appeared . . . small. As slight as a shadow. Ever since she'd arrived here, she had. Except for last night against her bedroom door. She'd been *very* noticeable then.

"Harry," she greeted him back, her hands folded in front of her. She appeared rather nervous about what he planned to do next. Everyone around them was kissing and murmuring sweet nothings.

So he bounded across the room to her, leaned in, and kissed her full on the mouth.

But he kept the kiss short. Too long, and he would get frustrated. He found the short kiss invigorating, to tell the truth. And it appeared to have the same effect of lifting Molly's spirits as well, which was a good thing.

Her cheeks reddened. "D-did you enjoy yourself?" She smelled deliciously of fresh bread somehow. And strawberries.

"Very much." He smiled and pulled her aside, as if they were having an intimate tête-à-tête like the others.

She nodded. "Bunny is very kind."

"I'm glad to hear you're doing . . . better," he said.

"One minute at a time is my new philosophy," she said. "I can always manage that."

Hmmm. Harry admired her spirit, but he wished she were having more *fun*. He rubbed his hands up and down her arms, hoping to relax her. "I'm to announce the first game now. Be prepared for anything, all right?"

He couldn't tell her any of the details—it wouldn't be fair to the other mistresses—but he did give her arms an encouraging squeeze.

"I'll try my best," she said.

And he knew she would. Molly didn't prevaricate in the least, quite a refreshing trait to observe in a mistress. His real ones had fibbed to him often.

"I hope your best includes more kissing practice," he whispered huskily, surprising himself.

Her face flushed pink. "Of—of course," she said. "When?"

"Now."

He wrapped his arms around her and kissed her the way he really wanted to kiss her. She responded by kissing him back with an intensity that surprised him, considering the presence of everyone else in the room.

He was well pleased. She was learning to put on a very good show. In fact, she did so well that when he pulled back, he was a little more heated than he'd intended to be.

"I've got to go now," he said low, and skimmed his thumb over her cheek. "But don't forget. Kissing practice is compulsory."

"I won't," she whispered back. "Um, when's our next lesson?"

He grinned. "After the first game."

"All right." She grinned back. "I'll be waiting."

He was sure she wouldn't be waiting for him after the first game, but he wasn't an Impossible Bachelor for nothing, was he?

So he kissed the back of her hand, allowing his lips to linger. "I'll hold you to that promise," he said, feeling the veriest cad when he saw the glow of pleasure in her eyes.

And he walked away to carry out Prinny's orders.

CHAPTER 13

Harry stood on a small ottoman to gain every person's attention—although Molly thought he really didn't need to do that as he had the sort of personality that drew attention like a magnet.

"We shall now gather on the side lawn for the first game—a sack race," he announced.

"A full accounting of which must be relayed to the Prince Regent," Maxwell reminded the crowd.

"Exactly," Harry said. "The winner of the sack race will accrue ten points in her favor, to be tallied into the final count at the end of the week. And don't forget, for both winners and losers, a fine picnic will be served afterward."

There was much clamoring to go out. It was a beautiful day, after all. And Molly was thrilled to hear the game was a sack race. She might not be a proper mistress, but she had a long history of winning sack races at the village fair.

And she'd always employed a brilliant strategy.

The women assembled at a chalky line drawn on the grass. Molly pulled the sack up over her shoes and gown to her waist. Her hands felt clammy, and her heart beat at a brisk pace already. She really needed to win this race, so she must—

Hop, she reminded herself as she gripped the edge of the sack. *Hop and don't stop*.

"I hope you trip," Joan said to her out of the corner of her mouth.

"I won't," she said, staring Joan down. "I've a strategy."

Joan curled her lip. "A strategy? For a sack race?"

But before Molly could reply, Harry blew a whistle, and they were off.

She'd forgotten how ridiculously awkward it was to make one's way forward inside a burlap bag. Holding tight to the sack, she hopped her way across the grounds. Hers was an unseemly, awkward advance, but it appeared that everyone else was having the same difficulties.

Out of the corner of her eye, she saw Joan fall, then Athena. Bunny was a few hops behind her, and Hildur was nowhere in sight.

Molly had the fleeting thought that she just might win this one!

She heard Harry saying "Go, Delilah, go!" and for a moment, she was upset at his lack of loyalty, but then she remembered *she* was Delilah.

She'd told him she wouldn't forget, and here she was forgetting—

But no time to think. It was time to hop for all she was worth. It was time to *win*. Yet she was laughing so hard at the madness of it all that she almost tripped and fell.

She caught Harry's eye and heard him urging her onward.

"I'm trying!" she yelled, but she was so out of breath, she didn't think Harry or anyone else heard.

Athena began catching up again. She was almost to Bunny, and then Bunny was almost to Molly.

She couldn't allow that, as much as she liked Bunny.

Hop, she urged herself when Bunny appeared at her elbow. *Hop and don't stop!* Lunging forward with all her might, Molly finally crossed the finish line—

In first place!

She dropped her sack, jumped up and down, and clapped her hands. Oh, to win! It was a lovely feeling.

She sought Harry's face, but he was still watching the other mistresses intently. All the men were, so Molly decided she must, too. She would stop clapping and be a good sport. So she praised the other women when they each crossed the finish line and helped them get out of their sacks.

When all was said and done, Bunny came in second; Athena, third; Joan, fourth; and Hildur, dead last.

"You'll do better in the next game," Molly said to Hildur, who gave her a look that could kill.

The men stood to the side, beneath a large oak tree, conferring. And none of the women congratulated Molly. She folded up her sack and pretended that it didn't hurt. Everyone was ignoring her silly victory. And the sack race had been so much *fun.*

Finally, Harry emerged from the circle of men. "We have our winner," he announced.

But Molly noticed that he wasn't making eye contact with her, and he didn't seem all that happy. Whyever not? Perhaps he had to hide his gladness so he would appear to be a fair master of ceremonies.

Yes, that was it, she decided.

"The winner," Harry said—Molly felt her face heat up, and she bit her lip so as not to giggle—"is . . . Joan."

Joan?

Joan jumped up and down and clapped her hands.

That made no sense at all!

Molly stared at Harry. She had obviously come in first place, and even if the men had judged her wrongly, Bunny had clearly come in second, followed by Athena. And *then* Joan, before Hildur.

Didn't the men have eyes in their heads?

Viscount Lumley went up to Joan and put a ribbon around her neck. "You had the bounciest pair of all," he murmured, his gaze lingering on her neckline.

Bounciest pair?

Molly looked down at her own neckline, where her cleavage was well in sight. Lumley couldn't mean *those*, could he? She looked up and stared at Harry, who was still evading her gaze, and her blood turned to fire. Was that how the men were judging this sack race?

The winner was the mistress who had the bounciest breasts?

"Yes," said Athena, guessing her pique. "Disgusting, isn't it? Especially as I'm sure Joan stuffs."

Molly blinked several times. She felt so . . . humiliated. And angry.

She'd won that sack race fair and square! But not only had she *not* been declared the winner, she'd fared poorly in a contest judging . . . bouncy breasts.

Not that *she* cared about having bouncy breasts. But somehow it hurt to know that the men—why, Prinny himself!—cared about that more than they did about the mistresses' ability to hop in burlap sacks, which was a silly skill, too, Molly knew, but—

At least it took some physical prowess to win the sack race.

One couldn't really control one's bouncy breasts, now could one?

Her blood grew hotter and hotter. She knew if Harry came over to her now, she wouldn't be able to contain herself. She wouldn't be biddable. *Nor* beguiling. She would not act like a mistress *at all*.

But there he was, striding toward her, his face carefully arranged in a pleasant mask. "Don't be too despondent," he said tersely. "It's how things are here. Prinny's orders."

"I see," she bit out.

She had to leave. She would cry if she stayed talking to Harry because she had never been more mortified in her life.

All that fun she'd had hopping. And yelling. She'd felt this wonderful feeling that had been buried deep inside her coming to the surface. But it was gone now.

The fun might as well have never happened.

"I'm sorry," Harry said. "It's nothing personal . . . Delilah."

She looked around to ensure no one was listening. Fortunately, the others were preoccupied with flirting, folding sacks, and setting out the picnic.

"Right," she whispered. "Thank you for reminding me that I shouldn't take offense."

He grabbed her hand. "Molly," he said. "I *told* you to expect the unexpected."

She tugged her hand back and strode off.

"What about the picnic?" he called after her.

She whipped around. "I'm not hungry," she said stoutly. "And kissing practice is canceled!"

"Molly—" Lines formed about Harry's eyes. "Please come back when you feel better. I'll miss you. And I mean that. According to most of the world's rules, you really did win the sack race, and I want to make it up to you somehow."

"I—I'll think about it," she said.

In a million years!

She turned her back on him. She didn't need his concern. She wanted to leave this place, and she didn't care if she looked like a poor sport. She headed toward the house, toward the paltry comfort of her bedchamber, where nothing was actually her own, except for her parasol and reticule and the now grimy walking dress she'd worn on her elopement day.

If only she could rewind time and go back to that inn, before Cedric met his Aphrodite. If only she could have made sure that they had left the inn and gone to Gretna. Right now she would be a married woman, and married to one of the handsomest—albeit annoying—men in England!

She forced herself to slow down and blow out a breath.

Who was she kidding? She didn't want Cedric. She deserved better. And after this miserable week was over, she was going to make sure her life *became* better.

But—she stopped walking and sighed—she needed Harry's help to do that. She obviously didn't understand men at *all*. She needed him to find a good one for her, a man who was the opposite of these ridiculous Impossible Bachelors.

Oh, dear. She would have to go back to the picnic, wouldn't she?

She looked back at the group, everyone laughing and talking and making merry. She would put on a cheerful face, too, like all the other mistresses. Bunny, especially, looked happy. If Bunny could pretend that everything was all right—when Sir Richard was so despicably rude and selfish—then so could Molly.

Harry had dreaded seeing Molly's face when he announced the winner of the sack race. She'd looked so damned happy when she'd crossed the finish line. And then her expression had changed, like a sunny sky going to gray in an instant.

He tried to be angry with her for ruining the fun of the game, but he couldn't. He'd felt like the worst scoundrel.

Especially when she came back to the picnic smiling,

doing her best to be dignified and pleasant to everyone—
even him—when he knew he didn't deserve it because he,
after all, was the one taking advantage of the fact that she
had damned little choice but to cooperate this week.

At supper, she was still showing the same dogged spirit.

Watching her now, as she labored at trying to entrance
her tablemates in the way *he* had advised her, Harry knew
it was all wrong, that she had not a hope of winning. But
he also had no alternative ideas to offer her, a fact that
made him entirely frustrated.

"Lord Maxwell," she was saying now, "you seem the
observant sort. Do you think dogs laugh with their tails?"

Athena narrowed her eyes at her.

Lord Maxwell looked thoughtfully at the tablecloth
then back at Molly. "I believe the tail wag signals a certain contentment on the part of the dog, but not laughter,
per se. Dogs don't laugh."

"But of course they do!" Molly said with surprise. "I
even had a dog who could talk. His name was Bounder.
Once he said 'Fork.' Clear as day. Right after he'd stolen
Papa's beefsteak off the table. And another time—"

"Delilah." Harry slammed his wine glass on the table.
A bit of it slopped onto the pristine white tablecloth. Not
that he really noticed or cared. It was his father's tablecloth, after all. "The men need to depart—to vote."

He was certainly not looking forward to adjourning to
the library to hear yet again how poorly his mistress was
performing in the competition.

Molly's brow puckered. "Already? We've still one course
to go."

"That's right," Harry said, drumming his fingers on
the table. "I meant *after* the last course."

"Oh." She stared at him as if he were from Bedlam,
then leaned closer to him. "Are you all right, Harry?" she
whispered.

"Fine," he muttered back.

Which was a lie. He felt the weight of an imminent wedding pressing on his head. He would be the groom, and Anne Riordan would be the bride.

CHAPTER 14

Goodness, Molly thought. Harry had put his wine glass down with such force! And his mouth was so tight. She knew he was disappointed in her lukewarm presence at the table.

As she was herself. Perhaps she'd overestimated her acting abilities. All she knew was that here, in this house, she felt overwhelmed and . . . and not delectable at all.

She thought she'd make a fine make-believe mistress but she'd have to talk about something *real* or she would *burst.* She'd been about to, when she'd spoken of Bounder, but Harry had cut her off, and then when she'd looked back, Lord Maxwell had been immersed in conversation with Athena.

Molly would try to speak to someone else.

"Viscount Lumley," she said, clenching her hands in her lap. "I—I have your tart to bake, and I must ask Cook to set aside the ingredients. Do you have a preference in fruit fillings?"

There was a silence around the table.

But Viscount Lumley came through soon enough, dear man. "I think I should prefer—"

"Delilah, whyever do you bother making *tarts*?" interrupted Joan. Her tone was snide.

"Because she's good at them," Bunny answered roundly for Molly. "What skills do *you* have, Joan?"

"Aside from the obvious ones, that is," said Sir Richard in his silky voice, and ran his licentious gaze over Joan's form.

Joan winked at him, then glared at Bunny. "What do you care?"

Bunny shrugged. "I was simply asking."

"Do less asking, Bunny." Sir Richard pressed his fingertips into her arm. Too hard.

Bunny blinked and turned red.

It was an obvious warning from Sir Richard, and Molly didn't like it. Not one bit.

She would return to the subject of her tarts. "If I don't have all the ingredients, I might have to go out and find them, Viscount Lumley. So do tell me your preference."

"Berries," he replied. "But I also love a good apple tart."

Harry eyed her, a small grin lifting the corner of his mouth. "We've loads of blackberries around the lake."

The lake?

Molly's heart raced. She wouldn't think of Harry swimming there . . . *naked,* or any other guests doing the same.

"Perhaps another expedition there is in order," Harry went on. "We missed the first one, remember?"

"Oh, no," Molly said hurriedly. "We needn't bother. I could always use apples instead."

"I ate the last apple just this morning," said Sir Richard.

Vile man.

"So we most certainly shall have to go to the lake," Harry said.

Oh, dear. Molly wasn't sure she could escape going to the lake *now*.

She absolutely refused to ponder how everyone at this

table would look naked, especially Sir Richard—although she noticed that refusing to ponder it just made her wonder all the more!

She was becoming just as bad as the rest of them.

She was relieved in a way when Harry suggested the men adjourn for the daily vote. She was glad they were leaving, but she wasn't pleased she wouldn't be getting any votes again. Of that, she was sure.

Fortunately, tonight the other women were too preoccupied with talking about how much they enjoyed the scandalous waltz, so none of them went to extraordinary, last-minute efforts to bewitch the men into voting for them, either.

Thank God. Molly didn't think she could take any more of Athena's drama or Joan's cleavage spilling out.

"After you," Harry said coolly to Sir Richard as they left the dining room to go vote in the library.

Molly could swear Harry stared daggers through Sir Richard even as he was being polite, but then again, she might be wrong. Harry might simply have indigestion. He'd been awfully grouchy all through supper, until the end, when he'd perked up a bit at the prospect of going to the lake.

Perhaps some brandy and a cheroot would improve his temper. Molly knew it was caused mainly by her weak showing as a mistress.

He turned back around to face her and the other women. "One last thing, ladies. In the drawing room, you'll find a note from the Prince Regent. He requests that you give it your most prompt attention."

And then he left.

Joan pushed back her chair, but Athena pushed hers back even faster. They raced each other through the door to the drawing room, Hildur not far behind them.

"Mine!" yelled Athena.

There was a loud noise of disgust, presumably from Joan.

By the time Molly and Bunny found their seats, Athena was standing by the pianoforte, her nose in the air, an eyebrow arched high. She held a large envelope in her hands. "Are you ready?"

She eyed the company quite as if she were already the winner of the Most Delectable Companion contest and the other ladies, her minions.

"Yes, we are, thank you," Bunny said in her soft voice.

Athena removed the wax seal on the back, pulled out the paper inside, and opened it with a flourish.

"Get on with it!" Joan snarled.

Athena narrowed her eyes at her then cleared her throat. "His Royal Highness, the Prince Regent," she read in stentorian tones, "requires all participants in the Most Delectable Companion contest to perform a dramatic reading at the conclusion of the house party, in a grand finale. You are to scour the library for your material."

She adjusted her chin one invisible notch higher: "Most of you have no chance to win this portion of the contest, so don't feel guilty about giving up in the face of better talent. Good luck, and Godspeed."

Oh, for goodness' sake! Molly rolled her eyes at Bunny, who responded with a stifled laugh.

Athena folded the paper and stuffed it back into the envelope.

"Let me see that." Joan grabbed the envelope from her hands, pulled out the note, and skimmed it. Her eyes snapped with unholy fire. "It doesn't say that last part! You *lied*!"

Athena colored. "I'm only trying to let you down easily. Of course I'll win this portion of the competition. I'm a trained actress."

Hildur's blond eyebrows flew up. "I don't understand. What is this thing we are to do that Athena lies about?"

Joan tossed the letter onto the pianoforte. "You must perform a dramatic reading." She spoke so slowly to Hildur, it was obvious she meant to be rude. "And Athena wasn't lying about you—you really *will* lose because you can barely speak English, much less read it from a book."

And then she laughed.

"Is not fair!" A sheen of tears appeared in Hildur's eyes.

Molly placed her hand on Hildur's arm. "*I* can help you."

But Hildur yanked her arm away, stomped to the windows, and pretended to look out at the grounds.

"You've no room to laugh, Joan," Bunny said in a gentle but chiding voice. "Athena's right. *She's* the actress among us."

Joan scowled. "That's not fair."

"Who said this contest had to be fair?" Athena tossed her hair.

Hildur was still pouting by the window. "Remember my offer," Molly told her, but the Icelandic beauty wouldn't answer. So Molly stood and bestowed an apologetic smile on Bunny. "Good night, ladies. I'll see you in the morning."

"Good night, Delilah." Bunny smiled back with understanding, but no one else said a word.

Molly sighed. At the moment she'd rather not think about Joan's and Athena's childishness. Nor about Hildur's pouting, nor about the dramatic reading, nor about the fairness versus unfairness of the whole competition.

But on her way out of the drawing room, she heard Athena whisper, "I'll bet she's going to stand outside the library and try to get in after the men leave. So she can get the best choice of reading material."

"Does she think we're stupid?" Joan whispered back. "I shall beat her to it!"

"So shall I!" said Athena.

Just in time, Molly flattened herself against the corridor wall to avoid being run over. Joan and Athena lifted their skirts and practically ran past her toward the library.

"You're right to get out of our way," Joan called back to her.

But Molly ignored the jibe and headed in the opposite direction. She had no intention of trying to get into the library. She was going to check with Cook to see if she'd any fruit for the tarts—perhaps Molly could avoid going to the lake to pick blackberries, after all.

But sadly, Cook had no fruit left. However, she did insist on showing Molly the tomatoes growing in the greenhouse. Ten very comforting minutes went by in which Cook and Molly held a plain conversation about sunlight and water and vegetables—with no double entendres or wagging eyebrows involved. Cook—well pleased by Molly's compliments on her tomatoes—finally went back to the kitchens, and Molly decided to stay outside and look at the stars.

The night was beautiful. Wending her way past a hedge of boxwood, she entered a more formal garden, where she wandered past lithesome statues and neatly trimmed rosebushes, eventually stopping to stare at the moon.

She sighed. In the grand scheme of things, even if she were to lose the competition, she'd land on her feet, wouldn't she? Harry would take her home at the end of this week, and no one there would be any the wiser about where she'd been.

So why did she feel so blue?

"You look alluring bending over that flower," a voice behind her said.

She jumped, and her heart began an immediate fast tattoo.

It was Sir Richard.

"Aren't you voting in the library?" she asked, and knew her voice sounded rather weak.

"We've finished faster than expected," he said. "Thanks to the disruption of Athena and Joan, who were whispering outside the door. Do you wonder if you received any votes?"

"No," she said more firmly, recovering somewhat from her surprise. "I assume I didn't."

Sir Richard laughed. "No one could ever call you a coquette." He advanced toward her. "I must say, I find you a most . . . *unusual* mistress."

She backed away, but a thorny rosebush stopped her retreat. "I think I shall be rejoining the others now. If you'll excuse me."

She attempted to walk around him.

Once again, he caught her before she could escape. "There must be something more to you," he murmured. "I would like to find out what it is."

Harry had spoken to her about mysterious women being so intriguing to men. She wasn't mysterious, but she *was* carrying a secret, wasn't she?

She was pretending to be a mistress.

"I assure you," she said, forcing a laugh, "there is nothing mysterious about *me*. I have no hidden fires. No secrets at *all*."

She hoped she was a good liar.

Sir Richard ran his hand up her arm. "You're a terrible liar," he said. "You're hiding something. And I shall find out what it is."

"I am *not* hiding anything," she said.

"I like when you get heated," he replied, his eyes getting darker.

"I'm not yours to like," she said, pulling away from him.

"You could be," he said. "What is your price?" His

hand was like a vise. She remembered how he'd used it on Bunny at supper and on her own wrist the first time she'd met him.

"Let go of me," she said, and slapped his hand. *Hard*. "I am *not* for sale."

He laughed, but his mouth thinned into an ugly line. "Showing some spirit now, eh?"

"Go away," she hissed.

She struggled and twisted, but he caught her from behind and held both her upper arms in a viselike grip.

"I shall have you before the week is out," he whispered in her ear.

"Never," she said, and threw her elbow back into his stomach. She was pleased to hear his sharp exhale. "Stay *away* from me."

She ran through the garden hedge, back to the kitchen garden, followed a small path, and slipped into the house through a side door. Leaning against it a moment, she caught her breath. It had been a bad idea to go into the garden alone at night. But she was in the country, and everyone had been occupied. She'd had no reason to worry! Or so she'd thought.

On trembling legs she crept up the back stairs to her bedchamber. She opened her door, stepped into her room, and closed the door behind her, feeling more alone than ever.

CHAPTER 15

Harry had begun to worry about Molly. No one knew where she was. Which left him with an unpleasant feeling in his gut, particularly as no one knew where Sir Richard was, either. So Harry had run upstairs, through his room and the dressing room connecting his room to Molly's, and found a blasted bureau blocking his way to her bed-chamber. After one quick shove to the door, he was in.

She was sitting on the bed, breathing hard, as if she'd been running. Two spots of color stained her cheeks.

"Where were you?" he demanded, probably more force-fully than he would have wished.

"Goodness, Harry." Molly placed her hand on her heart. "You frightened me, bursting in like that."

He was skeptical that he alone had caused her to be so jumpy. "You already looked frightened when I came in. And your hair is mussed. What happened? I went looking for you when I didn't see you in the drawing room. And Sir Richard disappeared, as well."

She smoothed her hair. "I was in the garden."

"And?" Harry felt very dangerous at the moment.

"And Sir Richard followed me. Or else he stumbled upon me while I was out there."

Harry took her shoulders. "Did he hurt you?"

"No." She smiled up at him, but it looked awfully wobbly. "I took care of him."

Harry pressed his lips into a thin line. Molly was part of *home,* part of what his *real* life was about, the rustic one that involved complimenting his mother on her flower beds and saying hello to the elderly people at the country church his parents attended and riding out to see the crops and visit with those who tended them. He didn't often acknowledge that life even when he was in the midst of it—he told himself it bored him—but he felt a sudden, fierce need to protect it now.

Harry's gut clamored to do battle with Sir Richard. And he felt an even greater need to wrap Molly in his arms and kiss away the anxiety he read in her eyes.

They were alone in her bedchamber. He grew heated just thinking about the fact that everyone in the house expected them to make love in her bed. And then *his* bed.

Perhaps a chair next.

Then against the wall.

Her legs wrapped around his waist.

His body loving hers in a mindless pleasure game.

All night long.

Harry sighed. He wanted to make her his. Primitive of him, yes. But in this house filled with men and their mistresses, he felt an illogical need to put his stamp upon her, a need that came straight from his groin and not his head.

"I shouldn't have brought you here," he said. "I always thought Bell rather weak, but he apparently means business. I'll talk to him. And if he bothers you again, I shall call him out."

"No." She laid a hand on his arm, and he was tempted to bring her palm to his mouth and press a hot kiss on it. "Sir Richard's not worth taking a bullet for. Although he really hates you, doesn't he? And he's attempting to get to you through me."

Harry released a fraction of his tension by taking both her hands. "You're certainly someone he might pursue for the sake of pursuing."

It was the gallant thing to say.

But she saw through his flattery right away. "Oh, Harry. I've been a little Miss Nobody here, hardly someone worth chasing through the garden. But he did say he found me mysterious. He said he knows I'm hiding something."

"Did he?"

"Yes. So I rather think you were right. Men like mystery."

Harry looked into her eyes and saw no mystery there— her gaze was open and earnest, as comforting as a feather bed. A swift pang of guilt shot through him because he felt an overwhelming urge to put something else in her eyes—

A blue flame of desire.

"You're not a little Miss Nobody," he said, and raised her chin with a gentle hand. "No one with any sense or character could think that of you."

And suddenly, he meant it. He rubbed his thumb across her bottom lip, and there was a beat of silence. He thought he saw an awakening in her eyes. A flicker of need.

But she's just had a scare, an annoying part of his brain chided him. *Step back.*

So he did, albeit reluctantly. And began to pace.

"I don't understand Bell," he said. "Tonight at the voting, he once again made insulting comments to me alone. No one else. I wonder why I offend him so? It's not as if I wield any power within my family. I'm the second son. The spare."

"Stop thinking about Sir Richard for a while," Molly said, and patted the bed. "Sit, why don't you?"

He paused and looked at her. Did she mean to look so

provocative, patting the bed like that? Or was his lust-filled brain imagining it?

Good God, of course it was. Molly didn't play coy games. She was his neighbor. He'd visited her at her father and mother's house the very day she'd been born!

He made the decision once more to behave, to sit next to her and draw comfort from the sensation of his shoulder touching hers. It meant she was safe.

"Harry," she ventured, swinging her legs the way she used to when they were children sitting on the ledge of the grand fountain outside his father's house.

"Yes?"

"You talk of yourself as if you're not important." Her legs stopped swinging.

He felt his chest clench, but he gave a huff of laughter. "I'm terribly important, Molly. I'm the son of a duke."

"Yes, I know." He was hoping she would have laughed with him, but her face was somber. "There was something in your voice when you said you were only the spare. What was it? Did you ever feel being the second son made you not important to your family?"

Harry met her open gaze. "I'm certainly not going to complain. I had a brother who doted on me, and a mother who did, as well. And as far as I know, they still do."

"What about your father?"

Harry's heart beat faster. "He's like most fathers," he said. "Immersed in his duties. Aloof."

Molly was silent a moment. "My father, too. I know he loves me. And he's a wonderful person. It's just that . . . once my mother died, he seemed to stop noticing me. Penelope was usually there for me, but not Papa. Especially after—"

Harry grinned. "The Christmas incident. You were sent away to that horrible school, so you saw your father even less."

"Yes. And the same for you. Although being forced to join the army was probably the best thing that could have happened to you, don't you think?"

"Why would you say that?"

She smiled. "I followed your progress. You did quite well for yourself. Even after . . ." She trailed off rather awkwardly.

"Even after my disgrace, you mean," he filled in for her.

She nodded. "Do you want to talk about it? I don't know exactly what happened. Papa's never told me."

"Ah. So he's alluded to it, then."

Molly lowered her eyes. "Yes."

Harry's chest tightened. "He probably told you to stay away from me. Be courteous, but don't spend too much time with me."

Molly looked up then. "He never said so directly. And as I'd already made clear my . . . my *disdain* for you"— she bit her lip—"I suppose he never felt the need to warn me off."

"It really doesn't matter what happened to me in the army." Harry strove for a light tone. "My father never notices my successes *or* failures."

"Then that's his loss, isn't it?" Molly said, edging a bit closer. "Families are funny things. I don't think your father means to overlook you. He might even feel you are overlooking *him*."

She smiled, and for some reason, he smiled back. She certainly had an interesting way of looking at things. And if she had any disdain for him, she wasn't showing it now. Her eyes were alight with an earnestness—a warm intensity—that he found entirely . . . adorable.

And irresistible.

He girded himself to be strong. Noble. Protective.

She leaned toward him and put a hand on his chest.

"Thank me, Harry," she said in a throaty whisper. "Because if I hadn't written that lovesick poem implicating you and Penelope while pouring out my undying love for Roderick—"

"No one would ever have known I kissed her mere weeks before their wedding," he whispered back. "And I never would have joined the army."

"And fought so well at Waterloo."

She knew about that? Of course, the gossip implicating him as a disgrace to the army canceled out any stories he had to tell about Waterloo, but still. She *knew.*

"How did you know?" he asked her.

"Roderick told Penelope. And she mentioned it in a letter to me."

The clock ticktocked on the mantel, and the wind moaned against the windowpane. Molly's eyes were wide and the warmest brown he had ever seen—still impish, but sparking with an invitation to—

God help him! Maybe he could simply be strong and noble—and give up on being protective.

"I know we're like a burr under the other's saddle," she said. "But I need the kissing practice, remember?"

"That's right." He swallowed. "Practice."

So he laid her back on the bed and kissed her thoroughly, to the point that he was beginning to take liberties that he really didn't need to take to prove she and he were together, as it were, at the house party.

But she was sunlight and ambrosia, and she stoked a heat in his veins that he feared would soon consume every ounce of his self-control. He kissed her again, cupping one of her perfect breasts in his palm and caressing its fullness.

"Harry," she whispered.

"Not Samson?" he murmured back, their lips still joined in deep, seductive play.

She shook her head.

Thank God for that.

He bent his head lower still, his tongue tracing her neckline where it plunged between those amazing breasts. She was intoxicating, and he wasn't sure why. Of course, he'd always noticed her luxuriant brown tresses, sweet face, and lithe figure, but they hadn't counted—she was Molly, after all, his neighbor and his nemesis.

When she wove her fingers through his hair and caressed his scalp with her fingers, it felt wickedly good, but not so good as his pushing down one side of her bodice and lavishing her pert and beautiful breast with more kisses.

"You're gorgeous," he murmured, and ran his tongue around her rosebud nipple.

"Oh, Harry." She moaned so loudly that he swiftly moved from her breast to her mouth to keep her quiet. She was driving him wild with her enthusiasm, but for her sake, he wanted no one else to hear her.

She was a lady. And he wouldn't have the others thinking he and Molly were up to no good in here—

Although that was exactly what he was supposed to want them to think. Wasn't it?

And they *were* up to no good, weren't they?

It was all very confusing.

When they came up for air, Molly's cheeks were pink and her eyes, a simmering brown. She looked incredibly desirable, Harry thought, more desirable than any mistress he'd ever had. But even through the blinding haze of his lust for her, his head was asking, Why? What was it about Molly that made his blood quicken to a fever pitch the moment his lips touched hers?

In light of their bitter history and the fact that he could very well wind up married to her if all went wrong with this caper, his desire for her made no sense. All she would

have to do was tell her father and his about their week at
the duke's hunting box, and Harry was a doomed man.

And she'd fare no better. Even he believed she deserved someone with an unsullied reputation, a husband
who could hold his head high and make a fitting partner
for her.

All the more reason for the fire between them to be
extinguished. If only he could resist her soft lips, he'd put
it out right now!

But Molly beat him to it. She pulled away from him
and stood, smoothing down her skirt. "It was once again
a very good practice," she said shyly. "I think everyone
will believe we're . . . a couple, don't you?"

He struggled to recover from the abrupt end to their
lovemaking by appearing completely aloof in expression.

"Yes, I do," he replied, but his voice was still gruff with
unspent desire and a need for something he couldn't name,
a vague something that went beyond a lustful bedding—
although he had no idea what it was.

He stood. "Keep your door locked," he instructed her
in the clipped way he would a foot soldier, "and come get
me if you're frightened."

Molly looked up at him with trust in her eyes. "I'll
knock on your door if I get scared. I know you'd make me
laugh, Harry."

And for some reason, that look of hers—and those simple words—*almost* penetrated the invisible armor he wore,
the armor that kept him detached and alone. She actually
seemed to need him, and no one had ever needed him before.

The army had needed the soldier. His family had needed
the second son. But who had ever really needed . . . Harry?
For being *Harry*?

Not a single person.

At least until now.

CHAPTER 16

The next morning, Molly woke up when the sun was already slanting across her pillow. She sat up and looked at the clock on the mantel. Nine! That was a late hour for her. But she didn't care. She felt happy for some reason, and then she remembered why.

Harry.

Well, Harry and Samuel Taylor Coleridge actually.

A smile tugged at her mouth. She'd gotten better acquainted with both of them last night. Her body literally tingled at the memory of Harry's kisses and caresses—and her heart beat faster thinking about the thrilling "Kubla Khan," which she'd decided to perform at the dramatic reading competition.

She wondered how Athena and Joan could have possibly overlooked Coleridge's poem, but when Molly had tiptoed down to the library with a candle in the middle of the night (she'd kept waking up and thinking about Harry), she'd found it on Harry's desk.

Then she'd realized Athena would no doubt read Shakespeare, and Joan—who knew what she'd read?

Molly had also found something she thought Hildur might like to explore with her, a book of poems by Lord

Byron. She'd approach her about it today if Hildur were in a better mood than she'd been yesterday evening.

She leaned back on her pillows to read "Kubla Khan" again when a tap sounded at the dressing room door.

She felt a quickening in her middle. It must be Harry! So she shut the book, placed it on her bed table, and threw the covers back. Then she pulled a luxurious wrap over her nightdress and turned the doorknob.

And there he was, leaning against the doorjamb, his arms crossed over his chest, his hair mussed and his eyes bright with mischief.

"My, my." He took in her state of dishabille and grinned. "Aren't you looking and acting like a mistress today!"

She blushed. "I've never had such, ah, lovely nightclothes. Nor slept so late, I admit."

"I thought I'd say good morning. The other bachelors and I—save Sir Richard—went out for an early morning ride. I believe he's still snoring away. And the others might have, um, returned to their beds."

But not to sleep, she guessed, and felt heat rise in her face.

There was an awkward beat of silence, and Harry pushed off the doorjamb. "May I come in, please? We've a business matter to discuss."

"Oh." She fumbled with her wrap. "Of course."

He entered the room, filling it with his presence. "I've been thinking about your dramatic reading," he said. "Something from Shakespeare might suit. A woman's soliloquy, perhaps? Or a sonnet?"

"I thought of that," Molly said. "But I couldn't hope to compete with Athena. No doubt she'll read from Shakespeare."

"Good point."

"But don't worry. I'm thrilled at what I've found—'Kubla Khan'!"

Harry brightened. "Excellent choice. I was reading it yesterday. Wait—when did you find the time to retrieve it from the library?"

Molly hesitated. "In the middle of the night. I took a candle."

"Molly," he chided her. "What about Sir Richard?"

She shrugged. "I had a candlestick in my possession, didn't I? And it's not as if you and the whole house wouldn't have been able to hear me if I screamed. Besides, he's too lazy to be up and about in the middle of the night. We both know that."

"Still, you should have come to get me if you couldn't sleep." Harry chucked her chin. "I would have escorted you."

"I wouldn't dare knock on your door at three in the morning!"

He lifted a brow. "Whyever not? Am I the big, bad wolf?"

She put her nose in the air. "Yes, as a matter of fact, you are. Why should a girl take any chances?"

Harry threw her a wry glance. "Let's get back to the dramatic reading, shall we? I'd like to hear you practice. Perhaps I could give you some tips."

"All right."

He sat in a chair by the window. "I'm ready when you are."

She took a moment to retrieve the book and find her place. Then, clearing her throat, she began to read aloud:

"In Xanadu did Kubla Khan
A stately pleasure-dome decree:
Where Alph, the sacred river, ran
Through caverns measureless to man
Down to a sunless sea."

Harry held up a palm. "Very nice," he said. "Although perhaps you could move about a bit while you read. The way a stage performer would. Remember that walk I taught you?"

"Oh, yes." She moved her hips back and forth.

"Perhaps you could also read the lines slower . . . and as you do, think about—"

He steepled his hands and thought for a moment.

"About what?" She blinked.

His mouth turned down. "With sincere apologies to Mr. Coleridge, I must say you'll have more of a chance to win the contest if you pretend Xanudu is the site where you and your lover escape to be together."

Molly pursed her lips. "That's rather ridiculous."

Harry gave a short laugh. "I know. But try it anyway. We want to win, remember. And Mr. Coleridge will never know."

Molly sighed. "Very well. Although it goes against everything in me to imbue his lovely poem with an . . . an overtone that's not there."

"If it's any comfort to you, no one is sure *how* to interpret 'Kubla Khan.' Look at the subtitle. He wrote it in some sort of opiate haze or dream."

"All right," Molly said, still feeling reluctant, although she did try to imagine what Harry had asked. But after a moment of quiet thinking, she released a frustrated breath. "I—I don't think I can do it. I'm sorry."

He stood. "Perhaps I can help you achieve the right frame of mind." His tone was kind and brisk. "Come to the window and see the beautiful morning." He beckoned her with a hand.

She rather doubted he knew what he was doing, but she did as he asked. He pushed the window up, and the sweet smell of morning rushed in.

When she leaned out to look, she saw that the day was, indeed, beautiful. A bit of mist still clung to the treetops. The dew had yet to dry off, as well, and several birds were busy flying from bush to tree, while others hopped about the grass, seeking their breakfasts.

When she straightened, Harry moved behind her. "Now I want you to pretend that just beyond those woods is Xanadu, the place where you and your lover meet." He pulled her close and wrapped his hands around her middle. "Lean back into me."

Carefully, she did.

"All right," he whispered, "pretend that we're there and that we're in love. Can you do that?"

Molly nodded slowly.

"I'm going to act like your lover while you read. You won't be able to move around this way, but you'll get a better feel for how I want you to sound. Understand?"

"Yes," she choked out.

He nuzzled her neck. "Relax."

She giggled.

He ran his hands up and down her waist, slowly, as if he were luxuriating in the feel of her, and she sort of melted into him.

"Better?" he asked her.

She nodded. Wonderful was more like it.

"Now," he said. "Start reading."

She took a moment to focus on the words, then began to read the poem aloud again:

> *"In Xanadu did Kubla Khan*
> *A stately pleasure-dome decree:"*

The difference in the sound of her voice was amazing! She went on, and as she read, Harry lifted aside her hair and pressed light kisses on her neck. And then her ear. And all the while, his hands worked their magic on her waist and hips.

At the third stanza, he pressed a hand to her stomach

and made lazy circles. At the same time, he slid a shoulder of her gown aside and pressed kisses on her shoulder.

The feeling was heavenly, and her legs could barely hold her up. But she continued reading:

> *"The shadow of the dome of pleasure*
> *Floated midway on the waves;*
> *Where was heard the mingled measure*
> *From the fountain and the caves."*

Meanwhile, the circles Harry was making with his hand went lower.

And lower.

"Harry," she said, overcome with sensation.

And dropped the book.

"You were perfect," he said in a hoarse whisper, and turned her slowly around. He smiled sweetly and pulled a lock of hair back from her face. "And I'm proud of you."

She couldn't look away. "Th-thank you." She felt the fullness of her mouth and couldn't make her lips meet, no matter how hard she tried. Her whole body felt open, like a flower. Ready to receive a honeybee's visit.

And then Harry put his hand at the back of her neck and oh so gently drew her face to his. The kiss was sweeter than any honey, and magical—absolutely magical.

He pulled back from her with a sigh, and she opened her eyes slowly and smiled.

Perhaps Xanadu wasn't so far away, after all.

"I hate to go," he said, his voice rough around the edges. "But as host, I'm in charge of the shooting every morning. And I've a few things to do in the stables, as well."

"That's fine," she said lightly. She didn't want him to see how much his touch enthralled her. "I'm famished, anyway. I'd like some breakfast."

"Good idea." He tugged on a lock of her hair. "A mistress needs to stay well nourished—not for all the lying about she does during the day, but for her more strenuous nighttime activities."

"Harry," she chided him. "You know *I* won't—"

But before she could think of a delicate way to express herself, he took her in his arms, leaned her back, and kissed her one last time.

"You know I'm only jesting," he said, a mere inch from her mouth. His eyes radiated heat, along with a healthy dose of good humor.

"I like seeing you happy," she whispered.

And he tilted her back up. "I'm always happy," he said, and swaggered toward the dressing room door.

"No you're not," said Molly. "Being an Impossible Bachelor isn't the same thing as being happy."

He rolled his eyes. "I'll leave you with the last word this morning." He opened the dressing room door and went through it, then popped his head back in. "Enjoy yourself with the ladies!"

And he shut the door.

Which meant he'd had the last word. Molly bit her thumb. Somehow she found she wasn't angry.

"Oh, well," she said. And sank onto the edge of her bed. It was time to stop thinking about Harry and how vexing and charming he could be, all at the same time, and how utterly disoriented she felt after being with him.

She must make some headway with the other mistresses.

CHAPTER 17

At breakfast, Hildur was delighted when Molly told her about the Byron volume.

"Your alphabet is rather similar," Molly said to her, as she broke her fast with some coddled eggs, bacon, and toast. "Although your pronunciations differ in some ways, of course. But I think that if we practice enough, you can succeed at reading one of Byron's poem in English. We'll find a shorter one. I know you admire him, don't you?"

"I love him." Hildur slapped her on the back and chuckled. "And I will win. The men hear my voice and want to bed me. Who cares I'm no actress?"

Molly almost choked—but didn't—on her toast.

Athena glared at Hildur then back at Molly. "You're being rather generous with your time, aren't you, Delilah?"

Molly smiled. "Why not?"

A vertical line formed on Joan's forehead. "Because you are setting up other people to defeat you, obviously."

Molly felt her cheeks redden. "I'm sorry you're unhappy about my arrangement with Hildur. But I shan't change my mind." She took a large bite of toast and gazed first at Athena, then at Joan, while she chewed it.

So much for trying to make headway.

Joan slammed her teacup onto her saucer. "I can't take any more of this nonsense." She pushed back her chair and left.

But then a loud exclamation came from the drawing room.

Hildur slipped a piece of bacon into her bodice, pushed back her chair, and hurried to the drawing room, Athena on her heels.

Molly exchanged an amused glance with Bunny, and then together they followed to see what the fuss was about.

"Well, blow me down," Hildur said.

"I told you," said Joan with a smirk.

"You did *not* tell. You *screamed*," corrected Athena.

But Joan, thank goodness, didn't bother to answer. She was staring, along with everyone else, at five chairs arranged in a semicircle. On the chair seats were small heaps of glittery baubles. And behind them, displayed on the chair backs, were five spectacular—and truly scandalous—gowns.

Molly could already tell all the bodices were too low. Her nipples would show, which was a problem she'd have to take up with Harry, although she knew what he'd say: she'd have to wear the luscious creation anyway, nipples be damned.

Joan waved a note. "We're to wear the gowns and the jewelry during the dramatic reading. Prinny's orders."

Damn Prinny and his blasted kissing closets and his blasted gowns! thought Molly treasonously.

Athena picked up a matching ruby necklace and bracelet and tossed them aside. "They're paste. We use them in the theater, so I should know."

Hildur let a pair of emerald earrings slide through her fingers and drop to the chair. "I have many jewels in Iceland," she said with contempt.

"But we can still have fun with them, can't we?" Molly held an earring to her ear.

"Indeed." Bunny stretched out her arm, adorned now with a diamond bracelet. "I feel like Cleopatra. And look at the gowns!" She picked one up and examined it. "This one's exquisite. Made by His Royal Highness's own seamstresses, no doubt."

Each gown was of a different design and color, all made with the finest silk and lavishly ornamented.

"Which gown belongs to whom?" Molly asked, and immediately regretted her words.

The other mistresses stopped oohing and ahhing over them. Then Athena sprang at one chair and snatched up a gown. "This one's *mine*!" she cried.

"And I've got this one!" echoed Joan, pushing past Bunny to get to a gown.

Hildur sat on a pile of jewels and crossed her arms over her ample bosom. *"Mine,"* was all she said.

Which left Bunny and Molly to choose a gown.

"I don't mind which one you take, Bunny," Molly said.

Bunny looked doubtful. "Are you sure I can choose first?"

"Of course I'm sure." Molly forced herself to smile. It was sad, really, how unused to kindness the other mistresses were.

Hildur looked at Molly suspiciously. "No friends. We are *enemies*."

"Why?" Molly's voice cracked. "Why can't we be friends?" It had been a difficult few days. Friends made things so much easier, didn't they?

Joan shook her head. "I wonder how you've ever survived as a mistress," she said to Molly, her mouth twisted in scorn.

Athena sighed. "There's your explanation, Delilah. It's a matter of survival. Mistresses can't afford to befriend one another. We are all one another's competition. One can never assume one's protector will remain faithful. There are always . . . other women." She looked Molly up and down as if she found her wanting. "Of course, some are more competition than others."

"But can't we—for this one week—let down our defenses?" Molly asked.

"When we are competing with each other not just in the usual underhanded way of women but *openly*, as well?" Joan shook her head. "I should think not."

"This is war," said Hildur. "And *I* sink all of you."

Bunny sighed. "Come now, ladies. The truth is, we're silly to fight about the gowns. We're of varying sizes. We may need to swap."

"Let's try them on *now*," Athena said, and shimmied out of her garish scarlet gown.

Molly tried not to stare. Athena's bare body was perfect, as sculpted as a goddess's. Hildur and Joan disrobed, too, and they were equally voluptuous, although Bunny's natural beauty outshone everyone's. She also appeared just as comfortable as the others being naked in the drawing room.

Molly bit her lip. No wonder all her competitors had found protectors! They seemed born to be mistresses!

"Delilah?" Bunny pointed to the gold gown that had become Molly's by default, still displayed on the chair.

"Oh, yes," Molly said. But her heart beat faster. The curtains weren't drawn, and the doors—

They most definitely weren't closed, and not one minute before, two footmen had walked by!

Joan laughed. "Delilah? Why do you hesitate to disrobe?" She was standing beneath the gown of her choice and pulling it over her head. When her head popped out, she said, "You are the oddest lightskirt I've ever known."

"There's not a thing wrong with modesty," Bunny said,

shimmying into a new gown. "Some men prefer their mistresses that way."

Molly tossed Bunny a grateful smile. "I'm perfectly amenable to disrobing," she said, as if she peeled off her clothes in a gentleman's drawing room all the time. "Once I even ran naked through a field."

"Did you?" Bunny looked most impressed.

"Yes," Molly lied, and casually made her way to a corner protected from prying eyes by a potted palm. She laid her new gold gown on a small table and began to remove her old one. "And a whole hunt party saw me," she said through an armhole.

If she were going to lie, she might as well make it an exciting one!

Joan rolled her eyes. "Why do I have trouble believing *you* would run through a field naked?"

"She lies," said Hildur.

Athena laughed. "Of course she's fibbing. My guess is you're trying to intimidate us, Delilah. But it won't work."

"I'm not trying to intimidate *anyone*," Molly said, naked now behind her old gown, which she held in front of her like a shield.

"Is that so?" Joan strode over and ripped the garment out of her hands."I dare you to run around the outside of the house and back here again. *Now*."

"Yes," said Athena. "If you don't, you'll look like a fool."

"Wait." Molly blinked hard at both of them and racked her brain for a reply. "You're trying to intimidate *me*."

"So?" Hildur chuckled. "You're scared. You hide."

Barely shielded by the potted palm, Molly shivered and—this being August—definitely not from the cold.

Bunny looked at her, concern in her eyes. And perhaps, Molly worried, even some questions.

"Something's funny about you, Delilah," Athena said,

tilting her head to the side, her shrewd eyes assessing her.

Molly swallowed and fingered a leaf of the palm. She suddenly knew, with a surety that made her tremble inside, that she had no choice. If she wanted to have any sort of chance to win this contest, everyone must believe she was a mistress.

And she wanted to win this contest.

Badly.

London called—plays, new gowns, a husband who indulged her every whim because he loved her and thought she was more fascinating than a broken vase. Or a statue missing an arm and sometimes a head.

If she wanted all that, she must run around the house naked—

Now.

"Just watch me," she said, and stepped out from behind the palm.

With not a stitch on.

She prayed fervently that the bachelors weren't nearby and that the footmen were occupied somewhere in the house, and that her mother was busy in heaven playing whist or baking bread, and not observing her daughter at the moment.

"If I do this," she said to the other mistresses, air swirling about her bare legs and torso, "no more fighting about the gowns, is that clear? Bunny will choose everyone's. She designs gowns herself and she knows best which of Prinny's creations would suit whom. If alterations must be made, she can do those, too, right, Bunny?"

Bunny nodded, and surprisingly, everyone else agreed to Molly's terms, as well.

Molly strode past them, her head held high, out the drawing room doors—she heard the other women run to the windows—and through the main corridor to the front door. She opened the door as quietly as she could, hoping not to draw Finkle's attention, and descended the three brick steps onto the gravel path.

The wind lofted her hair.

And then she ran. She felt like a deer as she sprinted round the house. She ran as fast as her feet could carry her. She even jumped over a squirrel.

And just as she came around the last corner of the house and had only a few seconds to go, she heard the sound of men talking and laughing, somewhere behind her, somewhere in the woods.

But she dared not look.

So she rushed through the open front door and back into the drawing room.

Her lungs were bursting. She took one, great breath through her nose and lowered herself slowly onto the settee. Then she crossed her legs and began to swing the top one slowly, like the pendulum of a clock.

"See?" she said.

All the women stared at her.

"She did it," said Bunny with a grin. "Just as I knew she would."

"Bitch," muttered Joan.

Hildur's shoulders sagged.

"Congratulations, Delilah." Actress though she was, Athena couldn't disguise the dismay in her eyes. "You've proven yourself."

Molly inclined her head. "Thank you," she said, her face straight. But inside she was grinning. Whooping, actually. And dancing.

She *had* rather proven herself, hadn't she?

CHAPTER 18

Later that afternoon, Harry excused himself from the company to oversee a carpentry project at the stables, which left Molly a brief hour to accomplish her secret mission to put everyone in a terrible mood.

"I can't wait to go to the lake," she lied to Athena, Lord Maxwell, and Viscount Lumley. They were in the drawing room playing whist. "It sounds like a romantic place."

She hoped she gave them a somewhat misty smile. Then she dropped a card on the table. Truth was, she was bored with the game. She'd rather be playing charades with the others, but she must act as if she enjoyed whist if she were to prevent the whole expedition to the lake.

She'd go on her own to find blackberries for the tart. She most certainly didn't want to go with all these people and wind up *naked* in the water with them. She'd had enough of being naked when she'd run around the house on her own, thank you very much.

The most dramatic person in the room was Athena. So Molly would begin with her.

"Lord Maxwell," Molly said, "what was the name of the character Athena played last at Drury Lane? I'm sorry it's slipped my memory, but surely you were present at every show."

Lord Maxwell's eyes hinted at mild annoyance. "I'm in the midst of analyzing probability here," he said, looking at his cards and the cards on the table, and thus avoiding the question.

Athena's cheeks grew rosy as she stared at her own cards, and her lovely winged brows narrowed over her nose.

Molly blithely smiled at Viscount Lumley.

"'Twas one of the hags, wasn't it?" Lumley said to Athena. "In *Macbeth*."

Athena grimaced. "I should have been Lady Macbeth. It was a tremendous oversight."

"Oh, *no*," said Lumley. "You made a most excellent hag."

Molly bit her lip to keep from grinning. Lumley, bless his kind heart, wasn't particularly adept at flattery.

"An astute observer would recall that Athena was the only witch the costumers couldn't make appear ugly," Maxwell said coolly. "And they didn't give her the part of Lady Macbeth because the scoundrel of a director was bedding the actress who got the part."

Athena gave him a glowing smile.

Oh, bother.

Molly must try again. She leaned toward Athena and put on her best "knowing mistress" look, but since she didn't know what a "knowing mistress" actually looked like, she merely raised her eyebrows. "He brought you your favorite flowers, didn't he?"

"I sent roses," Lord Maxwell said. "Every night."

Lumley grunted in approval.

"But they aren't my favorite flower, Nicholas," Athena said, looking down her nose as if she were Cleopatra on a barge on the Nile. "I prefer orchids." She paused, blinked several times. "If you knew me better, you'd know that."

"I know you better than you know yourself," said Maxwell rather dangerously.

Athena sniffed.

Lumley dropped a card, and Maxwell scooped it up.

"Well, you didn't bring me flowers in person," Athena protested.

Maxwell held his cards close to his chest. "Certainly I did." His eyes glinted with irritation. "On the one occasion I was there."

"Yes, the *one* occasion." Athena pursed her lips. "Otherwise, you sent them by courier. A toadlike man, too, with breath that smelled like onions."

"London bores me," Maxwell said coolly. "You already know that."

Athena gave a short nod. But her eyes began to fill with tears.

Oh, my, thought Molly. Her plan was working splendidly. She might go to hell for it, but she'd go to hell for swimming naked, too, so what was the difference?

"I wish you had been there on closing night," Athena whispered to Maxwell, her voice rising. "Or my birthday!"

Lumley almost gagged on his brandy.

"I should think the expensive baubles I provide you make up for my absence," Maxwell replied, unruffled, "which is made easier, no doubt, by the presence of your many adoring fans, who rightly call you the best actress on the London stage." He finished his own drink off with a flourish and dropped a card on the table. "Your turn, Lumley."

Molly sensed by the look Athena threw her that the actress was confused. Should she be angered or complimented by Lord Maxwell's remarks?

Molly decided to purse her mouth and slit her eyes to help Athena decide.

Athena huffed, then said shrilly, "What day *is* my birthday, Nicholas?"

Lord Maxwell sat like a stone, his eyes, half lidded, trained on his cards. Lumley grabbed at his cravat, watching the scene with what appeared to be horrified fascination.

"I believe you've won this trick." Maxwell finally looked over at Athena, his expression inscrutable.

"I most certainly did," Athena said, her chest heaving with emotion.

Molly stood up. "I—I'm feeling a trifle hot. Will you excuse me?"

Lumley and Maxwell stood to see her off.

Molly walked off, but not before she heard Athena say to Lord Maxwell, "I'm going to my room. *Alone.* And when I win Most Delectable Companion, if you expect me to be satisfied with a *wretched tiara of paste*"—the damning phrase hung in the air—"then you are a *fool*!"

Molly stopped breathing. She couldn't believe it! Athena had brought up the tiara! Next thing she knew, Hildur was practically breathing fire at Captain Arrow, complaining about the tiara. And Lumley was ashen and cowed by a similar tirade from Joan, which she hissed in his ear for all the company to hear.

If Molly weren't careful, she'd have a mistress mutiny on her hands!

She stood in the midst of the mayhem and said, "Would someone please tell me more about the trail leading over the hill to the lake? Is it a long walk?"

"I'm not going to the lake," Joan said, and flounced from the room.

"Count me out, then," said Lumley, with a lift of his glass, which he then drained.

"No lake." Hildur stared daggers at Captain Arrow and then followed Joan.

"I don't believe Athena will be enthused about going to the lake, either," said Lord Maxwell, looking up at the ceiling, presumably toward Athena's bedchamber.

"And I shan't enjoy going to the lake unless *all* the women go," Sir Richard said in that oily voice of his. Bunny sat next to him, quiet as a mouse.

Molly could tell Sir Richard was imagining all the women naked and frolicking together in the water.

The libertine.

But she must forget about Sir Richard and focus on saving what little virtue she had left.

"Oh, dear," she said. "No lake at *all*?"

The men all shook their heads.

"That's a shame." Molly smiled. "But would anyone care for another brandy?"

Every man nodded.

Done, she thought. She could go later for the blackberries. Alone.

"Pour one for me, too," she heard from the door. "A large one."

She looked over. There was Harry, looking splendidly handsome, *very* angry, and only mildly thirsty.

"Hello, Harry," she said, as pleasantly as she could.

"So, you've gotten the other mistresses riled up about that tiara, I see," he murmured for her ears only.

She shrugged. "Not really. It's just that a hundred pounds would be a better prize."

"Is that so?"

"Yes. Perhaps you could talk to the other Impossible Bachelors about it."

"Is that a threat?"

"Of course not," she lied.

He eyed her. "I'll look into it. Meanwhile, it's a shame

no one else wants to go to the lake. That means you and I shall have to collect those blackberries on our own. After I have a drink or two, of course."

And then he smiled at her.

The rat.

Harry glanced back at Molly and suppressed a grin. She wore a large straw bonnet and swung a tin pail and looked quite happy, trudging up the trail—and no wonder. The men had agreed to add—oh, all right, had been *coerced* into adding—a hundred-pound purse to the winnings allotted the Most Delectable Companion.

She was basking in her triumph and perhaps enjoying the splendid weather until she saw him turn to look at her.

And her scowl returned.

Molly definitely didn't want to go to the lake. Perhaps because he'd told her he swam in it naked on a regular basis and that all his guests were welcome to do the same.

She was doing her best to protect her virtue, which he found . . . endearing, considering she was already hopelessly compromised. Not that anyone else would ever find out. He'd get her back home safely before her father came home.

"Enjoying the views?" he asked her pleasantly.

"No," she replied in that airy way she had when she was up to something. "I told you on the first day, I might have a crumbling spine. I should return to the house immediately. Soon I shall collapse, and you will have to carry me back."

"Molly, exactly what *is* a crumbling spine?"

She pushed a branch out of her face. "Mrs. Turnbull has it. You know, the lady at church who walks with a cane."

"*You* don't walk with a cane."

"That's because I avoid hills at all costs."

"Oh, dear," he said. "Good thing this hill is not at all steep. It's more of a bump, really, than a hill."

"You're very lucky it is, Harry. I dread thinking what would happen if it were a tall hill. Swimming is also strictly forbidden for someone in my condition."

"Really? Could your crumbling spine *dissolve* in water?"

"Don't be ridiculous," Molly said. "I might land in a hole and be thrown off balance. That's all."

Harry bit his lip. "It's a very flat lake bottom."

"One can't take such chances."

"I'm certainly glad sack races are permitted with your condition."

The rustling of leaves behind him stopped.

He turned, saw her vexed look, and couldn't help laughing out loud. "Molly! I'm not going to swim naked! And I won't make you, either. Is that what you're worried about?"

Her brow smoothed out. "Are you sure, Harry?"

"Yes, you silly minx." He grabbed her hand and pulled her up next to him. They stood nose to chin, she looking up at him with an elfin grin. "I would never make you get naked when you don't *want* to."

He didn't mean for it to come out that way, all warm and gruff, but her nearness was affecting him, especially as they were surrounded by beautiful, leafy green trees and bushes and the occasional wildflower and a breeze that was softly blowing her skirt.

And privacy. Lots of privacy.

She didn't say anything back. Her eyes were focused on his, and hers were warm and oh so brown.

The cat had gotten his tongue, as well. It would be so easy, he thought, to lean down and—

No. He really must cease and desist that nonsense. No one was here to see them getting affectionate with each other, so what good would it do for his cause?

Which was to remain a *bachelor*.

And then Fate, thankfully, intervened. Somehow Molly's hair got caught in a twig.

"Oops," she said, and tried to move. But couldn't.

Harry gently removed the offending strands. "There." He grinned. "Might as well let down the rest. It's a hopeless mess."

She did as she was asked, pocketing her pins. Her hair fell around her in glorious toffee brown splendor, and she shook it out. "Oh, that feels good," she said with a sigh.

He was glad he was no longer standing close by. Because he was tempted to grab her and kiss her senseless.

There was a bounce in her step now, which he was heartened to see. "I'm so glad you Impossible Bachelors avoided a mistress mutiny, aren't you?" she said, skipping ahead with her pail.

Her curvaceous backside was temptingly near. "Yes," he said. "Amazing how it came out of nowhere, isn't it? Good thing it blew over. We couldn't have any of the ladies called up before Prinny's court for rebellion."

"Certainly not. You men would have never lived it down. I'm *so* glad we staved off almost certain embarrassment for all parties concerned, aren't you?"

"Indeed." He loaded the word with irony, which she conveniently ignored.

"Are there really lots of blackberries, Harry?"

"Yes," he said, enjoying the sight of her pixie grin. "And we'll pick them *all*."

"I can't wait!" she cried, and tumbled down the trail in front of him.

Crumbling spine, indeed.

CHAPTER 19

Molly swung her pail, pleased at its weight. They'd picked loads of blackberries and even some wild currants, enough to make four or five tarts! And she didn't know what she'd been so nervous about. It was a perfectly innocent lake, resting placidly in the sun. How could she have ever ascribed sinister motives to it? It was as pristine and clear as beautiful lakes come!

She'd let her nieces swim in this lake if they wanted to. Or her sister. Or even her best horse.

"See that?" Harry said, pointing at a large flat outcrop of rock bordering the western side. "That's where I jump in."

Naked? She wondered what he'd look like. She was insanely curious and losing her breath just thinking about it.

But all she said was, "It's very high."

"It's deep over there," he said, coming up behind her.

Indeed, that side of the lake looked darker, more brooding. As if it had secrets. She would steer clear of that side.

She felt Harry's warmth right behind her and had an odd temptation to lean back against him. She felt like doing that instead of talking.

In fact, she couldn't think of anything to say back to him. She'd developed this problem overnight, it seemed. He was suddenly a person she felt . . . nervous around. In a pleasantly unsettling way. If she didn't know herself better, she'd think she was developing a tendre for him.

But she *did* know herself better. And even if she were starting to feel all melty inside when he came near, she would do well to remember that he wanted to remain a bachelor.

She should also remind herself that were he to lose the contest completely, he would be forced to marry Anne Riordan. Molly wouldn't go to their wedding. She'd invent something if she had to. Something other than a crumbling spine because then Harry would tell everyone she'd made that up.

"Has Roderick ever brought Penelope up here? I wonder," Molly finally said.

"I don't think they've visited here," said Harry. "He and Penelope prefer the southern properties."

The wind blew across the lake, bringing with it a green scent mingled with the scent of flowers.

"I think this is the nicest one of all," said Molly.

"You haven't seen my family's other properties."

"I don't care," she said. "I like this one best."

"Me, too," said Harry.

They smiled at each other and sat on a log. There was a marvelous view across the water.

"Are you and Penelope good friends?" asked Harry. "Because I hope you don't mind my saying so, you're nothing alike."

Molly sifted some sand through her fingers. "Everyone says that."

Harry took a stick and made a circle in the silty earth. "Does that bother you?"

Molly shrugged. "I've overheard people say I'm a mere

shadow of Penelope. She has gorgeous chestnut hair, her face is that of a goddess, and she's very charming yet ladylike."

"And they say you are—?"

"You know, Harry. A hoyden. Perhaps not a genuine hoyden, but hoydenish." She sighed. "I always feel second-best next to Penelope. She never loses her temper or says stupid things. And she always looks exquisite."

He raked his hair back. "I feel the same about Roderick. He's the perfect son. It was why I kissed Penelope before their engagement was announced. I didn't even particularly *like* her at the time. She was too damned perfect, as well."

Molly chuckled. "It's rather annoying not to be able to find anything wrong with her. *Or* Roderick."

"Ah, yes." Harry's eyes twinkled as he gazed at her. "Those two deserve each other, don't they? As Cedric and Fiona do."

They both laughed at that.

Molly had outgrown her crush on her sister's husband long ago, but it wasn't until now that she realized why. She needed someone more fallible than Roderick. Someone imperfect. Someone funny. Even annoying sometimes.

Someone she could make up with by kissing . . .

A lot.

But it couldn't be Harry.

"You're bad." She elbowed him.

"And you're a hellcat." He tugged on a lock of her hair.

"You think so?" she said.

"Oh, yes. Running about the hunting box naked!"

"I don't know what you're talking about." She leaped up and scooped a small handful of blackberries out of the pail. "I'll give you ten seconds to grab your own and find a place to hide."

"Done," he said.

"This is war," she said.

"Of the best kind."

They were smiling at each other now. But they were circling, circling, just like the old days, when they'd been really young and country neighbors. She'd been about five or six. He'd been nine or ten.

She threw a few blackberries now, and they bounced off Harry's chest.

He roared and rushed right at her. She screamed and ran, but he was too fast for her.

He grabbed her from behind. She could feel her heart pounding.

"You're my captive," he said into her ear. "You must do as I say."

She stifled a giggle and pulled hard to get away. But he held her in a firm grip.

"Now," he said, "a gentleman doesn't throw blackberries at a lady. It simply isn't done. So you will have to eat these berries in my hand. That is your punishment for being caught so handily."

"All of them?" she asked.

"Yes."

"How many do you have?"

"I don't know. Maybe ten."

"All right. I *am* rather hungry."

"Close your eyes."

She did. Her heart was still racing from all the fun. And maybe from Harry's nearness, as well.

"Now turn around," he said. "Slowly."

She did.

"I'm releasing your arms," he said. "But don't run. I caught you fair and square, after all."

She stayed still, her eyes closed.

"Open your mouth," he commanded.

She did, and was somehow afraid. And then she was laughing. He laughed, too.

But then he was stern. "You must trust your captor, Molly. Always."

"I will," she said, and schooled her mouth to stop grinning and to make an *O* instead. It seemed to take forever, but then Harry finally placed a blackberry in her mouth. She bit down on it, enjoying the sweet spurt of the juice. Then she swallowed.

"Another," she demanded, her eyes still closed.

"This is supposed to be a punishment," Harry said, and plopped another in her mouth.

That one was delicious, as well. "You're too slow," she said, and opened her mouth.

This time Harry put in several. It took her a few moments more to chew and swallow those.

"Are we almost done?" she asked, her eyes still closed. "Your Majesty?"

"You are a most disrespectful captive. You're supposed to be frightened. Now open your mouth."

She opened her mouth. What was taking him so long?

And then she felt—rather than saw—his face moving toward hers. Perhaps he was blocking the sun. Before she could comprehend, his lips were on hers. He wrapped his strong arms around her waist, and his body pressed her close.

Closer.

She wanted to be so much closer, even though it didn't seem possible. His muscular thighs and chest enveloped her, it seemed, in a searing embrace.

"Harry," she whispered against his mouth.

"Hush, my captive," he said.

And their tongues melded, the remnants of blackberry juice lingering in her mouth, making the kiss particularly sweet.

Molly wrapped her arms around Harry's neck. They shouldn't be kissing. She wasn't really Harry's mistress.

Yet for the first time, she realized that she wanted to be.

If being a mistress meant this.

CHAPTER 20

Alone. They were alone. On a bright, beautiful afternoon at his favorite place—the lake.

Harry tore his lips away for a moment and picked Molly up. She coiled her hands about his neck and met his lips again with a fervor that he found entirely—

Entirely—

Oh, hell. He couldn't think. He could only do. And he wanted to do more. So much more.

"Harry," she murmured low in her throat when he laid her gently down on a soft, grassy bank dappled with an occasional shadow from passing clouds.

He felt the sun still warm and bright at his back, but he covered Molly with his body and plundered her mouth until they both broke away and stared at each other.

"I want more," she whispered. "I want—"

Her gaze grew frustrated. She put her hand on his jaw. "You do something to me, Harry. I—I can't stop thinking about you this way. Every time I look at you—"

"I can't stop thinking about you this way, either." He bent to kiss her. "And it's torture," he said against her lips.

"Yes," she murmured, and ran her palms up and down

his back, and then suddenly, her hands moved around to his middle and slid down to his groin.

Oh, God. He squeezed his eyes shut and tried to remember the Magna Carta. Or . . . or anything.

Anything but what Molly was doing to him now.

"Touching you here excites me like almost nothing else," she whispered in his ear. "I first felt it when I sat on your lap in the carriage. And then last night. And this morning, too, when you held me from behind during 'Kubla Khan.' "

He opened his eyes and groaned. "If only you knew how much it excites *me* when you touch me there."

And with all his willpower, he forced himself to remove her hand.

Her mouth dropped in disappointment. "I want to excite you that way, Harry. Please."

"You already do that—without even touching me," he said, then managed a grin. "It's a peril all men have to live with. Showing that, um, enthusiasm at inappropriate moments."

"But now *is* appropriate." She rubbed him again with her palm. "No one's looking."

No one is looking.

The invitation in her eyes was damned near impossible to resist. But who was he fooling? He'd have to be dead to resist it. No living male could turn away from those eyes. That mouth.

This girl.

"Molly—"

"Sssh," she said. "Show it to me. Please."

Hovering above her, Harry inhaled a great breath and began to unlace his breeches with one hand.

"Let me," said Molly, and pushed his hand away. Her hair was spread out like a fan on the grass.

"I'm flattered by your enthusiasm," he said, only half joking. He bent down and ravished her mouth while she played with the laces, finally loosened his breeches, and yanked on them until they were at his thighs.

And then she looked down. "Oh, my goodness," she whispered.

He grinned. "Kiss me back and stop talking."

She sighed and kissed him back, just as he'd asked, and the kisses became even more passionate when he felt a jolt of heat—

From her hands. They were touching him in a soft, curious way, and he couldn't help it. He ground himself into her palms and moaned at the delicious sensation.

Her palms pressed right back. "I love to see you this way, Harry," she murmured. "I want to touch you like this all the time."

"Any time you want," he choked out. "That is—"

"Kiss me back and stop talking," she mimicked him with a giggle.

He cupped the side of her face in his hand and looked directly into her eyes. "But I must tell you something now, Molly. I can't hold back much longer."

"Don't," she told him. "Don't hold back."

He would distract himself. He released her breasts into the sunlight and sighed with pleasure. He wished he could see all of her that way, but he couldn't. He had to show some restraint, didn't he?

"Where are those berries?" he said, as he swirled his tongue around her nipples.

"I don't know," she moaned, her fingers running through his hair. "I set them down somewhere."

"Wait." He jumped up and somehow managed to pull up his breeches over his hardness.

"No!" she cried. "Don't go!" She sat up on her elbows. "Harry!"

"I'll be right back," he assured her over his shoulder, and grinned. His delectable companion was most impatient. He ran for the bucket, swooped down and grabbed its handle, and ran right back.

"Lie back down," he said, when he'd reached her again.

"Pull your breeches down, Harry."

He laughed. "I will in a moment, hoyden. But first, be still."

She lay down, but he could tell that obeying him was costing her.

He squeezed a handful of berries over her nipples, and the juice ran down their soft mounds. With care, he lay over her again and suckled her.

All her impatience drained away. "You feel exquisite," she whispered, running her hand over the muscles in his arms. "But your breeches are still on."

She stretched out her hand toward his groin.

"In a minute," he said against her skin, and then gave in to an impulse. He pushed her gown up her leg.

"What are you doing?" she said breathily.

"Enjoying you," he said, and stroked her thigh with the flat of his palm. And then, in the middle of a lavish kiss to her breast, he moved his hand to her softest place, to the nub of her, careful not to enter her with his fingers.

It was her first time. He wanted to go slowly.

Her legs fell open to the sun. He explored her, exulting in the shivers that coursed through her and the soft moans she made in response to his touch. A moment later, with a cry and an arch of her back, she became the most desirable woman he'd ever known.

"So this is what being a mistress means," she said with a contented sigh, her arms still flung over her head.

She smiled at him from her grassy bed, and he laughed. Then he kissed her, glad to have pleasured her so well.

They lay in silence for a minute and listened to the wind play through the trees. Then she reached to remove his breeches again.

"You're a stubborn wench," he said.

A moment later, she was clasping his length. "I want the same thing to happen to *you*," she murmured.

"Are you sure?" He couldn't believe how much he longed to make love to her.

"I'm quite sure," she said.

Of course, a coupling was out of the question. But there were compensations for his restraint, nonetheless. Compensations in the form of an enthusiastic girl who seemed to care very much that he feel the same intense pleasure she'd felt a moment before.

When the inevitable approached, he rolled to the side so as not to muss her gown.

Afterward, they both lay on their backs again and stared at the sky.

"I don't know what to say," Molly said.

Harry turned his face to her. "You don't have to say anything."

"I've thought of something." Her smile was slow but real. "Can we do it again?"

Harry laughed. "No, you minx. We should probably get back to the house. We've several cantankerous couples to restore to good humor."

She propped herself up on an elbow and looked down at him. "I'm going to remove the bureau in front of that dressing room that connects our two bedchambers. You can come in whenever you like."

"I can't do that," he said, crossing his arms over his chest.

"But why?"

He pulled a lock of hair off her face and tucked it behind her ear. "Because it's nearly impossible to stop progressing once you get started doing what we did today. And we can't have you fully compromised, my girl. That leads to babies and"—he hesitated—"marriage."

Her face fell. "You're right." She laced up her bodice, smoothed her skirt, and stood up.

"You understand that having a child out of wedlock would be disastrous for you, don't you?" He clambered up and put his hands on her shoulders.

She wouldn't look directly at him. "Of course. It means you'd have to marry me. And that's an outcome to be avoided."

She stood back from him, and suddenly, the air was thick with awkwardness.

The whole way home from the lake, the awkwardness didn't leave them. Molly kept several paces ahead of him, walking steadily, never looking back.

Harry followed close behind, but he had no desire to speak, either. What could he say? They both knew that no matter what happened between them this week, they had no future together. Molly understood that. She was a willing partner in the dangerous pleasure game they were playing together.

So why did he feel so despicable?

CHAPTER 21

A lady should be able to conduct conversation anywhere, a voice in Molly's head said.

A lady is not afraid.

Often Molly pretended she was hearing the voice of her mother, saying things she wished Lady Sutton really *had* told her. But obviously, her mother hadn't. She'd died before she could give her daughter advice about life.

Which might explain why Molly usually made up things as she went along. She was at supper now with the rest of the company. Somehow, she'd muddled through this week.

It came to her then: *a lady* always *muddles through.*

There. Another homemade proverb to add to her repertoire.

"Wine," Athena was saying in that sultry voice of hers, "is the summation of all that is . . . eternal." She cast a mysterious glance around the table and smiled.

The table's occupants—save Harry, who was brooding, it seemed—appeared suitably impressed.

Indeed, Athena tended to spout inane sayings that Molly was sure that—being a muddler herself—her actress friend made up on the spot. Were her tablemates to review what Athena said, rather than be impressed by her tone of voice and nuance of expression, they would see that she was actually saying *nothing*.

Molly cleared her throat. "Tell me, Athena, what exactly do you mean by saying wine is the summation of all that is eternal?"

Athena clutched at her pearl strand. "Exactly what I said."

There was a silence.

"Then you mean that wine is . . . God?" Molly took a swig of her own wine for courage.

Athena's eyes widened.

"I'd rather not discuss religion," Joan said.

"I quite agree," said Sir Richard.

Of course he would. He was the devil himself, as far as Molly was concerned.

Athena opened her mouth, but nothing came out.

Lord Maxwell's mouth turned up, as if he himself had been aware of Athena's game and was amused that she'd been caught out.

Athena glared at Molly.

But Molly refused to be cowed. She smiled warmly at Athena in apology for understanding her *too* well. "Let us sidestep your remark. But perhaps everyone will consider mulling over *this* saying"—she looked around the table boldly, without any of the nuanced air of her actress rival—"'All's fair in love and war.'"

Harry put down his wine glass. "Why should we consider that?"

Molly mentally crossed her fingers. She'd figured out what had been bothering her so much about this week.

What felt . . . wrong.

What was making her peevish.

Even more so than the risqué nature of the wager.

She took a breath. "I believe this game you gentleman have been playing with us ladies as your pawns is a trifle one-sided. It's time to make the *men* competitors this week rather than observers. And we women will vote among ourselves to see who wins."

The other women gasped. The men were silent as stone. But Molly certainly had everyone's attention now.

"The men, competing?" Athena said, her brows arched high.

Molly nodded.

"And the women, voting?" Joan curled her lip.

Molly nodded again.

Hildur stared at her. "They shoot you in my country!"

"In this one, too," murmured Harry.

Molly cast a quick glance at him and was glad to see he didn't appear too terribly vexed with her. He actually had a little twinkle in his eye.

"Are you a bluestocking, Delilah?" Athena said with a bit of scorn, even though mere hours ago she'd been thrilled that Molly had wangled that hundred-pound purse.

"No, I'm not. I'm just a woman here for a week who would like to have more . . . *fun.*" She smiled at Harry, then took another sip of wine. "If the men dare allow it."

There was a warm, vibrant silence. She felt all the men's eyes upon her.

Oh, dear heavens. She believed she was flirting successfully with the entire table of bachelors. On *her* terms, too. She sensed that the women, as well, were finally aware that perhaps there was more to her than they'd assumed.

She took a large sip of wine. There was more to her than she *herself* had assumed!

It was those sayings of hers. *They* were helping her out. Especially the new one, the one about muddling through.

Harry finally spoke. "Delilah, need I remind you, the goal of this contest is to crown the best, er, *companion.*"

"Yes," she said, hardly able to restrain her excitement. "And you can win points for her in the men's game. An excellent mistress would choose no less than a skilled protector, would she not? So if everyone agrees, we can choose a game for the men now."

"Archery?" suggested Joan.

"A horse race, perhaps," Viscount Lumley said.

Several more suggestions were offered to mildly enthusiastic responses.

"How about fencing?" Molly remembered how often she'd seen Harry and Roderick fence as boys, with large sticks rather then real weapons. "I saw a collection of foils in a case in the library."

"Oh, yes!" said Athena, folding her hands in front of her bosom. "A fencing tournament!"

All the women clapped. "The gentleman who wins shall receive points for his lady," Molly suggested, "but the women will also be allowed to cast a vote for their favorite gentleman of the day, other than their own consort, of course."

Biting her lip, she wondered what the men would think. Lumley and Arrow shifted in their chairs. Lord Maxwell cleared his throat. Sir Richard stared at Molly as if she were the most fascinating creature on earth. Harry rubbed his chin and watched her with a small smile quirking his mouth.

"A fencing tournament, eh?" Harry said. "And a woman's vote at the end of the day? I believe this is a matter for our arbitration committee to discuss."

While Arrow and Lumley put their heads together, Molly discussed the possibilities with the other mistresses, all of whom were clearly as excited at the idea as she was.

After a moment, Lumley looked up, a big grin on his face. "As Prinny's arbitration committee, we declare that a slight change in the rules would be welcomed by His Royal Highness, who's not one to shirk a dare himself. Upon a show of hands signifying a majority, the fencing contest and women's vote will become an official part of the week's events, Lord Maxwell to record said changes."

"What *he* said," remarked Arrow with a lazy grin, and inclined his head at Lumley.

"All in favor?" Harry looked about the table.

Everyone raised his or her hand, even Sir Richard, who declared he could outfence everyone.

"Shall we adjourn to the library to cast our daily votes, gentlemen?" Harry asked the other Impossible Bachelors.

For the first time, Molly had hopes that she might receive one or more of those votes.

"No," said Hildur. "We *waltz*."

"That's right," said Viscount Lumley. "The ladies have been clamoring for a dance. Joan, shall you play for us? We can vote afterward."

Everyone stood up, even Sir Richard, who was rather pulled up from his seat by Lumley, and went to the drawing room. Joan scowled, but she moved to the piano and began to play.

Molly looked for Harry. She felt rather like a dying plant that needed water. Immediately.

He came straight to her side. "Shall we?" he asked her, his eyes a warmer brown than she had ever seen them.

She nodded, unable to speak. She'd always longed to waltz.

He took her waist and they clasped hands. "You look beautiful," he said. "Especially when you're causing trouble."

"Really?" She could barely get the word out. All she could think about when he was near was what magical things he'd done to her with his fingers and lips. And the odd effect he had on her thoughts.

In short, she *had* no thoughts when he was holding her.

Yet at the same time, she had so *many* thoughts when he held her that she was fairly bursting to share them with

him and to ask him *his* thoughts, too, about the silliest
things, such as what his favorite color was—hers was the
fresh spring green of new leaves, of course—and what
animal he'd be if he had to choose; she'd be a bird so she
could fly, although she despised worms and wouldn't
want to eat them, which meant she might choose to be a
squirrel because they leaped through trees and lived off
acorns, which weren't too terribly bad. She'd tasted one
once and had never told a soul.

Harry gave her a slow grin, then said, "What? No clever
retort?"

She held on to him tighter and shook her head.

All she knew was that she felt . . . happy.

Free.

And *herself.*

With him.

CHAPTER 22

The next morning, while the mistresses worked on their dramatic readings in the drawing room, Joan rose from her seat after a few minutes and began to pace by the large bay window.

No one else seemed to notice at first. Molly continued helping Hildur learn to read and recite her Byron poem in English, but all the while, she watched Joan out of the corner of her eye. After a few minutes, Bunny quit rehearsing her passage and looked up, as well.

Joan was still pacing.

"What do you think she's doing?" Bunny whispered to Molly.

"I don't know. But she certainly appears more agitated than usual."

"She's not exactly the sunny type as it is," Bunny quipped.

"No. But she's worse today, isn't she?"

"Yes. Something's amiss."

Molly gathered her courage. "Joan," she said in a clear, polite voice, "is everything all right?"

Joan whirled around. "I thought I told you—I don't want to be *friends*."

She went back to her pacing.

Athena and Hildur were watching her now.

Joan stopped. "Would you all leave me alone? I'm simply taking a turn about the room."

"But you're not turning," said Athena.

"You are a fish," said Hildur. "Flopping on the deck."

Joan made a noise. "So?"

"In *Macbeth* there's a great deal of pacing," said Athena. "On stage one paces when one is thinking deeply about something important. And it's usually troublesome."

Joan drew in a deep breath. "Whatever is important to *me* shouldn't matter a whit to any of *you*."

"But your reading," said Molly. "You must work on it for the finale."

Joan blew out a breath. "I don't care about the finale!"

There were gasps from Hildur and Athena.

"Why don't you care?" asked Bunny.

Joan trembled visibly. "Because as Athena said, I have other things on my mind, and they're burdensome."

"Joan," said Molly, "can you not tell us? I know you don't want—"

"Leave—me—*alone*." Joan's cheeks were bright red. She began to gather her reading materials, but in her haste to depart the room, she kept dropping things. First, a lovely red shawl. And then all her papers.

"Oh, bother!" she said and threw everything onto the floor.

Everyone was silent. No one dared move.

And then Joan collapsed in a chair. She inhaled and exhaled loudly, as if she couldn't catch her breath.

Molly flung aside her book and jumped up to go to her. Bunny did the same, even putting an arm around Joan's shoulders and saying, "There, there."

"You must tell us." Molly knelt before her. "Something's wrong, and we want to help."

"All right." Joan's hands were tightly clenched. "I'm going to be honest with all of you because"—her shoulders sagged—"as you said once, Delilah, we could be thrown over. At any time. There's no real security, is there, in our occupation?"

Her eyes looked so sad.

"Unfortunately not," Molly said. "But what security is there for women in *any* position?"

She felt a pang of guilt lying so handily. After all, she was no mistress and had no idea how Joan truly felt. But she had a good idea because she felt somewhat of a commodity herself. If her father weren't so preoccupied with his passion for treasure hunting, he could barter her through marriage to any man he saw fit.

"It's a man's world," said Athena.

Hildur and Bunny nodded their heads.

"It is," agreed Molly. "But we have this one week together. Let's use it to help each other. If we can."

She waited for Joan to speak.

Joan's brow was deeply furrowed, her mouth pressed in a long, thin line.

"My sister," she finally said, "lives in a small hamlet several miles to the north of the village nearest here. I haven't seen her in five years." She swallowed. *"Five whole years."* She looked up at Molly with large, unguarded eyes. "I've been in London all that time."

"How difficult for you." Molly would hate going that long without seeing Penelope.

Bunny rubbed Joan's shoulder.

"It's worse," said Joan. She took a deep breath. "My sister has had to be mother to . . . my baby boy."

Molly's heartbeat quickened. "A baby boy?"

Joan gave a little cry and nodded.

Bunny rubbed her shoulder even harder.

"Is he Lumley's?" Athena asked.

Joan shook her head. "A previous lover's. But I would like to see him. *And* my sister." She wiped at her eyes. "It's why I have been so wicked this week—I mean, more wicked than usual. I can hardly bear being here. It's torture to be so close and yet so far away."

"Oh, poor Joan!" Hildur squeezed in between Bunny and Molly and gripped Joan's hand.

Athena's jaw worked. She appeared to want to help, Molly noticed, but she didn't move.

"We must make a plan," Molly said. "We must get Joan to her child."

"If I could just *touch* him," Joan said. "Even for an hour. To hold him in my arms."

Hildur began to howl.

"Ssh," Molly soothed her. "We don't want the men to hear."

Hildur sniffed loudly and rubbed her nose.

"But how can Joan leave here?" Bunny asked, her beautiful almond eyes filled with worry. "Sir Richard watches *my* whereabouts very closely."

"The men have big eyes," said Hildur, shaking her head sadly.

"We'll have to make something up," said Molly. "Any ideas?"

"She can't take a horse," Athena finally contributed, her manner a little less stiff than a few minutes previous.

"It will take me over an hour to walk the trail to the village close by," said Joan. "And then another two hours to get to my sister's village. If I leave early in the morning, I can stay until early afternoon. Then I can make it back by nightfall."

"We still need a good story," Molly said.

They sat and thought. But no one could come up with anything.

"Can you not tell Lumley?" Bunny eventually asked.

Joan shook her head. "Never."

"He seems very kind." Molly waited for a sharp retort.

But Joan was quiet. "He is," she said eventually. "Which is why I don't want to tell him. I don't want him to have any excuse to"—she swallowed—"to get rid of me. He's the kindest protector I've ever had."

"I understand." Molly sighed. "Now, today we'll be doing other things, but don't despair. Everybody will be thinking. We'll come up with a plan for you to be gone tomorrow, all day."

Everyone murmured their agreement and went back to work on their dramatic readings. The atmosphere was noticeably charged, yet it was also a happier one.

While Hildur practiced her pronunciations, Molly wondered how to get Joan to her baby.

"I have an idea," Athena said a few moments later, her eyes sparkling. "Are you a good actress, Joan?"

"No. I've never done *any* acting." Joan's mouth drooped.

"Come now," Athena said with a conspiratorial smile. "We all act every day, don't we?"

"Whatever do you mean?" asked Bunny.

Athena chuckled. "Bunny, do you care deeply for Sir Richard?"

Bunny's eyes widened. "Why, no, but—"

"Don't you pretend . . . at certain times to be *wild* about him?"

Bunny's face reddened. "Well, yes."

"When I'm bored with a protector, I do the same," said Joan. "Although I haven't grown bored with Lumley." She actually giggled.

"Captain Arrow is not like other men. He reads women like sea charts. He always finds his destin—" She furrowed her brow.

"Destination?" Bunny asked.

"Oh, yes!" Hildur said with a broad grin.

Athena turned to Molly. "How about you, Delilah?"

Molly could hardly swallow. "I—I"—she struggled to say something—"I don't know what you mean," she finished lamely.

"You act like a virgin, Delilah." Joan chuckled. "Which men must find intriguing. You *are* a good actress, aren't you?"

Molly nodded hastily.

But Athena would not be dissuaded from her question. "Have you not had some experience, Molly, with faking your pleasure? Every mistress must be adept at this skill."

Molly had a small coughing fit. "No, actually," she said. "Um, Lord Harry is my first protector."

"That explains it," said Joan. "You're new to this. You *are* practically a virgin."

Hildur leaned in. "So he is good?" She waggled her eyebrows.

Molly's stomach was in knots. "He—he's quite nice," she said, remembering how she felt when he touched her. She got quite melty inside at the thought. "He's an amazing kisser. I—I quite enjoy it. And we—we laugh a lot together when we . . . kiss."

She blushed.

There was a big silence.

"You're not in love with him, are you, Delilah?" asked Joan.

"No," she said instantly. "Of course not."

"I hope not," said Athena. "That would be the worst thing for you."

"I know," said Molly. "I could be—"

"Abandoned," offered Joan.

"At any time," finished Molly.

"So don't let your heart get involved," Athena urged her.

Molly felt vaguely depressed, although why should

she? She was only pretending to be a mistress. And she knew she and Harry would part after this week anyway.

"Which reminds me," said Athena, "this whole conversation started when I suggested that you are more of an actress than you realize, Joan."

"And?" Joan looked intrigued.

"You must employ some of those same acting skills to convince the gentlemen you're ill."

"Moaning and groaning," said Hildur. "They love! Shrieking, too."

Athena smiled but shook her head. "That would appear unattractive in a female—in *this* situation."

Molly sat up straighter. She'd moaned when Harry had kissed her. And when he'd touched her. She'd thought that was a particular quirk—actually, a shortcoming—of hers. But perhaps the other women made . . . noises, as well.

She was afraid, however—and a little curious, she admitted—to contemplate in what circumstances shrieking would be considered appealing.

"We'll tell them you're indisposed for the day," said Bunny to Joan.

"But I won't be in my bedchamber," she replied. "What if Lumley comes looking for me?"

"We can tell him we put you in the nursery," said Bunny.

"Is there one?" asked Molly.

Bunny laughed. "Not that I know of."

Joan laughed, too.

"If Lumley goes searching for you, we'll tell him you need absolute quiet and that he should go have a brandy or two," said Molly.

The atmosphere was much more congenial now. The women continued practicing their dramatic readings, each pacing about in her own little corner, except for Molly and Hildur, who sat together on the couch. But this time,

Athena intervened and told Molly that Hildur would be much better off whispering a certain line of her poem than speaking it at a normal volume.

"Thank you, Athena," Molly said. "What a wonderful tip."

Joan stopped pacing and looked at Athena with worried eyes. "When should I . . . act sick?"

"You'll know," said Athena in a comforting tone. "And when you do, you'll have four nurses ready to take you to your bed."

Everyone chuckled.

But Molly realized something. "This plan seems most logical, but we don't want Joan to lose any ground in the contest, do we?"

"She shouldn't have to fall behind in the gentlemen's assessments as a result of her visiting her sister," agreed Bunny.

"But sick women aren't seen as very . . . tempting," said Athena thoughtfully.

"No man likes—" Hildur pointed to her throat and gagged.

"Exactly," said Molly. "So we need to find a way to make Joan's illness . . . alluring."

"Moaning and groaning," Hildur said again. "And shrieking."

"No," said Athena firmly. "Although I'm sure you mean well, Hildur." And Athena actually smiled at her.

"I agree with Athena," said Molly, pleased to see everyone being kind. "We don't want the men to see Joan . . . in an unappealing way."

"So how do you make illness *appealing*?" asked Bunny.

Molly thought for a moment. "It must be the circumstances in which she gets ill. You know how mothers"—she swallowed because this was her earliest memory of her own mother—"tell their children not to go out in the cold without wrapping up?"

Everyone nodded.

"So we can say Joan stripped off her clothes and bathed in the stream," Molly said. "And caught a chill as a result." She paused. "And I believe I've the perfect circumstance by which we can create that very scenario. One that will give us a few laughs—at the men's expense."

"Really?" Joan's brows were arched high, and she grinned.

"Really," said Molly. "Listen closely." She took her time explaining, and when she was done, the women laughed and clapped.

"It's perfect," said Athena.

"You're a genius, Delilah," said Bunny, and Hildur thumped Molly on the back.

"You're not nearly the featherbrain I thought you were," Joan admitted.

Molly bit her lip, incredibly pleased that they were all becoming friends. The easy companionship of other women might be the only type of intimacy she would have for the rest of her life.

She couldn't think about having a great love. Marriage was a contract. It was business. And dreaming about finding a husband who loved her and whom she loved back was crazy. The best she could hope for was a husband who was trustworthy. Hopefully fun and kind, too.

And if she won the Most Delectable Companion title, Harry was obligated to help her find him—a thought which didn't make her as happy as it had when she'd first come up with it.

CHAPTER 23

That afternoon Harry opened a small wooden chest by the library fireplace. Inside were the masks the men would use with their foils, and the wax Harry would form into buttons to blunt their tips. As he worked the wax, he relaxed a little. He'd simply have to focus during the tournament. Rely on his experience and his gut instinct.

He formed the wax into balls, stuck them rather viciously on the tips of the foils, and sighed.

Dammit all, he *couldn't* focus. He thought about Molly all the time, especially at night. As he tossed and turned in the sheets, his dreams were consumed with images of her, elusive pictures that were never clear in meaning. When he awakened, hard and frustrated, he knew exactly why—

Molly.

He hadn't had a decent night's rest since they'd arrived at the hunting box, to tell the truth. And he probably wouldn't have another one until he was safely away from her.

He gave a short laugh. *Safely away.* He was admitting that *he* needed protection from Molly. Today, especially, he had cause to be *en garde* in more ways than one. He had no doubt Molly would try something unusual while the women were in charge during the fencing tournament.

He couldn't imagine what. But he'd find out soon enough. It was time to take the foils and masks outside. The others were waiting. The mistresses laughed and chatted under the tree that had become their gathering spot of sorts. Harry sensed their added excitement—they were in charge today, after all.

The men, on the other hand, stood off to the side, silent and straight-faced, each one of them. There was an awkwardness about them that he'd never seen before. He felt it, too. And he suspected it came from knowing they were being judged by the women. No doubt all the Impossible Bachelors felt a new appreciation for what the mistresses had already endured this week.

The ladies clustered around him as he leaned the weapons against the tree and handed the masks to Molly. Bowing low, he said, "Enjoy. The game belongs to the ladies now."

There was a chorus of feminine cheers.

Molly smiled a bit giddily. She was to speak for the women, and Harry could tell she felt nervous about that. But excited, too. Which was exactly what worried him. With her in charge, anything could happen.

"It appears we're ready to begin the contest," she said to the men. "You've already chosen straws. Captain Arrow and Lord Maxwell will go first. The winner of that match will go up against Lord Harry; that winner, against Viscount Lumley; and that match's winner, against Sir Richard. The winner of each match will be the gentleman who completes the first touch to the chest, arms, or head." She paused. "Clear so far?"

"Clear!" said the men as one.

"All right, gentlemen," she went on, "the ladies won't presume to tell you how to fence properly, but we do have a few rules. You forfeit no points for losing a match, but the winner gains three. The champion of the tournament shall win ten. A word of warning"—she raised her index finger—"any man who leaves the tournament area before today's event is officially concluded will forfeit ten points for his lady at the end of the week."

Harry's stomach unclenched. He felt rather disappointed, actually. "We're not such poor sports that we would leave our competitors to struggle alone in their quest."

Molly smiled. "Of course not. We just want to be perfectly clear. Are there any questions?"

No man ventured one. Harry thought the rules seemed straightforward, if a little childish.

"Good." Molly looked toward the house and beckoned someone with her hand. "There is one more thing," she said, "though it's not a rule." She smiled at Harry, quite as if she were an angel.

Which didn't bode well, he knew.

"We shall ask Finkle to declare the winners of each match and mark the official conclusion of the tournament," Molly said. "He'll be assisted by two footmen if there's any confusion."

Harry turned around. Sure enough, Finkle was slowly walking toward him, accompanied by the footmen.

"Why Finkle?" Harry asked.

"Because we women shall be otherwise engaged," Molly replied, her tone rather too pert for her own good.

Harry narrowed his eyes at her. "Otherwise engaged doing what?"

"You won't be watching us?" cried Sir Richard.

"No," Molly and all the women said together, happy grins on their faces.

Blast it all. The proverbial axe was about to fall. Harry could see it in Molly's eyes.

"Why not watch us?" asked Captain Arrow. "I should

very much like to impress you with my parrying and, uh, thrusting skills."

He eyed Hildur with a lascivious grin. She batted her eyes at him.

Molly bit her lip. "We're—"

"Hot," said Athena, and began fanning her face.

"We need shade," said Joan.

"There's shade here, under the tree." Lumley threw out his arms.

"We're hotter than that," said Bunny. "We're going swimming."

"Where?" asked Harry.

"Over there," said Molly. "In the stream."

She pointed to a location surrounded by a thick grove of trees hugging the bank. "Have fun," she said brightly.

She headed toward the clump of trees. The other women followed. Soon every female had disappeared.

"What the devil—" said Lord Maxwell.

"What do they mean by swimming exactly?" said Lumley.

"Dipping their feet, no doubt," said Captain Arrow.

But there wasn't time to ponder anything else. Because Finkle called Captain Arrow and Lord Maxwell up and handed them their foils and masks.

Harry politely turned his attention to the match, although his insides were churning. What was Molly about, leaving the contest when she had been the one to think of it?

Arrow and Maxwell, meanwhile, had donned their masks, inspected the wax buttons at the end of their foils, and made a few practice thrusts.

"Salute," Finkle said.

The two men saluted each other with their weapons.

"En garde!" Finkle cried.

The two men posed for a brief second, and then Captain Arrow made an dramatic thrust, which was parried expertly by Lord Maxwell.

The foils hissed as they made contact, the blades sliding away in a blur of silver. Maxwell lunged to the left and, after a beat, attempted a quick thrust at Arrow's right shoulder. But Arrow sidestepped the maneuver, and the hissing of the foils began again.

Harry's heartbeat quickened. There was nothing like a good fencing match to get one's blood moving. The two men's styles were impressive, and at this point, he could see no clear leader.

The thrusting, parrying, and ripostes continued unabated. Arrow had just raised his foil to strike when something bright blue appeared on the grass near the clump of trees where the women were.

And then something red. And something green, and several beige items. Plus slippers—ten, to be exact, and they were tossed out of the bushes one by one.

"Oh, my God," said Sir Richard. "They're disrobing."

"Getting stark nekked, you think?" croaked Lumley.

There was a loud squeal of feminine laughter, followed by much chatter.

And splashing.

Bloody hell. Harry had known Molly would pull something extraordinary, but he hadn't envisioned this!

He crossed his arms and narrowed his eyes. She'd read them wrong, though. What sort of man would put a foil down or cease watching a manly contest such as this to go view women unclothed? In the stream? Splashing and playing and—

He swallowed hard. He'd like just one glimpse. *One* glimpse!

He was tempted to run right now, before his turn, but wait—that would be against the rules. He'd thought the rules redundant at the time, but now he saw why Molly had said them out loud. He couldn't leave. None of them could. Not unless they wanted to lose ten points.

Harry jetted a breath. Molly was turning the screws on the bachelors in the most frustrating way possible.

The vixen!

By the time the last match arrived, all the men were in foul moods. Maxwell had defeated both Arrow and Sir Richard. Lumley had won against Maxwell. And now Harry was in the midst of his bout against Lumley.

"This is torture," Lumley groaned.

And Harry knew he wasn't referring to the fencing match.

Lumley made an awkward thrust—not at all in character for him—and Harry evaded it in an equally inelegant way. Harry knew they were both losing their usual finesse with the foil—thanks to the women.

The splashing grew louder. "You're welcome to come join us, Viscount Lumley and Lord Harry!" the mistresses yelled as one.

Lumley gave his longest pause yet, his foil quivering. "Damn them!" he yelled, and made a thrust that narrowly missed Harry's chest.

The fencing went on, the squealing and giggling of the women did as well, and Harry did his best to channel every bit of his frustration into the foil.

Finkle called, "A hit!"

For a half second, Harry held the foil to Lumley's heart. When he pulled back, Lumley threw down his own foil and ripped off his mask.

Finally, the most frustrating fencing tournament in history appeared to be over.

Slowly, carefully, Finkle held up Harry's arm. "You're the winner, Lord Harry," the old servant rasped, "but I've yet to draw the event to a conclusion. That shall take a few more minutes. Footmen," he commanded, "do your duty."

The footmen were already over at the bushes, picking up the ladies' clothes and tossing them on top of the shrubbery hiding the women from view.

Harry gave a short laugh. Yes, Finkle had declared him the winner, but Harry was no fool. He and every other Impossible Bachelor knew who'd truly won this particular battle—and it wasn't anyone in breeches.

Molly watched from her perch in a tree as the footmen picked up the ladies' garments and laid them on the bushes near their bathing area. She couldn't help but chuckle when she saw how forlorn Harry appeared, the foil and mask dangling from his hand, even after he'd won the tournament so handily. The other bachelors appeared equally unhappy as well. Maxwell raked a hand through his hair and let out a gusty sigh. Captain Arrow stood with his legs apart and his fists balled on his hips. Sir Richard scowled, his arms folded. Lumley sat on the ground, his face in his hands.

The men couldn't leave the tournament area until Finkle called an official conclusion to the day's game. So they were trapped, watching helplessly as from behind the bushes, the women giggled and laughed and put their clothes back on.

It was too delicious. All Molly's frustration at losing the sack race, all that nervous energy she'd expended worrying while competing against the other women each day . . .

She'd gotten sweet revenge.

But no time to bask in it. Yet.

She'd told the other mistresses she'd be the lookout in the tree to ensure that the men played by the rules. But she'd had to throw her clothes out in the grass just like everyone else. Harry had sharp eyes. He would have noticed if she hadn't.

From her perch, which had been quite dangerous to arrive at safely without being poked in the wrong places by twigs, she'd arranged her body strategically so that the leafy branches below her masked her vulnerable state in much the way that Eve covered herself in the Garden of Eden.

As a crowd of men and women alike surged toward the house, Harry held aloft by Lumley and Arrow, Molly felt a thrill of happiness. She couldn't wait to tell him how proud she was of him! Of course, he'd done his best to triumph so he wouldn't have to get married, but—

She wouldn't think about that right now.

She'd be sure to kiss him in front of the others to celebrate his win. They'd expect that of her, wouldn't they? She must oblige. And truth be told, she'd be glad to oblige. Even now, watching him from behind, she grew breathless at the memory of his intimidating style in the tournament—his easy grace, his broad shoulders and muscular back, his fierce thrusts with the foil.

Wait a minute. How could she congratulate him while she was stuck up in this tree?

"Bunny? Athena? I need my clothes, please!" she called.

But no one answered.

Certainly, the other mistresses hadn't forgotten about her!

She'd try again. "Hello! Isn't anyone still down there?"

A few birds chirped, the wind blew through the branches—and a sick feeling grew in her middle. She'd been so wrapped up in enjoying her little prank and then being distracted by Harry's superb form that she'd lingered in the tree too long.

But she wouldn't worry. Surely her clothes were on top of the bushes.

Determinedly, she began her slow descent. Once halfway down the trunk, she peered below, hoping to catch a glimpse of her things. She bent out as far as she could to get a better view, but—an awful buzzing sensation began in her head and found its way down to her toes—her garments were nowhere to be found.

And everyone, absorbed as they'd been in rehashing the tournament and exclaiming over the women's mischievous role in it, had left her behind. Even Harry. Of course, he'd had little choice, being carried off like that. No doubt when he got put down, he'd realize she was missing.

But, still. She was alone.

The wind picked up, and her branch began to sway. To tell the truth, she was feeling a bit . . . vulnerable.

She dared another peek below to see if somehow she'd overlooked something.

And saw a masculine boot.

"Delilah," called Sir Richard in that oily voice of his. "I know you're in the tree. And I have your clothes."

Molly shook a branch in frustration. "Just leave them there, Sir Richard! And walk away."

"I don't see why I should," he said. "Everyone else forgot about you, after all. I'm the only one who noticed you were missing. You should be grateful."

"I'd be grateful," she bit out, "if you weren't such an ass."

He chuckled. "What's keeping you from coming down, Delilah, and taking them from me right now? All the other mistresses would prance before me naked. But then again, you're not like the other mistresses, are you?"

"I—I would take them from anyone but you," she said. "And I'm rather stuck on this branch."

"I'm not so sure about that. I wonder, Delilah, what your real story is."

Oh, dear.

"I don't know what you mean," she forced herself to say lightly.

Sir Richard laughed. "I have a proposal to make. I'll leave your clothes here, if—" He paused.

"If what?" she snapped.

"If you'll remember that you owe me a favor. And when I call it in, you must comply."

"I'd rather sit naked here all night than comply with your wishes, you beast."

"Then I shall leave you," he said. "*Without* your clothes."

"Fine," she said, suppressing her panic. "Someone else will find me soon enough."

"I don't think so," he said. "Bunny's telling everyone you repaired to your room for a nap because you had a headache. Your paramour is sitting in the dining room, eating and drinking and talking, quite oblivious to your actual plight."

"You rat. And how dare you involve Bunny in your sick games! She's much too good for you, you know."

"Just remember this," he said silkily, ignoring her jibe, "that I *will* have you someday. And you'll be obedient and respectful when I do."

She shook her branch again. "I'd rather die before I'm respectful and obedient to the likes of you."

Sir Richard laughed and walked away, dropping her garments on the far side of the lawn. She could never retrieve them without risking being sighted. But she'd rather catch cold than be caught naked by a footman or, God forbid, Sir Richard himself, who'd probably be watching her from a window somewhere to see if she'd dare to go after her clothes.

A bird twittered. The wind moaned low through the trees. A squirrel scampered up the tree trunk, saw Molly, and ran back down.

She shivered and wondered how long it would take Harry to realize she was missing—and how long it would take for Sir Richard to prove his suspicions that she was an imposter at the house party.

CHAPTER 24

Blast it all. Ever since the fencing contest, Harry had wanted to see Molly for conflicting reasons: to wring her neck for torturing the men so, and to bask in her admiration for winning the tournament. When he'd heard she'd gone straight to her room for a nap, he'd been sorely disappointed, but he'd curbed his impatience and waited a good while for her to come down. He and Arrow had gone out to practice their skills at archery, while the other bachelors and mistresses had gone about their own business.

But Harry had never been good at waiting, so he'd abandoned Arrow when Maxwell had shown up for a turn with the bow. And as Harry strode toward the house, feeling quite impatient to see Molly, he determined the three reasons he felt a particular need to have her near him as often as possible during the week.

One, to keep her out of trouble, of course.

Two, to protect her from Sir Richard.

And three, to keep up the pretense that they were lovers.

There were other reasons he kept her near, of course, which he brushed off as being inconsequential. She was very good company. He also enjoyed peering down her neckline when she wasn't looking. And then he also took pleasure in imagining his lips upon, oh, every part of her body.

But amusing pastimes aside, she was still his charge. And now she was missing.

He walked briskly into the drawing room, where Joan, Athena, and Hildur were idling on various sofas. "Where's Delilah?" he asked them without even a reference to their beauty or the mildness of the weather.

They looked at each other rather helplessly.

"I thought—" said Athena.

"She's sleeping," Hildur interrupted.

"No," Harry said, perhaps too firmly. "I just checked. She's not in her room. And her bed appears unslept in."

Joan's eyes widened. "But Bunny said she was napping."

Damn Sir Richard. Harry would like to kill him right now. He'd obviously misled Bunny.

"We shouldn't worry," said Athena. "Maybe Bunny and Delilah are together."

"But Sir Richard's absent, as well," said Joan.

"Oh." Athena put her hand to her cheek. "Then *he's* probably with Bunny."

Harry clenched his jaw. Sir Richard had damned well better be with Bunny and not Molly.

Joan gasped. "Could Delilah still be in the tree?"

"The tree? What tree?" Worry was making Harry rather impatient.

"The tree she sat in to observe the tournament and make sure all of you followed the rules," Joan said.

Athena put her hand to her mouth. "I had a cat once who got stuck in a tree. He didn't come down for two days."

Harry realized how inappropriate it would be under normal circumstances for a bachelor to rescue a young lady from a tree, presuming the lady in question were naked.

But these were not usual circumstances. Everyone here expected that he'd seen Molly with no clothes on many times.

"I'm going after her," he said grimly, and left the women to their lounging.

On his way out the terrace door, he saw Bunny and Sir Richard striding at a bold pace across the lawn toward the front of the house. Bunny's face was bright red. When she wiped at her eyes, her fingers trembled.

Sir Richard's brow was lowered dangerously over his eyes; his mouth appeared twisted in a cold rage.

Harry thought it looked to be more than your typical lovers' spat. Bunny was frightened, he could tell. Everything in him wanted to beat Sir Richard into a satisfying pulp, stuff him into a barrel, and drop him down a great river, someplace far from England, to float aimlessly forever.

But he couldn't do that. Ridding the world of the likes of Sir Richard would require a sterling sense of duty. And everyone knew Harry lacked that.

Besides, he had to rescue Molly at the moment. Hers was a problem he could solve easily—*if* she would let him help. That was always the question with her.

He made the turn to the grassy yard where they'd held the fencing contest.

"Delilah?" he shouted, and looked toward the treetops.

But there was no movement.

What the devil?

He strode to the tree and gazed up. It was impossible to see to the top from where he was. "Delilah?"

No answer was forthcoming.

He hitched himself up to a lower branch and made his way up.

What if she'd fallen asleep up there? One wrong movement and she could fall to her death! He'd best not call her name anymore, just in case he woke her.

He kept climbing, his muscles tensing.

But no. There was no one in the upper branches of the tree. Which meant Molly was still missing.

He climbed higher anyway and took a moment to look out at the grounds, hoping he might be able to see her. But there was nothing unusual. All was quiet, in fact.

Where *was* she?

He refused to panic. It wouldn't help the situation. But then he caught a slight movement near the house out of the corner of his eye. One of the bushes *moved*. And it had a tail, a pale blue tail.

Molly's gown! So that's where she was! But what was she doing? Harry allowed himself a small curve of a smile. Whatever it was, at least she was safe.

The bush hopped a few feet farther and stopped in a corner of the house, an inverted corner shaped like an L, forming an alcove of sorts. No one would be able to see her *there*.

The clump of leaves wavered, then somehow fell apart. Harry saw it was a collection of small branches, really. And then there was Molly, crouched low, her long brown hair covering her—

Her *nakedness*?

Why on God's earth was she still *naked*? The other women had donned their gowns long ago. Why hadn't she? She'd obviously been able to get down from the tree. Why hadn't she retrieved her clothes?

And then the answer dawned on him. Someone must have taken them. And she'd been forced to go after them herself, covering her form with a ridiculous—but serviceable—homemade bush.

Blood thrummed in Harry's ears.

Sir Richard.

But Harry wouldn't think about killing him now. He must wait until the wager was over, which would give him time to work up his fury into a healthy rage. Besides, at the moment he mustn't come crashing out of the tree and terrifying Molly. She shouldn't know he was here, watching her.

She leaned forward, seemingly looking to see if she had privacy.

A wave of guilt washed over him. He wouldn't think about her nakedness. Not yet. First, he'd acknowledge with a sort of pride that beneath her rather naïve exterior, she was a clever girl, the cleverest he'd ever met. Had she always been this resourceful as a child? Yes, she had, but he'd never wanted to acknowledge it, being the older, wiser neighbor. He'd always classified her as a young pest who made an occasional playmate when he'd nothing better to do—and nothing more.

Now she slowly stood, and he drew in a breath. All thoughts of her cleverness left his head. She was seashell pink. All over. And she was—he swallowed—absolutely breathtaking.

The kind of breathtaking that makes one ache deep inside.

He knew he shouldn't be watching her get dressed. But he—he couldn't help himself. And he couldn't help what he was doing to himself as he watched her.

God, he was an animal! But—

The whole world became Molly in the corner. She was what he wanted. More than anything.

He needed her.

He *wanted* her. More than anything he'd ever wanted before.

He—

He—

Was spent.

The birds twittered their frivolous song. Harry breathed in and out, stunned at the intense yearning he'd had for Molly. Not just for any woman—but for her.

When he looked up and saw her walk out from the corner of the house, fully dressed, her lovely head held high, he drew in a deep breath.

He was so confused.

And so very, very wicked.

Molly could hardly bear the thought of being in the same room with Sir Richard!

But she must.

She forced herself to smile when she entered the drawing room. Everyone was gathered there, save Harry. The men were playing cards, and the women, all in fresh gowns, were studying their dramatic readings, the only acceptable form of work this week for those who had to pretend indolence otherwise.

Athena stood, her expression stricken. "Delilah! Were you stuck in the tree?"

Molly caught Sir Richard's gaze and held it, just for a moment.

"Not at all," she said. "I was walking."

"That was rather a long walk." Sir Richard's lips were pursed in an ugly smirk.

She graced him with a small smile. "Yes, it was, wasn't it?" She sank into a chair. "But I find the outdoors so bracing. Don't you?"

There was a chorus of assents from men and women alike, except, of course, from Sir Richard.

Bunny barely looked at her. And no wonder. Molly wished she could take her friend's hand and squeeze it, tell her everything was all right. But she couldn't because things were far from all right. Molly really couldn't speak to Bunny until Harry helped her solve the problem of Sir Richard.

Speaking of which, where was Harry? She opened her mouth to ask, but he walked in, saving her the question.

His gaze was usually direct, but at the moment he couldn't seem to meet her eyes. Frankly, he appeared . . . guilty. But why should he? He'd had no idea she'd been without her clothes for so long and stuck in the tree!

She was curious, but when he kissed her hand, her curiosity dissolved in a charge of pleasure.

"I lost track of your whereabouts." His voice was apologetic but velvety warm.

When he released her fingers, she was sorry. She so wanted to tell him how handsome he'd been wielding that foil, how magnificent his form, when he'd been winning points for their cause—their *separate* causes, she must admit, but theirs, nonetheless.

At the very least she could tell him she was pleased he'd won. The other, giddier thoughts she would keep to herself.

"You needn't be sorry. I was out and about . . . enjoying the day. Perhaps we could take our own walk around the grounds?"

His eyes lit up. "Certainly. I would like that."

So would *she*.

"You just went on a two-hour walk, Delilah," said Sir Richard in a grouchy voice.

"One can never have too much of the outdoors, Sir Richard," she said. "Why, when I was small, I spent hours at a time sitting in trees."

"Is that so?" he said nastily.

She turned away before she stuck out her tongue at him.

When she and Harry got outside, she immediately took his arm and began to stroll with him. They must appear to be having a cozy tête-à-tête, she told herself, and brushed aside any other reasons she could think of to explain her need to touch him.

"We've some important things to discuss but, first, I

must congratulate you." She smiled up at him. "You won us a lovely number of points in the fencing tournament."

They stopped walking.

"I did, didn't I?" he said.

His eyes were that golden brown again. She was so tempted to reach up and kiss him. He was *hers,* after all.

"Molly—"

"Harry—"

They both spoke at once. The air between them was full of something invisible, tantalizing, out of reach— something that made her forget to breathe.

"I'm so sorry about what happened to you after the tournament was over." Harry brushed a curl from her face.

She blushed. "What do you mean?"

"You weren't napping." He hesitated. "I'm not sure where you were, but I know you were in trouble and that Sir Richard had something to do with it."

And then he moved closer, bent his head. She stood on tiptoe, and when their lips touched, it was like fire between them.

He pulled her close. She wrapped her arms around his neck. He deepened the kiss until she could barely stand. He tasted so good!

But they were playing a game, her common sense reminded her. Fooling the other participants in the wager with their kisses. Focused on winning points. Trying to reach goals that had nothing to do with each other.

And those goals were in jeopardy.

She forced herself to pull her lips away.

"What is it?" Harry whispered. His eyes, half lidded with passion mere seconds ago, were now wide open. Questioning.

She cleared her throat. "I—I'm doing my best to be a

good mistress," she said, "but Sir Richard is unceasingly suspicious and getting worse each day."

"I know," said Harry. "At every nightly vote, he mentions how unusual you are, as if he can't quite believe you're a mistress."

She sighed. "I was sitting in a tree, watching you being carried into the house after the fencing tournament, when Sir Richard stole my clothes. He promised to give them back to me if I came down, but when I refused, he grew more suspicious than ever that I'm no lightskirt. I told him I was stuck on a branch."

Harry's lips became a thin line. "I'll make him regret his rudeness next week, after the wager is over, when you're safely home and he can no longer jeopardize our standing in the wager. It riles me that he knows my hands are tied behind my back until then."

She laid her hand on his arm. "Harry—" How was she to say this? "I don't know if you can wait until next week to speak to him."

Harry stopped walking and gripped her shoulders. "Out with it, Molly," he said sharply. "What else has he done to you?"

She sighed. "It's not what he did to *me*. When I was, um, solving my problem and retrieving my clothes, Bunny came outside. I was hidden, so she didn't see me. But she went running to the tree, and I could tell she was looking for me."

"And you didn't call out to her?"

"No. Because right behind her came Sir Richard. He yelled at her for leaving the house. She told him she was worried about me, and angry at Sir Richard for making her tell everyone I was napping"—Molly looked down, still upset by the memory—"and he grabbed her by the hair. He pulled. Hard. Bunny cried out—"

Molly bit her lip. She had to stop talking.

"He's such a coward." Harry's eyes were stormy. "I saw them walking into the house. Bunny looked as though she'd been crying."

His agitation encouraged Molly. "We must do something, Harry, mustn't we? We can't stand by, even though Sir Richard may somehow find a way to unveil me—"

"There is nothing we can do," Harry interrupted her. "Nothing. As much as we hate what's going on between him and Bunny, it's not our business. She's chosen to stay with him. They've been together for years."

"It's not *right*." Molly felt her eyes pricking with tears. "It's . . . despicable."

"I know." Harry's tone was gentle but firm. "She isn't the only mistress treated this way. And you must know it happens to wives, as well."

Molly felt a raw ache in her middle. "So you're saying we do nothing."

"Exactly." Harry's gaze was unyielding. "We can't save the world, Molly. And we must protect our own interests. Do you want to leave here with your identity protected? And do you want to marry well?"

"Yes, but—"

"Then you must do your best not to antagonize Sir Richard further. Try to win the title of Most Delectable Companion. And accept the way things are."

Molly felt she couldn't breathe. How could she have wasted a single minute this week having tender feelings for Harry?

"I'm disappointed in you," she said, her voice hoarse with a jangle of emotions. "I—I thought you were better than that, no matter what everyone else said. But now—"

"Yes?" he challenged her.

"Now I don't want to speak to you."

Harry didn't say a word. His eyes were hooded now; his mouth, grim.

And as he strode away, back to the house, Molly felt the truth lance her heart: she would never, ever make the mistake again of believing he could be—she swallowed and blinked back a tear—her hero.

CHAPTER 25

Everything seemed gray and gloomy the next day to Molly. Her mood, her morning porridge, the sky, each cup of tea she poured for the ladies during dramatic reading practice, the limp cards she held during the incessant games of whist she played.

Athena had informed the men at noon, when they'd returned from shooting, that Joan was abed with a slight chill she'd acquired from romping about naked in the creek during the fencing tournament.

Their party was further depleted when Harry made himself scarce during much of the afternoon, claiming he had unexpected estate business to attend to in the library.

Molly suspected he was trying to avoid her as much as she was attempting to avoid him.

But at the dinner hour, he reappeared.

"You ladies are unusually quiet tonight," he said from the head of the table after the first course.

Molly exchanged a brief look with Bunny and Athena and read in their eyes the same concern she had: *Where was Joan? And how much longer could they cover for her?*

She should have been back by now. Dusk had fallen, and the woods were thick and deep.

"I'm simply famished," Bunny said hastily, and spooned some soup into her mouth.

"And I'm thinking about how ruggedly handsome all of you gentlemen are," said Athena, batting her eyelashes. "Shooting every morning has brought out the beast in each of you."

Molly thought Athena was taking her efforts to be distracting a little too far, but no man seemed at all suspicious that her remark wasn't sincere.

Oh, well. Molly was learning a lot about men this week.

She yawned modestly behind her hand. "I *am* a little tired."

"Me, too," said Hildur, yawning so wide Molly could see down her throat.

"Don't be too tired," said Sir Richard, chuckling with anticipation. "Tonight we have the kissing closet game. One more time, according to Prinny's schedule."

No. Molly had hoped never to deal with the kissing closet again! She didn't know if Lumley or any other bachelor would be content with conversation about tarts and family members this time.

And she would absolutely *die* if she wound up in the closet with Sir Richard.

Of course, there was the slight chance he wouldn't be . . . in good health by that time. He might retire to bed early.

Not that she knew of any reason *why,* she lied to herself on purpose.

Because if she thought about the truth at all, Harry and everybody else would see that she was guilty.

Not that she was guilty *yet.* But perhaps she soon would be, if Finkle and Cook had listened to instructions correctly.

To throw Harry off, she graced him with an angelic

smile. He really was a beast to ignore Bunny's unseemly situation as Sir Richard's mistress.

Molly couldn't wait to be rid of Harry at the end of the week, even though she was spending most of her time daydreaming about their bodies pressed close, and the way he'd . . . he'd brought her such incredible pleasure. And, um, the way she'd done the same for him.

Perhaps, if she won the contest, he would introduce her to a London gentleman who did all those things *better* than he did, although she had a gut feeling that no man did those things better than Harry did—or looked better than he did when he was doing them.

She sneaked a peek at his profile, at those lips that had aroused such delicious sensations in her, and the jaw that always scratched her mouth and breasts in the most pleasurable way when he kissed her. Then, of course, there were his hands, one of which was wrapped around his wine goblet right now. Those tapered, masculine fingers knew exactly where to touch her to make her—

Oh, dear. Her body was starting to wake up in, um, *that way.* She forced herself to stare intently at the footman, who was serving a course of lamb. Then she locked eyes with Athena, whose brow was furrowed with worry about Joan.

Joan.

A sliver of panic sliced through Molly's middle, dissolving the mental pictures she had of Harry naked and completely ruining her appetite. She moved her food around her plate and took the occasional sip of wine. But by the second-to-last course, there was still no sign of Joan.

Athena, Hildur, and Bunny had barely touched their plates, as well. Bunny's eyes were wider than usual, and there was the gleam of tears in them.

Finkle brought in the last course, thank God, a fine distraction for all the mistresses present.

It was a tart.

A tart Molly had made.

A tart she hoped no one else would notice she'd had a hand in creating.

"Oho!" said Lumley. "Did you make this tart, Delilah?"

"No," she lied. "Not this time." She lifted herself up to take a closer look at it. "How lovely! What kind is it?"

"Cook made the tart," said Finkle grandly to the room. "And it contains wild currants."

"Yum," said Lumley. "But it surely isn't as good as the blackberry tart Delilah made me yesterday."

Molly smiled at him. That *had* been a delicious tart.

"Shall I prepare a slice for everyone, milord?" Finkle addressed Harry.

Harry smiled. "Yes, Finkle. Do that."

There was a whimper from Hildur. Almost a small shriek, actually.

Everyone turned to look at her.

"Are you all right?" Captain Arrow asked her, and placed a hand on her back.

Hildur nodded glumly and sniffed. Finkle set a piece of tart in front of her, but she pushed it away. "I save this tart—for Joan." She gripped the edge of the table, her lower lip trembling.

Harry shifted in his seat. "Joan may have a piece when she feels better, Hildur. Please. Eat the tart."

Hildur lowered her brows and gave a low moan. Molly bit her lip and looked at Bunny. She saw reflected in her eyes her own panicky thoughts. Joan was either lost in the woods, or she was on her way home and about to be found out. Neither possibility was at all reassuring.

Harry looked at the frightened expressions on all the women's faces. Something was vastly wrong at the table tonight.

"We all miss Joan," said Molly in a calm, decisive voice to Hildur. "But she'll be better by morning."

"I should check on her," Lumley said. "After the last course. Where is she again?"

"The nursery," Athena said.

"We have no nursery," Harry said.

Molly smiled. "You might call it by another name. It's the room—"

"At the top of the house," Bunny said.

"To the right of the kitchens," said Athena at the same time.

What the devil?

Harry put his wine glass down. "So she is somewhere in this house," he said plainly.

"Yes," said Molly, and looked at Lumley. "And we mustn't disturb her, kind as you are, Viscount Lumley. She needs her sleep."

Hildur let out a small whimper, and the other women exchanged glances.

"Tell me, Lord Maxwell," said Harry, on high alert because really, *something was not right here* and Molly obviously wanted to change the subject. He trusted she had good reason, so he would. "Is it true that Parliament is—"

But Sir Richard made an odd noise. And spat something out on his plate. "What the hell is *that*?" He pushed his chair back, stood up, and pointed a finger at the—

What was it?

Harry leaned forward.

Oh, yes, a tiny, petrified frog—

No.

It couldn't possibly be!

Harry stared rather goggle-eyed at Sir Richard's plate, but he was in good company. Everyone was staring. There the offending frog lay, apparently smashed flat by a man's boot or a carriage wheel and left to dry in the sun.

Harry stole a quick glance at Molly. Her brow was smooth, and her hand covered her mouth. She appeared almost too shocked and not shocked enough—all at the same time.

She was a terrible actress.

He snapped his fingers. "Finkle?"

Finkle reappeared. "Yes, milord?"

"There appears to be a strange substance in the tart. I suggest you remove all our plates."

"Yes, milord."

Harry caught Molly's gaze again. She took a sip of wine, no doubt to conceal a triumphant smile, but her eyes gave her away. They were sparkling with satisfaction.

Satisfaction derived from petty revenge.

Finkle moved around the table, picked up the plates, and left the room.

Sir Richard wiped down his tongue with the edge of the tablecloth and was in the midst of taking a swig of wine, swishing it around his mouth, and spitting it back into a goblet when a loud crash resounded through the front hall.

Harry pushed back his chair.

"Finkle must have dropped something," Molly said quickly.

"I'll check," said Harry. Yes, he trusted Molly had her reasons for hiding something, but he also felt the need to know what was going on in his house, especially when dead frogs or loud crashes were involved.

Athena jumped up and posed at the entryway to the hall. "No leaving this room until you pay the toll, you *beast*." And she puckered her lips.

Harry paused only a moment. "No, thank you," he said, and tried to get around her.

But she threw her arms around his neck. "He's so handsome, ladies! Let us *all* kiss him!"

Harry was surrounded by feminine forms. Normally, he would have endured—perhaps even enjoyed—such over-the-top attention but not tonight. Not when something was badly out of place.

He tried to pry the women off, but the petting and kissing and hugging continued. "Enough, ladies!"

"*I* shall check on that noise for you, Traemore," said Captain Arrow and rose from the table.

Bunny and Hildur dropped their attention from Harry and moved to Arrow.

Which left Harry with Molly and Athena.

"No more," he said firmly to Athena—Molly seemed too nervous to kiss and hug him with much vigor—and in one quick movement, he slid out from under their grasp.

"Get him!" cried Athena, and lunged at Harry. But he slipped past and went out into the hall, certain he'd find *something* odd.

But there was nothing there.

At first. But then he saw a female outline backing out of the library, pulling the door shut behind her.

Joan.

He smelled fresh air. She'd obviously come into the house through the library window, which was low to the ground. Someone must have unlocked it for her.

A massive Grecian urn stood near that window, a Grecian urn which was probably no more.

When Joan turned around, her eyes flew open wide.

Harry pressed his mouth into a thin line.

Her gaze was beseeching. She pointed upstairs and mouthed some words.

Please, she was saying. *Let me go upstairs. Don't tell.*

Harry looked at her a split second longer, then he turned his back on her and returned to the dining room.

"Finkle must have cleaned it up," he said to the group.

The women all had expectant looks, as if they were afraid of something.

And now he knew why.

He took his seat again and sighed. He felt weary. Confused. What had Joan been up to? And why did she need the help of the other mistresses?

"I suggest we repair to the drawing room," said Captain Arrow.

"We've still the kissing closet to occupy," Sir Richard reminded everybody.

Harry restrained a sigh. Damned kissing closets. Why did Prinny ever think they were amusing?

"Very well," he said, ever the proper host. "To the drawing room."

Everyone stood. Molly bit her lip. Harry knew why. She dreaded meeting Sir Richard in the kissing closet. Every woman probably did, particularly after he'd almost swallowed a frog.

But the mood in the room swiftly improved when Joan walked in.

Viscount Lumley's eyes lit up. "Joan!" He went to her, drew both her hands to his lips, and kissed them, one by one. "I'm so glad to see you. Feeling more the thing?"

Harry tilted his mouth into a discreet but welcoming smile—the perfect host's smile. Whatever Joan had been up to, she looked quite well—in fact, better than she'd appeared all week. Her eyes were clear and full of something . . . happiness.

Harry looked at Molly, who was grinning like a fool, and lofted a brow.

I know, he meant the brow to convey.

He saw her intake of breath. *Are you angry?* she said back with her eyes.

He paused, thought, then shook his head.

Molly smiled.

And despite his best efforts—because he knew Molly had somehow arranged this escapade with Joan *and* put that frog in Sir Richard's tart—he couldn't help but smile back.

She had that effect on him.

The minx.

Molly, against her better judgment, couldn't help but be happy that she and Harry were communicating again, even if it was simply with their eyebrows. And she was so happy that Joan was back, and apparently much better for having made her trip. She carried herself like a new woman, and the light in her eyes was impossible to miss.

Joan chuckled. "I'm feeling *much* better, Lumley. All that sleeping did me good."

There were murmurs of affectionate greeting from everyone, except for Sir Richard, who stared malevolently at Molly.

Had he guessed about the frog? She tried her angelic smile on him and hoped it worked. But he turned away before she could see if it did.

"We were on our way to the drawing room," said Harry to Joan.

"To the kissing closet," said Sir Richard for the umpteenth time, leading the company to the drawing room.

Molly sat on the settee awaiting her turn, closed her eyes, and felt temporarily dizzy. Not only did she *not* want to participate in the silly kissing closet ritual, she didn't want Harry to, either.

It didn't feel right, his kissing someone else. Not after he'd kissed *her* and turned her whole world upside down! He couldn't go round making the world topsy-turvy for every female he met, now could he?

She opened her eyes. Athena walked into the closet, and Lumley followed her.

And now Molly must wait the three minutes. Everyone began to chat loudly—just like last time. But she was in no mood to join in. She didn't care how many votes she lost because of it. Her poor attitude tonight was her armor.

She wanted to be finished with being a false mistress!

She felt weary with pretending.

Weary with emotions she didn't understand.

She had a brief flash of her life the day before she and Cedric had eloped. She'd been so different then. So naïve. So untried.

Now she felt years older in less than a week's time.

And she wasn't sure why. She couldn't put her finger on it, but it had everything to do with Harry. Annoying, stubborn Harry, who'd thrown her over his shoulder and brought her here against her will.

Someone called her name, and she sighed. Time to go in the closet. But she didn't care. She would tell whoever came in that she was too tired to play silly games, and would they like to talk about politics instead?

Although if it was Sir Richard who entered, she would feign illness and beg to be excused. If he didn't let her, she—she didn't know what she would do. Pretend to faint, she supposed.

Please don't let it be Sir Richard, she begged God, and pulled the door shut behind her.

She waited, but no one came. She heard voices, low and insistent.

She waited some more.

Tapped her foot.

Tried to whistle.

Whatever they were talking about, it really was taking too long. She opened the door a crack and peeked. Everyone stood around Joan, who no longer had a blissful look on her face. Her lower lip pouted out, and her eyebrows were slashed low.

Oh, dear. Molly's heart sank to her feet. The old, angry Joan had returned!

CHAPTER 26

"You tell *me* why you think she has straw in her hair and stuck to the back of her gown, Traemore," Sir Richard said as if Harry were a dunce. "A woman lying in bed all day! I walked behind her from the dining room, and the straw fell out as we went. She's been tumbling someone in the stable. She wasn't ill at all."

"You're being ridiculous," Lumley said stoutly. "Joan has been resting."

"Unfortunately, she was sequestered in a seldom-used room." Harry was amazed how easily he fell into playing along with the mistresses' ruse, but whatever it was, it had done Joan a world of good. "The bed is often used by two of our sneakiest hounds. They traipse in with straw all the time. Mud, too."

Sir Richard looked temporarily appeased. But something else occurred to him. "Did anyone check on her today?"

"I did," said Athena. "And she was most certainly prone in that bed."

"Which was where?" Sir Richard asked.

"Under the eaves," said Athena.

"I thought someone said it was near the kitchens." Sir

Richard turned to Harry. "Do you have a bed in either place?"

"I don't see why it should matter to you," Harry said. "In fact, I would go so far as to say it's none of your business. Even if Joan weren't in her room all day, she has broken no rules of the game."

Sir Richard's face reddened even more. "Who's in charge here—we or they? Show me this room of yours, Traemore, under the eaves. Or is it by the kitchens?" he added nastily.

"*No,*" Joan said boldly. "Stop badgering Lord Harry. You're right. I wasn't in bed all day."

"See?" Sir Richard's face registered a mix of triumph and glee.

Joan's expression was cool yet defiant. "I went to a neighboring village. And I was fortunate to get a ride in a haywagon on part of the way back."

"Why did you go?" Sir Richard asked. "To lie with some farmer?

"Shut up, Bell," said Lumley, his fists clenched.

Joan shook her head. "I went to see my sister. And her— her baby."

"I didn't know you had family here," said Lumley. "I would've taken you."

"I didn't want you to know." Joan gave him a sad smile. "I thought you'd be angry."

"Why would I be angry?" Lumley's brow was puckered.

"Because we mistresses aren't supposed to have a life apart from our protectors," she replied in a low, bitter tone.

"That's right," said Sir Richard. "The other mistresses lied so you could shirk your duties."

"Yes," Joan said. "And I thank them for my few hours of freedom. They knew I wanted to see my family."

Sir Richard swiveled to Bunny. "You knew about this." It was a statement.

Bunny's face seemed almost pressed flat, as if she were anticipating being hurt. "Yes," she said in a soft voice.

Sir Richard raised his hand as if to strike her.

And before he could think, Harry grabbed Sir Richard's arm, right below the wrist. "Don't you *ever* lift a hand against Bunny in my house."

Sir Richard's face twisted in a satisfying grimace. "Let go of my arm."

"Not until I have your promise," Harry ground out. "Only cowards strike women."

Sir Richard narrowed his eyes. "All right."

Harry dropped his arm.

"Spineless fool." Sir Richard rubbed his arm, and his eyes glittered. "You've made a very bad mistake, Traemore. She's my property."

"I am *not* your property," said Bunny softly.

"What did you say?" Sir Richard was practically purple at this point.

"I am not yours," she said. "You pay me for my services, and I can leave whenever I choose."

"You *whore*," said Sir Richard.

Right, Harry thought. *That's it.*

He grabbed Sir Richard by the collar and almost lifted him off the floor. "Enough! Do you understand me?" He shoved him against a wall.

Sir Richard nodded, his eyes fearful—but full of hate.

Harry knew there was no turning back now. He dropped him with a thud. "If you ever strike Bunny again, or hurt her in any way, not only in this house but anywhere, I shall see to it that you will never do so again, if it means I have to call you out and put a bullet through your heart. Have I made myself clear?"

Sir Richard's mouth became a thin line. "Perfectly."

Captain Arrow came forward. "Are you still in the game, Bell? Or have you quit? Because if you do, you are by forfeit the next bachelor to marry."

"I'm in," Sir Richard said through gritted teeth.

"You're too riled to enter the kissing closet," said Harry, raking him with a scornful glance. "Joan, as well, is exhausted. I suggest we suspend that game for the remainder of the week."

It would be the cruelest joke to insist any woman here ever have to kiss Sir Richard.

Everyone appeared to understand Harry's meaning.

"As one half of the arbitration committee, I make a motion we suspend the kissing closet activity indefinitely," said Captain Arrow.

"As the other half of the committee, I second Arrow's motion," said Lumley. "Let's allow the ladies to have an early night, shall we? They need their beauty sleep."

"Excellent idea," said Harry. He took a breath, tried to calm down. "We've still the daily vote to do, gentlemen. Cheroots and brandy in the library in ten minutes."

There were awkward murmurs of agreement from all except Sir Richard, and then Harry's guests began filing out of the drawing room.

But there was Molly, still standing with her hand on the doorknob of the closet. Her eyes held a sheen of tears, and she smiled at Harry, a trembly, little . . . happy smile.

A smile he had no desire to resist.

Molly practically broke off the doorknob of the closet when Harry threw Sir Richard against the wall. Her knees were like water. But Harry was coming toward her now, striding with such purpose she felt a great joy surge through her. It propped up her knees and dried her eyes.

He'd done something heroic. And she was so very

proud of him. He didn't say a word, just backed her into the closet and shut the door.

They were in total darkness.

"Thank you, Harry," she whispered.

"You have nothing to thank me for. I should have done that long before now." He took her face in his hands and kissed her.

She couldn't see him, but she could feel him. He was like a beast, after all, pent up and fierce after the episode with Sir Richard. She sensed he needed solace, a refuge. So she roped her hands around his neck, smoothed his hair back from his face, and kissed him back for all she was worth.

"I want you, Molly," he murmured deep in his throat, and kneaded her hips as he plundered her mouth.

Inch by inch, he moved his hands higher, up to her waist, and then higher, until he was massaging one breast with one hand and pulling her backside as close to him as possible with the other, against his hardness.

But it wasn't enough.

It simply wasn't enough.

With a groan of frustration, he pulled apart from her, but she instantly molded herself back to his body.

"I want you, too, Harry," she said. "I know you only have a short time before the vote. But please. Show me the best three minutes you can imagine in a kissing closet. I'll never be in one again."

"Are you sure?" he whispered.

They were against the back wall of the space now, and he was leaving a trail of kisses down her neck. And somehow, he'd managed to pull down her neckline in the pitch-blackness and rub his thumb over her breast.

"Yes," she murmured.

"Good," he said back. And then he kissed and suckled her, rolling lazy circles around her nipple with his tongue.

It was just enough to drive her crazy with desire, a desire she felt at that hot point between her legs. The thrumming had become full-blown drumming, and her knees were weak.

While his mouth played with her breast, he moved one hand down her leg and pulled up her gown and shift.

She held her breath.

"Trust me," he whispered.

She would. She would trust him, the way she had at the lake. His warm, rough hand gently parted her legs. She couldn't see him, but she felt him move lower, his hair brushing lightly against her skin, his lips and that wonderfully scratchy jaw sending chills over her flesh as he left more hot trails of kisses.

He slung one of her legs over his shoulder, all the while keeping her propped against the back wall. And then she felt it, his warm mouth kissing the inside of her thighs, and his fingers—

She couldn't restrain a moan at the sensation of his fingers playing with her softest flesh. Sliding down the wall, she was helpless to stand, until he stopped her descent with a hand slung around her backside and his mouth.

His *mouth*.

He was licking and suckling her most womanly place. She arched her back and writhed with the delicious sensation.

"Harry." She could barely get the word out.

He murmured something back.

Which sent her to the next level of delight.

She had no idea what he was doing with his tongue, but whatever it was, she was suddenly caught—over and over—in a wave of exquisite pleasure even more intense, if possible, than what had happened between them at the lake.

When it subsided, she felt—

She didn't know how she felt. Sated. Thrilled. Wanting more.

Still pressed against the back of the closet, she took deep breaths. How could she ever have thought him selfish? He was always thinking of her pleasure. Always.

Harry partially stood, laid a light kiss on the fullest part of her left breast. "And that's the best three minutes in a kissing closet I hope you shall ever have."

She heard the smile in his voice and let out a shuddering breath. "Once again, I—I don't know what to say."

"Say nothing," he said warmly. "Leaving a woman speechless is every man's greatest delight."

"Harry." She giggled. "I want to do it again. It was . . . fun. More fun than I've ever had."

He stood up and took her face in his hands. "You're talking," he said softly.

"I can't help it."

"So it seems." Again, that smile in his voice.

"Is there a way . . . I can do that for you?" she whispered.

"Yes. Not that I expect you to. You're not supposed to be a true mistress, remember?" He managed to find her nose and tap it with a playful finger.

And before she could answer, he opened the door. A stab of light from the candles in the drawing room illuminated his face. He turned to gaze at her.

"I'd give anything for a cameo of you looking the way you do right now," he said, his voice so gruff and liquidy warm that she could hardly bear to let him go.

But he shut the door, and she heard his booted footsteps carry him away.

Away from her.

Away from her heart.

CHAPTER 27

Harry vowed to enjoy every minute of his last few days with Molly at the hunting box. Today was the treasure hunt, tomorrow evening was the big finale, and the day after *that,* the Impossible Bachelors and their mistresses were to go home. He knew what that meant—he and Molly would go their separate ways. And if he won the wager, he'd even have to help her find a husband.

After a filling lunch (with no tarts in sight), he sat on a bench outside the house with Molly and admired the soft, vulnerable tilt of her neck as she smoothed out the first page of directives Prinny's advisors had devised for the treasure hunt. Each couple had a different set of clues, but they all led to one, final hide site containing the treasure.

"Here goes," she said, then looked up at Harry. "First, there's a long word, a string of random letters that doesn't spell anything."

She held up the paper:

HTIHSERVOILYLALAHGIGEHNPEUSBS

"Hmmm," he said. "Gibberish, followed by a short verse."

"Yes," she said with a laugh. "Shall I read the verse aloud?"

"Of course. With fervor, please."

She cleared her throat:

A story of love you're commanded to find
About Woodhouse and Knightley and their meeting of
minds.

She lowered the paper. "That's *Emma*! You've read it, haven't you? It's not been out long."

"I can't say that I have," Harry confessed.

"Oh, but it's wonderful!" Molly wriggled in her seat. "It's all about this girl, Emma, who gets in the middle of everyone's business because she thinks *she* knows best—"

"Wait. Are you sure it's not called *Molly*?"

She gave him a droll look. "I believe I'll read the rest of the poem now."

"Go right ahead," Harry said, suppressing a grin.

Molly cleared her throat:

To whom does The Author dedicate this book?
Slash through those letters, then take a look
Your next move forward should be plain to see—
'Tis more than a destination—'tis your destiny.

"Our destiny?" Molly arched her delicate brows. "That's rather dramatic."

There was a tiny pause.

"And you love drama, don't you?" Harry grabbed her hand and squeezed.

"Oh, *yes*!" She squeezed right back.

He laughed. Seeing her so happy was his greatest pleasure.

"I suppose we should find out who *Emma* is dedicated to," she said thoughtfully, "and then we'll eliminate the letters comprising that person's name from this nonsensical word to find our next destination."

"You mean our destiny," Harry corrected her with a wink.

She rolled her eyes, but he could tell she was enjoying herself immensely, judging from the way she kept clasping her hands and speaking in that breathy way she did whenever she was excited. "I don't remember the dedication in *Emma* at all," she was saying. "I went straight to chapter one and began reading."

"Not to worry," said Harry. "Let's head to the library and find the book. No doubt Prinny's advisors have slipped it onto the shelves."

They entered the house and searched the library for several pensive minutes.

"Do you think we're in last place?" Molly asked in a small voice.

"I've no idea," said Harry. "But we can't worry about the others. We must focus if we want to win."

Another tense minute passed, and then his jaw relaxed— *Emma* was squeezed between two books, an older one about farming and the other, a treatise on the rights of man, by Thomas Paine.

"I've found it," he said, and braced himself.

Sure enough, Molly practically knocked him over when she rushed to his side. He turned over a page, and she looked over his shoulder. "It's dedicated to His Royal Highness, the Prince Regent!"

Harry gave a short laugh. "No wonder Prinny's advisors chose *Emma* as a clue."

He returned the book to the shelf, and when he turned around, Molly had already dipped a quill in the inkpot on the desk and was poised over the long collection of letters that made no sense. "I shall slash through 'The Prince Regent' and see what comes up," she said.

"Good idea." Harry was now looking over *her* shoulder. He was quite enjoying all the proximity the treasure hunt afforded.

Molly hesitated. "Wait. There's no *C* here, so the solution can't be 'The Prince Regent'—"

"Check 'His Royal Highness,'" suggested Harry.

Molly uttered each letter aloud as she scratched through them in the crazy word. *"H-I-S,"* she began, and then she went on to scratch out *R-O-Y-A-L* and finally *H-I-G-H-N-E-S-S*. After she finished, she put her hand to her mouth and laughed. "Oh, Harry." She turned her impish blue gaze to his. "So we're to find our destiny at *the village pub*?"

Harry grinned. "This is Prinny's treasure hunt. Are you surprised he might think a man can see his future in a pint of beer?"

"I suppose not," Molly replied.

"We've a good walk ahead of us," Harry said in the calmest voice he could muster. "Three miles at least, and the going isn't terribly smooth."

Molly was like a kettle on the boil. "Then let's set out immediately," she insisted.

"Very well," he said, pulling her close. "And no stopping to—shall we say—enjoy the scenery."

She wrapped her arms around his neck. "Absolutely not," she concurred, then drew back. "Wait. Do you mean—"

"Yes." He nodded gravely. "No kissing. Not if you truly want to win."

She pursed her lips. "Of course I do. We'll walk single file. Starting now."

"Yes, *sir*," he answered, and took up the rear position.

* * *

Molly was a bit leery but hopeful when they reached the thatch-roofed pub. It wasn't particularly large or impressive, but there was the jolly sound of a fiddle playing from within. "How could we possibly know where to look?" she asked Harry.

"I've no idea," he said. "The only hint we have is that we'll find our destiny here."

"A cryptic clue if there ever was one."

"Yes," Harry agreed. "So obscure that I believe we're to take it literally."

Molly's face brightened. "I see what you mean. Perhaps it's someone's name."

"Or a word written on the cover of a book," Harry suggested. "Who knows?"

Inside, the pub was packed with people. Molly noticed she and Harry got a few looks of curiosity, but almost everyone was focused on a pretty girl and a young man dancing merrily at the front of the room.

"Who are they?" Molly asked a smiling woman standing nearby. She was clapping her hands in time to the music, so Molly joined in.

"A young couple moving to America," the woman replied. "They sail next week."

"Oh, how exciting!" Molly hesitated. "Um, would you know if anyone here goes by the name of 'Destiny'?"

The woman drew in her chin and laughed. "Certainly not. What kind of name is that?" And she went back to her clapping.

Molly looked over her shoulder at Harry, and he shrugged. "So now we look for the word itself," he said in a reassuring voice. "Written somewhere in this pub."

But at that moment, the whole crowd, it seemed, began dancing the reel.

"It looks like so much fun!" Molly cried over the din to Harry.

"Then let's try it ourselves. We can look as we go." He grinned, led her by the waist, and they joined the two lines of dancers. Eventually, they made it to the top of the line, and together they skipped down the middle of the column and wound up breathless and laughing at the bottom.

And then they started up again.

The dancing went on for at least another ten minutes. Several times Harry hooked an arm about Molly's waist, spun her around, and stepped back again. Each time he did, Molly wanted to kiss him *and* keep dancing.

But finally, the fiddle music stopped. Everyone clapped, whistled, and shouted for more.

Molly could hardly breathe, and she was sticky with sweat. But she couldn't help it. She threw her arms about Harry's neck. "I loved that!" she said. "The dancing, the music, and—"

You.

She inhaled a little breath.

The room receded, and all she saw was Harry's golden brown eyes and the crinkle of a smile around them. She couldn't look away if someone had set fire to her skirt.

He wrapped his arms around her, and they touched noses. "You're . . . the most amusing companion a man could wish for," he said, in a warm, scratchy voice that made her melt inside. "Not to mention delectable."

"And you," she whispered, her forehead pressed to his, "you're—"

Amazing?

Wonderful?

Her one and only true love?

No. She couldn't say that. But suddenly, she knew that's what he was.

Her one and only true love.

Forever.

She bit her lip.

"What?" he whispered back, his mouth not half an inch from hers. "What am I?"

"A very good dancer?" she eked out.

And then she saw his mouth moving closer to hers. She felt his hands slide around her waist and pull her close. And he kissed her, right there in the crowd, a slow, luxurious kiss that made her heart beat hard against his chest.

No one seemed to notice—too much beer was flowing—but Molly knew when she drew away from Harry that *he* was her destiny.

And she wouldn't be able to stop loving him, even though she knew that someday, very soon . . .

Loving him would break her heart.

Harry knew he shouldn't have gotten distracted by the fiddle music. Because now, rather than look for hidden treasure, he wanted to stay here, in this pub, and dance all night with the girl who made him feel genuinely happy—for the first time in years.

The couple moving to America stood atop the bar and motioned for silence. When the room quieted, the young man raised a mug of beer skyward. "To our beloved home in England, our temporary home aboard the schooner *Megan Casey,* and the new home we'll establish in Boston. May we never forget from whence we came, yet may we always follow the tide of destiny!"

Everyone raised their mugs to the couple and cheered.

"Destiny!" Molly exclaimed to Harry.

"Surely that reference was mere coincidence," he said thoughtfully, "but his talk of tides and ships has given me an idea." He pointed at a wall covered with small and large oil paintings. "What if one of the ships in those oil paintings is named the *Destiny*?"

Molly gasped. "Of course! But I see at least"—she counted beneath her breath—"fifteen ships!" She was already running over to the paintings and examining them closely. Harry joined her, and thankfully, no one seemed to notice their interest as being anything out of the ordinary.

"Here it is!" Molly pointed at a medium-sized painting of a ship on rough seas.

It was, indeed, called the *Destiny.* As discreetly as possible, Harry felt around the edge of the frame and pulled out a piece of paper.

"I have a good feeling about this," Molly said. "But we'll need to hurry! What if the others are ahead of us?"

"Then we can always say we had more fun than they did," Harry reminded her.

And it was true. He *was* having fun. More fun than he'd had in years.

As he led Molly outside, he was oblivious for the moment to the crowds jostling around them, the cacophony that was the party, the smells of mutton and beer, and the continuing travails of the treasure hunt. Instead, he was distracted—and confused—by the sense of completeness that overcame him when he held Molly's soft, trusting hand in his own.

CHAPTER 28

A half hour later, after following detailed instructions on the paper she and Harry had found at the pub, Molly found herself in a fallow field, counting fence posts to find the place where Prinny's advisors had buried the treasure.

"Here," she said, pointing at a tuft of grass at the base of the fourth post to the right of a twisted oak tree.

Harry lifted the tuft right up, revealing a neat hole in the ground containing a small red leather box. "Shall I?" he asked her with a grin.

She clasped her hands and nodded.

He lifted the lid.

"Oh!" Molly was surprised to see a scroll inside. "I thought the actual treasure would be in the box."

"Maybe it's too big."

"Really." She imagined all sorts of possibilities: a chest filled with gold—a horse, perhaps! Or . . . or—

A monkey! She'd always wanted one of those. The kind with a little red hat and a striped shirt that rode along on your shoulder.

But she had no other ideas. She was simply too excited to think.

Harry seemed to read her mind. "Why don't we relax and read it together?" he asked her.

"Brilliant idea."

So they sat together, Molly between Harry's knees, and Harry leaning back on the fence post that had led them to the treasure.

Their fence post, she thought, smiling softly to herself. *Their* treasure.

She sighed and closed her eyes and listened to Harry open the scroll. He felt *so* good. And he smelled divine. Like the peppery scent of green grass baking in the sun. And the scent of fresh linen. And . . . and *man*.

But then she sat bold upright. "Tell me, Harry! What's the treasure?"

"A night together," he said, his voice husky. "An Arabian night, actually."

"What's that?"

He looked at her with an inscrutable expression. "Prinny's arranged to have a Moroccan tent set up by the lake and stocked it with a lavish feast, and we shall be waited upon by exotic servants."

"And—and we shall spend the night together in this tent?"

"Yes," he said thoughtfully, and rolled up the scroll again.

Her body flooded with all sorts of feelings—fear, worry, and . . . and if she were honest with herself, excitement. She would love to be held in Harry's arms all night.

But she *couldn't* spend the night with him!

By society's standards, she was already compromised, of course, but she was coming to believe there were *degrees*. At least in her bedchamber at the hunting box, she'd pushed that bureau in front of the door connecting her room to Harry's. But in the tent . . .

There would be nothing separating them. Nothing at all.

"We—we'll have to mark a line down the middle of the tent," she said.

Harry nodded slowly. "All right, if that's what you want."

Oh, dear, he'd left *that* sentence hanging. "You mean"— she dared to look up at him—"that's not what *you* want?"

Harry chuckled. "What do *you* think? But what I want and what I can have are two very different things."

Molly looked at her fingers. She was too embarrassed to look at *him*.

The man she loved.

He stood, and she was at eye level with his muscular thighs, encased in buffskin breeches. She forced herself to look away, to concentrate on the beautiful country scene in front of her.

"We'll make the best of it tonight," Harry said. "We worked hard for this, and there's really no way out without everyone figuring out our ruse. So let's enjoy it— we've won many points, after all—and I promise, I won't allow anything . . . unworthy of you to occur."

Points.

Yes, that's what this treasure hunt was all about, wasn't it? She mustn't forget that, even though in every other way his speech was noble. Endearing, even.

He held out his hand. She took it—and smiled wanly as he pulled her up.

"Thank you, Harry," she said, close enough to his face that he could kiss her with ease.

But he turned away instead and fiddled with the clasp on the leather box.

She suppressed her need to touch him and told herself to be glad. Harry was being wise. Prudent.

And she should follow suit.

* * *

"And I thought you were all brawn and no brains, Traemore!" The nasty voice rang out from somewhere to Harry's left.

He felt a huge black cloud of resentment when he turned and saw Sir Richard walking briskly down the field toward him and Molly, Bunny not far behind.

"Think again, Bell," Harry returned. "We beat you here, did we not?"

"Yes, well, no doubt luck played a role." Sir Richard stalked off to a nearby shady tree. He sprawled on the ground, opened a flask, and drank deeply from it.

Harry resisted the urge to roll his eyes.

"Congratulations, you two," said Bunny, a sweet smile on her face, a smile that couldn't disguise the signs of strain around her eyes.

No wonder. Sir Richard was an ass. And Harry would like nothing more than to kill him.

Molly hugged Bunny. "Thank you. We had such fun."

"De-li-lah!" Sir Richard called to her. His nasal voice was quite annoying.

Molly looked at Harry, then Bunny. "What does he want of *me*?"

"I've no idea," said Harry. "And you can ignore him if you'd like."

"I'm sure he means to insult you in some way," said Bunny. "And he is already calling you over as if you're a pet dog. *Do* ignore him, Delilah."

Molly pressed her lips together. "I think not. I'm going to tell him a thing or two."

And she strode off.

"He'd better watch out," Harry said with a chuckle, then turned and kissed Bunny's hand. "I hope you know I'm always glad to see *you*."

Bunny smiled. "Thank you for saving me from him last night. Although I don't feel I deserved your help. He insisted I tell everyone Delilah was napping, when she wasn't." Her mouth began to quiver. "Please tell her I'm sorry."

"Don't you dare apologize," Harry said. "We both know Sir Richard gave you no choice."

Bunny sighed. "That's no excuse." A tear trickled down her face.

He took her hand. "Don't be so hard on yourself. I can stop him if he ever attempts to harm you again, but I can't convince you to believe you deserve better. Please know Delilah and I both think you do."

Bunny blushed. "Thank you. I—I never realized how . . . lost I'd become until I met Delilah. She's helped me think about my life. And what I want." She looked furtively over at Molly and Sir Richard. "There's one way I'd like to repay you both. Something I stumbled upon this morning. You must know that Sir Richard wants to ruin any chances Delilah might have of being crowned Most Delectable Companion."

Harry pretended to be unperturbed. "What's he doing exactly?"

"I heard him speak to one of the servants. He said he wanted to send him to town with a letter for his ailing mother. I suspected he was up to no good, as he's been commenting this whole week on Delilah and how ill-suited she is to be in the running for the title. So I intercepted the letter before it went out. "

She reached into her reticule and pulled out the note.

Harry stuffed it in his pocket. "You've been a true friend to Delilah, and I appreciate that very much."

"I care for her," said Bunny, following Molly's movement about Sir Richard's resting place.

Harry watched her shake her finger at Sir Richard. She was telling him off about *something*. Even now, after his threats, she wasn't afraid of him.

"She's truly one of a kind," said Bunny with a laugh.

"That she is." He'd always known that about Molly. And he'd always thought her being one of a kind was a bad thing. A lady shouldn't be so *memorable*, should she?

Especially when you'd made a promise to forget her.

"Tell me, Delilah," Sir Richard was saying, "will Harry's soon-to-be-wife object to his keeping a mistress, or will you be seeking new employment after he loses the competition?"

"None of your business." Molly put her fists on her hips. "And I'm sure Harry wouldn't like to hear you speaking ill of him behind his back."

Sir Richard chuckled. "No need to be offended on his behalf. If Traemore must let you go, at least he'll have some compensation for your loss in the wit and beauty of his future wife."

Lovely.

Molly didn't need to hear how easily she'd be replaced after she and Harry parted ways. So she said nothing.

"Don't despair," Sir Richard said. "You may call on me if you're seeking a new protector. And I always pay a fair wage."

"Never in a million years," she returned blithely. "You're a despicable man, and I quite look forward to never seeing you again after this week."

She gave him a charming smile.

He stood up. "You think you're clever, don't you? You think Traemore will protect your interests." His voice was smug. "But I assure you, he's never shown loyalty. To anyone."

"Be quiet about Harry. You know nothing of him."

Sir Richard gave her a pitying look. "You sound like all the females who fall under his spell. Trust me, Delilah. Your illusions will soon be shattered. How do you think he came to be known as a ruthless ne'er-do-well? Mere rumor?"

"I said I'm not interested in listening to you!"

He laughed. "You may have heard he discredited himself in the army. Do you know how?"

"No. No one with good taste discusses it. I just know that he was doing very well in the army, and then suddenly . . . he was disgraced. But he continued on and made a splendid show of bravery at Waterloo."

"So what? A man can never shake off a truly despicable act, Delilah. Traemore was in the colonel's tent—seducing the colonel's wife—when his regiment was ambushed. No one could prove anything, however. He showed up at the ambush at the last minute, when it was too late to help. But for the remainder of his military career, he won no distinctions for meritorious service. He became known as a profligate woman-chaser, gambler, and drinker. Do you see now why he's called an Impossible Bachelor?"

She shook her head. "Why should I believe what you say? You hate him. And you make it obvious."

"Of course you wouldn't believe me," Sir Richard said. "You're as charmed by Lord Harry as the colonel's wife was!" He paused, pulled a small object out of his pocket, and carefully unfolded a layer of linen to reveal a cameo of a beautiful woman with burnished curls the same color as his own, and large gray eyes.

He handed the cameo to Molly. "You would hate him, too, if the colonel's wife were your *sister*."

Molly's lungs seemed to empty of air. She turned the cameo over—it had been painted on the first anniversary of the marriage of Colonel Frederick Smith to a Miss Abigail Bell.

"I just wish I had been there to protect her in her time

of vulnerability," Sir Richard whispered. "Her husband divorced her. She's been alone ever since that hour she spent alone in the tent with Traemore."

Molly fought against the light-headedness threatening to overwhelm her. Sir Richard's sister looked so happy in her portrait!

"How . . . how sad for her," Molly murmured, handing the cameo back to Sir Richard with trembling fingers.

He replaced it in his pocket with great care.

Molly couldn't help but note that his obvious soft spot for his sister was in stark contrast to the cruel way he treated Bunny.

"Why are you telling me all this?" Molly asked him coolly.

"You're linked to Traemore, and you two are obviously harboring a secret. If I can get to him another way—a way that has nothing to do with my sister—I will. Confess all to me, and we can bring Traemore down together. We'll get him legshackled, a fate which will bring him at least some misery. That alone would give me great pleasure."

Abruptly, Sir Richard strode away, back to where Bunny and Harry were talking. Molly stared after him. She still despised the man, but it seemed he had a legitimate reason to hate Harry.

Harry.

She turned her gaze to him. He was talking to Bunny, laughing at something she said.

Molly couldn't imagine him seducing the colonel's wife while the colonel was away. It was such a dishonorable thing. But he'd never claimed to be honorable, had he?

Perhaps the colonel's wife had lured him into her tent. He was a handsome man. Why wouldn't she?

But he should have said no *if that were the case,* a no-nonsense voice in Molly's head reminded her.

At this very moment, he was being a gentleman, speaking to Bunny with respectful attention. But try as she might to focus on the Harry she'd come to know, Molly's old distrust of him came back in suffocating waves. Women *did* fall under his spell. Even Penelope had—two weeks before her engagement!

Molly had proved to be no exception. This whole week her heart had been leading her head, she realized. It was time to get her head back into its rightful position.

Perhaps she didn't truly love Harry. Perhaps, like Penelope and myriad other women, she'd fallen for a man who had nothing more to recommend him than loads of empty charm and . . . and a family name that turned heads.

He was nothing more than a spare, her head told her decisively. A spare who'd gone to rack and ruin, whose heroics at Waterloo were probably as short-lived and insubstantial as a curl of smoke from a fired musket.

CHAPTER 29

Harry guessed that Arrow and Hildur, Joan and Lumley, and Maxwell and Athena arrived at the final site of the treasure hunt about half an hour after Sir Richard and Bunny had.

Athena was in a terrible snit. "I despise caves," she said, her hair rather more wild than usual. "I will *die* before I set foot in another one."

"She only stood at the entrance," Maxwell muttered to Harry. "And a bat flew in her hair. You'd think it was the end of the world. It took me a good thirty minutes to calm her."

Arrow and Hildur both looked half dressed, and their hair was damp. "We lost track of the time," Arrow said, quite good-naturedly. "We really did intend to win."

Hildur laughed. "I *like* waterfalls, Captain Arrow." She threw him a smoldering glance.

"You do, don't you?" He shook out his cuffs and winked at Harry.

Joan was in a foul mood, as well. "Those ruins," she said, "are *fake*."

"It's all the thing, don't you know," said Lumley with a shrug. "Build your own ruins, invite friends over."

"But we were *trespassing*," Joan said. "And they caught us."

"It wouldn't have been a problem if, um—" Lumley stopped talking and looked worriedly at Molly.

Harry noticed that ever since their time together in the kissing closet, Lumley treated Molly with special deference. She'd asked after his mother's health, after all. And made him a lovely tart.

"If what, Lumley?" Sir Richard asked nastily.

"If we weren't naked," Joan said with asperity.

Harry looked swiftly at Molly. The word *naked* apparently wasn't bothering her as much anymore. She appeared to be laughing behind her hand!

The minx.

He caught her eye and grinned, but her expression instantly became serious again.

And it hadn't improved, all the way back to the hunting box, where they immediately trooped into the drawing room for a late afternoon cup of tea.

Captain Arrow flicked back the curtains. "We'd all best batten down the hatches tonight," he said. "We had a devil of a red sky this morning. I predict a vast downpour. And gusty winds."

"But the sky is clear," said Athena, "save for a few fluffy clouds."

"Red sky at morning, sailors take warning," said Captain Arrow. "I'm sorry for Harry and Delilah, though."

"We'll be fine," said Harry, trying to boost Molly's spirits.

She didn't say a word.

"Delilah, aren't you excited about your impending Arabian night?" asked Joan.

Molly sat up in her chair. "Of course I'm excited," she said, and tried to smile.

But she was a terrible actress, Harry thought for the

umpteenth time. She looked as though she'd rather be drawn and quartered than sleep in a Moroccan tent with him.

Athena puckered her brow. "Are you all right, Delilah?"

Molly nodded. "I—I'm fine."

"I should hope so," Sir Richard huffed. "While we'll have roast beef and pudding, you'll be treated to a lavish meal served by exotic menservants."

"Where are they?" Molly asked.

No one knew.

But the piece of paper detailing their prize made it clear that the servants would be at the site on the hill near the lake sometime soon after sundown.

Which was in fifteen minutes. So it was time to go.

After many wishes for a pleasant evening from everyone except Sir Richard, Harry found himself alone again on the trail with Molly. She was lagging behind him, perhaps without realizing it.

"Tell me truthfully," he asked her. "Are you all right?"

"My slipper's loose," she said. "That's all."

"I could carry you," he offered with a grin. "It could be fun."

"No, thank you," she responded politely, but her smile was weak.

Approaching a bend in the trail, Harry racked his brain for something that would restore the affectionate, cheerful Molly to him. Without her, he was becoming cross. And damned if his head wasn't beginning to ache. For the first time, his usual charm was failing him utterly, and he couldn't think how to . . . how to *win* her back. She'd been ignoring him, ever since she'd talked to Sir Richard after the treasure hunt.

Wait—

Sir Richard.

Harry braced himself to ask Molly what had transpired between them, but she was staring over his shoulder.

"Oh!" she cried. "I've never seen anything like it!"

Straight ahead, shimmering like a jewel among the trees on the side of the hill facing the lake, was a scarlet and white striped Moroccan tent.

"It *is* rather splendid." Harry squeezed her hand, encouraged by her enthusiastic reaction.

She didn't lag behind anymore. In fact, he had to walk faster to keep up with her. All thoughts of asking her about Sir Richard went out of his head. Harry was hopeful that Molly was back, *his* Molly, the one who made him feel as if every day were an adventure.

A few minutes later, when they actually got to the campsite, there didn't appear to be anyone nearby, even though there was a small fire and a well-roasted suckling pig crackling and hissing away on a spit above the flames.

"You're late," Harry heard from behind him.

"*Oh!*" said Molly, and whirled around.

In the split second he took to turn, Harry girded himself. He knew that voice, even as the commonsensical part of him insisted that it couldn't be that person—it couldn't! Not out here in the middle of nowhere.

But there he was—Prinny himself, sitting in a grand chair between two trees. He was surrounded by two Indian servants waving large feather fans behind his head. And he held an open bottle of wine in his hand.

"Your Royal Highness," Molly said in a trembling voice, and dropped a low curtsy.

"Your Highness," Harry said in his crispest tone. "Welcome to my family's property." He gave a swooping bow.

Prinny chuckled. "My, my, my," he said. "So *you* won the treasure hunt, Harry." His gaze raked boldly over Molly. "Did this fair lady assist you?"

Harry took a step forward. "Yes, Your Highness, she

did. She was indispensable, actually. Never would have won it without her."

Prinny took a swig from the bottle. "It gave me great pleasure to arrange that treasure hunt. I'm surrounded by very capable advisors"—he paused—"and some dolts, as well, who think I should attend to state matters *all* the time. But everyone knows a man must have his fun, eh?"

The prince leaned on an elbow and eyed Molly. "Tell me your name, my dear."

Harry almost couldn't breathe.

"D-Delilah, Your Highness." She smiled at Prinny, and Harry prayed Molly's heavy eye makeup and rouge would disguise her, in case the Prince Regent ever saw her about town.

"You've intelligence and a bit of spirit in your gaze," Prinny said. "I like you. Don't you, Harry?"

"Most definitely, Your Highness."

"I shan't stay." Prinny stood on rather wobbly legs. "And my servants shall leave after they've fed you—they'll sleep in your stables tonight, Harry, and clean up here tomorrow."

"I'm happy to offer them a room, Your Highness, and access to the kitchens."

Prinny nodded. "Just as well. As for me, I've a horse and a servant nearby, and a carriage awaiting me in the village. A good friend—a rather delicious friend—lives not five miles from here." He gave them a breezy salute. "I hope you'll enjoy your Arabian night, my friends."

And he turned to walk away.

"Wait!" Molly cried.

Prinny paused and turned back around.

"I mean, Your Royal Highness," Molly amended with an apologetic smile. "We would be honored to have you stay and sup with us."

Prinny chuckled. "You don't want old Prinny about.

One more bottle of this stuff"—he held up the wine bottle—"and I shan't be so civilized. Besides, I'd rather think about what will happen here after I *leave*."

He waggled his brows.

Molly turned beet red.

Harry cleared his throat. "We're certainly grateful for your patronage, Your Highness. Safe journey."

Prinny eyed him. "Safe journey to you, too, as you navigate your way through this wager. I hope you come out the other end of it the way you wish."

"Thank you, Your Highness."

"And you, young lady." Prinny pointed the bottle in Molly's direction. "Don't settle for a ne'er-do-well, eh? Make sure you find yourself a protector who knows your worth. I can already see that very few gentlemen deserve to win you."

Molly smiled and curtsied. "Thank you, Your Highness."

He skewered Harry with a steely look. "Take it from me, Traemore, the whole world might hate you for one reason or another, but if you've a good woman by your side, you can still enjoy life. And it don't matter if she's a duchess or the winner of the Most Delectable Companion contest."

Harry grinned. "I shan't forget, Your Highness."

They watched him walk away.

But as soon as he disappeared, Molly's energy—her brightness, her spirit—seemed to flag again, even as they sat by the fire and ate a sumptuous feast, complemented by a very fine bottle of wine.

After they finished their meal and said good-bye to the servants, Harry said, "You seem preoccupied tonight. You haven't even looked inside the tent."

"No doubt I'm still rather in shock," she said, "as we were just visited by the Regent of England. Out here in the woods." She gave a little laugh.

But the Molly Harry had grown familiar with wasn't so understated. Nor so lacking in curiosity.

"I hate to add to your discomfiture, but Bunny gave me something today that you should read." Reaching into his pocket, he handed Molly Sir Richard's letter.

Skimming the lines, Molly's face registered worry. "He's hired someone local to check all the posting inns from here to London for a woman of my description. I thought I was a good actress, but the truth is, I make a terrible mistress. And Sir Richard has figured that out."

"A young lady isn't *supposed* to make a good mistress." Harry hated to see her so burdened with remorse. "Besides, I'm just as guilty as you of being a poor actor. Even though we've"—how should he say it?—"*transgressed* certain boundaries, I can't forget that you're a lady. No doubt it shows in my manner."

Her face looked particularly pained when he mentioned she was a lady. Was she worried that this week's events had somehow stripped her of that distinction?

He laid a hand over hers. "Molly, you've done nothing wrong. And you'll be all right. I shall see to that. We've got one more day to go, and then I'll take you home, no one the wiser. You *must* trust me."

They locked gazes, but the look in her eye was far from trusting. She swallowed. Her mouth trembled. And she was wary of him. He could tell. It was as if this week of getting closer had never happened.

Standing up, he ignored the hurt he felt somewhere near his heart. "I'm going to chop wood," he said gruffly.

They didn't *need* any more wood. The Indian servants had left them some. But Harry had discovered in the army that hard work was a good way to forget that the people you cared about didn't expect much of you—and it was also a good way to prove them wrong.

CHAPTER 30

Staring into the fire, alone now with her thoughts, Molly knew she'd made the biggest mistake of her life when she'd eloped with Cedric. Had she never left home, she'd never have fallen in love with Harry.

She closed her eyes tight. *If only she could pretend he didn't exist!*

But she could hear him, whistling under his breath as he chopped wood.

And if she were a little bit closer, she could smell him—that fresh-as-the-outdoors Harry smell that made her want to press her cheek close to his and inhale. It was mixed with an elusive scent as comforting to her—but as indefinable—as that of her favorite bed pillow. She would never forget it.

The way she would never forget his touch.

Or the look in his eyes every time he wanted to kiss her.

She opened her eyes. She must remember that marrying was not in his plans. Not for a long time. And when he did eventually marry, it would be against his will. He was a profligate gamer, drinker, and chaser of women.

He walked over to her now, the axe dangling from his

hand. "Needless task, I suppose, but highly satisfying." He pointed to the new stack of wood in the clearing. "Especially when one is playing a waiting game. Are you looking forward to the finale?"

"I suppose," she said. But her heart wasn't in her words.

Harry crouched beside her. "Out with it, Molly," he said quietly. "What's the matter?"

She swallowed, avoided his eyes.

But she must be brave.

She must *ask*.

So she met his gaze directly. "I want you to answer a question for me, Harry, about your service in the army."

He sprawled on the ground beside her. "Fire away."

She gathered her courage. "Did you seduce the colonel's wife? And . . . and forbear from defending your comrades in the midst of an ambush?"

His eyes flared with something she didn't understand. "Why are you asking me this?"

She must stay strong, immune to his charms. "Sir Richard told me it's why you were disgraced in the army. The colonel's wife is his sister."

Harry blew out a breath. "That explains his particular hatred of me. I had no idea the two were connected. She was married, of course. I didn't know her maiden name."

"Yes." Molly felt a stab of pain near her heart. "She was *married*."

Did he not see how wicked he'd been to seduce a married woman?

Harry said nothing. His mouth was a straight line.

"Is it true then?" she whispered.

"Yes. It's true." Harry didn't blink, and his tone was neutral. "I *was* with the colonel's wife while my friends got ambushed. But it's not how it looks."

Molly's eyes stung, but she wouldn't cry. "What do you mean?"

His eyes were hard. "It's not my secret to tell."

She felt sick. He was acting like a stranger—cold, unyielding. "Harry, *tell* me. Please." She laid a hand on his arm, but he brushed her hand away.

"I told you. I can't." His words were clipped. "Do you trust me? You said once that you did."

She stared at him. Her whole insides felt stripped away. But she couldn't say yes.

She simply couldn't.

He stared at her a moment, his expression impenetrable. "Very well, then," he said, like a stranger again.

And moved past her.

She watched him stride away.

Is he not going to say anything else?

Her heart was beating so hard, she felt it would burst out of her chest. "Where are you going?"

"To the lake," he responded curtly. "You'll be fine."

"Of course I will!" She felt her cheeks heat up. "Why wouldn't I be?"

"And I won't be back for hours," he said, as if she hadn't spoken, and strode down the trail.

"Fine!" she called after him.

She watched until his figure disappeared over a crest.

Let him stew and sulk at the lake. She would do well up here on the hill all by herself. It was what she wanted anyway. He'd best not try to come back any time soon, either. If he did, she would tell him exactly what she thought of him and his Impossible Bachelor ways.

They were far more lethal than she'd realized. And she would *not* succumb to them.

She made sure she was still scowling when she walked through a flap in the front of the tent—and stopped short.

She'd no idea that the interior of the tent would be so gorgeous!

The floor was covered in colorful rugs strewn with

large silk pillows in exotic patterns. A small wooden chest to one side held an ornate brass lamp and a pitcher with two goblets. Several fringed blankets were folded in one corner, and in another, hanging from a tent pole, was a beautiful outfit, the likes of which she'd never seen. A small moan of appreciation escaped her when she touched it—it was see-through in parts, silky, and had slits in the oddest places. She wasn't quite sure how to wear it. But she knew if she tried it on, she'd want to twirl in it. Or stand on the hillside and let the wind blow through it while she stretched out her arms like a butterfly.

She looked down at her own gown that had been in service all day. It was covered with little bits of leaves and dirt.

Very well. She'd change into the harem outfit, not to play dress-up or to please Harry but to be more comfortable.

After several attempts, she finally figured out how to don the exotic costume. Leaving off the veils she surmised were meant to cover her head and face, she lay down on the luxurious pillows, closed her eyes, and said her prayers. God could help her avoid total ruin, couldn't He?

But why would He want to? She'd been flouting every bit of wisdom she'd ever heard!

She may have been a false mistress, but she'd also been a *fool*.

She closed her eyes and vowed to get a good night's sleep.

Five minutes went by. Then ten. Still no ridiculous man returning to apologize *or* explain his disgraceful behavior.

A lone bird cawed.

Molly opened her eyes and stared at the colorful walls of the tent.

"Harry," she whispered, a tear slipping down her cheek.

She would never let him know how she felt about him.

She'd endure until this ridiculous week was over, and if all went well, she'd go back to her old life.

A life without Harry.

But a life of respectability.

She unfolded the second blanket and drew it up to her chin. Even though it was soft and of a pleasant weight, it was no comfort at all. Sort of like her existence would be when she left this glorious place.

The place where Harry was.

Another bird sang its nighttime song, and she sighed. Stupid bird! Didn't it know her life was practically in ruins?

Yet somehow her eyelids felt heavy, and despite her cheerless thoughts—or maybe because of them—she slipped into a deep, dreamless sleep.

Around Molly Harry had kept his anger banked to a slow burn, but when he'd left Prinny's camp, he'd let it flare. On the trail he stomped and fumed and eventually gave up on reaching the lake the civilized way. He headed straight into the woods, crashing through brush to get to the water faster. Once there, he'd headed straight for the diving rock, stripped off his clothes, and plunged in. He'd suffered a few scratches of thistle and thorn in the woods, and those cuts now stung.

But he wanted the pain. And the coldness of the lake. It almost helped him stop thinking about Molly.

And his past.

He swam to the shore, and when he strode onto the beach, the moon was climbing the sky, illuminating a bank of clouds in the west. A soft breeze rippled the lake surface and flirted with the trees.

Arrow had been right. A storm was likely on the way.

Harry retrieved his clothes and put them back on, but he wasn't ready to go back to the camp. Bending down, he picked up some flat rocks, skimmed them over the lake's mirror surface, and watched them skip and sink. Sort of like his mood today. It had started out so well. And now—

Now he felt like he had lead in his stomach.

It was a moment for him to face some truths.

Doing his duty had gotten him into trouble in the army, hadn't it? He'd given up on leading a respectable life and fully immersed himself in the lifestyle of an Impossible Bachelor—a title he'd spent several debauched years earning.

He'd deserved Molly's rejection of him tonight.

Based on what she'd heard from friends and family alike, she was right not to trust him—not to *believe* he could protect her. He was the one who pursued women as playthings, wasn't he? The one who didn't care what happened to them after he crawled out of their warm beds at night.

Knowing what she knew of him, Molly was right to be frightened about her future. How could a wayward bachelor protect her from the likes of Sir Richard? If he uncovered her identity, she'd be hopelessly ruined. She'd spend all her time at the side of her cousin Augusta, and after Cousin Augusta departed this world, she'd be lucky to go back to her father's house. There would be no assemblies, no church bazaars. No family of her own. No husband to love her and for her to love back.

She would be hidden away. Disgraced.

And it would be all Harry's fault.

He should have forfeited the damned wager and taken her straight back home from that blasted inn.

He dropped the rock still in his hand. He was a cad. A coxcomb. And if Molly were ruined, he'd never forgive himself. He kicked up some sand and began heading back to camp.

She was probably asleep. He wanted her to feel safe. So

he would sleep outside the tent. Perhaps it was the only way to show her that his intentions toward her were—if not entirely honorable (his mad lust for her had already disproved that)—at least not despicable. He wanted her to leave this week at the hunting box with her reputation intact. And he wanted her to be able to marry a good man who would appreciate her humor, wit, and beauty.

He would do whatever it took to make sure her reputation was secure. And to hell with their previous agreement. He'd find her a good man, even if she didn't win the contest. He owed her that.

There was the sweet, cushiony hush of nighttime in the woods. By the time he reached the camp, he felt much better. At peace somehow.

He added a log to the fire and lay down by it, flat on his back, his hands folded under his head. Looking up, he could see some stars through the branches overhead. Beneath him the ground was hard and unyielding, but he embraced the discomfort.

He would show Molly how much he respected her by staying far away. Closing his eyes, he heard a distant rumble of thunder. Was God going to test him so soon?

But five whole minutes went by in relative silence. Perhaps the storm would blow to the north, he thought.

Then a splash of freezing cold water fell directly on his eyelid. And another, on his forehead. His experience in the army had taught him that in a rain, he'd get no more than chilled. Perhaps he'd suffer a few sniffles later, but he never got colds.

He was too manly for that, at least according to Fiona.

Why, the very day Fiona had run off with the pompous Cedric, she'd told Harry he was the handsomest, most charming man in all of England.

He felt the veriest stooge. The fire sizzled as the raindrops came down faster, erasing all illusions he'd had about his worth as a man. Fiona had been paid to flatter him, and he'd actually believed her. He'd believed every last word.

He'd believed he was a veritable *god*.

The truth was, he was beginning to think he was a big baby.

The rain came down steadily now. He sat up, drew his knees to his chest, and wrapped his arms around them. He would watch the fire as long as it lasted, which, judging from the increasing intensity of the rainfall, wouldn't be longer than another ten seconds.

But he wouldn't move. He'd sit here all night.

For Molly.

CHAPTER 31

Molly lay on her side, her hands tucked beneath her head, and opened one eye. It was definitely raining. She heard it pelting the roof of the tent, and sat up, surrounded by darkness.

Where was Harry?

A thin slice of moonlight shone through a crack in the tent flap as she padded to the entrance and peered out. There was a small break in the cloud cover, enough to see the fire was out. The rain had seen to that.

She scanned the rest of the campsite.

Heavens. There he was—at least she thought that soaked form was Harry—sitting up against a tree trunk, his eyes closed. Of course he must be awake—the branches of the tree deflected some rain but certainly not all. No one could sleep through being rained on, could they?

"Harry!" she called in a loud voice. The noise of the rain would be certain to drown her out, otherwise. "What are you doing out there?"

He instantly opened his eyes. "Trying to sleep. At least until—"

"You can't sleep out there!"

"You forget I was in the army."

"I don't care." Molly's mother hen instincts were clamoring to get him out of the elements. "Come out of the rain. You'll catch a chill!"

"I'm *fine*."

"No, you're *not*. Get in here, Harry!"

"I'll just make you wet if I do that."

"Nonsense." The rain began to come down even harder.

"Go back to sleep," he insisted. "I'm already soaked through, and joining you won't make me any drier."

She could barely hear him over the tumult. "Come inside! Or I shall come out there after you!"

"No you wouldn't."

"Yes I would!"

Their gazes locked. This need for Harry to come into the tent went beyond Molly's mother hen instincts. She had a hollow feeling in her stomach. An ache. She wanted to be with him as only a false mistress could be, which meant not *really* with him, but with him in a *way*.

She hated the ambiguity. But she loved Harry. And she would take him any way she could get him.

"I'm coming to get you." She thrust one leg outside the flap of the tent.

"Get back in there!" Harry strode over to her.

She pulled her leg back inside.

"Don't you even *think* of coming out," he said.

Despite the threat in his voice, she couldn't help reaching out a hand to touch his cheek. It was rough, cold, and wet.

Very wet.

"I *do* trust you, Harry," she said. "I believe you have good reason not to tell me what happened to you in the army."

Even in the darkness, and with rain pelting down, she saw his eyes flare with something fierce. And yet there was something tremendously vulnerable in his gaze, too. She was reminded of the days when she'd watch him from a stone wall as he played at sword fighting with Roderick before the church service. They'd both grab long sticks and have at it, Roderick large and looming, Harry full of bravado, even as his smaller hands had trembled on his makeshift weapon.

"Really?" he said.

Now Molly could only nod, too full of emotions to speak.

But she must be practical. "Come inside and get out of those wet clothes before you catch cold." She swallowed. "You could, um, wrap up in a blanket. Unless there are some clothes for you, as well. I didn't see any."

"Thank you for the kind invitation, but I can't come in." His tone was warm but firm. "I'll see you in the morning."

He turned away.

"Harry!" She gulped.

Slowly, reluctantly, he turned back around.

"If you don't come in, I'll quit the competition," she said, her chin in the air.

"You wouldn't."

"I would."

"Then do it." He sighed bitterly. "I should have taken you home long ago. We'll leave at first light."

Oh, God, he wasn't supposed to give *in* like that! He was supposed to want to stay, to *win*!

She sighed. "Never mind. If we leave, you'll be forced to marry. And I don't want that to happen to you."

She pleaded with him with her eyes. *Please, Harry. Come into the tent!*

He scratched his forehead and sighed. "All right, I'll come. But only because you're too stubborn for your own good. *And* mine."

She smiled and felt shy all of a sudden. "I'm glad. About everything. About being stubborn. About you entering the tent. About this week and about our friendship."

He gazed at her a long moment. "Me, too," he finally said, and stepped through the flap. "My goodness. You look . . . lovely."

She felt heat rise on her cheeks. "Thank you. Wait until you see the rest of the place."

He held the tent flap higher and peered closer at the interior. "I see a lamp and a pitcher on a wooden chest. And pillows. Lots of pillows."

"You should see it in the daylight. It's so exotic. And pretty."

He secured the flap so that a block of moonlight found its way inside.

"I'll bet it's even prettier when the lamp is lit," he said. "I'll do that now, if you wouldn't mind."

"Not at all." She smiled at him and knelt by him at the wooden chest, his nearness reassuring, even though his clothes were, of course, still cold and damp.

"How to light it," he muttered.

"Are there no matches?"

"None that I can see or feel. Perhaps in the chest. To keep them dry."

"That makes sense."

Together they removed the items on the chest, and Harry lifted the lid. "Aha!" he said, and withdrew a leather pouch. "I feel them in here."

"Very good." She felt quite cozy and happy.

He lit the oil lamp and held it up. The makeshift room took on a warm glow. "It's very attractive, this place. And you"—his voice was warm—"you look more beautiful—and alluring—than I've ever seen you."

"Thank you," Molly said, feeling shy again. She was about to shut the lid of the chest when she saw a bundle in the bottom. "Oh! Perhaps these are clothes!"

She pulled the bundle out and shut the lid. Harry put

the lamp back on top of it and crouched next to her. It was a drawstring bag, and not very light.

"Too lumpy and heavy to be clothes," she said, disappointed.

He smiled at her reassuringly. "I can wear a blanket."

She sighed. "I suppose that's better than nothing."

"I suppose," he said with an awkward laugh.

Too late, she realized her gaffe. She reddened and busied herself opening the drawstring bag. "What's this?" She pulled out a small, primitive-appearing statue.

Harry studied it. "Prinny, you dog," he muttered, his eyes alight with amusement.

Molly swallowed. "It's . . . it's two people."

Harry traced the entwined limbs with his index finger. "They're rather involved with each other."

Molly's heart raced. "You mean they're—"

"Yes," said Harry. "They are." His eyes snapped with mischief. And heat.

She shoved the bag at him. "Perhaps *you* should look. There's more."

"All right." He reached in with a grin and pulled out a book with gorgeously rendered script on the front in an unfamiliar language.

"Oh!" sighed Molly, her hand on Harry's arm. "It's beautiful! And old, I think."

"I think you're right." Gently, he opened the book to a random page.

An illustration of two people, um, doing the same thing as the people on the statue stared up at them!

"Shut it, Harry!" Molly cried.

Harry shut the book, but not before staring at the picture a few more seconds. "Are you sure you don't want to see more?"

"No."

"No?" His eyes flickered with a challenge.

She stuck her chin in the air. "Absolutely not. You need to get warm and dry, and we need sleep. I, for one, am perfectly exhausted." She made herself yawn, and then scrambled onto some pillows, and pulled an emerald green woven blanket about her head. "I'll wait beneath this until you're dressed."

"Very well," he said. "No peeking."

"As if I would!"

He laughed, and she heard him pull off his breeches. Her breath grew a bit short—no doubt because of the blanket smothering her. "Are you wrapped up yet?" she called impatiently.

"Yes. You can come out now. I'm perfectly respectable."

Feeling a tiny bit afraid, she let the blanket slide off her head.

He was lying on his side, facing her, his head propped on his elbow, his own bold yellow and black blanket not sufficient to cover his chest nor his strong, shapely calves. His hair was a wet mess, but somehow on him it looked charming, particularly that curl pressed to his forehead. She had a desire to touch it, to straighten it, to *play* with it, but she wouldn't.

"I won't bite, you know." His tone was serious, but he had a twinkle in his eye.

She narrowed her gaze. "Harry, this is a serious breach of etiquette. But under the circumstances—"

"Oh, you don't have to be all prim and proper. I know you wouldn't have called me in except for the rain. And I wouldn't have come, but you're stubborn. You would have yelled all night and had no voice left for tomorrow. We can't have that."

"That's not true."

"You're not stubborn?"

"No." She lowered her eyes, afraid to meet his. "It wasn't *only* because of the rain I called you in. Although that was part of it."

"Really?" His voice was warm.

She would be brave. After all, she didn't have much more time with him. "I wanted you here."

"I wanted to be here," he said rather hoarsely.

She liked that kind of voice in Harry. It usually promised kisses.

He leaned closer. "I understand why you'd assume the worst of me concerning this army incident. I've earned my bad reputation. Which makes your trust in me that much more . . . meaningful. No one else, save a few close friends and my brother, believes I am any more than a wastrel. Including my father."

He gave her a heartrending smile.

She couldn't bear to see him so sad!

"Harry—"

He put a finger to her lips. "I'm sorry if I've pressed myself on you this week. It was not well done of me. In fact, I regret every moment I've ever made you feel uncomfortable."

"It's not that I was uncomfortable exactly—" She stopped speaking. "And you didn't exactly press yourself—"

Actually, he had. He'd pressed himself on her in the most delicious ways. She felt her whole body warming up at the memory of the most recent time he had, in the kissing closet.

His mouth curved in a small smile. And her knees melted. *Everything* in her melted.

"Oh, Harry," she whispered. She *so* wanted him to kiss her. But he was *so* bad for her.

Wasn't he?

"I know," he said, a world of understanding in his voice. And reached over to lay a gentle kiss on her lips.

She closed her eyes. It truly was the sweetest kiss he had ever bestowed on her. He *knew*. He knew that *she* knew that *he* was—

Oh, bother. He simply *knew*. And that was all that mattered.

She opened her eyes.

"Now, Molly," he said firmly, "as you've already pointed out, we should sleep." He rolled onto his back, folded his hands behind his head, and closed his eyes.

She felt the beginnings of a childish tantrum build within her chest. She didn't *want* to sleep. Especially now that they understood each other so much better.

And there was that book. She was a bit curious, and she was with Harry, after all. *He* wouldn't tell anyone if they took another peek.

She sighed loudly and shut her eyes.

The rain still fell steadily, but not as strongly as five minutes before.

"Are *you* sleepy?" she asked.

"Not at all," Harry said pleasantly. "But you're exhausted, of course."

She nudged his leg with her big toe. "I hope we win tomorrow."

He shifted a bit. "Me, too."

She sighed, rolled over, and faced her side of the tent again. No matter how much she knew she shouldn't be behaving the way she was behaving, it was as if she couldn't help herself. Harry had some kind of mysterious pull on her. He made her forget everything she knew to be right.

He was simply so . . .

Handsome.

And lovable.

And funny, when he wasn't being a stubborn mule.

And he understood her. Better than anyone.

She pushed her foot backward and made contact with his leg again.

"What're you doing?" he said, not angry. Not even annoyed. But alert.

"Nothing." She suddenly felt stupid. She would quit bothering him.

So she stared at a pillow this time and decided to count the number of feathery shapes woven into the fabric. Maybe that would help her sleep. The cozy patter of the rain on the tent lulled her somewhat, but still she went on, doggedly counting.

She'd reached forty-five when she felt a warm, solid arm drape itself over her body.

He pulled her closer. "You can't sleep, can you?"

Oh. Her back was against his chest now. They fit together like two spoons. And he was toasty warm.

"I think I'll be able to. *Now.*" Molly smiled, sighed, and closed her eyes.

But then she opened them again. "I forgot to say good night."

"Oh?" said Harry softly, but he had a big, bearlike voice, the kind he got in *special* circumstances. Her heart skipped a beat, and she twisted her body to face him.

"Good night," she whispered, and laid her palms against his chest. Because it was there. In the way.

She couldn't help herself. She had to rub that chest with her palm. It was so warm, and beautiful, with those fine, jet black hairs sprinkled across it.

"I thought you were exhausted."

She sighed. "Me, too." But then she wrapped her bare feet around his calves. Harry made her feel so . . . cozy. And this tent of Prinny's was perfect.

"You've got cold feet," he said, still with that bear voice she felt flattered to have caused him to employ.

He rubbed her back with his free hand.

"Sorry." She grinned, and wrapped her feet around him even more.

He began a long, luxurious sweep of warm palm over her bottom. "You're beautiful," he whispered. "Even when you're perfectly annoying."

She kissed his chest and looked up, into his brown eyes glinted with flecks of gold. Their color was like a favorite autumn leaf she'd pressed into her diary. "You, too," she said.

Which was a perfectly good hint that she wanted him to kiss her. Would he understand?

But wait.

"Harry." She lifted her head. "The lamp's still burning."

"I know." He smiled, lifted his head, oh-so-gently pushed her on her back, and began to ravish her mouth with a warm, slow kiss. "I suspected you wouldn't be as ready for sleep as you claimed to be."

She knew she should be offended. But all she could think, as she kissed him back, was that this moment was bliss.

Pure bliss.

CHAPTER 32

He shouldn't be doing this, Harry's conscience said to him while he kissed Molly. He'd told himself he would stay away.

But she was so . . . irresistible. Why else would he ignore every ounce of common sense he had and persist?

Perhaps it was because she wore that exotic harem outfit. Or because her body strained toward him, and her mouth was so eager. And perhaps it was because she was simply . . . Molly.

He lifted his head. "We should stop now," he forced himself to say.

Molly had that same dreamy look she'd had in the carriage the first time he'd kissed her. "I don't want to," she whispered, and began to play with his hair.

"You shouldn't say things like that," he groaned, his elbows propped on either side of her head. He was extremely aroused and was doing his best to keep his lower half away from her.

She sat up, her hair flying forward and settling on her shoulders. "Harry," she said, quite agitated. "I want to be your true mistress."

He sighed. "Molly—"

"Really." She moved even closer to him. "I don't want to marry a boring old squire and have his brats. And what are my chances in London of finding someone who . . . who understands me?"

"It will happen," he soothed her.

"No," she said with conviction. "I'll reject all of them. Because once they discover what I'm really like—which is very trying, I'm well aware, and quite fond of kissing— I'll be kept up in a turret or something." She crossed her arms and stared at him.

He played with her hair. "It's healthy to want to do what we do together."

"Really?"

"Yes. Your husband will not have a disgust of you. He'll want to be with you this way all the time. He won't want to keep you in a turret."

Her eyes clouded.

"What is it?" He hated to see her eyes like that.

"I—I don't like knowing you'll be with Anne Riordan this way," she said. "Although it's almost inevitable, isn't it?"

"We must stay confident," he said as brightly as he could.

"Right." She sighed. "But if I do win Most Delectable Companion, you must find me a husband."

"I know."

She stared at him. "I wish—"

"What?"

She swallowed. "I wish it could be you."

Oh, God. She was breaking his heart.

"Molly." How could he say this? "I—I'm not good enough for you. You deserve—"

"You mean you're not ready to stop being an Impossible Bachelor." Her eyes got a little glassy.

Was she going to cry?

He sat silent for a moment. He didn't want hers to be another heart he broke. He cared about her far too much.

"No," he said, struggling to identify what it really was that kept him from marrying. "It's not that. It's just that . . . I have nothing to offer."

That was it.

"Why?" she asked.

Indeed. Why?

Whose fault was it, really, that other than that brief moment in the army when he'd performed his duty to the best of his ability, he'd accomplished nothing else in his adult life of any benefit to anyone?

His father's fault?

The fault of all the gossips and naysayers in his life?

Or his own?

Deuce take it, it was his own damned fault! Of course it was. Yet he still had too many questions to answer. Too many feelings to sift through, the main one being, how could he make up for lost time? How could he try to bring honor to the house of Mallan, even though no one believed he could?

He pulled a curl off Molly's face. "You are a most desirable woman," he said softly. "You've exceeded all my expectations of what a false mistress should be. Any man would be extraordinarily lucky to claim you for his wife. But"—he swallowed—"I cannot be that man."

Molly blinked.

"For obvious reasons, of course," he went on doggedly. "Such as the possible obligations of this wager."

She still said nothing.

He grappled for words. "But also because I need time. To think. To become . . ." He paused. "Something."

She lay quietly, her expression open yet inscrutable. He continued stroking her hair. "You're my friend, Molly. And I want you to be happy." He rose up over her, the blanket wrapped around his waist so she couldn't get her hands on him. If she did, he couldn't trust himself to control the urge he had to make her his own completely.

She said nothing.

He leaned down, brushed a warm kiss over her lips. "Please. Let me make you happy. Even if it's only for a few minutes."

Still nothing.

"Molly?"

He kissed her again. Pulled back. And looked at her face.

"Harry!" She smiled brilliantly at him. "You're so easy to tease." She sat up on her elbow. "I don't *truly* want to marry you."

He let out a gusty sigh. "Really?"

"Sometimes, yes, I think you might make a girl a wonderful husband. You *are* fun. But we both know you're not ready. Who knows if you'll ever be?"

"You minx!" He threw himself on his back and stared at the scarlet and white striped roof above his head. Then he leaned over and kissed her.

He felt a shiver pass through her.

"Let's look at that book," she whispered.

"Which book?"

She nudged him, her eyes luminous. "*You* know which one."

"You're sure?"

"Yes."

So he clutched the blanket about his middle, moved the oil lamp, opened the chest, and withdrew the book. After he replaced the lamp, he went back to Molly, who'd made a little nook for them by stacking pillows in a circle.

Once he was situated, she sat back in the circle of his arms, pressed close to him.

He turned the pages of the book slowly, and neither of

them said a word. But he felt her body tense and her heart speed up.

He rubbed her shoulder. "Are you all right?"

"Yes," she whispered.

He kissed her neck then, very gently, and she tilted her head so he could have even more access to her.

"I know you said we can't be together completely," she whispered. "But I want to get as close to *completely* as possible. Can we?"

He hesitated. "Do you really want to?"

She nodded. "More than anything."

He put the book down and turned her to face him. "I have to admit—I do, too."

"It's our last chance," she said.

"To make an incredible memory," he whispered.

Their gazes locked, and she said nothing as he lowered her onto some pillows. Slowly, he slid her harem outfit off her arms, then down her waist, and finally, off her body altogether. Her ripened breasts, her slender legs, and the essence of her femininity . . . all were bared in the light of the lamp.

She was exquisite.

When he bent low to kiss her belly, she cupped his jaw and caressed it with her thumb—a tiny gesture that affected him deeply. *She trusted him.* And her future husband had best be worthy of that trust, Harry thought, a fierce protectiveness rising up in him. Or he would see to it that whoever the groom was would suffer greatly.

The rain came down, softer and quieter now.

"We really should get some sleep," she murmured. "After."

Yes. *After.*

He grinned, marveling at how lacking in artifice she was. "That *was* you, wasn't it?" he said. "Running around the house naked."

She nodded and smiled. "I had to. The other mistresses were starting to doubt me."

"I have a secret, too," he admitted. "I saw you change into your clothes outside the house."

Her mouth dropped open. "Really? Where were you?"

"In the tree—looking for you."

She gasped.

"I didn't mean to see you, of course. And no one else did, I assure you," he was quick to add.

She smiled. "I'm glad you did. You know how I feel about being naked, Harry. If it were any man but you—"

"Right." He suckled her breast, then looked up at her. "But I didn't simply watch, Molly."

She drew back. "You didn't?"

"No."

It took her a moment, but then she laughed. A sweet, husky laugh. "Oh, Harry. I like thinking about you watching me and doing that." She shuddered and ran her fingers through his hair. "We've known each other so long."

He stopped for a moment, wanting confirmation. Because it was simply unbelievable that—

"You really do trust me, don't you?" he asked her.

"Implicitly," she said, with a smile that took his breath away.

My God. That was rather . . . something, wasn't it?

Harry was feeling, at the moment, many feelings. He didn't usually like to feel feelings. They were such a hindrance to having fun. But today, for some reason, they weren't.

"I—I like you, Harry," she said. "Very much. No matter what anyone says about you. I know"—she hesitated—"I know you're brave. And kind. Even if you *are* an Impossible Bachelor."

And it was at that moment he realized that he'd never wanted to pleasure a woman as much as he wanted to pleasure this one. Nudging her leg over, he lifted her knee and kissed the inside of her soft, deliciously scented thigh.

"Harry." She moaned. "I love this, but I want the closest thing. Show me. *Please.*"

He looked up. "We're just warming up." He leaned forward and kissed her, his shaft pressed against her warm, silky belly. Then he flipped her on top of him, loving the feeling of her breasts pressed against his chest. "The closest thing I know involves some acrobatics," he said. "You got a glimpse of some acrobatics in that book. Are you prepared?"

She giggled. "Yes!"

"Then stay where you are, but get on your hands and knees."

She did as he asked.

He ran the backs of his hands over her nipples, and she arched her back like a cat.

"Now I'd like you to turn around," he said. "I'm going to kiss you again, the way I did in the kissing closet. And while I do that, you can explore me. However you want."

Her eyes widened, but she looked excited. Not afraid. "I'll get to kiss you *that way*?"

"Yes," he said. "If you remember to. You might be slightly . . . distracted."

"Of course I'll remember," she said stoutly, and maneuvered herself over him so that her sex was mere inches from his mouth, ready for intimate exploration.

He let out a sharp breath. She'd already found his most vulnerable flesh and tentatively circled it with her tongue.

"Is this right?" Her voice was alluringly low as she bestowed a wet kiss on the tip.

"Anything's right." He suppressed a groan of pleasure and reminded himself to be strong—he wanted to bring her to pleasure first. Embracing her thighs with his hands,

he lifted his head to her most intimate spot, letting his tongue flick in and out.

In—

Her legs buckled, and he caught her, pulling her even closer to his mouth.

And out.

All the while, she moaned against his own sex and suckled it. Stroked it with her hands. Licked it and kissed it.

He kept her petal-soft core close and loved her with his tongue and his mouth.

"I—" She struggled to stay on her knees. "I can't wait—" She sucked him and caressed him—she was driving him wild.

He intensified his efforts. She moaned, gyrated.

Immersed in the dual pleasure of loving her and receiving her own enthusiastic, sensual ministrations, he wondered: what was this woman doing to him? It went well beyond the exquisite gratification he was experiencing at the moment. She was imprinting herself upon him in a way no other female ever had.

"Harry," she whispered raggedly. "With me. Please. I—I'm ready. I want it. I remember from last time. What will happen."

"You're sure?"

"Yes," she sighed. "*With* me."

"Together," he murmured against her flesh and gripped her buttocks, plundering her with his tongue. She bucked. He gripped her tighter and felt her shudder around his mouth.

"Har-eeeeee!" she shrieked.

And then he let himself go, as well. Into her mouth. And she welcomed his seed, her hands splayed around the base of his shaft as if she were holding on to the edge of the earth. Then she collapsed, rolled to the side, her arms thrown out.

"Oh," she said, her voice trembling. *"Oh."*

Harry sighed, sat up on his elbow, and pulled on her hand. "Come here," he managed to whisper. She was like a rag doll, but she came and flopped onto his chest.

She'd depleted him as well, in more ways than one.

"That was as close as we could get," he said, his chin resting on her hair. "Without . . . complications."

She sighed and snuggled against him. "I—I don't see how it could get better. I *shrieked,* Harry. Just like Hildur said."

He lifted his head. "Exactly what did Hildur say?"

Molly giggled. "Never mind. It was girl talk."

They lapsed into a comfortable silence. No real coupling he'd ever had had come near what he and Molly had shared tonight—the closeness and the intense, unfamiliar emotions he'd felt, as well as the exquisite pleasure.

"Just wait," he whispered to her. Her breathing was evening out. Soon she'd be asleep. "There's more. But all in good time."

Although she would experience it with another man.

That was the part that was killing Harry, and the reason he made sure that when he eventually got up to extinguish the lamp, he crawled under a blanket on the other side of the tent.

CHAPTER 33

When Harry woke up the next morning, he saw that Molly was still sound asleep, her mouth slack, one arm thrown up above her head.

He grabbed his wet clothes, turned away, and stepped out of the tent into the fresh morning air, allowing himself only the smallest of sentimental grins. Last night had been . . . amazing, yes. But he couldn't think about Molly that way anymore. He must think of her as his entry in the contest instead. *She* must, too. Neither of them could afford to forget he had a one-in-five chance of getting leg-shackled to another woman.

Thankfully, she'd made it clear last night she agreed with him wholeheartedly—there could be no serious attachment between them.

It was time to win.

He eyed his wet breeches distastefully before pulling them on.

And just in time.

"Good morning!" Molly poked her head out of the tent and smiled broadly at him. Her long lustrous brown hair hung free, and she was once more back in her own gown.

It seemed her usual vigor had been restored by a good couple of hours of sleep . . . *after.*

He grinned. "Ready to head back? Prinny's servants will clean up here."

"All right. But . . . I—I need to fold some blankets first."

"Oh." He fumbled for an excuse to give her a few minutes alone. "I just remembered I need to inspect a tree down the trail. Why don't I do that and come back . . . soon?"

"Thank you," she said, looking relieved. "You're very thoughtful."

He smiled, gave her a little salute, and took off down the trail. Somehow Molly made him feel like a hero about the smallest things, which was quite nice. And different from the way Fiona and his other mistresses had complimented him. They'd always flattered him with a lofted brow, a pursed mouth. The old come-hither look.

Molly treated him more like a friend.

He'd never had a woman he'd seen up close and naked treat him like a friend. Was it lowering? An affront to his pride?

Or refreshing?

He stopped, took a moment to inhale the fresh morning air, washed clean by last night's rain.

Refreshing, he decided.

In fact, for some reason he felt like a new man this morning, ready for anything. Sir Richard's threats seemed far away. And so did his departure from this place and from Molly. He vowed to enjoy every minute of their last full day together.

Molly splashed water on her face from a bucket of water left by one of Prinny's servants. And blushed. Harry had once again performed wonders on her last night.

He'd seen her completely naked, too. Up close!

She couldn't believe it!

But she must not think of that. It was daylight now. The truth was plain—she and Harry had one more day together, and then they each must go to their other lives.

She would be practical. So she went back into the tent and folded the blankets, all the while trying to focus on the finale—not on Harry.

She would win tonight! Everyone would be amazed!

But she *did* wish she could see Harry naked again. And she wished he could do more things to her, and she to him.

Oh, dear. She would have to stop those thoughts for the rest of the day. She would think about the competition instead.

But hadn't she already told herself that?

She shook her head, hoping to loosen Harry's hold on her thoughts.

"All set then?" Harry was back.

"Yes," she replied, and wondered what he was thinking.

He opened the tent flap for her, and she stepped out.

"We have a big day ahead of us," he said, his face unreadable. "We must do our very best to win the finale."

"I know." She hesitated, but then just came out with it. "You won't be thinking of me naked, will you, Harry? Because I really need to concentrate."

"You can rest assured I won't be thinking of you naked all day," he said, with what she thought was admirable fighting spirit.

"Thank you. And I won't be thinking of you naked, either."

There was the tiniest of pauses.

"Let's just focus on today," he finally said. "And remember we're a team. We want to win big. Think of how we both shall benefit."

"Yes," she said, with equal spirit. "A team."

Harry stuck out his arm, and she took it. But not before she looked one last time at the campsite and committed the scene to memory.

CHAPTER 34

Harry made sure the day went by in a flurry of recreational activities. A bit of shooting for the men, some lawn bowls for the women while they were gone, and charades in the afternoon. Molly went upstairs to take a nap after tea, and he made sure he'd be nowhere near, or he'd have been tempted to enter her room and repeat what they'd done last night in the tent.

All day he'd had to remind himself not to think about what had transpired in that tent, which of course meant the goings-on there—and Molly—were seldom far from his thoughts.

Now they had about an hour of sunlight left. Harry led the group over the hill to the side of the lake, where Finkle and his two footmen assistants had prepared a crude stage, a rustic dressing area, and a picnic supper to be enjoyed before the dramatic reading.

Each step of the way toward the site of the finale, Harry felt a pang of longing for Molly.

There was the tree on the trail where he'd pulled her hair off a twig and they'd been so happy in their own little leafy world.

And then the campsite Prinny had devised and visited,

to his and Molly's amazement. Although Harry thought the royal welcome paled in comparison to the memories created there after Prinny had left!

A few minutes later, there was the log at the lakeside where Harry and Molly had sat cozily together, discussed their families, and shared blackberry kisses.

And when they all filed by the grassy bank where he'd first introduced Molly to the more intimate delights a man and woman could share, Harry could hardly bear the emotions surging in his chest.

The next day, he and Molly would go their separate ways, and he would miss her. He would miss her very much, but he refused to examine the feeling too closely. He'd immediate responsibilities, after all, as host of this gathering, which was being watched very closely by the Prince Regent himself.

By necessity, Harry kept his churning thoughts to himself, although during the meal, he watched Molly as often as he could without staring. And he laughed. He laughed quite frequently. Lumley and Arrow were particularly witty that night, and the women were sparkling.

Especially Molly.

"You're awfully quiet tonight," she whispered in his ear. "Are you all right?"

"Never better," he said, forcing himself to grin. She must be in the best of spirits for her performance. "And you?"

"Prepared to win." Her tone was brisk, but then her gaze softened. "Thanks for the coaching, Harry. And for all your support this week."

"It was my pleasure," he said, his voice a bit gruff. In the old days, he could always disguise when he wanted a woman. But with Molly, it was becoming increasingly difficult to hide his feelings.

Their gazes locked—and then she ran off because Athena was threatening to pour lake water over her head if she didn't leave the picnic blankets to ready herself for the entertainment *immediately*. Their gowns and reading materials awaited them behind the dressing area, which was composed of two blankets tacked onto overhanging tree branches, a small table, and a lantern.

"Good luck, ladies," Lumley called out to all of them. "We gentlemen shall be waiting with bated breath!"

It was, indeed, time for the show. The footmen had already lit the torches. Two velvet curtains were rigged to open between two trees nearby, forming the makeshift stage. The men sprawled out on the linens, awaiting the fate of their mistresses by lighting cheroots and opening flasks of brandy.

According to the selection of straws, Bunny would go first, followed by Athena, Joan, Hildur, and Molly.

Harry would have to wait longer than any other bachelor to see how his companion fared. But he had faith in her—he'd seen her perform "Kubla Khan." He took a thoughtful sip from his flask and thought that victory might very well be the last thing they'd share, he and Molly. But the thought didn't buoy him as he expected it should.

Behind the curtain shielding the makeshift dressing area, Molly and the other mistresses were frozen in place, staring at the tree branch that held the women's special evening gowns. Someone had slashed through Molly's, apparently with a knife. The skirt hung in tatters, and there was a gaping hole in the bodice and one on the lower back.

"No," she whispered.

"Oh, Delilah!" Bunny put her hand to her mouth.

Hildur held up the ruined gown and looked through one of the jagged holes. "It is a fishnet now."

"I know it was Sir Richard," Molly said without emotion. She'd known all along Sir Richard was after her. And now he'd made his mark.

Bunny's eyes were wide. "I saw him over here earlier. But I thought he was simply being nosy, as he always is."

"He hates me," Molly said flatly.

Bunny squeezed her hand.

"He hates everyone," Athena said, her eyebrow raised in a weary arch. "But he does seem to hate Lord Harry especially."

"Yes, he does, doesn't he?" Joan put an arm around Molly's shoulder. "He thinks he's a coward. But we all know Lord Harry is worth a thousand Sir Richards. I don't care what people say about his army disgrace."

"Do you know what happened there, Delilah?" Athena asked her.

Molly's face reddened. She couldn't tell any of them why Sir Richard hated Harry. Or that Harry was innocent of all accusations. "No," she said. "But I know Harry. And he *is* a good man. He's told me he's done nothing to hurt Sir Richard, and I believe him."

"We *kill* Sir Richard," Hildur said. "Right now." She pulled Molly toward the curtain.

"*No,*" said Athena firmly. "Not now. The show *must* go on. Kill him *later.*"

Hildur hesitated, and Molly released her hand. "Thank you"—she smiled at Hildur, then looked at Athena—"but you're right. The show must go on. And I can wear the gown I have on now."

It was the bishop's blue muslin, the first dress of Fiona's she'd ever worn. She'd donned it this afternoon especially for Harry, a parting gift to him. Because after tonight, he wouldn't see her in scandalous gowns anymore! He'd be married to Anne Riordan, and Molly would be on the shelf, still pouring out tea for Cousin Augusta.

Or he'd be carousing about London with not a care in the world, the winner of the Impossible Bachelors wager— and if not that, at least one of the losing bachelors who'd slipped past parson's noose by drawing a saving straw at the end of the bet.

She'd be without Harry, of course. Either way. And wearing modest gowns as the years passed and this week's contest became a distant memory.

She bit her lip. She must stay focused on what was happening now. Not depressing thoughts of the future.

"I know this is probably a silly question, but is the gown at all fixable, Bunny?" Joan asked.

"No, not even if I were near my sewing box." Bunny looked sadly at Molly. Then she gazed around at the others. "But I have an idea. And if you're willing to go along with it, Delilah will have as much a chance as any of us to win the finale."

"Then let's do it," said Athena.

Bunny's face lit up. "I'll be right back." And she lifted up her gown and ran to the men. When she reappeared a minute later, she said, "I brought something that will allow us to remove beauty from the criteria for judging." Her eyes sparkled. "Or, depending on your perspective— that is, if you're a male—we might use this tool to *accentuate* our beauty."

She opened her palms to reveal three small knives. "Every man had one on his person, of course. I brought several back and told them some of us needed to clean our fingernails and teeth." She giggled.

"None of them particularly enjoyed hearing that, I'm sure," said Joan with a grin.

Bunny nodded. "Sir Richard was the most horrified of all. I think it's because he could see from my expression that I knew exactly what he'd done to Delilah's gown."

"And that we *kill* him with these knives," said Hildur between gritted teeth.

Molly laid a hand on her arm. "It's all right to hate him

on my behalf, but I really don't think we have to, um, kill him."

Hildur's shoulders sagged.

"We can cope with this ourselves in the way women do, Hildur," said Bunny. "We shall simply outsmart Sir Richard."

"Yes," said Joan, her eyes bright with interest. "Are you proposing what I'm thinking you're proposing with these knives?"

"I think she is," said Athena. "And I do believe she's brilliant!"

"You mean—" Hildur made a cutting motion with her hand. "To *my* dress. And yours."

Bunny nodded, her mouth curved in a mischievous smile.

"Goodness, no!" Molly blurted out. "I couldn't ask that of any of you." She laid a hand on Bunny's arm. "Thank you so much for the thought. But . . . no. I can wear what I have on."

"But Delilah," exclaimed Bunny in the most impassioned voice Molly had ever heard her use, "Lovely as you appear, your gown isn't nearly as splendid as these creations made by Prinny's orders! I want us to match, all of us." Bunny's eyes grew a bit shiny, and she looked around at all the women. "I haven't known any of you longer than this week, but I—I feel like we're sort of . . . sisters. And—"

"And sisters, on special occasions, wear matching dresses," interjected Athena.

"Exactly," replied Bunny. "We shall all be almost naked . . . together."

"And no one mistress will look better than the other," said Joan.

"They'll be driven mad with indecision." Athena laughed.

"So many tits to choose from!" Hildur threw her arms wide.

Molly chuckled and wiped her eyes. "You're too kind. All of you."

She'd feel *special* romping about near-naked with these suddenly dear friends—Athena, Joan, Hildur, and Bunny. They were going to ruin their gowns on purpose—to help *her*.

One of their own.

Molly got a lump in her throat. Maybe she wasn't a real mistress, but she'd been included in their number, and it felt like the highest honor. She would miss them all deeply, she thought, as she hugged each of them separately, saving Bunny for last.

Because Bunny was her very special friend.

CHAPTER 35

The men were getting impatient. It was taking longer for the ladies to get ready than they'd anticipated, so they lit more cheroots and drank more brandy.

Sir Richard leaned over to Harry. "I still believe something's not quite right with you and Delilah, Traemore, and I shan't give up trying to find out." He'd spoken loud enough for all the men to hear.

Now that Harry knew why Sir Richard disliked him more than he disliked everyone else, he tried to be— maybe not completely kind, but kinder. Especially as he was still not at liberty to divulge the truth to Bell about what had really happened to his sister.

"Try all you want, " Harry told him. "I couldn't give a fig, to tell the truth. Would you like a light for that cheroot?"

"No." Sir Richard scowled. "Not from you."

"Do you really think any of us will be inclined to wish you good luck tonight when you are such a horse's ass, Bell?" said Maxwell, blowing a smoke ring in his direction.

"I don't need your good wishes," Sir Richard replied. "You are obligated by oath to choose the best mistress tonight. I know how honorable you gentlemen are. You won't allow personal differences to stand in the way of fairness."

"If you mean we won't let Bunny pay the price for your shortcomings, then I suppose you're right," said Arrow.

"See?" said Sir Richard. "I can count on you fools to be sickeningly honest in your assessments of the women."

"We most definitely can't count on *you* to do the same," stated Lumley.

"An Impossible Bachelor stops at nothing to retain his lofty status as a man among men," said Sir Richard. "My tactics are perfectly unexceptional and, sadly for you dolts, unidentifiable. They shall remain locked in the vault of my brain, only to be shared perhaps with the occasional by-blow who might seek advice about how to avoid the parson's mousetrap."

"Advice which includes ensnaring respectable virgins and seducing them," said Arrow, "then threatening to deny everything if they dare tell their mamas how you crawled through their windows past midnight to deflower them."

"And you object to that sort of thing?" Sir Richard said in that world-weary voice of his.

Harry stamped out his cheroot. Sir Richard was an enigma. He was angry because he was sure Harry had seduced his sister, yet his whole adult life he'd prided himself on seducing everyone *else's* sisters.

"I object to *any* young lady being taken advantage of, Bell," said Harry.

"I don't believe that," Sir Richard growled. "Your history says otherwise. Prove it by marrying one of those young ladies, Traemore. I'll be laughing from the back of the church."

Ouch. Harry knew he *should* marry Molly, shouldn't he? He was suddenly unable to think of a single retort.

Lumley filled in for him. "Don't be so sure *you* won't be the one at the altar, Bell."

Bunny came to the curtain and announced that the ladies were ready.

Harry stood, vowing not to let Sir Richard disturb his equanimity again tonight. Facing the other bachelors, he held up an envelope. "Tonight we come to our last competition. According to Prinny's wishes, the women will perform dramatic readings they've selected themselves. I've a note from His Royal Highness that I must read aloud to you."

He took a few seconds to remove the note from the envelope, and read:

My Impossible Bachelors, you shall judge the ladies tonight on many things: beauty, comportment, originality, charm, and dramatic skills. But, above all, before you cast your last vote for this year's Most Delectable Companion, you might ask yourself the following crucial question: Which lady, other than my own, is the most unforgettable, and why?

Of course, at the start of this week, you might have wondered why your Prince Regent takes so much interest in your lives that I would arrange this extensive wager and command you to participate.

Gentlemen, I write to you in confidence. The people claim the merry path I've chosen has exacted a great price not only on my country—but on my very soul. I am ceaselessly urged to bolster the health of both.

Well, my friends, you must know serious endeavors bore me. But in a nod to my detractors—and with a devilish wish to irk them as well—I created this frivolous bet as a means to share with you, the next generation of English gentlemen, what paltry wisdom I may have accrued in this lifetime.

You know as well as I how difficult it is to behave. A wastrel they may call me, but I'm not completely addled. And one thing I've learned in this wicked life of mine is that women don't need us as much as we need them.

Lowering, isn't it, to find that your own best destinies may very well lie in the hearts of those women who deign to love you?

My Impossible Bachelors, I leave you to ponder that possibility in your own brandy-soaked hearts. Good luck and Godspeed.

His Royal Highness, the Prince Regent

"Ye gads," said Sir Richard.

Harry folded the note and put it in his breast pocket. "I rather like Prinny better when he's not so acute in his perceptions," he drawled.

"Those moments are brief, I assure you," Maxwell commented dryly.

Lumley scratched his head. "The woman he was with at the club probably dictated that in his ear."

"Must forget the letter ever happened," Arrow muttered around his cheroot. He waved at Harry. "Let's move on, as quickly as possible."

There was a chorus of affirmatives.

Harry was glad to know he wasn't the only bachelor discomfited by Prinny's words. "Remember," he said, "at the conclusion of the show, we shall tally the votes, add them to those accrued by the mistresses all week, and if all goes accordingly, present the title of Most Delectable Companion to one of these lovely ladies."

He went to the curtain and pulled it to the side. "Let the finale begin!"

CHAPTER 36

Molly was last in the lineup, her stomach in knots. Last night, when she'd let slip that crazy idea that Harry should marry her, and he'd soundly but kindly rejected the notion, she'd faced up to facts. She and Harry were best together as friends. Friends who occasionally removed each other's clothes and kissed each other senseless.

It sounded rather like an arrangement between a man and his mistress, didn't it? A romp between the sheets, a good laugh, and . . .

No commitment.

If she won tonight, his inevitable fate—marrying Anne Riordan—would be delayed. But only for another year. Anne was bound to catch up with him sometime.

And if Molly lost, he would help her find another man to marry.

She released a shaky breath. Why was there no good solution? She was damned if she won and damned if she lost.

Either way, she and Harry would be apart. Forever.

But friends, she consoled herself, until one of them got married.

Friends of a special nature.

He didn't know it, but that was what she was going to tell him after this week was over, that she would be his mistress. And just as he did last night when she'd suggested the same thing, he would balk, he would say no, and she would simply carry the day by kissing him and getting him to change his mind.

It was as fine a solution as any to her constant emotional turmoil.

Wasn't it?

From behind the makeshift dressing room's curtain, Molly could see Bunny walk on stage in her extremely revealing gown. She curtsied to her male audience, all of whom clapped madly for her and whistled. The light from the torches flickered over her body, highlighting her curves, exposing flesh beneath the gaping holes in her gown, and leaving shadows in all the right places. The jewels she wore in her hair, on her neck, and on her wrists glinted and sparkled.

She'd never appeared more beautiful, Molly thought.

The men quieted for a moment, the mood expectant, as Bunny opened the book *Tristram Shandy*. But when she began to read a portion of the familiar and hilarious tale of the long-nosed stranger from Strasbourg, they chuckled.

" 'I have made a vow to St. Nicholas this day, said the stranger, that my nose shall not be touched,' " read Bunny in a pompous voice, and as she continued the tale, the bachelors laughed—everyone but Sir Richard, that is. He sat with his arms crossed over his chest, and his lower lip stuck out.

And no wonder. *He* could be the long-nosed stranger from Strasbourg!

Molly wondered if that was Bunny's intent all along.

When she exited the stage with a bright smile on her face, Molly hugged her. "Were you doing what I think you were doing?"

"Yes," Bunny said, her voice catching, "and I'm never going to be alone with him again. Lord Harry's promised me a footman to guard my bedchamber tonight, and he's also informing Sir Richard he has the choice of sleeping in the stables or leaving this evening after the program. He assures me Sir Richard will stay far away from me from now on, and he's teaching me how to shoot a pistol just in case he ever shows up again!"

"Wonderful!" Molly hugged her again.

Athena strode past them to the stage. "I need silence," she hissed.

"Sorry," whispered Molly—too late—and looked at Bunny.

They both had to bite their lips to keep from laughing. Athena, much as they'd come to appreciate her, was always . . . Athena.

She positioned herself center stage, her shoulders thrown back. And with a twist of her lips, an arch of her brow, and an unholy glint in her eye—transformed herself into Lady Macbeth.

> "Come, you spirits
> That tend on mortal thoughts! unsex me here,
> And fill me from the crown to the toe top full
> Of direst cruelty; make thick my blood . . ."

Of course, Molly noted with envy, Athena had refused to *read* her passage. She'd memorized it, as all good actresses do. And at the moment she was living and breathing it, as all *great* actresses do.

She'd positioned herself so the torchlight cast shadows under her face, making her appear even more evil and demented than she sounded. The tattered, gaping dress added to the effect, especially when she swung her arms madly as she stalked about the stage.

"She appears possessed by a demon," Bunny whispered, and grabbed Molly's arm, which had gotten goose bumps as soon as Athena had begun speaking.

"Look at the men," Molly whispered back.

The bachelors sat in stunned silence. Sir Richard loosened his cravat. Lumley cringed as Athena swept by him, and even Lord Maxwell's stoic expression faltered. He blinked several times and drank from his flask when she demanded:

> *"Come to my woman's breasts,*
> *And take my milk for gall, you murdering*
> *ministers . . . !"*

At one point, she made a face so frightening that Hildur announced quite loudly, "She is a hound from hell!" into a void of silence. For at that exact moment, Athena ceased her performance.

She stood there, trembling, and for a few seconds, no one spoke or moved. But Lord Maxwell began a slow clapping. And all the other bachelors joined in until they were all applauding madly—with admiration and possibly a little relief, Molly surmised.

She couldn't help being glad the performance was over herself. When a moment later, a depleted Athena rejoined the mistresses, Molly swallowed and tried to say, "Well done," but she only got as far as "Well—" before her throat tightened.

"Yes, very—" Bunny began, but her voice trembled so much, she shut her mouth.

"Oh, it's just me now, you ninnies," Athena said. "Not Lady Macbeth."

But her lips curved in a self-satisfied smile. Apparently, she was well pleased to have frightened them so.

The whole mood changed when Joan walked onto the crude stage next.

"She's so different now, isn't she?" Molly asked Bunny. "She's no longer bitter and angry. She seems . . . at peace."

"Tonight, especially," Bunny replied. "And she looks glorious."

Yes, she did, thought Molly. Joan's gown was slit every which way, a chaotic golden backdrop in deep contrast to her stark beauty.

"I shall read 'Lullaby of an Infant Chief,' " she said in a clear, strong voice, and smiled serenely at her audience. "Composed by Sir Walter Scott."

Molly drew in a sharp breath of recognition. She suspected Joan had chosen the poem in honor of her own son. No wonder she wouldn't share any information with the ladies about what she was to read! Up until a few days ago, hers had been a private pain.

Joan knelt on the ground, bowed her head, and closed her eyes, as if preparing herself. When she opened her eyes a few seconds later, she made a curve of her left arm and gazed at the empty space there, as if she were cradling a baby.

"Oh!" said Bunny, and looked at Molly, little tears in her eyes.

Molly immediately welled up, too.

Joan began to rock slowly back and forth. And from a paper held in her right hand, she read:

"O hush thee, my babie, thy sire was a knight,
Thy mother a lady, both lovely and bright.
The woods and the glens, from the towers
*   which we see,*
They are all belonging, dear babie, to thee . . ."

The men were silent, but Molly could tell by their respectful faces they enjoyed Joan's solemn but heartfelt reading. Lumley even surreptitiously wiped at his cheek with a handkerchief.

When she was done, the men again clapped madly. She curtsied, threw them kisses, and left the stage.

"You were wonderful!" Bunny told her.

Molly hugged Joan. "We're so proud of you."

"Thank you both," she said with a sniffle.

Athena came running up. "Where's Hildur? She goes on next! We can't have a delay."

But she'd disappeared. Molly's heart skittered. She'd worked so hard with Hildur on her poem! What could have happened to her? Where could she be?

Thirty seconds passed, which was an age in the theater, according to Athena. With the aplomb of a seasoned actress, she walked onto the stage area, folded her hands, and said, "We shall have a brief intermission as it seems that Hildur is missing—"

"Wait!" Hildur cried from somewhere in the shadows. "I am *here*!"

And she entered stage left, a large scroll in one hand, as well as a stripped tree branch in the other.

Before Athena exited stage right, she threw a brief, concerned glance at the other mistresses.

"What's Hildur about?" Molly said. "The scroll is her poem, but why the branch?"

"And the sly smile?" Joan added.

"I've no idea," Bunny replied, "but I'm worried."

Athena shuddered. "Up close, she had a fierce Icelandic look in her eye that almost struck fear in my bold English heart. I believe it was the same look her ancestors had when they invaded other countries."

"Everything all right, Hildur?" Captain Arrow called out to her from the audience.

Hildur's brow was smooth, like an ice queen's, but then it furrowed. She stamped the butt of the tree branch on the ground and said, "No! It's not all right!" And she threw the branch to the ground.

CHAPTER 37

The mistresses inhaled a collective breath.

"Oh, dear," murmured Molly. "I believe all my tutoring has been for naught."

Hildur gave a small roar, held up the scroll, and ripped it down the middle. And then she ripped those pieces again—and again—and stomped on the pieces until they were a pulpy mess.

Why?

Molly had carefully copied the poem in large letters on the scroll, for easier reading. "Let's go, ladies," she said. "I sense she'll need many handlers."

Onstage Hildur was holding her branch again.

"Hildur," Molly whispered, and beckoned her offstage. "What will you do now? Do you remember the poem?"

"No," Hildur said, a sheen of tears in her eyes. "I don't want Byron's poem. He's no good. He loves too many women. So Cook tells me this very morning."

Athena sighed. "Joan tried to tell you the same thing. Days ago!"

Hildur shrugged. "Captain Arrow is much better than Byron. Captain Arrow likes Icelandic girls." She smiled. "I have a better plan for tonight."

"Tell us," said Athena.

"A story. From my country." And before any of the mistresses could counsel her further, she approached center stage.

Molly crossed her fingers and hoped for the best as Hildur told the tale in her beautiful, exotic language.

Which no one understood.

Nevertheless, there were highlights. First, her voice carried well, especially when she shrieked. And she was adept at walking like an old woman. And sucking her thumb like a baby. And then somehow she was the old woman spanking the baby, all at the same time.

"She's, um, quite a versatile actress," Bunny murmured.

"Either that, or she's crazy," Joan said.

Hildur raised her tree branch in the air and roared.

"Crazy," said Athena, her brow puckering. "Definitely crazy."

Molly couldn't help but chuckle. Hildur was her own woman, as the men were discovering.

And while no one understood her story, she certainly deserved points for trying her best.

She said something exuberant in Icelandic, beamed, and threw her arms in the air.

And the men clapped—politely at first, but then they began clapping in time, whistling, and yelling, "Brava! Brava!"

Athena came forward and addressed the audience. "We beg your patience as we take a moment to rest before we begin the last performance of the night—Delilah's."

Molly's relieved and happy mood changed in an instant. Her heart seemed to fall to her feet, and she couldn't feel her hands or legs anymore, from sheer terror.

She must do her own dramatic reading! Somehow she'd forgotten all about her own performance. She pretended that all was well as the mistresses returned to the dressing area and she told herself she'd practiced her poem several times. And she'd have the book right in front of her, wouldn't she? She'd simply read the words, read them the way Harry had taught her. And she'd sway as she walked—the way an alluring mistress would.

She'd forget about the long-ago Christmas incident, where she'd read a heartfelt poem and been severely punished as a consequence.

"Where's my book?" she said, but the excited chatter of the ladies was too loud for anyone to notice what she'd asked.

She tossed aside some of the gowns. "Where *is* my book?" The other mistresses were finally paying attention. "I left it right here. I'm reading 'Kubla Khan.'"

"I know," said Bunny. "It was right here. I saw it before we went to counsel Hildur."

Everyone looked, but no one found it.

Joan's eyes widened. "You don't think Sir Richard—"

"He couldn't have done it," Athena said. "He was in the audience."

"The whole time?" Bunny asked.

"I've no idea," said Molly. "And it got rather prickly there when Hildur, um, expressed her feelings before her performance. Perhaps he slipped away then."

"And did what with the book?" Bunny's eyes were wide with worry.

"Most likely destroyed it," Athena said.

Hildur narrowed her eyes. "I go get him. I find that book! And then I *kill* him!"

Joan laid a hand on her arm. "I'm sure it's too late. He probably dumped it in the lake."

"It's the only logical conclusion." Athena sighed.

Bunny shook her head. "I'm so sorry, Delilah."

"Let's tell the men," Joan said. "At the very least, they'll pummel him. And perhaps there's a slight chance he still has it on his person."

Molly looked out over the lake, which shimmered in the moonlight. She heard the murmur of the men's voices, an occasional chuckle, and swung back around to face the other mistresses. "Sir Richard's not that stupid. He would have gotten rid of it right away. Joan's right—he'd have thrown it out there." She gestured at the lake. "All he had to do was swing his arm, and it would have sailed out far enough that no one would ever know for sure whether he did it."

All the mistresses sighed.

"What will you do, Delilah?" Bunny laid a hand on her arm.

"I'll employ the same strategy we used with the gown debacle." Molly gave her a weak smile. "I'll outsmart him."

"How?" Hildur asked, her sky-blue eyes wide with concern.

"I'm not sure yet," said Molly. She tapped her index finger to her mouth. "The poem was too long—I didn't even attempt to memorize it."

"You can read from *Tristram Shandy*," offered Bunny.

"Thank you." Molly smiled. "But that was *your* reading. I wouldn't feel right doing the same thing."

And then she stopped breathing.

The same thing.

She had an idea—a very *good* one!

If she didn't lose her nerve.

She blew out an unsteady breath. "I'll read *your* poem, Hildur."

"But Delilah." Athena gave a light laugh. "She tore it up."

"I know." Molly's heart beat faster. "But it's not that long, and we went over it so many times, I—I think I can do it."

She blinked rapidly.

"I know you can," Bunny said, and gave her a hug.

Hildur patted her on the back. Too hard, of course. Joan fixed one of her stray curls, and Athena squeezed her hand. "Break a leg," she urged her.

Molly walked briskly to the stage. Alone. Except for a poem inside her that she must get out if she wanted to have any chance to win the Most Delectable Companion contest.

Harry noted, with a sort of wondrous pride, that Molly carried herself with confidence when she entered the makeshift stage, even though—

Good God. Even though the torchlight illuminated a goodly portion of her left breast! And there was another gaping hole in her gown, slightly above her thigh . . .

No. He wasn't seeing what he thought he was seeing. It was a trick of the light. Or perhaps it was the brandy.

"God help me," he muttered. It was bad enough that as she performed tonight, he'd be recalling the morning she'd read 'Kubla Khan' in his arms. Now he'd also be dreaming of her in that gown, imagining reaching his hand into one of those holes cut in the fabric and playing with that pert breast and—

He forced himself to stop indulging in such a fantasy. In less than an hour, Molly's time as his own very delectable companion would be over.

And they would be back to being country neighbors related by marriage.

But he had to give her credit. Without even trying, over this week she'd developed a mistress persona and protected her true identity. That was a marvel in itself. No one had come forward and unmasked her.

She'd managed to preserve the mystery.

Yet she'd also done the opposite. She'd worn her heart

on her sleeve, told everyone what she was thinking—
most noticeably, about the inequality of the games—and
offered her friendship to the whole company.

And in private, she'd held nothing back, either—when
they'd kissed and explored each other's bodies, when she
talked about her family and his, and most touching of all,
when she'd told him what was in her heart.

Harry sighed. How had she inverted everything he
thought he'd known best about women and men and created something . . . better?

That Molly, he must admit—the generous-hearted,
imaginative Molly—was the one who had him and everyone else here (save Sir Richard) wrapped around her
little finger.

"Hello," she said, and made a small arc with her right
hand.

"Hello," Harry and the other men said back.

There was a long silence.

There she stood, wringing her hands and staring out at
her small but captive audience. Harry smiled encourag-
ingly at her, but she seemed distracted. Unfocused.

Almost bleak.

"You can do it." He willed her under his breath to remember the morning they'd looked out her bedchamber
window and pretended that Xanadu was just through the
woods.

He saw her visibly inhale and exhale.

What was wrong, exactly? Something seemed off . . .
missing.

Wait—

Where was her copy of "Kubla Khan"? There was no
way she could have memorized it! It was much too long,
and she hadn't had time—

Harry half leaped up from the picnic cloth. "Delilah!"
he whispered loudly.

It was a question of sorts. But how would she answer it?

She looked directly at him, then said with a surety that stunned him, " 'When We Two Parted,' by Lord Byron."

Harry sensed immediately that the steely way she eyed him was her way of telling him to sit down—

Behave—

And believe.

In *her*.

Slowly, he sank back down to the ground, worried. Not so much about losing the competition. He was more concerned about Molly's own state of mind. Ever since the Christmas incident, she hadn't been able to speak in public.

So why was she changing course? Putting herself in what for her must be a terrifying position?

He didn't know. But he certainly couldn't ask her now.

She folded her hands in front of her and looked out over the men's heads toward the lake and the moon, where it had risen over the opposite shore.

" 'When we two parted,' " she began. " 'In silence and tears . . .' "

Her voice quavered—not a good start for her—and Harry's stomach clenched. But he forced himself to smile at her in support.

" 'Half broken-hearted,' " she said. " 'To sever for years . . .' " She didn't seem to notice him or anyone else at all.

" 'Pale grew thy cheek and cold,' " she struggled on. " 'Colder than thy kiss.' "

She was twisting her hands now, and he began to sweat. But then she took a breath: " 'Truly that hour foretold sorrow to this.' "

Thank God. She'd made it through a whole verse, with little pause. Harry forced himself to sprawl on the blanket and listen to her start the next verse as if he hadn't a care in the world. But he was seriously agitated. She might know the words, but she *must* relax more—put more feeling into the lines—if she were to charm his fellow Impossible Bachelors.

Then again, this particular poem wasn't one he'd have chosen to charm *anyone,* especially careless gentlemen. It was sad, after all. About two lovers parting ways—

Harry closed his eyes. Tried not to think.

Oh, God.

Two lovers.

Parting ways.

"'The dew of the morning,'" she said with more strength now. "'Sunk chill on my brow. It felt like a warning of what I feel now.'"

When he opened his eyes again, she was looking directly at him. Not at the lake. Not at anyone else. And it was as if she'd woken from a long slumber. Her eyes were expressive now, not distant. And her mouth, too. It was soft. Vulnerable.

By God, the words tumbled out of her, one by one, monuments each to something big and true and . . . *aching* inside of her. Harry couldn't stop listening, as much as he wanted to. And neither, apparently, could the other bachelors.

There was another verse—and more agonizing truth spilling from her whole being. She was talking about him, wasn't she? About loving him. And having to separate from him.

Him.

Harry swallowed hard. He saw Arrow cast a glance in his direction. And then Lumley and Maxwell and Bell. He sensed the mistresses were probably staring at him, as well.

"'In secret we met—'" Molly said, as earnest and

open as a flower. " 'In silence I grieve, that thy heart could forget, thy spirit deceive.' "

A gust of wind blew off the lake and shook the torch flames.

Molly was looking at her entire audience now. And it seemed as if it were composed of more than the bachelors and the mistresses . . . it was the very stars and moon above her head. The trees leaning in. The crickets chirping softly in time with the cadence of her words.

" 'If I should meet thee, After long years.' " She swallowed hard. " 'How should I greet thee?' "

" 'With silence,' " she eventually whispered, " 'and tears.' "

Harry couldn't move, even as the other bachelors began clapping for Molly—all of them but Sir Richard, of course. He sat sulking.

"She's something," Lumley called to Harry above the sound of the clapping and whistling.

"You're a lucky man," Arrow leaned over to say.

"I know it." Harry could barely utter the words.

He tensed his jaw to keep from showing any emotion. He felt too many. And they threatened to overwhelm him. So he began to clap—

For Molly.

When she finally looked up from her slippers, out at him and the other Impossible Bachelors, a soft smile played about her lips. A smile of triumph, of pride.

Not of sorrow.

The other mistresses came and hugged her close.

"We did it," Harry heard Molly say to them. "We *all* did it."

And they all began to laugh and talk at once.

They don't need us as much as we need them. Prinny's words echoed in Harry's mind as he uncorked his flask and found it empty.

Lumley tossed him his.

"Thanks." The brandy burned a hot trail down Harry's throat, and he wiped his mouth. "Let's get the votes counted," he said perfunctorily and tossed the flask back to Lumley.

Harry decided then and there he wouldn't try to understand. Anything. He simply needed to make it through this night. And get back to the life he had before this week began—a life that seemed far away and rather pathetic, but was most certainly easier to live.

CHAPTER 38

Molly walked with the other women to the log she and Harry had sat on so recently, and she felt a wisp of loneliness curl in her belly.

She and Harry would never sit on this log together again.

In a few moments, she'd find out if she had won the Most Delectable Companion contest. If so, Harry would win another year of freedom. If not, he'd be among those bachelors forced to pull straws, one of whom would find out tonight if he was to get legshackled to a woman of his club's choosing.

"How will you feel," said Molly to the other mistresses when she sat down, "if your bachelor is the one forced to marry?"

Bunny squeezed in next to her. "You know I wouldn't care. I shall be leaving him anyway."

"Really?" Athena was astounded. And so it seemed were Joan and Hildur.

Bunny nodded. "Yes. I was on the verge of telling Delilah earlier that I've a friend I can stay with in London. She's an assistant to a seamstress with a thriving business. I think she might be able to get me work."

Molly hugged her. "That would be too, too wonderful!"

Bunny smiled. "You inspired me, Delilah. Thank you for believing in me."

"The truth is, ladies," said Athena, "whether or not Maxwell draws the short straw, we shall soon part ways. He's not the sort to stay with one woman for long. And my career as an actress is providing me with sufficient income to live comfortably. I shall no longer require a protector."

"That's marvelous!" Molly said, and everyone clapped.

"Perhaps I can help with your costumes?" Bunny asked Athena. "And your gowns, as well, if you'd like."

Athena smiled and tossed her hair. "You must come to Drury Lane to visit me at your earliest convenience."

When it came to Joan's turn, she chuckled. "I have great affection for Lumley, of course. Who wouldn't?"

Molly knew exactly what Joan meant. Lumley had such a big heart.

"But he is more like a brother to me now," Joan went on. "And I say that as the highest compliment." Her eyes brimmed with tears. "He's providing me with sufficient funds to move north and be with my son and my sister. And then he's sending my son to a good school not far away from home."

There were gasps along the log, and happy tears were shed by all for some few minutes.

"And you, Hildur?" Molly eventually asked. "What will you do if Captain Arrow must marry?"

"I go where it's *hot*. I'm a pirate."

"You mean you'll find a pirate protector on an island somewhere?" asked Bunny.

"No," said Hildur, pointing to her chest. "*I* steal gold."

"Arrow told her he'd arrange her passage," Athena said, rolling her eyes.

Molly grinned. She could actually imagine Hildur as a female pirate!

"What are your plans, Delilah, if Lord Harry must get legshackled?" Joan asked. "Will you stay with him? When you performed tonight"—she hesitated—"it seemed as if you would be truly pained to be parted from him."

Molly looked around at the other mistresses. She'd been kidding herself, hadn't she? She'd tried so hard not to care about Harry beyond their friendship and kisses and jokes, but she loved him.

She loved him, and she wanted to be more than his mistress.

She did!

She wanted to be his *wife*.

She sighed. "I believe Harry, once settled into marriage, won't be the type of man to seek out a mistress. He would devote himself to his wife, whoever she is."

Whoever is lucky enough to win him, she thought.

There was a long silence.

"For Impossible Bachelors, this group is certainly more serious-minded than anyone thought, aren't they?" Joan said.

"Except for Sir Richard, of course," Bunny interjected.

"Yes," said Athena. "Except for him, they're all good men." She put her hand over Molly's. "If Lord Harry decides to have both wife *and* mistress, will you stay with him?"

Molly shook her head.

And then she had to shut her eyes. She felt that hot sand welling behind them that signaled tears about to flow. She squeezed her eyes shut harder, but one, lone tear escaped.

There was a painful silence.

"You *do* love him, don't you?" said Bunny.

Molly nodded, still unable to speak.

There were many sighs from the other mistresses.

"I understand why you wouldn't want to share the man you love with another woman," said Athena gently. "But sometimes it's the only way."

"That's the lot of the mistress," Joan reminded her.

Molly blew out a shaky breath. "I can't do that," she said. "I would rather be . . . *alone*."

And now she realized that she would. She couldn't be Harry's mistress. Not when he was a bachelor *or* married. Not when there were other women in his life.

Hildur patted her shoulder. "Start over."

"In a new life," said Bunny.

Or in her old one, Molly thought. Could she pick up where she'd left off? Could she go back to being the person she was before she'd taken off with Cedric on their ill-fated elopement?

She wasn't sure she could. She would have to take each day as it came. At least for now.

Athena stared at her, a thoughtful crease on her brow. "You're the only one of us here who really has a stake in this competition," she said. "If you won, it would mean another year of freedom for Lord Harry. A year he could spend with you."

Molly wished she could tell them that tonight, no matter what, was her last night with Harry. Because if she won, he was obligated to help her find a husband. And he'd made no promises to her that he'd be anything but his old, dissolute self, biding his time until he had to marry Anne Riordan.

But she couldn't tell her new friends. She'd promised Harry she would play the role of his mistress.

And she must play it to the end of the competition.

Would the other mistresses hate her if they found out her true identity was not that of a mistress at all? She hoped not, but she wouldn't blame them if they did.

"I want you to know," she said carefully, "your friendship has meant the world to me this week. The absolute world. I was so scared. And—and you made me feel at home."

Hildur wiped at her eyes. "I don't know what you say, but it's sad."

Molly patted her hand. "Whatever happens, I hope you know that I care for you all. Very much."

"And we, you, Delilah," said Bunny.

"It's time, ladies!" Harry's voice rang out.

The women exchanged hugs and best wishes.

And for the last time, they journeyed to the curtain.

CHAPTER 39

Once at the curtain, Molly noticed right away that the men had moved back far enough from the torches so their faces were in shadows.

"Ladies," she heard Harry say, "you've all done marvelously well this week. We wish all of you could win the title of Most Delectable Companion."

Lumley clapped and hooted.

"But we must choose only one winner," Harry went on. "We've tallied the votes, double-checked our figures, and now are proud to announce . . ."

Molly felt as if time slowed down then, even though Lumley slapped his thighs in a rapid tattoo, in imitation of a drum roll.

"The winner of the Most Delectable Companion title is—" Harry paused.

Molly clutched hands with Bunny and Athena.

"Delilah!"

Molly blinked. It didn't seem possible! *She?* The most delectable companion?

The other mistresses hugged her and congratulated her. But it was as if she were in a dream. She felt the same way when the men came forward. All of them wished her many happy returns, except Sir Richard, who stood alone, his lip curled.

Harry had a pleasant smile on his face but his gaze was carefully neutral. She supposed as host he didn't want to go overboard showing his joy at being the lucky bachelor whose name didn't have to go into the hat. That wouldn't have been sporting of him.

But she knew, however much she pretended not to care, that he must be thrilled to have another year of freedom. He despised the parson's mousetrap. He'd made that clear in his words and actions for years.

He held out the sparkling tiara. It was beautiful, Molly, thought, but it was made of worthless paste.

It was a sham.

Like her.

Like her week with Harry had been.

"Congratulations, Delilah," he said, rather formally.

"Thank you," she responded in kind.

And he kissed her cheek. It was a polite kiss, nothing more, signifying no connection between them beyond their obligations to each other as coconspirators in a fraudulent endeavor.

When Harry pulled back, Bunny took the crown from him and placed it on Molly's hair.

Lumley draped a beautiful purple cape over her shoulders, patted her back, and said, "Well deserved! You've got some money coming to you, you know. Don't forget that hundred pounds."

She leaned over to Bunny. "I'm giving *you* the money."

Bunny's eyes widened. "Whatever for? *You'll* need it."

"No. I—I've made an arrangement with Harry. If he throws me over, he'll pay me a great sum. Besides, if I keep the money, I'll waste it on . . . queen cakes. I have an obsession with them."

"A lady shouldn't overindulge in queen cakes, Delilah," Bunny scolded her affectionately.

Molly grinned. "Which is exactly why you shall use my winnings to start your own sewing business. No arguments."

"You're too generous." Bunny threw her arms around her and squeezed.

Molly forced herself to smile, to act happy. She would simply hang on until they left this place—until she could be completely alone somewhere and cry her heart out.

She spun for all the company, allowing her beautiful purple cape to billow and sink back around her legs, her crown to sparkle in the torchlight.

Why was love such torture? she wondered, as she smiled at her well-wishers.

And why were happy endings as impossible as the bachelor she so desperately wanted?

CHAPTER 40

It was four-thirty in the morning. And Harry was properly drunk, as the winner of the Impossible Bachelors wager should be, in his estimation. He lay sprawled on his back on the floor of the library, Maxwell, Lumley, and Arrow lounging in leather seats surrounding him. The fire was low. An empty decanter of brandy sat on Harry's father's desk.

"You know, Delilah's not a real mistresh," Harry mumbled, looking up at the ceiling, which began to spin slowly to the right. It was such a dizzying sight, he accidentally let his empty glass roll out of his palm. "She's falsh. Falsh as they come."

And God, it was driving him crazy.

Maxwell rubbed his eyes. "If Delilah's not a real mistress, then I'm a *woman*."

Arrow laughed. He laughed so hard he snorted brandy through his nose.

"Really," said Harry, turning his face toward the men. The Aubusson rug scratched his cheek. "She's a virgin, dammit." And he shook his head and moaned. Because shaking his head hurt. And spending all his time pining after a virgin was . . . torture.

Lumley threw a cheroot at him, and it bounced off Harry's nose. "Shuddup. Arrow's the good joke teller. Not you. Stick to riding curricles to Brighton."

"We don't need jokes anyway," Maxwell said to them all, and rubbed his eyes. "We've another year in which to run riot."

"Egg-zhackly," muttered Arrow.

Maxwell raised his glass. "Here's to . . . escaping the marital noose," he said. "And to Sir Richard's choosing the short straw instead."

"Hear, hear!" came the chorus from Harry and the others.

Lumley hiccupped. "And to Sir Richard's shoon-to-be bride. The poor woman. Whoever the club board chose for him."

"Yessss," Harry said. "I feel for her."

Everyone but Harry touched snifters. His was somewhere near the hearth, out of reach.

"We must let Bell know she's off limits for beatings, too," said Harry. "Else we shall make him most unhappy."

There was a murmur of assent.

"Where *is* Bell?" asked Maxwell.

"He took off . . . in a *snit*," said Lumley. "Got a servant to prepare his carriage. And Bunny wouldn't go with him. She says Delilah gave her the hundred pounds she won. Bunny's setting up her own sewing shop."

"Good for her!" said Harry.

"Here's to Delilah, as well," said Lumley. "She should set up her own tart shop." He paused and thought for a moment. "Not *that* kind of tart. The kind you bake in the oven. With losh and losh of apples."

Harry contemplated that possible future for Molly for a fuzzy minute.

Arrow sighed. "I suppose I'm free now to go on another voyage round the Cape."

"How many times is that?" Harry asked.

"Five," Arrow replied.

Maxwell lofted a brow. "And I'll continue minding my own business when I'm not pulling my brother out of scrapes."

"Sounds . . . thrilling," said Harry.

"I'll travel to my new castle," said Lumley, kicking his shoe at nothing.

"You've another?" Harry laughed.

Lumley sighed. "It's in the north of Scotland." He turned his brandy glass upside down and held it over his mouth. One drop fell out. "I think I'll learn how to shear sheep. You know how difficult that izzh?"

None of them did.

"Izzh difficult," said Lumley sadly. "Sheep shmell. Would any of you like to try?"

Arrow shrugged. "Sure. Why not shear sheep?"

"Tha's right," said Maxwell. "Ish as good an occupation as any."

"And no one'll miss me if I take a bit of shore leave," said Arrow.

"I'm up for it," said Harry. Certainly, no one would miss him, either. Except, perhaps, Anne Riordan.

"Good. I'll lesh you know when." Lumley turned to Harry. "What will you do in the meanwhile, Traemore?"

Harry scratched the side of his nose. "Oh, you know. The usual. Go to London, meet some beautiful women."

"Izzhat all?" asked Arrow.

Harry shrugged. "I suppose."

He had something *else* to do in London, but he couldn't remember it at the moment. It was the real reason he'd gotten so drunk tonight.

What was it again? It caused his gut to ache, but for the life of him, he couldn't remember.

Good.

Because he didn't *want* to remember.

There was a bleak silence in the room.

Harry rolled over onto his stomach. The rug fibers tickled his nose enough that he found the focus he needed to stand on rather wobbly legs. "Thank God we've made it, gentlemen. But I think I'll retire now. My head . . . ish becoming a bit sore."

"More drink will cure that," said Maxwell, with a hiccup. He handed Harry his empty brandy glass. "Here. Have mine."

Harry stared at it. "Thank you, Maxwell."

"You're welcome, my friend." And then Maxwell's head fell back and he began to snore.

"Lesh carry him up," said Lumley. "Whaddya say?"

Harry took Maxwell's arms. Arrow and Lumley took his legs. And somehow they managed to get him up the stairs and to his bedchamber.

Harry made it to his own, even though the hallway was spinning. He wished it would stop.

Molly. He needed Molly.

She would help his bedchamber stop spinning. And she would kiss him and tuck him in and maybe get under the sheets with him. He wouldn't bother her. He just wanted her to sleep next to him.

He would hug her close because it was going to be a chilly night and he didn't want her to catch cold.

A gray light seeped between his bedroom curtains. Was it close to morning already?

Damn, but he was starting to feel chilled. And his room was still spinning. He'd best get Molly. She was only next door.

Molly gave a shriek. There was a ghostlike figure, smelling strongly of spirits, swaying right above her. "Harry. What are *you* doing in here?"

"The room's spinning, Molly. I need—" He paused as if he couldn't remember what to say.

"What do you need?" she asked.

"You," he said.

"Whatever for?"

He shrugged. "Because. Just because."

"Harry." Molly blew out a breath. "You're drunk."

"I am?"

"Yes." She threw back the covers. "Now come with me."

She took his arm and led him from her room, through the dressing room, and into his own.

He groaned a little. "D'ya have to go so fast?"

He stood near the side of his bed and she pushed him down on it. He immediately lay back and groaned some more.

She took off his boots.

"You're so pretty," he mumbled. "I can't stop thinking about that dress you wore tonight. The one with the holes . . ."

He trailed off.

"You need to sleep," she said, and laid a blanket from the bottom of his bed over him.

He patted the bed. "Come lie down with me. I won't touch you. I just want . . . a kiss. How's that?"

"How can you *not* touch me—and kiss me—at the same time?"

"Wha'?" He lifted his head for a moment and let it drop.

She leaned over him, pushed his jet-black hair out of his eyes. "You sleep, Harry. We're leaving here in a few hours. I suspect you'll be miserable, but at least sleep now."

He grabbed her elbow. "I want you to stay."

She shook her head. "No, Harry."

"But you're my mishtresh," he said.

"You know I'm not," she said back. "I'm a respectable female again."

He closed his eyes and groaned. "Oh, God. I remember now."

"Remember what?"

"Nothing."

But a terrible crease furrowed his brow. He'd surely remembered something unpleasant. Or perhaps he was ill from drink. She'd heard of men getting awful headaches after a night of drinking. She'd be cruel to leave him in such a state.

She went to the other side of the bed, crawled onto the feather ticking, and lay down gently beside him. "I'm here," she whispered.

"Good," he said, his eyes still closed.

She didn't know who made the move first—it seemed as if they'd both thought of it together—but they laced hands.

"G'night, Molly." He gave her hand a little squeeze. "Don't forget, all right?"

"Don't forget what?"

"The Moroccan tent," he whispered. "Or the lake. When we threw the blackberries."

She bit her lip. Hard. The pain helped her keep the crying at bay. "I won't, Harry," she eventually managed to say back.

But he was already fast asleep.

CHAPTER 41

An hour later, Molly slipped out of Harry's bed before he awoke and met the mistresses for an early breakfast. Molly doubted she would ever see them again. She couldn't very well give them her address at Marble Hill, could she?

But saying good-bye to Bunny was proving to be too difficult. The footman left the dining room to bring several platters back to the kitchen, and the other mistresses excused themselves to finish packing.

Both Molly and Bunny stood in the doorway, watching Athena, Joan, and Hildur ascend the stairs.

Bunny turned back to her. "Before I go, I must thank you again, Delilah, for the money." She hugged Molly, then drew back and took her by the shoulders. "I know I'll never forget you. And I hope you shan't forget me."

Bunny's gaze was warm, trusting. It was enough to make Molly come to a decision.

"Of course I won't forget you," she said. "And perhaps I'm rash to confide in you, but—" She swallowed hard. How could she tell her friend that she'd lied all week?

Bunny took her arm and drew her deeper into the drawing room, to the corner by the sideboard. "Please do tell me what's bothering you," she said, affectionate concern in her voice. "You've always been such a help to me."

Molly bit her lip. "Would you hate me too terribly much if"—she turned to face her friend squarely—"if I told you that I'm not a *real* mistress?"

Bunny blinked several times. Then she put her hand to her mouth, which was open in a wide O, and after an awkward few seconds, she dropped her hand and chuckled. "Delilah, are you telling another amusing anecdote?"

Molly shook her head. "It's true. I—I've been an imposter. All week."

Bunny went back to the dining room table and sank into a chair. Molly sat down next to her, took Bunny's hand, and squeezed it. Then she proceeded to explain, in a low voice, how she'd come to be at the house party.

Bunny pressed a palm to her chest. "So your real name is Molly." She smiled. "It suits you."

Thank God. Thank God she hadn't gotten up and walked away in a huff.

"Yes," said Molly weakly. "I like it better than Mary. I'm actually . . . Lady Mary Fairbanks. My father is the Earl of Sutton."

Bunny's mouth fell open again. *"No."*

Molly nodded vigorously.

Bunny clapped her hand over her mouth to stifle a giggle. But she couldn't. She laughed aloud, her beautiful face alight with mirth. "Oh, Molly!"

Molly laughed, too. She should have known—Bunny was a true friend.

Bunny sighed. "What a *tale*. But I'm delighted. I'm so happy to know that"—she hesitated, looked around to make sure the footman hadn't come back, nor any other guests—"perhaps you have a chance with Lord Harry."

Molly's heart sank. Just thinking of Harry and how

unattainable he was made her depressed. "I don't think so, Bunny. He enjoys being a bachelor."

Bunny squeezed her elbow. "They all fall at some point. And I—I think he has feelings for you. In fact, I'm sure of it. Please don't give up hope."

The footman came back then, and their cozy talk was over. But when Molly hugged Bunny good-bye this time, she felt worlds better, even as her heart was heavy about Harry. If he had feelings for her, nothing would stop him from acting upon them! And he hadn't acted. So that was Molly's answer.

She gave Bunny her address at Marble Hill and begged her to write as soon as she got settled into her new situation, which Bunny promised to do.

And then it was time to leave.

The subsequent journey to London was a miserable affair. Molly had to endure the powder and rouge and kohl for another day, and she wore Fiona's most voluminous bonnet. It wasn't safe to be seen so far from home without a disguise.

Harry had to exit the carriage twice within the first hour of leaving the hunting box to be sick. Eventually, he decided to ride on top of the carriage with his coachman.

But Molly wasn't alone in the interior of Harry's vehicle. He'd procured a maid from the village to act as chaperone. All morning, she chattered away. Molly barely listened. Instead, she reflected on the fact that she was going back home to her old life.

Without Cedric, thank God.

But still. Her old life.

She tried to be excited about the possibilities, but she couldn't. What possibilities were there? Too much had happened in the past week, the main thing being that she'd fallen in love—with the wrong man.

"You all right, miss?" the maid asked her sometime after the sun had risen above the trees.

Molly sighed. "I'm fine, thanks."

"We'll be stopping soon." She took Molly's shawl and draped it over her. "You seem a bit ill. Perhaps a special punch would do you good."

An hour later at a small posting inn, Molly shared a "special punch," prepared at the maid's direction, with Harry.

"Good afternoon," he said to her, his voice rough. He drained his cup of punch and stared at her, quite as if he didn't see her at all.

It was the first they'd spoken all day.

"Good afternoon," she said back, and took a reluctant sip of her punch. But it was good, and powerful. It warmed her, so she finished it quickly.

"It seems we're both under the weather." The corners of Harry's eyes were etched with creases.

"Perhaps the punch will do the trick and return us to fine fettle." Molly gave him a wan smile to mask how little she believed that.

"Indeed." He cleared his throat. "I've been meaning to tell you: I haven't forgotten our bargain."

"Oh?" She pretended she'd forgotten, when really, it had been all she could think about since she'd won . . . Harry going back to his disgraceful ways. And Harry using those selfsame skills to weed out bad potential mates for her.

"Yes," he said rather stiffly. "Our bargain. You won the contest, so I shall be looking for a suitable husband for you in London."

"Oh. How kind of you." She didn't know what else to say.

His eyebrows lowered. "I'm not being at all kind. A man doesn't go back on his word."

She clenched her reticule and backed away. "Very well. I think I shall go back to the carriage now. If you don't mind."

He seemed to realize he'd been not as charming as he should. "Wait. Please."

She hesitated.

He attempted a smile. "Pray forgive me my ill manners today. I was foolish to overindulge in spirits the night before a long journey."

She nodded and withdrew her hand. "Apology accepted."

Oh, well.

Her ills wouldn't be cured after a day, that was certain.

She hastened back to the carriage.

CHAPTER 42

Harry sat at his club, nursing a brandy a little past noon. He was reading the newspaper and contemplating how he would spend the rest of his day. Gaming right here at the club? More boxing at Gentleman Jackson's? Or finally calling upon the widow who'd been pestering him for a discreet affair?

None of those options appealed to him—the affair, least of all.

Clamoring in his brain was a tiny yet strong voice, the one he'd first heard in Molly's presence. Dare he? Dare he attempt to follow through on what he'd told her?

He wanted to do something—*be* something—of value.

After all, look at the other Impossible Bachelors: Maxwell, with his scientific papers; Arrow, the brave sea captain.; and Lumley, who was capable of running more than several estates and managing a very large fortune.

Tentatively, Harry put aside his newspaper and pulled a small notebook out of his pocket. He would call for a quill and some ink. And then he would write down all his plans.

"Enjoying yourself, eh?" said an old gent, Lord Humphries.

Harry raised his glass and quirked his mouth in a pleasant grin. "That I am, sir."

Lord Humphries laughed and punched his shoulder.

Dear God. The shoulder punch. Harry knew what *that* signified. He forced himself to smile at Lord Humphries . . . and waited to hear the dreaded words.

The old gentleman opened his mouth. "If only I were—" he began.

"Excuse me!" Harry leaped up. *If only I were your age again* was surely the phrase Lord Humphries was about to utter. "I believe someone is calling your name for a game of whist, sir."

"Whist?" Lord Humphries eyed the crowd at the tables. "Who? Where?"

"I—I'm not sure." Harry gave the man a respectful bow, scooped up his notebook, and left his half-drunk glass of brandy on the table. He didn't know how many more congratulations he could take. Or the punches to the shoulder. Or the reminiscences of youth.

Really, being the winning Impossible Bachelor had its merits, but it had its flaws, too. Every rout, every ball, he attended in town in the Little Season was but a precursor to what he was to expect when a greater portion of the *ton* descended upon London for the regular Season come springtime.

Already matchmaking mothers, restrained by Prinny's decree from pestering him, spoke about him from behind their fans and gave him calculating looks. Young misses ran as if he were a scary monster rather than a mere rake of somewhat undeserved repute. The men mobbed him, peppering him with questions about what it was like to be able to remain free—free of legshackles.

Free of expectations.

He'd always been free of expectations, hadn't he? So this notoriety—as well as every man-about-town activity he'd once viewed with enthusiasm and pleasure—was actually somewhat . . .

Boring.

Predictable.

Harry was at serious loose ends, for the first time in his bachelor existence. Which was why he would hold on to this idea of his. And if he worked hard enough, he could present it to his father next time he saw him.

Which would be soon. The duke had summoned Harry to come home for a small country ball to be held in honor of Roderick and Penelope's return from Italy. And Harry was actually looking forward to going. Not so much to see Roderick and Penelope and their girls—although he had a great deal of affection for all of them—but in the hopes that he'd see Molly there.

Everything he'd done since the week of the wager, he wondered what she would think of the activity. Which was why he'd been with no lightskirt or society widow since he'd last seen her.

He'd feel . . . disloyal somehow.

Not prepared for the anonymity of the act when it took place with a hired girl—and certainly not ready for the jaded outlook of the widows who made clear their desire to be with him . . . *that way.*

He smiled to himself. *That way.* It sounded like something Molly would say.

But then he frowned. Because, really, he must find her a suitable husband. It was another duty of his.

Perhaps he could kill two birds with one stone, bring several potential grooms with him for Molly *and* pay his respects to his father and the rest of his family.

That's what he'd do.

He looked around him. The club was full. Surely in the next half hour, he could drum up three or four respectable friends who'd be willing to come with him to his father's country ball. On the way down, he'd drop little hints about the wonderful young ladies they'd be sure to meet there, especially one named Molly Fairbanks, a sweet little heiress whose father had buried her in the country the past three years. But had she been to London, he'd tell them, she would have taken it by storm.

And she would have, he thought, as he searched the gaming tables, and even the seats in the bow window, for appropriate candidates for her hand.

If only she'd been given the chance.

Any woman who could win the title of Most Delectable Companion when she wasn't even a mistress could even take *Paris* by storm, much less stuffy old London. Not that he could put it quite that way to his friends. But somehow, he would convey her allure. And were he to fail, when they saw her in person they would understand.

If they didn't, they'd have to be asleep. Or dead.

Of course, he hadn't noticed her allure until recently himself. But that was because of their long history, starting with that damned Christmas incident.

Suddenly, he felt the fiercest anger about that. He and Molly had been children. Penelope, too, for that matter. But for years Harry and Molly had paid the price for that one, silly kiss between him and Penelope, and a poem expressing a young girl's infatuation with an unattainable boy. It was time for a new page in their lives, wasn't it? It was time to get past that Christmas incident once and for all.

Harry would dance with Molly at the ball. Not twice, of course. That would signify a special attachment between them. He would dance with her just to show the neighbors how distant the past truly was.

And how exciting the future could be. Because Harry intended to announce his plan at the ball. And if his father liked it, he could thank that long ago day—the Christmas incident—for providing Harry the inspiration.

"Are you sure you're well, Molly?" Lord Sutton growled at her one morning, about a month after her return home. He'd been none the wiser about her absence. Neither had the servants or Cousin Augusta. She'd laid the ground well before she'd eloped with Cedric, little realizing how differently things would turn out.

She poked at her eggs. "Yes, Papa. I'm well."

"You usually eat like a horse."

She shrugged. "I'm feeling quite the thing, I assure you."

Which was an out-and-out lie. She'd never been more miserable.

Lord Sutton cut into his morning beefsteak. "You haven't been the same since I got back." He chewed, stared at her, and swallowed. "And quite frankly, neither have I. I'm still baffled by Cedric's disappearance. I'm considering employing another assistant unless I hear from him in the next day or two. Are you sure he didn't say where he was going?"

Molly felt her face flame red.

"Oho!" Her father eyed her suspiciously. "Was something going on between you and Cedric that I didn't know about?"

"No, Papa. Nothing. And I don't miss Cedric. Not one bit. I hope he never returns."

"The lady doth protest too much," Lord Sutton said with a chuckle. He took a sip of beer, gave a lip-smacking sigh, and set his tankard on the table with a great thunk. "Tell you what," he said. "I shall speak with him when he returns. You two should marry. The more I think about it, the more I like the idea. *You*—and Cedric!" He chuckled with delight. "You'll stay with me forever and keep making me those delicious tarts—and he'll be my assistant and watch over my artifacts when I die."

Papa appeared very pleased with himself.

Molly put down her fork. "*No,* thank you, Papa. And I—I've been meaning to discuss something with you."

"What?"

"Cedric and I are not suited"—she paused, took a breath—"but I certainly would like a Season in town."

"You're too old for a Season!" Lord Sutton sputtered. "You're practically on the shelf!"

She felt her mouth tremble. "And I have you to thank for that, Papa. You've kept me buried here with Cousin Augusta. Why?"

Lord Sutton's face turned red. "How dare you question my judgment? I know what's best for you."

Molly sighed and walked around the table to be close to her father. Sinking into a chair next to him, she said, "All these years, ever since that unfortunate Christmas incident, I've either gone to a very strict school or I've been here with you and Cousin Augusta. I love you, Papa, but I've missed countless balls in London. I've never had flowers delivered to my door after a soiree or rout. And I've been becoming a spinster, slowly but surely."

Lord Sutton's shoulders sank a few inches.

Molly put her hand on top of his and schooled her voice to be gentle. "You taught me yourself, through your work to preserve the past, to not let life pass me by without truly seeing it as it unravels. Please." She gave him a beseeching gaze. "I would like to have some memories of a London Season."

Lord Sutton sighed. "All right," he said. "One Season." He chucked her chin. "Are you sure you won't have Cedric?"

"I'm sure, Papa." She leaned over and kissed his cheek. "And thank you for being so understanding."

He grimaced, never one to like displays of affection.

"You're very welcome," he granted her. "It is but the beginning of October. You have several months to wait. We'll rent my good friend's house on Jermyn Street from January to June."

"And meanwhile, we might have to make a trip up to London, so I can shop for a new wardrobe," she said, brightening at the thought.

Lord Sutton rolled his eyes. "I suppose that might be necessary. We shall leave tomorrow."

"Why so soon?"

"You'll need some clothes sooner than you think," he said. "There is to be a small ball in a fortnight at the duke's residence. To celebrate Penelope and Roderick's return from Italy."

Molly blinked. "Of course. I should have thought of that. Do you suppose Harry will be there?"

Lord Sutton frowned. "Why should we care? But I suppose he probably will."

Molly's curiosity about Harry was soon put to rest. She was pruning some roses in the garden later that afternoon when a housemaid came to her with a note.

"A letter for you, Lady Molly." The maid bobbed a curtsy and left her with the shears dangling from one hand and the letter in the other.

Molly's heart raced. She put the shears down and broke the seal. It was a note from Harry. After much deciphering of his appalling scrawl, she figured out that he would be coming to the ball.

Harry! At the ball! She held the paper to her lips and savored the news for a moment. But as she continued reading, a cold chill spread from her feet to her hands. Harry wrote that he'd be bringing some friends down from London who would be suitable marriage prospects for her. And she should be ready to flirt.

Of course she should. She sighed, folded the letter. He was only doing as she asked, so why was she so . . . disappointed?

She fingered a rose and tried to swallow the lump in her throat.

Oh, she was more than disappointed, wasn't she? She was heartbroken. That was her problem. She loved Harry. And he—

He obviously didn't love her.

They'd had fun together, yes! The most fun she'd ever had with anyone.

But he didn't love her.

She stared at the bottom of the note. He'd signed his name with a large *H* followed by some more indecipherable scribble.

Harry.

Molly folded the letter and tucked it in the pocket of her garden apron. Harry's teachers must have despaired of his handwriting when he was a boy. So typical of him not to care.

Yet so endearing, too.

But she couldn't smile.

No, she had to stop thinking of him. Stop thinking of all those things she loved about him.

She put away her shears. Then she walked into the house, up her father's wide staircase, and to her room to pack for the trip to London. She was in the market for a husband. Perennial bachelors with bad penmanship simply wouldn't do.

CHAPTER 43

"I've got big news, brother," Roderick said, tying his cravat in the looking glass.

"Let me guess." Harry took a sip of his brandy.

It was early evening, and his parents' ball would commence in less than an hour. Harry was in the opulent suite Roderick and Penelope shared when they stayed with the duke and duchess.

"You know already, don't you?" Roderick smiled.

Harry put the brandy down and stood up. "I can tell just by that grin on your face. Your fertility *and* your legacy are assured. Penelope is with child, and you think it's a boy."

Roderick laughed. "Yes, you devil. Is it that obvious I'm proud to have caused my beautiful wife to breed yet again?"

"Yes, it is." Harry slapped him on the back. "Well done. And how are you so sure this time that she'll produce a son?"

Roderick sighed. "She feels different, she said. And her maid did some kind of trick with a spoon on a string and proclaimed the babe to be a boy. But truth be told, if we have another little Penelope, I'd be equally glad."

"You know what this means, don't you?" asked Harry.

"Not exactly," Roderick replied, pouring himself his own brandy.

"If you have a boy, I will no longer be the spare."

Roderick paused. "You're right."

"I shall be released from the one duty I've been carrying all my life."

Roderick gazed at him. "I can't tell if you're relieved—or will somehow miss it."

Harry raked a hand through his hair. "I'm mixed, actually. Being the spare has defined me all these years. As being the heir has defined you."

Roderick nodded in understanding. "It does get rather wearying, doesn't it?"

The brothers both sat on the edge of the bed. "I sometimes think, Roderick"—Harry felt his jaw clenching—"that even now, Father doesn't know me. Or care to."

Roderick sat silent for a moment, then said, "He isn't the most affectionate of men." He lightly punched Harry's arm. "I should have noticed you more. Given you that attention every boy needs."

"You needed it, too."

Roderick shrugged. "I got plenty of attention from Father. It might not have been warm, or particularly personal, but I *did* feel important." Roderick threw out an arm and intoned, "What would happen to the world without the house of Mallan? It would stop spinning." He grinned, but it was wistful. "That was the feeling I got from Father."

They sat quietly again, and Harry noticed he felt happy, despite the awkwardness of their conversation. It was good to sit with his brother and be . . . accepted.

"I knew I always had you," Harry blurted out, his voice hoarse. With emotion, he supposed. Ever since that week at the hunting box with Molly, and all the feelings he'd felt there, he'd been more emotional than he'd ever been. He swallowed hard. "Thank you for believing in me when the whole world didn't."

Roderick lowered his brandy. "You mean . . . about what happened to you in the army?"

Harry nodded. "It's been difficult. Really difficult. To not be able to defend myself."

Roderick sighed. "Is that why you've simply . . . given in? Been what everyone expects of you?"

"Yes," Harry said. "Part of it. Especially because Father expects so little of me. I'm not quite sure he believes I was protecting a lady's honor. And still am."

"Harry," Roderick remonstrated with him. "As much as Father knows you're doing the right thing, the frustrated parent in him doesn't like standing by doing nothing. Trust me, I know, now that I'm a father myself, how much I'd hate to feel useless if one of our girls were in trouble."

Harry sighed.

"He may not show it," Roderick said, "but he loves you. He does. Feel sorry for him that he can't show it more readily." Roderick paused. "Do you love *him*, Harry?"

Harry stared at the floor. Did he? Did he love the man who'd shown him almost no attention and definitely no affection—for his entire life?

His brow creased. "Yes," he said, looking at Roderick. "I do. I don't know why, but I do."

"Then tell him. Don't wait for him to tell *you*. That might never happen, but you can tell him. And be at peace. Finally. That's another reason you're an Impossible Bachelor, isn't it? Because you're angry."

Harry stared at Roderick. "Yes," he said. "I'm angry."

Roderick's gaze locked onto his. His expression was concerned. Accepting.

Hopeful.

Harry smiled. "It's time to move on, isn't it?"

Roderick nodded. "I'm proud of you for realizing it. I knew it long ago, but unless it comes from your own heart—it can't happen, can it?"

They both stood. A beat passed, and then Harry threw his arms around his brother and squeezed him hard.

"Thanks," he whispered.

Roderick hugged him back. "No. Thank *you* for being there for *me*. Now that I look back on it, you always have been."

Harry laughed. "Except for one time."

"Oh, yes," Roderick drawled. "When you kissed *my wife*."

"She wasn't your wife *then*."

Roderick laughed. "Actually, that episode brought me around. I'm afraid I'd been taking her a bit for granted. I've never taken her for granted since."

"Well, you'd best not quit now. We're five minutes late, you know, for the gathering in the drawing room."

Roderick rolled his eyes in mock horror. "There'll be hell to pay from Mother *and* Penelope, won't there?"

"Yes, but I'm used to it from Mother," said Harry.

"Just wait until you get married."

"That'll be the day," Harry murmured with a wicked grin.

They both chuckled and bounded down the stairs. Harry watched Roderick sail to Penelope's side and kiss her soundly.

The retorts Harry used to defend his bachelor status were so habitual he could recite them in his sleep. But somehow, today, in light of Roderick and Penelope's wonderful news and their . . . *togetherness*, those platitudes rang false even to his own ears.

Which was rather disconcerting.

Was he losing his touch?

He decided he rather didn't care at the moment.

There were more important things to think about. Like family. And friends. And having a good time at a small country ball thrown by an overbearing duke who just might happen to love him, after all.

CHAPTER 44

Molly's palms were damp. She couldn't wait to see Harry. It had been six long weeks! How would she act toward him? And how would he act toward her?

She knew she was a fool to wonder. Harry was free to be a bachelor and, as far as she knew, that's exactly what he'd been doing. According to the gossip rags, he'd been out and about all over London, although she noticed that in no report did his actions appear to be more dissolute than any other bachelor's.

They were dissolute enough, however, to bring her pain. Was he already entangled with another woman?

At least she knew she looked her best. Her gown came straight from London. Papa, dear man, had spared no expense. It was a pale rose colored muslin—almost white—with the most delicate sheer sleeves. The neckline was modest enough, but the skirt was sprinkled with translucent beading which shimmered as she moved. And in her hair, which was miraculously holding its curl, she wore a cluster of pale pink roses.

At the balcony overlooking the ballroom, Molly waited in the receiving line to greet her host and hostess, after which she'd descend the massive staircase to join the festive crowds below. She realized she should be quite comfortable—the duke's home was practically her home. She'd been coming here since she was a baby, and her sister was now the duke's daughter-in-law.

But things had forever changed after the house party. And now, she couldn't believe how she'd never noticed Harry before that time . . . in the way a woman notices a man.

She lost her father on the staircase—he was somewhere in the crowd below her.

But then he found her and touched her arm. "Go on without me, Molly. I must have a chat with Lord Winston, and I left my spectacles in the carriage. I shall be back momentarily."

She was on close enough terms with Harry's family to go through the receiving line on her own, of course.

"As you wish, Papa," she said, and proceeded onward.

She couldn't look down the line for Harry—she was much too preoccupied with greeting his parents. She wondered if she'd ever stop being intimidated by His Grace. She somehow doubted it, but the duchess made up for his controlled, intimidating manner.

"So good to see you, Molly." The duchess smiled rather tenderly and squeezed her hand. "Do you know you look more like your mother with each passing day?"

Molly felt a rush of warmth fill her. "I do?"

"Most certainly," replied the duchess. "I hope you enjoy yourself tonight, dear."

Molly thanked the duchess and moved on to Penelope and Roderick, who were even more pleased to see her, of course. She gave them both the warmest of embraces.

"You look gorgeous," Penelope gushed. "And it's been an agony not seeing you sooner." She hadn't had a moment to travel over to Marble Hill with the girls since coming home from Italy three days ago. She and the duchess had been busy with the ball preparations.

But Molly understood. And she couldn't wait to have time alone with her big sister. She had a glow about her—it was love, of course. Love given *and* returned. Something that she felt destined never to experience herself. But she could be happy for Penelope, and she was. Genuinely so.

And in the midst of that happiness for Penelope, Molly sensed, rather than saw, that the object of her unrequited affections was very near. While she spoke to her sister about her favorite Italian haunts, she heard Roderick turn to his left and say, "Here's the little hellion that caused you to join the army, Harry."

And that's when she saw him. Her insides instantly turned to jelly. In his perfectly cut evening clothes, Harry was more handsome than ever. Yet there was also a solitariness about him, a reserve, that he hadn't had at the hunting box. Perhaps it was because he was around his family.

Molly could tell by the light in his eye that he was well pleased to see her. He kissed the back of her hand, and the shock of his touch sent ripples of pleasure through her.

"My friends from London shall be asking you to dance," he continued rather low, even thought Roderick and Penelope were now immersed in conversation with two old spinsters. "I shall introduce you to them myself when I'm done here."

Molly felt her bubble of happiness deflate. "Thank you, Harry." She managed a smile. "I'm most obliged."

"It is my firmest desire to fulfill my promise to you," he said with a gravity to his tone that she'd never heard before.

He took her hand once more and kissed it. She made sure her smile stayed frozen in place until she was free of the receiving line—as she must be free of him.

He'd made a promise to help her find a husband. But

did he have to be so happy to fulfill it? She must move on. She'd flirt with his friends. And if all went well, perhaps tonight she would dance with the man she would marry.

Harry didn't mind that he'd got caught up in a circle of women surrounding his mother. She'd called him over to answer questions from them about his plans for the future. His parents and their cronies were *always* asking him his plans for the future.

For the first time, he had some. "I'm starting a small press," he told the ladies.

His mother gasped. She smiled. And then tears sprang to her eyes.

Harry was rather overwhelmed with emotion himself.

"Mother, dear." He took her hand and smiled. "My first effort at the Traemore Press shall be a compilation of children's riddles, jokes, and poems. It shall be called *A Christmas Pageant Collection for Children*. All the profits from each printing—I intend to update the collection each year—will go to the local orphanage."

There were murmurs of approval from the women.

"I'll also be putting together various other charitable projects," Harry went on, "such as an advice manual for women seeking safe and honest work in London, which we'll dispense in churches and poorhouses around the city."

"My goodness!" one elderly woman piped up, her quizzing glass to her eye. "Whatever has happened to the Harry of old?"

Harry turned to her. "I'm the same person, Countess. Only better."

All the women laughed.

"Does your father know, Harry?" His mother's eyes were bright with hope.

He shook his head. "Not yet. I've not had a chance to tell him. But I shall. Later tonight."

"Good," she said. "Tell us more."

Harry grinned at her enthusiasm. And he wished that he'd figured out, long ago, that nothing—not his father, and not even his disgrace in the army—had been holding him back. Only *he* had.

"Eventually," he told the company of women, "I'll branch out into acquiring amusing novels, books of poetry for adults, and learned tomes, but I shall never forget my initial inspiration"—he lifted his mother's knuckles to his lips and kissed them tenderly—"which is yourself, dear lady, a most loving mother who taught me to do what is right and leave off that which is wrong."

The duchess was speechless. So were her friends. In fact, not one of them had a dry eye. Harry got more hugs and well wishes than he'd ever gotten in his life, and strangely enough, he was all right with that. He could accept the past. Because he was more than that now. Bigger, somehow.

And, as he'd told the dowager countess, *better.*

But while the women waxed on about his business venture and paid him the most flattering attention, he yet sought an avenue of escape. Because over his shoulder, he'd caught a glimpse of Molly. She was dancing with his friend Alfred, who must have said something witty because the minx threw her head back and laughed.

Which was when Harry got his first stab of jealousy. The slender column of Molly's throat, he knew from experience, was soft and warm, smelling of strawberries and sweet promises.

He didn't like the idea of her offering her neck to Alfred. And Harry despised imagining Alfred pressing kisses to it.

"You seem distracted, Harry," said his mother, laying

her hand on his arm. "And no wonder, with a fine future beckoning you."

"Would you like to dance?" asked Lady Gregory. "My Anne would make a fine partner."

Good God. There stood Anne Riordan, most likely his future bride. She was of impeccable lineage and substantial wealth. In the eyes of the *ton*, there was no reason why he shouldn't offer for the chit.

"Hello, Lord Harry." Anne squinted up at him.

"Er, good to see you, Lady Anne." He tried to smile at her.

"We know you're off limits in town," Lady Gregory said to him, "but surely not at your mother's house?"

Harry understood Lady Gregory well. Bet or no bet, he was still his parents' son, and he would comply with their traditions. He held out his arm to Anne. "I would be honored to dance with you," he said, striving to sound gallant.

She gripped his arm as if she were headed for the gallows.

My God, Harry thought as he carried her off, his neck reddening at the twittering of the ladies behind them. Were the banns already being read and someone forgot to tell him?

Holding a meaningful conversation while Anne constantly stepped on his feet was difficult, but he managed. And when a fop in a pink waistcoat bumped into them with *his* dance partner, Anne appeared to almost faint from the shock.

Of course, Harry offered her some lemonade at that point, but she declined with a small shake of her head.

"Thank you for a lovely dance," he told her at its conclusion, and passed her over to the fop in the pink waistcoat, declaring her to be the finest dancer and most pleasant company he'd encountered yet at the ball that evening.

Duty done.

Now he could go search for Alfred. A few moments later, he caught up with him at a linen-covered serving table adorned with ivy-wrapped candles and two epergnes loaded with hothouse orchids. Penelope's favorite flower, Harry knew from Roderick.

A maid, her hair tucked neatly beneath her frilly cap, ladled out a light, iced punch. "Here you are, Lord Harry." With a warm smile, she handed him a brimming cup.

"Thanks very much." Harry raised the cup and grinned at her. It felt good to be welcomed back home, even by the servants.

Alfred asked for two cups of the stuff and turned back to Harry with a confiding air. "You did me a great service. I like your Molly. She's a wit *and* a pleasure to look at. In fact, I'm bringing her some refreshment now. She said she might go out on the terrace with me."

"I don't think so," said Harry. "She's not to go out on the terrace with anyone. Her father's orders."

Alfred drew in his chin. "Who are *you* to listen to fathers?"

Harry attempted a jovial smile, but he was afraid it came out a bit threatening. "Molly's different. She's not someone to toy with."

"I'm not *toying* with her," Alfred said, his back obviously up. "I might even decide to court her, but—" His face turned red. "Now see what you've done."

Harry followed his bitter gaze. Molly was surrounded by the other three friends he'd brought down from London.

Alfred sighed and put the cups down on the punch table.

"I'm sorry," Harry said, not feeling sorry at all that Alfred had lost a chance to get to know her more intimately. "You won't win her without a fight."

Alfred looked at him quizzically. "Do *you* like her?"

Harry gave a short laugh. "Of course I do. She's my neighbor. I've known her since she was an infant."

"You're acting awfully put out that I was bringing her punch."

Harry cleared his throat. "I feel a certain protectiveness toward her, yes."

"As you would to a sister?"

Harry smiled. "Exactly."

"Then I shall stay far away," Alfred said gloomily. "I have a sister myself." And he left Harry, presumably in search of other female quarry.

If Alfred was so easily dissuaded, he didn't deserve to be in the running for Molly's hand in marriage, Harry thought, feeling vindicated for having weeded out one unworthy bachelor.

But then he looked over and saw the other three still hovering. And one of them—Lord Michael Bannister—asked Molly to dance to the waltz.

Really, Harry thought, what was his mother thinking, allowing such a scandalous dance to be performed? It must be Penelope's influence.

His throat tightened. Michael was a Romeo—a good man, but with a bag of wild oats he'd made very clear he had yet to sow. Molly was chatting avidly with him during their waltz—looking at him with those large, always curious brown eyes of hers.

And it was when Harry saw that sweet openness in her gaze not directed toward him but toward someone else—that he knew.

He already knew he felt lust for Molly. And a healthy dose of friendly feelings.

But he felt more than that.

He didn't want to share her with any other man. At all. *Ever.*

He'd never felt that way before. When he'd had his dalliances, he'd been perfectly amenable to the lady moving on to someone else after their own affair had run its course.

But he didn't feel that way about Molly. She was no longer involved with him *that way,* but he most certainly didn't want his bachelor friends chatting away with her, all the while imagining taking her to bed.

He didn't want his friends to *dare* have those thoughts about her. Now or in the future.

He felt a possessiveness that threatened to unravel him if he didn't get control of himself. Uncurling his fists, he strode across the room and tapped Michael's shoulder. "I'll take over," he said in a short tone.

Michael stopped, looked rather confused.

"I'll explain later," Harry said.

And he would. He would explain to the whole company present that Molly was to be his. No one else's. He was free to marry whom he wished, and he would marry *her*.

He would make her his wife and never have to worry about other men approaching her again.

Because he *loved* her! How could he have been so thickheaded, taking so long to realize that his crazy, mixed-up feelings—his constant thoughts of Molly—were nothing less than love?

He truly *was* a dunderhead.

But no more.

No more!

Michael relinquished Molly's hand, and Harry gripped it.

But she didn't look happy about the switch in partners. "What, pray tell, are you doing?"

They took up the waltz where she and Michael had left off. "You shouldn't waltz with just anyone," Harry said, and to make his point, pulled her closer. "You never know their intentions. I'm merely keeping the wolves at bay, as I promised. And admit it. You want another Queen cake. I saw you eating one in the corner not ten minutes ago. I shall procure one for you as soon as this waltz is over."

"I'll admit your mother's recipe for Queen cakes is the best I've ever tasted, and I wouldn't mind having another." Molly pressed her lips together and didn't speak for a moment. She swallowed hard, as if she were gulping back tears.

Harry felt a twinge of alarm. "Are you all right?"

She gave a rather bitter laugh and didn't answer. He spun her around the floor and tried to think of something to say to get her past this odd mood she was in. But he felt tongue-tied. Probably because when they made direct eye contact, she immediately glanced away.

She wasn't happy. She wasn't happy at all. With *him*!

He prayed he wasn't too late to win her.

"Molly," he began, gripping her hand tighter. "Have I offended you in some way?"

She inhaled a deep breath. "Answer me this, Harry. Why do you bother noticing what I like?"

"Because"—he paused—"I feel it's my duty to know all about you."

"When you're arranging for me to marry someone else?" She shook her head, her tone incredulous. "And why is it you call the men you arranged to meet me—all of whom appear perfectly respectable—'wolves'? Many people would call *you* one. The papers say you're taking full advantage of your unfettered bachelor status."

Harry couldn't deny it. He had. But now he knew it was because he'd been trying to forget *her*.

"Don't believe everything you read." He certainly hadn't slept with any other woman since he'd been with her. "And I called your previous dance partners wolves because"—he paused—"they're not right for you."

She sighed. "You're supposed to help me *find* a husband, not shoo them away. This isn't helping, your hovering over me like a big, black cloud."

"Do I look threatening?"

She nodded.

"Good," he said, and swung her around the floor. "I plan on keeping all your new acquaintances away."

"Why?" she complained. "Harry—"

"Because I have found the perfect husband for you already." He smiled.

Her brows flew up. "Have you? *Who?*"

Couldn't she see? Couldn't she see it in his eyes? "Molly," he groaned. "We must go out in the garden, as soon as this waltz is over."

And without even realizing it, he slowed until they came to a perfect standstill in the middle of the floor.

"Harry?" Molly's brown eyes registered confusion.

But just then there was a clamor from the stair landing—loud words exchanged, and the sharp, guttural sound of someone being punched in the middle and gasping for breath.

The musicians stopped playing.

"Oh, heavens," Molly whispered.

Harry looked up. A footman lay crumpled in a heap. Two other footmen gripped a wild-haired man by either arm. Yet even though the man was trapped, and struggling, he had a triumphant gleam in his eye.

It was Sir Richard. And hovering near him, her beseeching eyes focused on Harry alone, was the lovely— yet insipid—Fiona.

CHAPTER 45

When Molly saw Sir Richard accompanied by Harry's old mistress, her heart beat so fast, she was afraid she might faint.

"I have an announcement to make," yelled Sir Richard from the balcony at the top of the staircase into the silent ballroom. "And it's of vital importance for the Duke of Mallan and all this company to hear it, if they value honor!"

Molly locked gazes with Harry.

Their charade was over.

She fought to maintain decorum as the footmen struggled to contain Sir Richard.

"Your Grace! I implore you to hear me out!" Sir Richard cried.

The footmen managed to drag him almost to a doorway, but he kicked and struggled all the way. Fiona appeared unmoved by his distress and not at all surprised by it, either.

"Release him!" commanded the duke from the ballroom floor.

The footmen were slow to do so. But they finally dropped Sir Richard's arms, and he stood, his chest heaving.

"What have you to say?" the duke called up to him from the ballroom floor.

But before Sir Richard could answer, a rather ridiculous thing happened. Molly's father appeared at the entrance to the ballroom, nimbly sidestepping the gasping Sir Richard and the two footmen.

"What the devil is going on here?" Lord Sutton asked over his spectacles to no one in particular.

Oh, Papa.

Molly so wished he weren't here to witness his daughter's downfall.

He was followed into the ballroom by a man with golden hair and the face of an angel.

Cedric.

Molly gasped. What was *he* doing here? Unless her father had concocted some sort of plan after all, a last-minute effort to get Cedric and Molly married before she had a Season in London.

Or perhaps Cedric himself had had second thoughts about abandoning her.

Harry moved a step forward, his hands clenched into fists. "Alliston . . . the bastard."

Molly laid a hand on Harry's arm. "No," she insisted.

He mustn't waste his time on Cedric. Because, after all, what did his perfidy matter now anyway? She had no future. And Harry's was sealed. He would be marrying Anne Riordan once Sir Richard revealed the lie they'd perpetrated at the Most Delectable Companion contest.

She kept her hand on Harry's arm and saw him uncurl his fist. But he looked as if he could murder a whole slew of giants if he wanted to.

She stood quietly, refusing to think about her father and his desire that she marry Cedric. Both of them stood next to Sir Richard. Her father ogled him as if he were a strange sea creature. And Cedric, the fool, was looking at

Fiona with poorly masked horror, which only proved to Molly that he was once more angling for her hand.

She felt only indifference and a vague pity for the man. And a weary acknowledgment of her father's refusal to hear what she wanted or didn't want in a husband.

Their indifference to her desires seemed less important than what was happening now, in this ballroom, the same ballroom where she'd stood at age thirteen concocting dreams that never came to pass.

Now she was like a criminal at the guillotine, hands tied, eyes bound, waiting for a final, miserable fate to befall her.

And it wasn't long in coming.

Sir Richard pointed a trembling finger at Harry. "Your son, Your Grace, was conscripted into Prinny's Impossible Bachelor wager."

"Yes, we all know of the wager, Bell." The duke sounded weary. It wasn't his first ball to be ruined by a shocking display. "Do get on with it."

The crowd was perfectly still. Molly could hear her blood pounding in her ears.

Sir Richard lofted a brow. "As you know, I am also one of this year's five Impossible Bachelors." He was obviously quite impressed with himself. "Each of us was to bring a mistress—"

"*Roger!*" That was Harry's mother remonstrating with the duke.

Molly saw the duke put his hand over hers. "We are all adults here, Jane. But any lady who cares not to hear may leave the room at once."

There was a stirring and a shifting of the crowd, but not a single female left the room. Not even the vicar's wife.

The focus of attention returned to Sir Richard.

He strutted to his left, then turned and strutted to his

right, stopped, and cleared his throat. "To see the wager through," he said in that pompous voice of his, "we were each required to bring a mistress to a week's house party. To be held at one of your hunting properties, Your Grace. My understanding is that we used your *favorite* hunting box."

There was a huge rumble of protest in the room. The noise went on and on, and Molly looked at Harry. "Wasn't the hunting box *yours*?" she whispered.

Harry shook his head. "I've much to explain about me and my father," he whispered. "But it's all past now. I was planning on talking to him tonight. And to you, too, Molly."

He sounded fierce. Desperate. Yet there was also something warm and true and so . . . *loving* in his eyes. Could he—*did* he—have feelings for her?

He squeezed her hand. "I want to tell you everything. I—I was trying to get the words out during our waltz. I want to *be* with you." He took a sharp breath. "More than anything else in the world."

Molly nodded, her heart in her throat. "I want to be with you, too, Harry."

The loud, condemning voices around them continued, but for at least a few seconds, nothing came between Molly and a huge surge of happiness and love welling inside her.

But the duke's voice, commanding everyone to silence, drew her out of her reverie. Harry, too.

When order reigned once again, Sir Richard continued his speech. "According to the rules of the wager," he said, "the women at the house party were to compete for the title of Most Delectable Companion. And the bachelor whose mistress won the title at the end of the week would be guaranteed another year of freedom from the marital noose. The rest would have to draw straws to see who

would be required to get legshackled." Sir Richard stared
at Harry. "Your younger son, Your Grace, won the wager
and was exempt from the drawing."

"Yes," the duke drawled. "We know. As does every
disappointed virgin and matchmaking mama in town."

There was a ripple of laughter.

Molly kept her hand on Harry's arm. His mouth was a
thin, threatening line. And his eyes—hard and cold—
were locked on Sir Richard's.

"But it has come to light, Your Grace," said Sir Richard, "that your son violated the rules of the contest. And
he should thereby forfeit his win."

There was another huge rumble from the crowd.

"How so?" asked the duke equably.

My goodness, the man was cool under pressure, thought
Molly. And she began to admire him.

Sir Richard scratched his chin. "Your son's mistress
abandoned him at an inn the day the contest was to begin.
In fact, she is here, to prove my story." He looked at Fiona.

"I am that woman," she said in a soft, breathy voice. "I
did, indeed, leave Harry. There are many witnesses at the
inn to support my claim. He wouldn't let me bring my
lapdog to the house party! And he didn't even care when
I *cried*." She batted her lashes and put her fists on her
curvaceous hips.

The crowd went mad.

"Silence!" the duke's voice rang out once more.

There was one last gasp from somewhere to Molly's
left, and then utter quiet once again.

"Do go on, Sir Richard," the duke said.

Sir Richard drew a breath. "Your son didn't know what
to do, Your Grace. If a bachelor arrives at the site of the
wager without a mistress, he forfeits the wager and must
propose to a young lady almost immediately."

The men in the ballroom looked warily at each other.

What a nightmare! their glances said. And the women in the room seemed to roll a collective eye.

"As I was saying," Sir Richard asserted, "your son would forfeit the wager unless he brought a mistress with him. So in place of a real mistress in the competition, he put a *false mistress.*"

There were more gasps. Even a shriek.

"What in the world is a false mistress?" someone near Molly called out to the company.

"A false mistress," Sir Richard explained, "is a mistress *in name only.*"

"How do you know she was a mistress in name only?" another anonymous nosy-body cried.

"Because the two parties involved had a shouting match about it outside the inn where they met," Sir Richard said with a laugh. "Their terms were clearly outlined and overheard by the innkeeper and his barmaid. As well, the imposter masquerading as a mistress barred her bedchamber door."

Molly gripped Harry's arm and her eyes widened.

"I heard her myself," said Sir Richard. "Every night, she'd push a large piece of furniture across the floor." He had the effrontery to yawn. "There were *no* shenanigans going on in that room, I assure you."

There was yet another clamor from the floor. When it died down to a murmur, Sir Richard crossed his arms, tapped his foot, and looked accusingly at Harry. "As a consequence, this woman's claim to the title of Most Delectable Companion is invalid. Which, in turn, makes your son's win of the general wager, Your Grace, invalid, as well."

More gasps from the crowd.

Sir Richard raised his hand in the air. "I'm no longer the loser of the wager. And I'll not propose to the young miss ascribed to me by the board of our club. *Your* son is the loser, Your Grace, by default. *He* is the bachelor to be legshackled, and according to the club's wishes, to none other than Anne Riordan, who is in this very room."

Molly's knees turned to jelly. But she straightened them. She must. If not for herself, then for poor Anne. Granted, she was a squint-faced bore, but to be considered the punishment for the loser of the wager?

No one deserved such ignominy.

"If all you say is true," said the duke to Sir Richard, "then so it shall be done."

Sir Richard smiled and bowed in the duke's direction.

Harry's jaw clenched.

"Is that all you have to say, Bell?" the duke went on.

"No," he said. "Because the perfidy of your son goes beyond this, Your Grace."

The crowd was silent, the mood of the room having grown noticeably more tense.

Harry took Molly's hand.

Sir Richard looked directly at them both. "Your son, Your Grace, has ruined a respectable young woman, the one who played at being his mistress. She is in this very room."

There were so many gasps, Molly almost screamed at everyone to shut up and raised her hand to confess. But she couldn't do it. Not with her father looking on.

"And your son should be challenged to a duel," Sir Richard said.

A duel? Why, that was ridiculous! Molly looked helplessly at Harry, but his eyes were frozen on Sir Richard's face.

"A duel, my friends," Sir Richard went on bitterly. "For he shall not be able to reverse the fate of this heretofore respectable young woman. He's to marry Anne Riordan, after all."

Molly's heart sank at those words.

Sir Richard lowered his brows. "The pity is, Your Grace, that the girl's father is too old to avenge her honor in a duel. So her brother-in-law must."

And he looked directly at Roderick.

As one, the whole crowd swung around to look at Roderick. If he was the brother-in-law, then who—

The mass of people pivoted to look at *Molly,* including her father, who peered at her from over his spectacles and gave a start so sudden that a footman took his arm to steady him.

"Molly?" Lord Sutton called out, his voice wavering. "You have nothing to do with this, have you?"

A spark of understanding traveled through the crowd at lightning speed. If Molly were Harry's false mistress, then Roderick would have to challenge *his own brother* to a duel!

The room broke out in noise so overwhelming, the massive chandelier above the ballroom floor trembled.

Molly felt her face redden, but she kept her chin high and said nothing.

Which, as far as the duke's guests were concerned, was acknowledgment of guilt.

The duke strode up the ballroom stairs, his hands clenched at his sides, and got in Sir Richard's face.

"Who—was—that—false—mistress?" the duke asked, his voice a low growl.

Sir Richard kept his gaze on Molly. "Lady Mary— *Molly*—Fairbanks," he said calmly.

Harry's mother fell in a dead faint.

"No, Molly, no!" Penelope shrieked, and then *she* fainted, too, right into Roderick's arms.

"The baby!" he cried, and lifted Penelope up, cradling her to his chest. "Dr. Krauss. Are you still here?" He began to stroke Penelope's hair.

Molly felt the blood fall to her feet. Penelope was to have another baby? And now she'd received a great shock—

Molly put her hands to her mouth to keep her lips from trembling. She was blinking so hard, she almost couldn't see. And then it seemed all the women in the audience began to cry, or faint, or yell in Penelope's general direction.

The news about the baby couldn't have come at a worse—or more appropriate—time. Because Roderick's life might very well be in danger.

The house of Mallan was vulnerable!

Pray that the child is a son!, Molly heard over and over. She leaned into Harry.

"Hold on," he said. "Don't let them—"

"Penelope—" Molly could barely speak.

"She'll be fine. So will Mother. Everyone will be."

"But my father—"

Lord Sutton was still staring at her, thunderstruck.

And then, in the midst of the chaos—after Dr. Krauss had removed Penelope from Roderick's arms—Roderick looked at Harry, and Harry looked at him.

Time stood still.

And for a moment, Molly felt as if she were back at the Christmas ball when she was thirteen.

Penelope had fainted again, yes. But her chagrin would be far worse this time around because Harry and Roderick wouldn't simply exchange punches. If Roderick were to defend her honor, he would be compelled to challenge Harry to a duel.

For a moment, all Molly knew was a swirl of color, and loud, jangling noises. But then she felt Harry's hand touch hers. And he gripped it. His hard, warm palm cradled her own.

She would focus on the warmth of Harry's hand and not on what was happening on the stair landing. Yes, she would hold on to Harry's hand for all she was worth. And she would think about how much she loved him, that despite everything going on around her—despite her world crashing around her shoulders—she loved Harry. And always would.

With a capital *L*.

And it seemed that maybe—oh, bother with *maybe,* she was sure!—he loved her, too.

She lifted her chin and stared defiantly at Sir Richard. At Roderick. At the duke. At her father. At the world. She would endure the clamor and pray her father and sister and Harry's family would forgive her. But if they didn't— what was done was done.

She was Harry's forever.

"That despicable vermin said it rightly, Father," Harry's voice rang out, more threatening than she had ever heard it. "Molly Fairbanks *was* my false mistress, emphasis on *false*. She incurred no wrong. And she will pay no price."

Molly trembled next to him.

Harry's words were heroic, but she knew that she *would* pay a price, as much as Harry hated for it to be so.

Sir Richard chuckled. "How naïve of you, Traemore. Rest assured, at the very least, *you* shall certainly pay a price. There are members of our club here tonight who—if they value obeying their Prince Regent—will step forward and demand you make restitution for your perfidy by immediately proposing to Anne Riordan."

The duke's face was grave. "As I am well aware of the details of Prinny's wager—having read the Impossible Bachelors decree numerous times at my club—I must validate Bell's concerns."

Molly's fingers went icy as the duke turned to look at her father and said, "Forgive me for what I am about to demand, Sutton."

Molly knew what that demand was. And with all her being, she wished it didn't have to be so.

The duke looked at Harry. "You shall propose marriage to Lady Anne Riordan immediately."

Molly swallowed hard. Lord Sutton looked about to cry. She was ruined. Completely. And she and her father both knew it. Any plans he had to marry her off to Cedric would be cast aside now. She was a fallen woman. No respectable man would have her.

Thank God Penelope had been carried out of the room.

Harry looked at Molly, a world of pain and regret in his eyes. "I'm so sorry," he whispered.

She knew he was. The whole thing had gotten out of control, hadn't it? They'd both made stupid decisions, but somehow in the middle of it all, she'd discovered the center of her being, the place where you knew you were whole.

And Harry was there. Harry was a part of her. No matter what happened.

"I understand you have no choice," she whispered back. "I knew it all along." She squeezed his hand. "Harry, you *must* propose to Anne."

He squeezed her hand back so hard, she wanted to wince. But she wouldn't. She would remain strong for him. She would never let him know how much it hurt to let him go.

He left her side, and something inside Molly went numb, in the very center of her heart. She knew she would never be truly happy again.

CHAPTER 46

Harry looked at the duke. It was time to do his duty. He'd avoided marrying because he knew his father would be happy to see him married, and no matter what, Harry hadn't wanted to make his father happy.

Because he'd thought the duke didn't love him.

But he saw today that he did. His father may never have said it out loud, but the cool way he'd handled Sir Richard—his entire commanding demeanor—suggested to Harry that his father loved his family above all things and would defend it to his dying breath.

Harry was part of that family. He was the one who seemed to make a mess of things, but his father had never thrown him out of his life. He'd always included Harry, in his own way.

"I shall do my duty, Father," he said to the duke. "A man of honor must always satisfy his obligation to a bet." He paused. "But in hindsight I see that he has an even greater obligation to question a wager which compromises the dignity of so many, a duty which I shirked. Perhaps, had I spoken up, I could have steered Prinny in a different direction."

The duke cleared his throat. "As a longtime acquaintance of the Prince Regent, I should have requested a meeting with him to air my concerns, especially as his plan involved my son. Had I been more attentive, perhaps it wouldn't have come to this . . . end."

He looked so sorrowful that Harry had to choke back a lump in his throat.

"Don't be sorry," he told the duke. "Soon I shall fulfill my obligations to the bet and restore honor to the family—but meanwhile, I've an even higher duty to heed. A duty of the heart."

Harry strode up the stairs two at a time to the balcony. Sir Richard jumped behind a footman and cowered, but Harry wasn't wasting any more time on him.

"You *jackal*," he said, grabbing Cedric's lapels. "Before I propose marriage to the highly esteemed Anne Riordan, a sad victim of this brutish bet—and before Sir Richard Bell manages to pit my beloved brother against me to avenge his sister-in-law's honor—I demand that you restore that honor immediately, by proposing marriage to Lady Molly Fairbanks. She is in this coil because of *you,* you slimy reprobate."

And he shook Cedric so hard, his teeth rattled.

"She asked *me* to elope." Cedric's sickeningly beautiful face winced.

Lord Sutton's mouth dropped open. "You eloped with my Molly? How could that be? She doesn't even *like* you!"

Harry dropped Cedric with a thud. "This coward had no intention of ever marrying your daughter, Lord Sutton. Molly made an error in judgment—she felt she'd rather marry Cedric than be a spinster—so they started off on a journey to Gretna Green while you were away. And then the despicable rat"—he snarled at Cedric—"abandoned her at a dangerous inn and took off with *her.*"

Harry pointed to Fiona.

Molly's father visibly trembled. "Because of my indifference, my overabsorption in my work—and because I've been making her pay the price for years for a silly poem she wrote when she was a mere child—my daughter is suffering this shame."

"No, Father!" Molly cried out. Her eyes were bright with unshed tears but her voice was strong. "It's not your fault! You are the best of men!"

Harry's throat tightened. Molly was so selfless. And good. And brave.

And he loved her.

She was Molly, *his* Molly, who had read a silly love poem when she was thirteen, a poem that tore straight to the heart of so many different matters in both their families: jealousies, demands, misunderstandings—all stemming from the need to be noticed. To be loved. And to love in return.

Lord Sutton swallowed hard when he looked at Molly. "I won't turn my back on you this time, daughter. No matter what happens today, you are still my beloved child." He wagged an index finger at the crowd. "And no one shall cut you without having to cut me first. Is that clear?"

He stared at the crowd over his spectacles, daring them to say anything untoward.

But no one said a word.

Lord Sutton turned back to Fiona. "Is this true what Harry said? Did you go off with Cedric while he was in the midst of eloping with my daughter?"

Fiona stuck out her lower lip. "Yes. Cedric said he'd take me to Gretna in your daughter's place, but he didn't. He took me to another inn, ravished me, and deserted me, as well, the villain!"

Several women in the crowd swooned. One had to be carried out by two footmen.

Molly's father turned to Cedric. "You shall propose to

my daughter immediately," he said in such a dangerous voice that Molly worried for his health.

Cedric inhaled a great breath. And exhaled. "As you wish," he said dramatically.

Harry saw Molly shut her eyes. He knew she was thinking that being married to a pompous ass like Cedric was a horrible fate. And he agreed. But it was a better fate than her total ruin. As a married woman, Molly would still maintain her respectability, which Harry craved for her above all things. He knew that if she thought long enough, Molly would never want to pull down the reputation of the rest of her family. So she would marry Cedric for Penelope and her father's sake.

And for the sake of both their families. Harry would never raise a pistol against Roderick, and he knew in his heart that Roderick felt the same way about him. But a duel between brothers, called out of the necessity of avenging Molly's honor—even if both brothers shot into the ground—was a scenario that neither family would wish. It would be talked about for years.

And Molly knew this.

Harry saw the moment when she'd come to a decision. She opened her eyes, straightened her shoulders, and walked through the crowd, looking neither right nor left.

She ascended the stairs to the balcony and curtsied before Cedric. "I accept your proposal," she said, loud and clear.

At which point, Harry breathed a sigh of relief.

But as Cedric took Molly's hand and placed a reluctant kiss on it, claiming her for his bride, Harry realized that his soul was empty.

And would remain that way indefinitely.

Because Molly, his dear, *dear* Molly, was lost to him forever.

CHAPTER 47

Molly stood next to Cedric and looked out over the crowd. She would keep her head high. She'd made mistakes, yes. But everyone she loved had done the same, hadn't they?

Her father was standing by her. No matter what. That was something. And she was standing by him.

That, in fact, was what love was all about.

Understanding that the other person is only human.

And forgiving.

She watched as Harry made his way over to Anne Riordan. Her parents flanked her, and it looked as though they held her up by the elbows. Molly wouldn't be surprised if Anne's knees were jelly. She'd been humiliated beyond belief, and now the strongest, handsomest, kindest, funniest man in all of England was approaching her to . . .

To make it all better.

Molly bit her lip as Harry got down on one knee before Anne. He took her slender little hand in his.

"Anne Riordan," he said loud and clear for all the company to hear, "would you do me the great honor of becoming my wife?"

Molly heard the spit of several candles in a wall sconce behind her head. And the labored breathing of the still shaken Cedric. Her own heart pounded in her ears. She clasped her icy fingers together and waited.

Please, God.

She didn't know what she prayed for. Perhaps an angel, one that could sweep away the general ache she felt inside.

Or was she praying for time to have passed another twenty years, making this horrible scene a distant memory?

"No," said Anne loudly. Suddenly and with force.

Molly jumped. It seemed everyone did. And then there was a silence that stretched for eternity.

What had Anne said? Molly strained her ears.

"No," Anne said again. "No, no, *no!*"

But Harry didn't move. He held on to her hand and stared at her. He was like a statue.

"Pardon?" he finally croaked.

"I like you, Harry," said Anne, in a thin but clear voice. "Very much. But like you, I tire of having to fulfill tedious obligations for the sake of my family name." She turned to her father. "I shan't have him, Papa. I don't care what you or Prinny or the fuddy-duddies at your club expect! I want Gregory Westfield, the vicar's visiting cousin!"

"And I want *her!*" called out a fop in a pink waistcoat, his cheeks flaming.

Anne burst into tears, yanked her hand out of Harry's grasp, and ran into her beloved's arms.

Molly felt her mouth hanging open in shock, and remembered to shut it for decorum's sake, although the night had been rife with rather . . . indecorous events.

Harry slowly stood. He looked at his father. Both seemed stunned by the turn of events.

A gentleman stepped forward from the crowd.

Molly looked closer. It was Maxwell. Dear Lord Maxwell! How had she missed his presence?

"As a member of Harry's club in good standing," he

said, "I submit to the company here that Harry's obligation to the bet has been fulfilled. He is under no obligation to marry anyone at this time. I request that another
member of the club present—Harry's family excluded—
also come forward and concur."

And he stepped back into the crowd.

"I concur," said another man. He had the most lovely
smile.

Lumley.

Molly broke into a grin.

Another man stepped forward. Oh, dear. It was Captain Arrow! And he looked magnificent in his naval uniform, Molly thought.

"I also concur." He looked at Harry. "As a member of
the Impossible Bachelor's arbitration committee, I con-
firm that the bet stipulates only that you *propose* to Anne
Riordan. It makes no provisions for a circumstance in
which she rejects you. Therefore, you are free of all obligation to the club and its members, as well as all obligations to the Prince Regent's wager."

Molly could see Harry taking a deep breath. Then she
saw his gaze scan the room slowly, lingering on his parents and brother, and finally coming to a rest . . .

On her.

Harry took a deep breath. Good God, was he dreaming?
Or was he really still an unfettered bachelor?

One look at Molly's expression—at the joy he could
see in her eyes even from a distance—confirmed the
truth that he had, indeed, dodged a bullet that would have
made both him and Anne Riordan—dear Anne, to him
now—absolutely miserable.

He kept his gaze on Molly's and wended his way through
the crowd toward her. The walk, which took place in total
silence—except for the rustle of skirts and squeak of heels

as his parents' guests made room for him to pass—seemed to last a lifetime.

Molly stood near her father, who'd suddenly moved between her and Cedric. Her hands were folded in front of her, and Harry could see her pinky finger fluttering.

She was nervous. It pained him to see her suffer even a moment longer, so he went up the stairs three at a time and stood facing her, mere inches from her beloved face.

The crowd began to murmur.

"What's going on?" he heard over and over from different corners of the room.

"Molly," he said. And it was like breathing pure mountain air just to say her name out loud.

"Harry." Her mouth trembled.

He grasped both her hands in his own and lifted them to his lips. *How close he had come,* he thought, his mouth pressed to her knuckles. *How close he had come to losing her.*

Was it yet too late?

Slowly, solemnly, he got down on one knee.

She looked down at him, a misty smile on her face.

"You're not thinking of Samson, are you?" he asked her, his voice hoarse with emotion—

With love.

She shook her head. "No. Just *you.*"

"I have something to propose to *you,*" he murmured for her ears only. "But before I do, would you be patient a moment?"

She nodded. Smiled.

Little did she know, her trust in him was all his strength. Harry stood again, strode ten feet over to where Sir Richard cowered, still craven, behind a footman.

"Wait!" someone called from the crowd. "Please! Don't punch him! At least not yet!"

A woman strode to the front of the crowd. It was a

maidservant—the one, in fact, who had served Harry a cup of punch and greeted him so warmly.

He looked closer at her. Who was she? He recognized her vaguely, but—

She took off her cap.

That hair.

That *hair*.

He looked at Sir Richard's hair. It was the same burnished chestnut color.

"Peggy!" Sir Richard cried. His upper half appeared from behind the footman.

"Dickie!" she called back.

Harry looked between them.

Sir Richard's sister.

Now Harry knew who she was! The colonel's wife. He hadn't laid eyes on her in six years.

Or so he'd thought. She was apparently a servant in his father's household.

He looked at his father, wondering if he knew—

Gad. He *did* know. His expression was resigned, bemused. As if it were all out of his hands now.

And Sir Richard appeared totally confused but delighted to see his sister. Peggy, on the other hand, was looking at her brother with distress evident in her eyes.

"You've made a huge mistake!" she cried up to him. "And it is all *my* fault."

Sir Richard grabbed at his cravat. "Wh-what do you mean?"

Peggy pointed to Harry. "This man has been nothing but good to me. Six years ago he saved me from being ravished by two French soldiers who were among the first to ambush my husband's regiment. While the rest of the regiment defended themselves, Lord Harry heard me scream and came to my immediate defense in my husband's tent. When it was over, I begged him to tell no one else how close I had come to being completely ruined. And he's kept his promise all these years, despite the fact that telling someone my secret would have absolved him of all false accusations against him."

There was a big murmur of interest from the crowd.

The maid waited until the buzzing ceased. "My husband refused to believe my wretched story," she continued. "He chose to divorce me instead and spread malicious, unfounded gossip about Lord Harry. When I heard how pitilessly he was treated by the army and the *ton,* how he was vilified for being a lecher and a coward, I should have stepped forward. But I did not. I was frightened. And alone. I'm ashamed of my conduct. Terribly ashamed."

She looked at the duke. "And then one day, I received an unexpected blessing. Until that point, the vengefulness of my husband had almost destroyed me. He'd ensured I had no place to stay. No means of earning my bread. No friends. But the Duke of Mallan found me. He said he didn't believe a word that anyone was saying about his son. The duke knew Lord Harry was protecting a lady's honor and couldn't speak. Rightfully assuming I was the lady in question, the duke offered me a respectable position in his household, where I have been now for five years. Tonight is the first time he's heard what truly happened."

"You've been here *five years*?" Harry asked Peggy.

She nodded.

Harry made eye contact with his father. The duke allowed himself a smile, and Harry felt a tear form in his eye. Not that he would let it fall, of course. He was of the house of Mallan, made of stern stuff. "Thank you, Father," he said gruffly.

The duke nodded, a gleam of something warm and . . . and *loving* in his gaze. "You're welcome, son."

Peggy smiled. "I've been safe here. And quite happy."

She looked at Sir Richard. "You never knew where I was. I was afraid to let you know."

"I wish you had," Sir Richard rasped. His face was extremely red.

She smiled at him. "I love you, Dickie, but what used to be your playful naughtiness as a bachelor has turned into villainy. I've heard wretched stories about you. I couldn't contact you for fear of losing my position."

"Me?" Sir Richard laughed. "A villain? Of course I haven't been."

Peggy frowned. "I don't believe you. And while I appreciate your caring for me, Dickie, you really must stop being such an ass to the rest of the world. Once you have, feel free to contact me again."

She stepped back into the crowd.

Harry punched Sir Richard solidly in the nose, and he fell to the floor with a thunk.

"I propose Sir Richard Bell be removed from the club roster," Harry said to the company.

"Done," said his father.

Lumley, Maxwell, and Arrow stepped forward. "We needlessly concur," said Maxwell, "but it gives us great pleasure to do so."

"Indeed," said Captain Arrow.

"We propose that we remove him right now from the premises of the ducal estate," said Lumley, rolling up his sleeves.

"Agreed," Harry said. "Along with his companion, if you don't mind."

Fiona gasped. "Me?"

Harry looked at her. "Yes, you. How did Bell ever uncover you and your role in the events that transpired?"

She sniffed. "I'm beautiful, remember? Innkeepers aren't likely to forget me. Or the people with me. I'm quite easy to track down."

Lord Sutton stepped forward. "I would appreciate the removal of another beautiful but soulless person from the premises—Mr. Cedric Alliston, whose duplicity is such that I hope he will never feel welcome in this corner of England again."

The duke laughed. "I shall ensure he's welcome in *no* part of England. Be gone with you, Alliston."

"But—" Cedric spluttered, his face beet red.

"I'm sorry, Cedric," Molly said sweetly. "But it is what it is—isn't it?"

Cedric narrowed his eyes at her, and Harry chuckled. The minx!

As much as Harry enjoyed watching Cedric exit the ballroom as fast as his feet could carry him, he also regretted not punching him before he went. But really. He was tired of the endless delays. He wanted to get to *Molly*.

His false mistress.

And his one, true love.

With the atmosphere, should he say, restored to a congenial one, he once again took up his position in front of his intended bride. His knee was taking rather a beating. But it was all for a good cause, wasn't it?

His and Molly's future happiness.

He grinned up at her and took that dear hand of hers. What was he talking about, *future* happiness? They were *already* happy.

Here.

She smiled a breathtaking smile.

Now.

She nodded, even before he could ask the question.

And for always.

EPILOGUE

"Thank God for special banns," Harry said, sweeping Molly up into his arms and carrying her over the threshold of their new home on Bruton Street in London. It was such a relief—and a joy—to know she was his at last. He stopped where he was, right in the middle of the corridor leading to the kitchens, and kissed her.

It was like sinking into happiness. A dream come true.

When he pulled back, she sighed, but her gaze was a little strained.

"Hungry?" he guessed.

She nodded. "I haven't been able to eat all morning. First, we'd the wedding, then the nuptial breakfast at Penelope and Roderick's—"

"You don't mind that we'll be living right around the corner from them when they come to town?"

"*Mind?* I'm thrilled! I think I lost my appetite because Cousin Augusta was staring at me so, as if she knew I'd already seen you"—she blushed—"naked."

"Oho!"

"And then Imogen twirled one time too many and got sick—"

"Children seem to do that when they're wearing their best clothes."

"Yes, and Papa insisted on dancing with me, which made me cry . . . and—"

She stopped.

"And?"

"Every time I looked at you, I became excited thinking about . . . *now*."

He grinned. "Now?"

She nodded. "It's been so *long,* Harry. Since that night in Prinny's tent." A becoming pink crept up her cheeks.

"Yes, three months and five days ago," he murmured, glad he'd told the servants to disappear until morning.

"And thirteen hours," she said simply.

"Indeed." He continued carrying her down the corridor. "But there's food to be obtained. At our very own, intimate wedding feast."

She kicked her legs. "Lovely!"

In the kitchens, he set her on her feet and looked around, wondering if Cook had followed orders.

Ah, there it was.

He strode to a large, well-worn table and whipped off a napkin. A delicate plate of iced Queen cakes appeared. And to the side was a sweating pitcher of milk.

He'd not been oblivious to Molly's lack of appetite that morning. So he'd sent a runner round to their new residence and given orders for this little meal to be provided. Cook must have left the premises not thirty minutes ago, judging from the coldness of the pitcher.

Molly clasped her hands together. "Oh, Harry. You're *so* thoughtful."

"Am I?"

She went to him and kissed him soundly. "Yes. You are."

Then she sat at the chair and devoured two Queen

cakes in a row before she swallowed half a glass of milk.

She sighed, a contented sigh this time, he thought. And then she stood. "I think—"

"No thinking," Harry said, unwrapping his cravat. "Doing. That's what we're up to right now."

"Really?" She gave him an impish grin and pulled off his cravat.

"Yes, really." He bent and kissed her, his hands wrapped around her waist, and then he pulled her closer.

"Harry," she murmured. "I can't wait any longer."

"I believe I've heard you say that before," he teased her.

"It's true." She drew back. "No more talking."

"Yes, no more talking. At least until we're naked."

And before they knew it, their clothes lay in a heap on the kitchen floor.

"We're supposed to do this upstairs, in our marriage bed," Harry murmured against her breast. "Shall I carry you there now?"

"No," Molly gasped. "I can't wait that long."

"I see. Only Queen cakes can divert you from your sensual purpose, eh?"

"Not even Queen cakes now," she said, her breath feather light on his jaw.

"I'm honored. I think." Harry kissed her without stopping and lifted her to sit on the table. "You know," he whispered in her ear, "I might want a Queen cake, as well."

"Really?"

He nodded. Then swiped a finger through the icing of one of the cakes on the plate.

She had an adorably befuddled look on her face.

"Part your legs, my sweet," he murmured against her mouth.

She gulped. "Oh, my God. You're—you're—"

"Hungry." He smiled into her eyes, then slowly ran his iced finger over her sweetest, most vulnerable flesh.

"Harry."

He sank down before her and plundered her with his tongue. She ran her fingers through his hair, leaned on his shoulders, and moaned her delight.

"I need a little more icing," he said at one particularly luscious moment, and took his time running his finger through the top of another cake.

"Please," Molly cried. "Hurry up!"

He laughed, and when he returned to her, he lavished her with every bit of loving attention he could give his new bride. After a few more heady moments, she arched her back and called his name.

It was the sweetest sound he'd ever heard.

When she was done, her whole body was rosy.

He pulled her up and kissed her. "You're beautiful," he said. "And quite delicious. I'll have to share Queen cakes with you more often."

She smiled. "You're wicked, you know that? And I love you. More than words can say."

There was a silence between them, a shimmering, golden silence.

"I love you, too," he said. "And you're right—words can't express—" He sighed and ran a finger down her cheek. "Come. Let me show you."

Molly held Harry's hand tightly as they climbed the stairs.

Last night—her last as an unmarried woman—she'd been visited by Penelope in her bedchamber at Lord Sutton's rented mansion on Jermyn Street. Penelope had held her hands, and they'd cried together, both of them wishing aloud that their mother could have been there to speak to Molly about her wedding night.

Penelope, of course, knew Molly and Harry had already, ahem, spent time together—what were sisters for, after all, but to share in such wondrous news?

"But nothing can prepare you," Penelope had said, swallowing hard and rubbing the backs of Molly's hands with her thumbs, "for the actual . . . act."

"Really?" Molly grew breathless just thinking about the possibilities.

Penelope nodded emphatically. "Oh, yes. There's nothing like it. Especially when you're in love."

"And are you in love with Roderick, still?" Molly whispered, and pulled her hand out of Penelope's to push a curl behind her ear.

Tears flooded Penelope's eyes. "More than ever. If Harry is at all like him—and of course, we know he's cut of the same noble, kind, handsome, and irresistibly amusing cloth—you'll be tremendously happy as his wife."

"And married to two brothers, our sister bond will be stronger than ever, won't it?" Molly said, wiping at her own eyes.

"Stronger than ever," Penelope choked out.

They hugged. And cried a few more happy tears.

Now Molly was about to find out what Penelope had been talking about so feelingly. Penelope and Harry's mother—now Molly's mother-in-law—had seen to it that their bedchamber was warm and welcoming. Vases of white roses decorated both sides of the mantel. The bedclothes had been drawn back, and a small, cheerful fire laid.

Molly looked at the far wall, where Harry was staring. It held numerous oil paintings in gilded frames, fronted by a bust of Lord Nelson on a pedestal, a gift from Captain Arrow, who practically worshiped the man.

"What is it?" she asked.

"See that picture of the hunting box?" Harry said.

"Father told me we'd find another wedding present in our bedchamber. I've always loved that painting. So has he. He probably has a dark rectangle on the wall in his library where it's resided for decades."

Molly smiled. "How sweet of him to give it to us."

Harry gripped her hand. "No, Molly. You don't understand. This means . . . he's given us the hunting box, as well."

"It *does*?"

Harry gave a soft laugh. "Father's a slave to family tradition and expects me to know every nuance of it, as well. In our family, whoever owns the painting owns the property."

He turned to her and kissed her, his naked form pressed firmly against her own.

"He must know it's special to us," she murmured against his lips.

"It's where we fell in love," Harry said, his hands kneading her bottom, her hips, and then sliding up to cup her breasts.

Several delicious moments later, they were on the bed, wrapped in each other's arms, their kiss unbroken, the need between them palpable. He was hard against her belly. She could barely breathe when he nipped teasingly at her breasts and then suckled them. And the exciting way he pinned her arms above her head and kissed her as he stroked the soft core of her drove her mad with longing.

She loved him. She loved him so much it left a knot in her middle that begged to be loosened. Harry, she knew, was the only one who had the power to do so.

"Please, Harry," she managed to say around their kisses.

He was already between her legs. "This might hurt," he said. "But just for a moment. If you can trust me—"

"You know I do." She smiled at him, drew an invisible

line down his cheek with her index finger, a line that ended at his lips.

He grabbed her hand and kissed her fingertips. "Molly—" he whispered raggedly.

And then he was inside her.

There was a split second of pain between her legs, but she hardly noticed. Because Harry was kissing her mouth and then her breasts as he began a sweet tempo of movement. The feeling of fullness inside her was so pleasurable—so *right*—that she lifted her hips to bring him deeper.

"Oh, Harry . . ." she whispered.

Everything they'd shared before this moment was in his gaze—their outrageous, thrilling courtship, their childhood, their years of separation and suffering, and the wedding promises they'd made that very morning.

He pressed a hand against her brow and swept her hair back. "You're my love," he said simply. "Forever."

"And you're mine," she said, smiling at him. "Forever."

But words, wonderful as they were, and so true—were not enough.

Molly felt Harry's fierceness, his craving, as their rhythm took on a new intensity. He dipped his head and kissed her, holding her tight in his embrace as their tongues melded in a dance of desire. She clung to him, wanting . . . wanting—

And then she was suddenly there—she'd no idea where she began and where Harry ended. All she knew was wave after wave of intense pleasure.

Of love.

Of oneness.

All in a rapturous moment.

She was exactly where she belonged—with Harry.

Her husband, her lover, and her best friend.

Sighing, she sank back down into the pillows, her arms still wrapped around his neck.

He rolled to the side and pulled her on top of him, a lazy smile on his lips. "So, Lady Harry—" he said in his very best Adorable Man voice.

She laughed. "Is that my new name?"

"Only at stuffy social occasions." He grinned and wrapped one of her curls around his finger. "I've a question."

"Ask away, my lord."

"How do you feel about Lord Nelson being so close by? Arrow insisted he must reside in our bedchamber. He said something about hoping his presence would ensure we become the parents of at least one great naval hero."

She turned around and stared at the bust of the revered admiral, who appeared to be watching them with a grim, determined expression. "He's welcome to stay, of course," she said blithely. "But I can tell by the look in his eye, he expects us to do our duty often."

"And with the uncommon zeal particular to sailors and their wenches," Harry added.

Molly grinned, laid her cheek on his chest, and listened to the beating of his heart. "What about Maxwell and Lumley? Did they give us a present?"

"They did, as a matter of fact."

Molly lifted her head and gazed around the bedchamber. "I don't see anything . . . out of the ordinary."

"Well, the presents aren't exactly here. Lumley has purchased and named a noble ram after me and a gorgeous ewe after you at his newest estate in Scotland. He has high hopes, he says, for a magnificent herd to rise from their union. And if you look in the little greenhouse in the back garden, you'll see that Maxwell's commissioned a botanist to experiment with cultivating a white rosebush named Harry with a pink rosebush named Molly in one pot. He predicts they'll spawn a new, hearty, attractive, and clever generation of rosebush."

"*Clever* roses?" Molly laughed.

"Yes. Clever. And I told Maxwell I insist one or two must have your hair color." He kissed the tip of her nose.

She grinned. "And they must have *your* smile."

Harry chuckled. "We're no botanists, obviously."

"Nor sheep breeders. But clearly we've deduced your Impossible Bachelor friends are trying to tell us something."

"That they are," Harry replied, and rolled her beneath him again. "Shall we get started proving them right, my love?"

Read on for an excerpt from the next book
by Kieran Kramer

DUKES TO THE LEFT OF ME, PRINCES TO THE RIGHT

Coming soon from St. Martin's Paperbacks

In a proper English drawing room on Clifford Street in London's Mayfair district, Lady Poppy Smith-Barnes, daughter of the widowed Earl of Derby, threw down the newspaper and stood up on shaky legs. Finally, the secret passion she'd been carrying around with her for almost six years would have its day in the sun.

"He's here," she announced to Aunt Charlotte. "Sergei's in England."

She could hardly believe it. She'd resigned herself to being a Spinster—she was in good company, after all. But now . . . in a matter of a moment, everything had changed.

Her prince had arrived.

Aunt Charlotte, tiny in her voluminous, outmoded gown, stopped her knitting. "Are you sure?"

Poppy found the paper again and put it under her aunt's nose. "He and his sister are touring with their uncle's last portrait and unveiling it for the very first time here in London. They intend to enjoy the social whirl while they're visiting, of course."

"Oh, Poppy!" Aunt Charlotte's eyes were a bright, mischievous blue above her spectacles, and her powdered white wig sat slightly askew on her head. "He's the only man on earth who could coax you out of the Spinsters Club."

"Indeed, he is." She hurried to the front window and looked out, expecting *something* to be different. But the day appeared like any other day. She knew, however, that it wasn't. It was special.

Sergei—the perfect boy, and now the perfect man— was in town.

She spun around to her aunt. "Do you think he'll remember me? It's been six long years. I was fifteen. We had only a week. It seems a lifetime ago."

"How could he forget you?"

She shrugged. "So much has happened to him. He's been traveling, he was in the military—I kept up with him as best I could through the papers. I'm afraid . . . I'm afraid he'll see me at a ball and walk right by me."

Aunt Charlotte laughed. "No one walks right by you, dear. Not with that fiery hair of yours. Or that mischievous grin. You're an impudent thing, you know. Just like me. He'll notice you, all right."

Poppy went to her and squeezed her hand. "But I've got to get through Eversly's proposal first. I'm dreading it, Aunt, more than any other offer I've ever had. He's such an amiable sort."

Aunt Charlotte calmly resumed her knitting. "Yes, he is. But you must stay true to yourself. He'll survive the turn-down, and you will, too. It's not as if you haven't had a great deal of practice."

Eversly was due to arrive within the hour, and his would be the twelfth marriage proposal Poppy had turned down in the three years she'd been out. Two of those offers had rather predictably taken place during the fireworks at Vauxhall. Another two had transpired at Rotten Row in Hyde Park at the fashionable hour, both times while she'd sat astride docile mares (Papa wouldn't let her take out the prime-goers). One proposal had taken place in front of a portrait of a spouting whale at the British Museum at eleven in the morning and two more at the conclusion of routs that had dragged on until dawn. One had transpired in the buffet line at a Venetian breakfast after she'd overfilled her plate with wedges of lemon tart to make up for the dull company, two had occurred in her drawing room over cold cups of tea—tepid because her suitors had prosed on so long about themselves—and one had taken place, inexplicably, at a haberdashery, where she'd gone to buy buttons for Papa's favorite hunting coat.

Two barons, a baronet, three viscounts, four earls (one of them only nine years old at the time), and one marquess had proposed to her. Two had had large ears. Five had had small eyes. Three had smelled of brandy, and one had lost his breeches in a fountain. One had been missing his front teeth (and it hadn't been the boy).

Stay calm, she told herself. *More than ever, you have a reason to say* no *to Eversly.*

As the clock ticked closer toward the earl's arrival, Aunt Charlotte kissed her on the cheek and left the room. Poppy waited another agonizing twenty minutes. Finally, there was a knock at the front door, and she put her newspaper under a pillow. Kettle, Lord Derby's elderly butler, greeted the visitor in his usual sober way.

Poppy stood.

Then she sat.

And then she stood.

Finally, the earl, a veritable Adonis, entered the room. He had gleaming blue eyes, a golden curl on his forehead, and shoulders so broad she should feel weak in the knees.

But her knees stayed firm.

"You're alone." Eversly's eyes were warm. She could tell he had genuine affection for her, and she did for him, actually. He was sporting, congenial company, but she couldn't help thinking of him only as a friend. It was always that way with her suitors, as if there were a big *NO* stamped on all their foreheads.

Thanks to Sergei.

"Yes," she told Eversly, swallowing hard. "I *am* alone."

They both knew what *that* meant. Without her father or Aunt Charlotte by her side, she was unchaperoned. Only an engaged or married woman could meet a man alone in a room.

But she wasn't quite alone, was she? There was her mother—sedate, mature—smiling down at her from her portrait, her wedding rings sparkling on her pale, slender hand. Her hair was the same shining copper color as Poppy's own wavy locks; her eyes, the identical emerald green.

Lord Eversly moved toward Poppy, skirting a small table and rounding a chair. He lifted her hand to his lips and brushed a soft kiss against her knuckles. "We shall do well together," he said, in a low-timbered voice which should have sent shivers up Poppy's spine.

But it didn't.

She stole a glance at his perfect lips. She'd heard from her aunt's maid, who'd heard from the maid of a widow who'd had an affair with him, that he was a splendid kisser.

"We should," she said with a little intake of breath, "were we to marry."

Lord Eversly arched an eyebrow. "Aren't we?"

"No, we aren't," she said in a small voice.

"What?" The earl's voice became a mere squeak.

Poppy bit her lip. It was always at this point she reminded herself of the Spinsters Club and the vow she'd made with her two very best friends, Lady Eleanor Gibbs and Lady Beatrice Bentley. None of them would marry except for love.

And then, to inspire herself further, she imagined herself kissing Sergei.

"I can't marry you," she said to Lord Eversly, feeling braver now. "I'm so sorry."

And she did feel sorry. He was such a dear.

He winced. "But your father said—"

Poppy blinked. "He doesn't know."

"Doesn't know what?"

She was reluctant to hurt him, but she told her usual story. "I'm to be engaged," she said. "And it's a love match. Surely you understand."

"I demand to know his name," the earl said rather breathlessly.

Sergei, she wanted to say. But instead she said, "The Duke of Drummond." Her tone was firm but gentle. She'd been through this scenario many times before.

Her other suitors believed she'd met the Duke of Drummond on a walking tour she'd taken in the Cotswolds, but he was totally fictitious, actually, a product of Cook's lurid imagination. Cook enjoyed making up tales as she stirred her pots and chopped her vegetables, but that was part of her charm (if a floury-faced, wild-haired harridan in the kitchen who tippled occasionally could be called charming).

Indeed, just this morning, Cook had told Poppy another outlandish tale about the duke. Poppy already knew he was the mightiest, fiercest duke ever to have walked the earth. And she knew as well that his ancestral castle jutted out over a cliff above the swirling waters of the North Sea. According to Cook, he'd murdered his brother so he could become duke, and to forget his guilt, regularly plunged off this cliff for a swim. Occasionally, he came back up from the depths with a writhing sea creature under his arm, usually one with large, snapping teeth.

Today, Poppy learned the dreaded duke had even fought an octopus the size of a Royal Mail coach—and won.

"Did you say the Duke of Drummond?" the earl demanded.

Poppy yawned. "Yes, he rusticates somewhere far away."

Eversly drew in his chin. "Never heard of him."

"He's quite wicked."

"Wicked?" The earl raised his brow.

"Wickedly handsome, that is," Poppy recovered. She thought again of Sergei. "We met three years ago. Remember the year I missed that impromptu boat race on the Thames?"

"Oh, yes. I do recall. My side won, actually. I had a prime spot at the front of the boat, and Miles Fosberry fell in the river. We couldn't fish him out until we'd finished."

"Right." She gave him a sheepish smile. "Well, while you and your team were rowing past your less-favored acquaintances, I was on a walking tour of the Cotswolds. The duke was on one, too. We met at a village fair."

"But your father—" The earl's brow puckered. "Lord Derby never mentioned it. He said you were free to accept my offer."

"Drummond hasn't exactly *offered* for me yet," she explained. "But he's"—she paused—"on the verge."

She'd been quite clever to have come up with that phrase—*on the verge*. Her previous suitors had found it suitably vague, so that when they saw her dancing for weeks and months—and some, for *years* after her rejection of them—they didn't think to question her story.

"It's simply a matter of time," she said. "I've never told my father. It's my secret"—she laid a hand on her heart—"my secret of the heart." She allowed her voice to go a bit trembly. "And I'm not willing to reveal it yet, even to Papa."

Lord Derby would be furious, of course, that she'd turned down the earl's suit. But surely he'd recover. He was far too busy toiling away for England to waste time being angry at her for long, especially if she cried and told him she was waiting for a true love match, like his and Mama's.

The earl looked down at his well-polished Hessian boots, and when he looked up again, his gaze was both besotted and disappointed.

"I still like you," Poppy protested. "As a friend. This little . . . engagement thing between us—let's forget it, shall we? I'll see you throughout the Season, won't I? We can share a waltz." Although her dream was to share her next waltz with Sergei.

She dared to lean forward and give Eversly a small kiss on his cheek. She wasn't one to dispense her kisses lightly, and the whole *ton* knew this of her.

"I shall hold you to that waltz," the earl said, a little gruff. She could tell he genuinely cared for her. Nevertheless, his old good cheer sneaked back into his tone.

"I look forward to it." She smiled. "Meanwhile, I know I can count on you to be discreet. Please don't say a word to anyone about our . . . conversation."

"I wouldn't dream of it." The earl bowed and left the drawing room without another word.

She waited a few seconds for Kettle to open the front door, then she ran to the window and looked out. Lord Eversly descended the front steps rather slowly. Poppy recognized that walk. It was the gait of a jilted bachelor. She'd induced it in many men.

But by the time he ascended the steps of his fine carriage waiting on the street, the earl's pace had picked up to his regular jolly one. And why shouldn't it? He was a wealthy, handsome peer of the realm with tremendous charm. Plenty of women would accept his suit. Why, she'd put a bug in several girls' ears this very week.

She turned around to see Aunt Charlotte standing in the door, a loose curl from her wig hanging in her eye and making her look quite the scamp. "I heard every word," she whispered loudly. "I'm *so* proud of you for following your heart. But—"

"But what?"

"We're doomed. I hope your emergency suitcase is packed."

"It is," Poppy said in a thin voice.

"You know the procedure. Now that Waterloo is behind us, Spinsters in untenable situations no longer retreat to the north of Scotland. We're forced to go to Paris!"

Aunt Charlotte appeared delighted at the prospect.

"*Poppy*?" It was her father's voice. She could hear him in his boots, clomping down the hall toward the drawing room. "That wasn't the earl leaving, was it? I've brandy and cigars in the library to celebrate your betrothal."

Outside, Lord Eversly's coachman cracked his whip, and he was gone.

But Poppy's problems had only begun.

Be sure to check out the companion blog to

WHEN HARRY MET MOLLY

at

www.musingsofthemistresses.blogspot.com

The musings of Athena, Bunny, Hildur, and Joan—the four mistresses who befriend Molly—are amusing indeed. Visit them now!

…and don't miss the blog belonging to Poppy's Aunt Charlotte of

DUKES TO THE LEFT OF ME, PRINCES TO THE RIGHT

www.thespinstersclub.blogspot.com

You'll love spending time in her splendiferous Spinster world!

Coming soon…

Don't miss the next novel in Kieran Kramer's
Impossible Bachelors series

CLOUDY WITH A CHANCE OF MARRIAGE

ISBN: 978-0-312-37403-7

Available in May 2011 from St. Martin's Paperbacks

"Delectable."
—Julia Quinn, *New York Times* bestselling author